About the a

Steve Harper was born into a service family and travelled the world with his parents, living in Germany, Northern Island and Aden. He was sent to a mixed boarding school in 1963 and expelled in 1965. He lasted another year in a grammar school until he was again expelled. Seeking employment, he then got a job working for the Board of Trade where he studied at Bletchley Park. On finishing college, he applied for a job with the GPO as an engineer. Thankfully they took him on as he married Judy in 1970 and needed to pay the bills. Their two children, Daniel and Lindsay, were born in 1974 and 1979 while the family moved around Cambridge. In 2000 Steve took early retirement and he and Judy moved to Norfolk. Here he joined the local amateur dramatics society writing several plays, some of which were published and won prizes. He now paints, writes and plays bass guitar for two local bands. He smiles a lot.

JOSHUA'S TRUMPET

JOSHUA'S TRUMPET

STEVE HARPER

Vanguard Press

VANGUARD PAPERBACK

© Copyright 2021
Steve Harper

A CIP catalogue record for this title is
available from the British Library.

ISBN 978 1 80016 203 7

*Vanguard Press is an imprint of
Pegasus Elliot MacKenzie Publishers Ltd.*
www.pegasuspublishers.com

First Published in 2021

**Vanguard Press
Sheraton House Castle Park
Cambridge England**

Printed & Bound in Great Britain

Chapter 1
Dob Dob Dob

Me and Arthur Wells grew up together. We went to primary school together, we played football together, we joined the GPO together, and, in 1940, we committed murder together. It was an accident, we didn't mean it to happen, but it did, and it changed everything.

I met Arthur when I joined the 1st Welling cub scouts in 1926. He had joined two weeks earlier and knew more of the rules than I did. He already had a green pullover with badges, a proper neckerchief with a woggle, and a cap. My mum had sent me along in my ordinary school clothes, I looked like a civilian. As the obvious new boy, I was open for a ritual blooding. Seven-year-old boys can be as predatory as sharks.

I stood on the side lines watching the 'Pack Howl'," and listening to the notifications about 'Bob a Job' week. Mrs Brown, the akela, introduced me as a new recruit. "I expect a lot of you know James Jones, well now that he is seven, he has come to join the pack. I expect everyone to help him out, because a lot of what we do will be new to him. Right James, you will be in orange six, which is Peter Mellor's, do you know Peter?" I nodded. "That's good. Now I just need to pop out for a moment, go and sit next to Peter and we will play a game." She watched as the chairs were arranged, and then nodding left the room. "Michael, see that they play without messing about."

Three of the older boys, who were all sixers, sat on chairs. They were the judge, the captain and the whacker. Everyone else had a number, I was number five. I can't remember what the game was called, but the objective was that when challenged you replied with ritual phrases until you in turn, could accuse somebody else. If you made a mistake and deviated from the ritual you had to bend over and the whacker hit you with a knotted neckerchief. It should have been harmless fun. It wasn't.

Mrs Brown had gone to talk to her mother, leaving Michael Phillips, the senior sixer, in charge. He had a lot of badges but was small and exuded little authority. He had been a cub longer than any of the others, but nobody seemed to pay him much regard.

He started the game with an opening gambit of accusing the captain. The captain, Derek Murphy, was a tough ten-year-old. He had a big scab on his knee and a bigger brother who would duff you up as soon as look at you. He checked we were alone before flicking a 'V' at Phillips. That made everybody laugh because we all knew it meant something very rude. The game however continued; it was too good not to. "Who me, sir?" Murphy replied.

"Yes, you, sir," said Phillips looking down at his shoes.

"Not I, sir," said Derek elongating the I. That made us all laugh again, which is OK when you are not the object of ridicule.

"If not you sir, then who, sir?" replied the senior sixer completing his part of the ritual and sitting down gratefully now safely out of the game. Murphy played to the audience turning his head slowly, looking for a victim. I sat there in my grey school pullover, new, alone, vulnerable.

Derek smiled. "I accuse number five sir." All eyes turned to me. I knew I had to reply, but panic made me confused and I couldn't remember what I was supposed to say. "I call for the whacker," shouted Derek spreading his arms and turning through a slow semicircle. His audience responded.

They all took up the chant, "Whacker, whacker, whacker." I was led to the whacker's chair and forced to bend over it. Being hit on the backside with a knotted cotton scarf shouldn't be painful. I suspect, with adult hindsight, it is only included in the game to signify corporal punishment for the losers. I mean nobody would want to deliberately hurt little boys in a game, would they? Well adults don't want to hurt anybody, but Derek Murphy wasn't an adult. The whacker hit me an overhead blow. It wasn't very hard and was greeted with a cheer. It didn't hurt, but I was pleased it was over. I resolved to learn the lines for next week. Most importantly I had not cried.

It was then that Derek decided to intervene. "Call yourself a whacker," he jeered. "I'll show you how to do it, hold him." He then took off his own neckerchief, rolled it into a tight roll and gave me a vicious whip crack on the top of my unprotected leg. It hurt, it really hurt. I cried out and felt the tears pricking at my eyes. Although I struggled, I was held fast.

I knew this was bad, there were no adults to rescue me. I was going to be sacrificed, and then the tears came. "Oh look, Jimmy's a cry baby, poor little Jimmy riddle, have you wet your pants Jimmy riddle?" I knew he was drawing back to hit me again, when a voice intervened. It cut through the excitement like a knife.

"Pack it in Murphy." The silence that followed was charged. Nobody challenged the Murphys, they didn't play by the rules. Now something bad was going to happen. Hands fell away from me, until I was able to turn and see my rescuer. Arthur wasn't particularly big or brawny, he wore glasses and looked as though he had another six months growth to fill out his uniform. There was, however, a sense of determination that you wouldn't normally notice, but it was there.

Murphy looked at him with disdain. "What did you say Wells?"

"I said pack it in. You've hurt him, no call for that."

Murphy threw the neckerchief to Arthur. "All right you give him a whacking, and let's see if you know what to do with this." Arthur caught the scarf in his left hand and, without taking his eyes off of Murphy, blew his nose loudly on it. He then threw it at Murphy's feet. Murphy's reaction was very fast. In an uncontrollable rage he threw himself at Arthur. He was bigger, stronger and angrier. How dare this little shit humiliate him?

Years later, when Mr Pomeroy taught us how to kill, he explained that when the red mist is behind the eyes, it stops rational thinking. "A great asset in hand-to-hand combat gentlemen," he would say. Arthur had somehow instinctively known this, and had deliberately goaded Murphy into an enraged attack.

What all of us had failed to notice was that Arthur's right hand was curled into a fist. It was curled into a fist because Arthur had scooped a handful of sand out of the fire bucket in the corner. His hand shot up as though he was bowling underarm and he released the sand into the accelerating face of Derek Murphy. It went into his eyes, his mouth and even up his nose. It must have been extremely painful, to say nothing of the shock. It seemed to those that witnessed it, that a giant hand had picked Murphy up and slammed him back on the floor. You could hear the breath driven out of him, and he lay kicking his legs unable to inhale. Mrs Brown choose that moment to re-join us. She saw a group standing round one of her sixers who was writhing on the floor. "Michael, what on earth has happened?" she demanded of the senior sixer.

She grasped Derek to her, his breath was now coming in long shuddering heaves. "Nothing Akela," lied Phillips. "We changed the game to British bulldog, and Derek got knocked over." If there was ever a badge for lying through your teeth, that lad should have had it pinned to his chest and received a kiss on both cheeks. She looked suspiciously at all of us, but small boys are very adroit at looking totally innocent whilst lying.

Not one of that group came to Derek's rescue. They had all been subjected to his nasty bullying, and now there was a new cock of the walk. Arthur was a new and unlikely hero. "Are you feeling a bit better Derek?" she asked.

Derek glowered at the rest of us. "That Arthur Wells hit us, Akela," he said.

Mrs Brown turned, bringing the full weight of her authority to focus on Arthur. "Arthur Wells," she said. "Did you hit Derek?" You could hear a pin drop. Arthur appeared to be considering the question. "Well?"

Arthur looked her in the eye. "No, Akela, I didn't hit him," he replied. Mrs Brown looked at the two boys. Murphy, feral, two years Arthur's senior and a close-cropped haircut that made him look like a Victorian felon. Arthur, bespectacled, thin and what she thought of as 'from good stock'. It seemed most unlikely.

"Well," she said. "No more rough games for a bit, we don't want anybody getting hurt now do we? Do we pack?"

"No Akela," we all chanted.

"All right Derek?" she asked.

Derek wasn't clever, but he knew he had lost this battle, he knew better than to make accusations without a friend to back him up. "Yes Akela," he said.

"You just play too rough you boys," she continued. She took out a handkerchief, spat on it and wiped Derek's face. "Just look at you Derek

Murphy, you have dirt all over your face. Is that sand in your hair? You need a good bath when you get home." Personally, she thought that an unlikely prospect. "Now come and sit quietly with me. The rest of you, knots. Michael gets the box of ropes out. Sheepshanks boys, sheepshanks."

Although I had been allocated to the orange six, I walked across to Arthur in the blue area. He looked up. "I just wanted to say thanks mate," I said.

He looked at me for a few seconds. "Did it really hurt?" I felt the tears coming back, more the humiliation of the helplessness. I pulled up my trouser leg and revealed the red welt on my thigh. Arthur looked.

"Yeah," he said. "That hurt, but don't call me mate, kid."

I was stung, I had done the right thing and acknowledged his bravery only to be rebuffed.

"Don't call me kid, mate," I retorted. We glared at each other for a few seconds until Arthur's face cracked into a smile.

"You're tougher than you look, ain't you. Thing is, Jimmy, it is Jimmy, isn't it?" I nodded. "Thing is, I made an enemy tonight. Derek won't come back for more on his own, but he's got a brother who might."

"I'm sorry," I said.

"Balls to sorry," he grinned. "I need a mate to be in my gang."

We looked at each for a moment then I stuck my hand out. Surprisingly Arthur took a step back and put his hand into his armpits. I learnt later that he wasn't comfortable with handshakes. Then very awkwardly he stepped forward and briefly grasped my hand. I somehow knew that had taken a lot, but having done it, we were friends for life.

Chapter 2
The Addicks

The winter of 1930 wasn't as bad as the blizzards of the previous year, but it was still very cold. It had snowed overnight and two inches had settled, bringing a muffled brightness to town. Me and Arthur were snuggled in our favourite spot, next to the cooker. Arthur's mum had sent him out with a bag of oranges to share, she believed they had great preventative powers against winter ailments, so the kitchen now smelt very seasonal. We had put old cushions on the floor and emptied our bag of comics between us. Christmas was only ten days away so we were both on best behaviour. I wanted an air gun and Arthur wanted a model plane with a real petrol engine. In reality neither of us held out too much hope. Arthur lived alone with his mum because his dad had died of TB in 1922. Dad said he had caught it at Passchendaele, and never recovered. "Bastard war," he said. Dad got a job with the bus company after he came home.

Mum said we were lucky, but money was still tight. "Sometimes," she said, "we just couldn't get everything we wanted." Mum was usually right. She appeared from the lounge and told us that the flats needed sweeping. Arthur groaned and rolled his eyes. "Yes, I know," she said, "but the sooner you start, the sooner you can get back to Micky Mouse, and I'll make you hot chocolate." We didn't have a plan B.

Mum and Dad lived over Zimmerman's carpet shop. It was a two-storey flat with three bedrooms and a bathroom at the top. Downstairs had a big lounge, a kitchen and a dining room. Mr Zimmerman had been in the war with Dad, and he let us have it at what mum called a 'reasonable rent'. Arthur and I liked Mr Zimmerman, it was his sixpence that had bought our comics. He was also our main supplier of acid drops and coconut ice. "One of your own," Dad said.

The kitchen and the dining room looked out on to the flat roof of Mr Zimmerman's stock room. Dad had put flower tubs and a coal bunker on it, but the waterproofing had started to perish, and standing water would leak through. My job was to sweep water off. Dad had built a broom that had no bristles, but a strip of rubber instead. It worked well with water, but snow was hard work.

We put on our gabardine macs, caps and gloves and trudged out on to the flats. By the time we had taken turns at pushing all the snow over the edge, we were both hot, and our woollen gloves were wet. I heard the creek of the iron staircase that linked the ground floor garden to the flats.

Arthur didn't, and the snowball hit him on the left shoulder spinning him round and splashing wet snow up his neck. As I turned, the second one hit me in the chest exploding snow up into my chin. "Up the buffs," shouted Mr Zimmerman releasing the third of his stock. Arthur threw down the broom, and scooped up a wet glove full of snow.

"Surrender or die," Arthur shouted at Mr Zimmerman. I also scooped up snow and threw it at Mr Zimmerman's trilby.

"Get him," shouted Arthur. "Pincer movement." Two on to one soon prevailed and eventually Mr Zimmerman threw up his hands.

"Pax, pax," he shouted. "I surrender, spare me, and I will make it worth your while." Laughing we brushed the snow off and, pushing each other, we fought our way back into the warmth.

"All done?" Mum called through.

"They have done a grand job," Mr Zimmerman shouted back.

"Hello Harry, I didn't see you there," said Mum. "Have you been playing snowballs?" Mr Zimmerman looked at the snow still adorning his grey trilby.

"I was assaulted by a gang of shaygets," he answered.

"Who threw the first one?" Mum was not easily fooled.

"Well, I may have got my retaliation in first, but that's modern warfare for you."

"So my 'little rascals', were only defending themselves?"

Mr Zimmerman conceded defeat for a second time. "Any chance of tea?" Mum smiled and went back to her kitchen. Mr Zimmerman took off his good woollen overcoat and folded it carefully on the back of a dining room chair. He always wore smart clothes, and sometimes had a flower in his lapel.

"Dapper," Mum had once said to Dad.

He sat in Dad's armchair pulling his trousers up to maintain the creases. "How old are you two rascals?" he asked taking an envelope out of his inside pocket.

Arthur and I exchanged glances. "We're eleven," he said.

"Old enough then," replied Mr Zimmerman. "I think it's time you two were introduced to the beautiful game. On Saturday Charlton are playing Nottingham Forest, and I happen to have three tickets!" He waved the envelope. We sat in stunned silence, we both loved football.

We played on the cinders of the cinema car park next door, and sometimes went to Dansen Park to watch the local amateurs, but neither of us had been to a professional match. Charlton Athletic was our local team, but too far and too expensive for us.

Mum came in with a tray of hot drinks. "Mum, please Mum, Mr Zimmerman has got tickets for Charlton, Mum can we go, can we…"

"I heard," said Mum. "There are two conditions. You must go home and ask your mum, Arthur, and we must contribute to the cost."

Mr Zimmerman held up his hand, "Permission yes, but this is my treat, I'm looking to recruit two new supporters for the future."

"Wow we would be Redbreasts," said Arthur.

"No, you wouldn't," said Mr Zimmerman. "You would be Addicks.

"Not sure I like the sound of that," said Mum.

Mr Zimmerman laughed. "We used to be called the Redbreasts because of the strip. Bright red jerseys, you see. But now it's all changed, the trainer has them on a high protein diet of haddock and chips, so now we're the Addicks; haddocks get it?"

We certainly did, and thought it the best joke ever, we were going to be Addicks, and we laughed and laughed. "All right boys, it's not that funny," said Mum. "Arthur, go and ask your mum." Twenty minutes later he was back having run all the way.

"Mum says, thank you very much," he panted.

"Right," said our benefactor. "I'll pick you up at two o'clock Saturday."

It took a long time for Saturday afternoon to come. Eventually, however, Mr Zimmerman arrived. He had his usual woollen coat on, but now he also wore a bright red Charlton scarf. Best of all he carried a wooden rattle with red ribbons on it. "Play up the Addicks," he shouted whirling his rattle.

Mum put her hands over her ears and ushered us outside. "Have fun," she shouted as she shut the door

We crossed the road and caught a four-eight-six bus from the stop by the wool shop. As we climbed on, several boys a bit older than us whirled their rattles and cheered. "All right, all right, keep it down," yelled the conductor. "One and two halves to Floyd Road, is it?"

"It certainly is," said Mr Zimmerman proffering coins. "And don't spare the horses."

The stadium was the biggest thing we had ever seen. Mr Zimmerman told us that when it was finished it would be the biggest in Europe. We went through the turnstile and made our way to our stand.

Lots of the men there knew Mr Zimmerman and made sure Arthur and I could see the pitch. "New recruits?" said one of the men who had a red and white rosette in his hat.

"Size of this place, we are going to need all the help we can get to fill it," Mr Zimmerman replied. "This is Jimmy and this is Arthur, boys this is Wilf, Joe and Bernie." They all said hello to us, and then talked tactics and league tables until the teams ran out, and the game began.

Nottingham Forest was a Midlands team. They weren't as skilful as us, and our star players Dai Astley, George Armitage and Ted Ballentyne soon had them on the defensive. Two certainties from Astley hit the cross bar of the Nottingham Forest goal without the keeper moving.

We cheered and cheered; it was the most exciting afternoon we had ever had. Everything was in our favour until just before half time when the visiting centre forward made a break and ran down the left wing for our goal. Armitage spun round and was on his heels in an instant. He managed to catch him on the edge of the penalty area, but as soon as he sensed a challenge, the Nottingham player threw himself full length on the ground. The referee eventually catching up pointed to the penalty spot. The crowd went wild, booing echoed round the ground. "That's not fair," shouted Arthur. "He cheated, he cheated."

"He bloody did son," said the man with the rosette. There was still a sense of fair play then. The centre forward got to his feet, placed the ball on the penalty spot and, with the referee's whistle, drove the ball into the back of our net. One — nil.

At half time we had hot Bovril. The mood had changed, and everyone seemed a bit despondent. "Sorry about this, boys," said Mr Zimmerman. "Thought we would win this one."

Arthur turned to him and said, "It's all right, we are not going to lose, Mr Zimmerman."

The man with the rosette looked at Arthur. "What makes you say that lad?"

"Well," said Arthur. "I have been reading up about statistics and tactics. We have a younger more skilled side and we are playing with the wingers further forward. We should have been two up before that man cheated. If they rely on that, they won't stand against us. A draw if we are unlucky, a win if there is any justice." There was a moment's silence.

"How old are they, Zimmey," somebody asked.

"Eleven," he replied. "But they have brains."

"I think the lad has got a point," said the rosette man. Arthur blushed with the pride of acceptance. Once he became interested in something he soaked up knowledge like a sponge, everything else was ignored. He had always been like that.

The second half started, and again two good attempts were saved by their goalie. The pressure that Charlton put on the visitors eventually paid off when six precision passes put George Armitage in their penalty area. He fired off a shot that left the keeper with no chance and stinging hands. The ball hit the netting at the back of their goal. One — one. Although Charlton should have scored again, it wasn't to be. One went over the crossbar, and one was desperately blocked by the left back. By the time the referee blew for full time our mood had improved wonderfully, it didn't feel like a draw, we knew it should have been a win.

We clapped the players off the pitch, then headed for the bus stop. We were Addicks, we were the best, and life was good. As we left one of the other men shouted, "You bring 'em again Zimmey, they're good luck." That was a good day.

Chapter 3
Christmas

I woke early on Christmas morning, it was Sunday, it was 1932 and it was cold. As a thirteen-year-old I was far too grown up to believe in Father Christmas, but I was also very reluctant to abandon my Christmas stocking. Thirteen is still young enough to want one and, true to form Mum and Dad had left a pillowcase at the end of the bed. I knew presents were opened after dinner, but this was an oasis of childhood, a moment of pure indulgence.

I ripped off wrapping paper to discover a Bakelite maze with a blob of mercury in it that you had to get to the centre. A cone that fired a ping-pong ball up in the air, to be recaught. A liquorice smoker's set with a pipe, cigarettes, matches and chewing tobacco. A jigsaw of Charles Lindberg flying over the white cliffs of Dover and a yo-yo. But best of all a book. Mum and Dad always put a book in my stocking because it let them have an extra half hour in bed while I read.

This year it was the new Hardy Boys mystery called *While the Clock Ticked*. A ripping story of secret passages in Dalrymple mansion. I had just got to the bit where Frank and Jo were locked in a dungeon room with water gushing in when Dad stuck his head round the bedroom door. "Happy Christmas, old man," he grinned. "Want a cuppa?"

"It's an ace book, Dad," I said. "Best one I've read."

"That's great," he grinned gathering his dressing gown round him. "I'll put the kettle on and light a fire." I put on my slippers and dressing gown and went down with him to help.

While the kettle boiled, Dad laid kindling on yesterday's evening news and carefully placed lumps of coal round it. The trick was to hold a double newspaper page over the front of the fire so that a draught was sucked up the chimney making the coals glow. You had to be careful, because if it got too hot, a brown spot would appear in the middle of the paper just before it burst into flames. Dad was an expert and at the very last moment let the roaring fire suck in his burning paper. "That should do it," he said. "Right, I'll take this up to Mum, you get yourself up, and we'll see about breakfast. Always eat when you get the chance, my RSM used to say, and we have the hordes coming across no man's land at eleven o'clock."

"Nan and Granddad aren't hordes, Dad."

He grinned. "Well maybe not Nan!"

We were having Arthur and his mum, and Nan and Granddad for Christmas dinner. Mum had ordered a big capon, but was concerned that it wouldn't stretch to seven. Dad said not to worry, because he had done pigs in blankets and everybody was bringing something. I don't think Mum was convinced. Dad poured her a big sherry and started peeling the potatoes.

First to arrive was Nan and Granddad, they had to come from Willesden Green so they had caught a cab. Nan said she felt like royalty, Granddad said she had sat in the back and waved like the King does. They had lots of string bags that chinked, a sherry trifle, Granddad's ukulele case and a special bag of presents. Mum took the coats, Dad got a port and lemon for Nan and poured Granddad a pint of best bitter from the barrel he had set up in the dining room. Granddad went into the lounge to inspect our Christmas tree with the new electric lights that Dad had bought from a man at work. Nan went to help mum in the kitchen and to tell her the latest about Mrs Palmers' divorce. Dad got himself a glass of beer, and me a lemonade.

"What do you think about this depression thing that's happening in America then?" said Dad.

"Bloody yanks," replied Granddad. "They can't do nothing right."

"Well, they did fight with us, Dad, we would probably still be in the trenches without them."

"Gammon," said Granddad. "They didn't get there until it was nearly all over, 1917, bastards. What was it Wilson said, 'Peace without victory', I'd bloody give him peace without victory. He was never crouched in a trench with whizz bangs ranging in. Bastard." Dad gave me a look, Granddad had strong opinions about the war.

"Do you like our decorations, Granddad," I asked. "Dad and me put them up last weekend."

"I think they're bloody marvellous Jimmy, and to celebrate, I'm going to have another pint. Come on then Stanley, let the dog see the rabbit." Dad grinned and led the way back to the barrel.

I was saved further discussions about the war by the doorbell. Arthur and his mum had arrived. I rushed through and opened the door. "Merry Christmas mate," I shouted.

"Merry Christmas, kid," he replied. It had become our private joke.

"Hope you like sprouts and bacon Jimmy," Arthur's mum said, carrying in a suspiciously large dish.

"Sprouts make you fart," said Granddad taking some of the bags. "Merry Christmas, Ivy, what you drinking?" He held a sprig of mistletoe over her head.

"I'll have a gin and lime please, Reg," said Mrs Wells giving him a quick kiss on the cheek.

"How about you Arthur?" said Granddad.

Arthur pulled a face. "No, I don't want a kiss."

"No, you nincompoop, do you want a drink? How about a pint of wallop?"

"He'll have a lemonade, same as Jimmy, thank you very much," replied Mrs Wells.

Mum came through with Nan and Dad. There was a lot more kissing, and merry Christmasing, so Arthur and I got lemonades and went up to my bedroom. I showed him my new book and the toys from my stocking. He had got a plaster of Paris kit, a new pullover, a Charlton football book and a pair of roller skates, but he hadn't been able to bring them. What he had brought was a bag of oranges. Arthur's mum was a great believer in medicinal powers of vitamin C. She had a friend who worked down on the docks who could get oranges when they came in. They were seasonal and, depending on the time of year, came from Egypt or Spain. These were Egyptian, they were a bit sharp but we ate them and my smoker's kit.

At two o'clock Mum called us down for dinner. All of them had been celebrating enthusiastically, and seemed to find the slightest thing funny. We sat round the table on an assortment of chairs while Dad carved the chicken and all the ladies dished out the trimmings. There was enough, but only just.

There were real crackers that banged and we pulled them with whoever sat opposite. We all put on our paper hats, and Granddad proposed a toast to Mum for our, "Splendid and superlative," dinner.

Dad shouted, "Hear, hear," and the other ladies clapped politely. There were also jokes and mottos in the crackers. When Mrs Wells read one about one snowman asking another if he could smell carrots, Nan laughed so much that port and lemon came out of her nose. Her trifle was all right, but it tasted a bit strange. Granddad told me that was the goodness in it. Dad said it was the whole bottle of sherry in it, and they all laughed as though that was really funny.

At three o'clock all the plates were cleared away and Dad turned the wireless on to warm up. King George was going to wish everybody a happy Christmas, and read a speech that Rudyard Kipling the famous writer had done for him. Dad tuned the radio into the Empire Service. After a lot of crackling a man came on and told us the King would talk to us from Sandringham, which is near the seaside. The speech wasn't very good. He said through the marvels of science he could talk to all his subjects. He told us his life's work was to serve, and his only reward was our loyalty and confidence in him. Granddad stood to attention saluting; Nanny kept toasting the radio with her glass. Mrs Wells cried into her serviette and Mum and Dad held hands.

When it finished Dad turned off the set and said, "Well the King in our living room, isn't that grand."

Nan shouted, "God bless him."

And Granddad held his salute. "That's why we've got a bloody empire Stanley, because we're bloody British," he said. I think he had a tear in his eye and he was sounding a bit slurry. He went off to blow his nose, recharge his pint, and get an ashtray.

Mrs Wells said she thought we were all very lucky to have had such a special day, and she touched Mum's arm as she said it. Mum put her hand on Mrs Wells' and said, "You're welcome Ivy, it's so nice to have you and Arthur with us." Granddad came back with ashtrays and everybody smoked. Dad had got cigars for him and Granddad, but the ladies had cigarettes, Nan rolled her own. We had just settled down and were at last about to open presents when there was a knock at the door.

"Who on earth can that be?" said Mum.

"Well only one way to find out," said Dad, and went through.

It was Mr Zimmerman. "A merry Christmas to all," he greeted us. "I know I'm interrupting, but I just wanted to give you a little seasonal something." He offered Dad a parcel.

"Harry, there really is no need," said Dad.

"Bobbymyseh," said Mr Zimmerman. "A small token of friendship." Dad opened it to reveal a bottle of good French brandy. Granddad vanished, only to quickly reappear with a mixture of glasses, which he put in front of Dad.

"Come on Stanley," he said. "It would be rude not to toast Harry." He seized Dad's bottle and poured a generous splash into six glasses. I noticed as toast master he kept the most generous. He raised his glass. "To friends at Christmas." We all toasted each other in French brandy, Arthur and I had ginger beer.

"And, of course, a little something for my fellow Addicks," he said.

Arthur and I both got an envelope, which we tore open. Inside there was a ticket for tomorrow's game against Tottenham and a big white five-pound note. Neither of us had ever owned so much. He fended off our thanks and promised to pick us up on Boxing Day. They don't make them like Mr Zimmerman any more.

After he had gone, Granddad told us Mr Zimmerman had won the Military Medal at the battle of Cambrai. He had been wounded, but had wiped out a machine gun nest. "Do you know," said Granddad, "I asked him once why he did it, because, well because he should have been killed instantaneously. Do you know what he said?" Arthur and I both said we didn't. "He said they got his dander up," said Granddad. "Got his bloody dander up, he killed three of them. That gentleman is a genuine hero." Granddad had another tear in his eye.

Finally, the presents came out. Mum got a new coat with a fur collar. She kept saying, "Oh Stan it's so..." but we never got to hear what, because Mum had to wipe her eyes a lot. I think she liked it. Nan got a new cardigan, some lily of the valley scent, a pack of Golden Virginia and a watch. Granddad got new gloves, a pipe, a razor and some regimental cufflinks.

Dad got a smart new shirt, some aftershave that made Granddad wolf whistle at him, and a bottle of Irish whiskey. We had bought Mrs

Wells a scarf and some chocolates. Granddad had bought her a pair of silk stockings. Nan seemed quite surprised that he had been so thoughtful.

Arthur and I got presents from everybody, the best one was from Mum and Dad, we each got a 'cat's whisker' radio set. Dad said he would help us build them. "We'll take the accumulators down to the radio shop on Tuesday, and get them charged," he said. Arthur had to explain that all the power came through the amplitude modulated wave picked up through the aerial. Dad said, "Yes of course," and nodded a lot.

Nan asked how they worked so Arthur started to explain about crystals, demodulators and headphones. She said that she wished she, "hadn't bloody asked." Granddad said in the army they had this thing called PFM that made everything work. Dad got him another brandy to shut him up.

We played lots of a games. One that Granddad showed us was called Where are you Moriarty? First Granddad was blindfolded and given a rolled-up newspaper, then Arthur was treated the same. Granddad had to shout out, "Where are you Moriarty?" and Arthur had to try and hit him guided by the sound.

It was very funny because what Arthur didn't know was that as soon as he was blindfolded, Granddad took his off. He easily dodged Arthur's blows, but scored a direct hit every time it was his go. Although Arthur wasn't pleased when he found out, he saw the funny side.

Mum and Dad did a magic trick. Dad went out of the room and Mum put three glasses on the table. Nan had to go and touch one of the glasses, then Dad came back in and had to guess which one it was. He was amazing, and got it right every time. He said he was guided by the ghost of the great Houdini.

We all tried, but no matter what we did he always got it right. It was Arthur who finally twigged that Mum put her cigarette on the left, right or middle of her mouth to show dad which one to pick. We eventually ended up round the piano. Mum and Nan played and we all sang. It was dead good. Granddad had brought his ukulele and sang 'Chinese Laundry Blues' which made us all laugh. Mum brought in a plate of ham sandwiches and pickles, which we all tucked into until I thought I would burst. Arthur and his mum stayed until half past eight, they put their hats and coats on and waved, shouting, "Happy Christmas" as they walked home. We agreed it had been the best Christmas ever, and arranged to meet on Boxing Day. Tottenham Hotspur would be a difficult match, but we thought a win might be possible. We also had to discuss what we were going to do with our five pounds.

I put my pyjamas on and stayed up late playing cards. We played Newmarket. Nan cheated and took all the pennies in the pot, but nobody was brave enough to accuse her. Eventually Mum said it was time for bed. I got a hug from everybody, and even though I said I wasn't tired, I was asleep before I had read any of my new book.

Chapter 4
The Beating

Boxing Day was on a Monday, Arthur came round on his own at eleven. He said his mum was going to have a quiet day in listening to the radio. Nan and Granddad had stayed the night. They had a lay in, but didn't have a lot of breakfast. I heard Nan say, "I'll give you bloody silk stockings, you dirty old git."

Granddad had called her, "My sweet," a lot, but seemed to be out of favour. Mum and Dad decided that after Mr Zimmerman had collected Arthur and me, they would all have a walk to the park, and perhaps call in to the Polly Clean Stairs pub on the way home. "Blow the cobwebs away," said Mum.

Mr Zimmerman was a bit early, he had been round at his business partner's and decided to beat the rush to the ground. He wore a brand-new coat that had been a Christmas present. Mum said it was cashmere camel, and made him look distinguished. He said he had a friend in the business, and that he had got it 'trade'. We put our Charlton scarves on and walked to the bus stop. "What do you think Arthur?" said Mr Zimmerman.

"I'm not sure," he replied. "Tottenham are an excellent team, but they play completely different tactics to us. I suppose it will depend on our line up."

"Sounds sensible," said Mr Zimmerman. "Should be a good game though."

There were a lot more people than normal with it being Boxing Day. The away supporters' end was packed, because White Hart Lane was only a bus ride away. Although it was a local derby, the mood was still Christmassy in the ground, and lots of people wore their new pullovers. Mr Zimmerman's friends were all there, and we were now allowed to call them Bernie, Wilf and Jo. They had got themselves hot drinks, and had topped them up from a hip flask. There was one for Mr Zimmerman, and two hot chocolates for me and Arthur.

At three o'clock we kicked off. The game was very exciting with lots of near misses at both ends. Tottenham scored, but almost immediately we equalised. Just before half time there was a scuffle in the goal mouth and the ball trickled over the line despite our goalie desperately clawing it out. "Oh, bugger off," shouted Wilf. "Are you blind ref, that was never a goal." But it was, and we went into half time a goal down.

Five minutes into the second half I felt unwell. It might have been the oranges, the sprouts, or the smoker's set but, all of a sudden, I really needed to go to the toilet. "Mr Zimmerman I really want the toilet," I pleaded.

He saw the urgency in my eyes. "Come on then Jimmy, I could do with a whizz myself." We walked quickly to the toilet block with the cramps gripping my stomach. Luckily the toilet was empty.

"Go on Jimmy, I'll wait out here for you," he said. I didn't hesitate and just managed to get my trousers down in time. The relief was immediate. As I sat on the toilet, I heard more people coming in, their voices loud and aggressive. They didn't sound friendly.

"Hey look, Pete, there's an old Yid, hanging about the shithouse."

"Dirty old kike, what you doing? Waiting for little uns to suck your knob?" There was mean laughter.

I heard Mr Zimmerman reply, "Gentlemen, I don't want trouble, I am just waiting for a friend. Just leave me alone, go and watch the match."

"Or what? You old Yid bastard, this is our manor, we are the BUF and we don't want your sort round here." It sounded bad. I hoped that if I came out Mr Zimmerman and I could get out and go back to the others. I flushed the toilet and made my way to his side. It only made it worse. There were three of them, they were pulling scarves up to hide their lower faces.

The smallest one said, "Bloody hell the old Jew boy is queer, look he's got a kid with him." I only glimpsed him for a moment before he pulled his scarf over his face, but I knew who it was. He glared at me, and I knew we were in real trouble. The face I had just seen was Patrick Murphy, Derek Murphy's elder brother.

Mr Zimmerman put his arm round me and turned for the door.

"Get him, Pete," one of them said.

"No, you don't, you shirt lifter, come here," said the biggest one. He made a grab for Mr Zimmerman. It was a mistake.

Years later I was trained to fight; not boxing or ju-jitsu, real fighting, commando fighting. It was based on three things, speed, surprise and pure viciousness. You got in first, and you made sure your opponent was not capable of fighting back. I suspect somewhere in his army service Mr Zimmerman had been taught something similar.

Even though he must have been at least sixty, Mr Zimmerman pivoted on his left foot, his right arm followed through and he hit the biggest one with the heel of his hand in the face. He didn't hit him on the chin, he hit him straight into his nose. The man fell backwards his hands instinctively grasping for his broken nose.

The blood poured between his fingers. "Aghhh, bastard," he screamed. "Get him, kill the fucking kike." Blood bubbled from his nose and mouth as he shouted. There comes a moment when you know there is no way back from the inevitable, when that decision has been made you can accept your fate, or go down fighting. My friend, Mr Zimmerman, chose to attack. It so damn nearly worked, but he wasn't a commando, he sold carpets. Speed and surprise had worked, but this was peace time and violence of the required degree was no longer acceptable. Mr Zimmerman stopped and turned to grab me. The second man jumped on to his back and, despite his efforts to twist him off, they both crashed to the toilet floor. I saw him reach a hand out to claw Mr Zimmerman's eyes, it had a blue tattoo on the inside of his wrist. It was a funny square with a cross in it but bits were missing.

Once he was down, they all turned on him with all the savagery of a hunting pack. They kicked him with their boots, hard kicks to the body and head. He tried to rise but there were too many of them, and the killing lust had them in its grasp. They kicked him again and again. I screamed and threw myself at Patrick Murphy, trying to claw his face. He grabbed me by the scruff of the neck, I saw the flash of something bright, and then my face exploded into pain.

He had used an open razor to cut my cheek. I felt the blood splash on to my coat, then a wave of nausea hit me and I sat heavily on the floor feeling dizzy and sick. It stopped the other two from the attack on the now unconscious Mr Zimmerman, they must have realised the enormity of what they had done, and pausing only to spit at us, they ran out into the crowd.

I will never forget the appalling image of my friend laying too still on the toilet floor. His blood slowly seeping into his new coat and turning it dark brown. He lay with his leg at an unnatural angle and his arm in the urinal.

We were lucky, the next man to use the toilet was an off-duty ambulance driver. He pushed his handkerchief into my cut, and told me to hold it tight. He then rolled Mr Zimmerman onto his back, and quickly felt for broken bones. Then I remember him bellowing very loudly for help. Other men came in, and a policeman was found. I felt very light headed and wanted to cry. The policeman told me I would have to go to hospital with Mr Zimmerman. He asked what my name was and if I had come with my parents. I told him about Arthur, and he said he would sort that all out.

I remembered our stand number and told him, and then the tears came. "He'll be all right, won't he?" I asked.

"Have to see Jimmy," he said. "Have to see." I heard the bells of the ambulance, then two men appeared and put Mr Zimmerman on a stretcher.

"Can you walk son?" they asked. I nodded and followed them to the ambulance. The man who sat in the back with us was called Norman, he put some gauze and some sticky tape on my face.

Does it hurt a lot he asked? The truth was it didn't, everything was just numb. We should have been cheering our team on and going home for Boxing Day tea, not going away in an ambulance. They took us to the hospital on Shooters Hill, doctors and nurses were waiting and they rushed Mr Zimmerman away. A nice nurse took me into a cubicle and cleaned my face up. She went and got a doctor who came to look at me. He examined me, smiled and said he would put a few stitches in.

"Be brave, Jimmy," he said. "I'll give you something for the pain." He took the nurse by the arm and took her outside the cubicle, but I could still hear. "Jesus, Gwen," he said. "He can't be more than fourteen, that's a razor cut he's got there. We ought to notify the police."

"They brought him in," she replied. "He was with the elderly man who got beaten at the football match."

"You mean that they assaulted him as well? Hell, Gwen, what's the world coming to?"

"How is the old boy?" she asked him.

"Not good, broken leg, broken ribs and it looks like a bleed on the brain. Mr Warrington is with him now."

"Well at least he's got the best we can offer," she said.

They came back in and the doctor propped me up with pillows.

"Right, Jimmy lets sort you out shall we." Gwen the nurse went and got a syringe in a kidney shaped bowl. She rolled me onto my side and stuck it into my bottom. At first it hurt, but then a warmth spread over me, and I felt very sleepy. The doctor reached over and pinched my earlobe, it was quite hard, but it didn't hurt at all.

"Right, let's suture this closed," he said. "Six, ought to do it, hold his head Gwen." The next thing I remember was being in pyjamas, and being tucked into a big bed. I slept.

When I woke up it was Tuesday, Mum was sitting by the bed looking worried. "Mum," I whispered.

She was on me in a flash. "Oh Jimmy, my baby, what have they done to you?"

"I'm all right, Mum," I said. "How's Mr Zimmerman?"

She looked pensive. "He's not well Jimmy" she told me. "The doctors operated on him last night, and they say all we can do is wait. He's a tough old bird though is Harry, he'll pull through."

I was very thirsty, and Mum made me an orange juice. "Did Arthur get home all right?" I asked. I had forgotten he had been left with Wilf, Bernie and Jo.

"Yes, he's fine," said Mum. "They put an announcement out on the tannoy system and those friends of Harry got him home. He wants to come and see you, but we said wait until you were home."

There was a knock at the door, and the same policeman I had seen at the grounds came in. He winced when he saw my face. "Morning

Jimmy," he said, taking off his helmet. "Do you think he's up to answering a few questions Mrs Jones?"

"Not for too long," said Mum. He nodded and pulled a chair up to my bed.

"Right Jimmy, tell me everything you can remember about yesterday. How did it all start?" I told him about needing the toilet, Mr Zimmerman taking me there, the men that had come in while I was in the cubicle. "Can you describe them for me," he said.

"Well, they had scarves pulled up over their faces, but the big one was called Pete, and he told us he was BUFs." The policeman looked up from his notebook.

"They said they were members of the BUF did they?"

"Yes," I said. "But I don't know what that is."

He scowled. "It's the British Union of Fascists." He turned to Mum. "Mosley's lot." Mum nodded. "Any other names you heard Jimmy?" he asked.

"No but I know who one of them was," I said. The policeman looked up from his notebook again.

"Do you now?" he said.

"Yes, it was Patrick Murphy, I know his brother."

"Well, I know most of the Murphys and you might have just helped put one of them away Jimmy, well done."

I began to feel tearful again at the image I had of Mr Zimmerman laying on the toilet floor. "I think that will do for now, constable," Mum said. "Can you come back later, and give him a break?"

"Yes, of course," said the policeman getting up. "Well done, Jimmy, that's excellent, that's really first class."

"I'll go and have a little chat with Patrick Murphy." He put his helmet on and left.

Mum told me that they wanted to keep me in for one more night, for what she called observation. I wanted to go home, but Mum stayed and read me my new book. I had liver and onions for tea. My face had started to hurt, so one of the nurses gave me a pill and I went to sleep.

The next morning both Mum and Dad came to get me. The doctor looked at my cut, said it was healing nicely although it was red and swollen, and gave mum some pills in case it started to hurt again. He said to go to the doctors on Friday just to check. Mum asked if it would leave a scar. He said it would, but because of my age, it wouldn't be disfiguring. Mum started to cry, so Dad put his arm round her. He put his other arm round me. "Chin up, old man," he said. "Worse things happen at sea." We took the bus home, people looked at me because of the big piece of gauze taped to my face. It was embarrassing. Mum said we could have fish and chips for tea as a treat.

In the afternoon Arthur came round, his mum had sent a bag of oranges. He stared at my bandage. "You all right kid?" he asked,

"Yeah, I'm on the mend, mate," I replied.

"How's Mr Zimmerman?" Arthur asked.

I paused. "Not good, I heard a doctor saying he had a bleed on the brain. They cut the top of his head off to operate!"

Arthur looked shocked. "But he'll be all right, won't he?" I said I didn't know, Dad was going to visit that night, and would report back. "Why did they hurt him?" Arthur asked, he looked close to tears.

"Don't know," I said again. "Because he was Jewish?"

Arthur went very pale. "You think they did that to him just because he was Jewish?"

"I don't know," I said for a third time. "You know when somebody wants to fight you at school, there doesn't have to be a reason, they just want a fight, and no matter what, they will fight you anyway?" He nodded. "Well, that's what it was like, they came into the toilet looking for somebody, anybody, to fight. It was my fault for making him take me there."

Arthur shook his head. "No, you can't say that. There are only three people to blame and they will be sorry." Arthur wasn't given to empty threats. I knew then that he meant what he said.

Chapter 5
Rabbi Abraham and the Bad Prognosis

At first Arthur and I went to see Mr Zimmerman two or three times a week. We would report on football matches, school and what was happening around Welling. He always seemed pleased to see us, but couldn't concentrate for too long. Sometimes he would be in bed, occasionally he would sit in his chair, but he started to look like an old man. There was always a bottle of Robinson's orange on his bedside table, and sometimes there would be grapes which he let us eat. But it was as though he wasn't connected to the real world. Once a nurse dropped a metal tray, and he jumped out of his skin, and started to cry. He had a tick under his left eye and couldn't remember anything about Boxing Day. The doctor came to see him once while we were there, he asked Mr Zimmerman if he knew who the prime minister was, and how many ounces there were in a pound. Mr Zimmerman didn't. He told Mr Zimmerman he was recovering very nicely, but we saw him shake his head when he looked at the chart on the end of the bed. Mum or Dad would go in the evening. They didn't stop for very long because Mr Zimmerman was always tired, and wanted to sleep. Eventually Mum told me he was being let out of hospital to go home. Mum went round to his house, and gave it a good going over. She did some shopping and cooked him a steak and kidney pie. Dad laid a fire. She collected some fresh clothes, and took his second-best woollen coat for him to come home in. They got a taxi and collected him from the hospital. Mum said he didn't seem to know what was going on, she said that was so sad because he had lost his chutzpa.

We weren't the only ones who tried to help. Mr Bloom his business partner bought him out, and because he was also a friend, paid him an income from the shop. Mum hired a lady she knew, to be Mr Zimmerman's housekeeper. Her name was Beryl and she went in every day to cook and clean, but he didn't even talk to her a lot. Wilf, Joe and

Bernie tried to get him to play cards, and took a medicinal bottle of brandy round for him. They ended up going less and less because even they couldn't raise his spirits, it was as though something in the old Mr Zimmerman had died early.

The police came round to our house twice. They took statements of what I had seen at the football on Boxing Day. They explained to Dad, that Mr Zimmerman would not be called as a witness because he was too frail, and couldn't remember anything. Dad said, "In that case, you will be the witness for both of us." He put his arm round me and gave me a squeeze when he said that. "All right, old man?" he asked.

"Yes Dad, I can tell what happened," I said. I didn't feel scared, I just wanted the men who had hurt Mr Zimmerman to go to prison.

They arrested the big man, Peter Summersgill, and Patrick Murphy. I had to go to an identity parade at Blackheath police station. They sent a police car for Dad and me. It was dead easy, because I knew Patrick Murphy, and Peter Summersgill had a broken nose where Mr Zimmerman had hit him. I picked them both out straight away. Inspector Richards ruffled my hair, and said, "Good lad Jimmy, good lad." They hadn't been able to find out who the third man was, and neither of the other two would say. "Don't worry Jimmy, we'll get him," said the inspector. "They use the birch on the Isle of White, and that's where those two will be going."

In June I had to go to court as the only witness to what had happened. Mr Zimmerman still couldn't remember anything. The police had taken a lot of statements from me, but I just told them everything I had heard or seen over and over. Inspector Richards, told me he was very impressed, and said when I was asked questions in court, I should talk directly to the judge, just like I had spoken to him.

The trial lasted for three days. The judge asked me, if I was certain it was Peter Summersgill and Patrick Murphy that had beaten Mr Zimmerman and cut my face. I said I was. The defence lawyer asked me how I could be sure as the assailants had their faces covered. I explained that I had seen Murphy's face before he covered it up, and that the other man still had a broken nose where Mr Zimmerman had punched him. People in the gallery laughed and Wilf shouted out, "You tell him Jimmy." The judge said nobody was to shout out, but he had a bit of a smile as well. Patrick Murphy looked at me as though he would like to kill me.

The jury took twenty minutes to reach a verdict: guilty. The judge said that the King himself had directed the judiciary were to punish violent crimes severely. Peter Summersgill got eight years hard labour with a recommendation that he be flogged, Patrick Murphy got six and a recommendation he receive fifteen cuts of the birch. He started to cry. Dad put his arm round me and said, "That's one for Mr Zimmerman and you Jimmy." Inspector Richards came up and shook my hand.

"Thank you, Mr Jones," he said to me. "If all my constables gave evidence as well as you, I would be very pleased." He gave me a police whistle on a chain, and told me to consider the force as a career.

Me and Arthur went straight round to Mr Zimmerman's house after the trial. Mum said I should be the one to tell him the verdict. Arthur rang his doorbell, and eventually he opened the door a few inches. "What do you want?" he asked.

"It's us, Mr Zimmerman," I said. "We've come to tell you about what happened at the trial."

He scowled. "What trial? I don't want none, go away." He slammed the door. We knew sometimes he got confused, and thought he was either back in hospital or living in Lithuania where his family came from.

"Give it another go," said Arthur. I reached up and rang the bell again. He tore the door open and glowered at us.

"You young rips, bugger off and leave me alone. I'm not Jewish, you can't prove anything. Leave me alone." There were tears in his eyes when he slammed the door. We were a bit shocked. Mr Zimmerman had never been so aggressive with us. Something was very wrong.

While we stood there confused another man came up the garden path, he was tall and dressed in a black coat and a homburg hat. "Hello boys, come to see Mr Zimmerman?" he asked.

"Yes," Arthur replied, "but he won't let us in."

"Oh dear, let's see if I can persuade him," the stranger said. "I'm Rabbi Abrahams, I'm sure he will be more hospitable if I ask." He looked at my red scar. "Are you Mr Jimmy Jones by any chance?" he asked, raising one eyebrow. I said I was. "And you're here about the trial no doubt," he said. We nodded. He asked, "Have they reached a

33

verdict?" We nodded again. "And you want to be the ones to let him know? Oi vey, what am I saying? Of course you want to be the ones to tell him." With that he knocked on Mr Zimmerman's door with three firm knocks, *bang, bang, bang*. Nothing happened.

The rabbi sighed. He banged again, harder this time. "Come on Harry, its Rabbi Abrahams, open your door or I shall huff and puff and blow your house down." At first nothing happened, then slowly the door opened.

Mr Zimmerman peered out. "Ah, Rabbi," he said. "Come in, come in."

"And I'm sure your hospitality extends to your very good friends Mr Wells and Mr Jones, after everything you have told me about them?"

Mr Zimmerman took a moment to think. "Of course, of course, boys come in," he said softly.

Rabbi Abrahams made tea in Mr Zimmerman's kitchen, he also found a packet of ginger nuts. "Now, Jimmy, do you have something to tell us?" asked the rabbi helping himself to at least three biscuits.

I nodded. "Mr Zimmerman, do you remember the men that hurt us?" I asked.

Mr Zimmerman's expression changed, he looked furtive. "Don't remember," he said.

"That's a shame," said Rabbi Abrahams. "Because these two young men have come all the way over here to tell you what happened to the men who attacked you."

"So what happened?" Mr Zimmerman asked, while gazing down at the floor.

"The big one that you knocked down got eight years hard labour, and Patrick Murphy, he's the one that cut me, he got six years." Rabbi Abrahams nodded; Mr Zimmerman looked at him.

"So an end to it Harry, a time to restart, get your life back on track, you won't see those two paskudniks ever again."

Mr Zimmerman got up and shuffled out to the toilet. Rabbi Abrahams waited until he was gone. "Boys," he said. "It's probably best if we go now. He will need time to think about this." He paused, "Do you like real Italian ice cream?" Arthur admitted that we had never tasted it. "No!" said the Rabbi. "Well, we shall have to go to Tony Willimott's shop, he does the best pistachio ice cream in London." He raised his voice. "We're off Harry, I'll pop back later for a chat. Yom Tov."

As promised Rabbi Abrahams took us to the ice cream parlour. It was a little cafe near Bexleyheath. I had never tasted anything so good. I had the pistachio like Rabbi Abrahams, and Arthur had Neapolitan. We ate in silence for a while. Eventually Rabbi Abrahams put his spoon down. "Boys," he said. "I have heard a lot about you from Harry. How you visited him in hospital, went to report on the football, and well, just cared for him."

"He is our friend," said Arthur. "That's what you do for friends."

"Indeed, it is," said the Rabbi. "And I hope you will think of me as a friend as well." It sounded somewhat ominous.

"Why?" said Arthur.

"Because I have to tell you about your friend Mr Zimmerman."

We sat up. "I have known Harry for a long time," he said. "He came to this country from a place in Europe called Lithuania. He was twenty-two when he arrived, both his parents had been killed, and Harry should have died many times on his journey. Being Jewish back then was, well, difficult and dangerous. He worked very hard, and started to build up his business with his friend, Michael Bloom. In 1914, he was one of the first to volunteer to fight for this country. He ended up as a captain in the East Kent regiment, and he won a military medal. He's a good man, boys, a good man that was beaten because he is a Jew."

"Why?" said Arthur. "I don't understand why you would want to hurt somebody just because they are different."

Rabbi Abrahams smiled. "That is very intuitive Arthur, you have just summed up two thousand years of Jewish persecution in one sentence. Because we are different."

I interrupted him. "But this was Mr Zimmerman, he's not different."

Rabbi Abrahams shook his head. "I know, I know," he said. "Boys, the world can sometimes be a very unfair place." He paused. "Do you know why he is acting like he is?"

"Is it because he's had brain surgery?" I said.

"Yes, it is," the Rabbi replied. "Do you know what the word prognosis means?" We said we didn't. "It's what the doctors at the hospital think will happen to Harry, sorry Mr Zimmerman. They are pretty certain he won't get better, boys, he will only get worse." Arthur looked away; this is not what we wanted to hear. "Better that you understand why he is acting like he is, than to think it is something you have done," Rabbi Abrahams said. "I'm afraid he can't go on much longer, there are blood clots in his brain they couldn't remove, one of the top brain surgeons in the country operated on him, but even he couldn't do enough to save him. I'm sorry boys, but you need to understand. He will need you to be his friend, no matter what he does or says. Do you understand?"

Our journey home was very subdued. Obviously, a Rabbi wouldn't lie. But the thought of Mr Zimmerman just getting worse and worse was awful. When we got in, Mum and Dad wanted to know how Mr Zimmerman had taken the news. We told them about Rabbi Abrahams, and Dad nodded. "He shouldn't have told you," he said. "But it's true. The doctors at the hospital told Mum and me, because we are the nearest thing to family he has." Mum said it was just as well we knew, and no matter what Mr Zimmerman said, it wasn't the same man that had been our friend.

We still went round to see him. Sometimes it was just like our old friend. He would tell jokes, and read bits from his books that he thought were particularly grand. At other times he seemed to resent us being there. Once he shouted at Arthur and accused him of being the leader of a pogrom. We didn't know what a pogrom was, but we knew how to deal with his mood changes by now, so Arthur told him to salute when a senior officer was present, and to stop talking balderdash. He stood up, saluted and shouted, "Sorry sir, won't happen again, sir."

It took Mr Zimmerman two years to die. As Rabbi Abrahams predicted he never recovered from the beating he had received. One side of his face now looked lower than the other, and he dribbled out of the corner of his mouth. He walked by leaning heavily on a stick but the worse thing was the haunted look in his eyes. Arthur and I still went occasionally, but by now he just didn't know who we were. One morning Rabbi Abrahams came to see us and told us Mr Zimmerman had passed away in his sleep, he was sixty-three. Mum and me cried, Dad just held us very tight.

Mrs Wells, Arthur and Beryl came with us to the funeral at Manor Park. He didn't have any family, but a lot of his friends from the war came from all over the country. Wilf, Joe and Bert were there, they all wore medals, and carried the coffin with Dad.

Beryl and Mum had made a tea for after the service. We all went back to Mr Zimmerman's, there was beer, whisky and sherry. Arthur and I were allowed to have a beer to wash the spam and piccalilli sandwiches down.

Granddad said we should have a proper drink to toast Harry with. That was the first, and only, time I saw Arthur cry. His shoulders shook, and his mum cuddled him. She kept saying, "It's all right Arthur, it's all right." But it wasn't.

He told me later that he was going to find the third man, and make sure he was sorry for what he had done to our friend. I believed him.

Mr Zimmerman did one final act of kindness to our family. He left Mum and Dad the flat. Dad said it must be worth at least six hundred pounds. The money didn't matter because it was our home, but it meant we would never have to pay rent again. As Dad said, "We were fortunate to know Harry Zimmerman, they don't make them like him any more." Arthur and I never forgot him.

Chapter 6
Employment

The years rolled by and, in 1935 we took our School Certificates. I did all right with five passes. Arthur was far more academic. He got distinctions in physics, chemistry, maths and credits in history, geography, German, English and technical drawing. He had also taken some City and Guilds in radio and line transmission, which he did for fun!

I wanted to leave school and get a job, but was a bit surprised when Arthur said he was leaving as well. Everybody thought he would stay on and do a Higher Certificate.

What we all forgot was Arthur's passion for radio and telegraphy. Ever since our first introduction with our cat's whisker radios in 1932, Arthur had become fascinated. He subscribed to *Amateur Radio* magazine and his mum had let him build a workshop in the old garage. I liked the crackly old crystal sets, but Arthur was designing and building his own multivalve receivers by the time he was fifteen. He just seemed to have a natural aptitude for it and, as in everything he was interested in, he soaked up knowledge. He got an amateur radio licence, learned Morse code and got a Saturday job down at Albert Gee's store. Albert sold electronic components, resistors, capacitors, transformers, in fact, everything a radio enthusiast could want. Arthur often knew more than Albert, and would often help the customers out. If they didn't have a particular valve, he would nearly always have a suggestion for an alternative. He got paid in components and a little cash, which suited them both. Albert offered Arthur a job when he left school, but Arthur had other ideas.

We both went for an interview with the General Post Office as telephone engineers. We wore our best clothes, and Dad had insisted that I had a haircut and polished my shoes. "Always makes a good impression does a well-polished pair of shoes," he said. The interview was at Dollis

Hill exchange. On the bus ride over, we talked about the possibilities of getting a job.

I wanted to work outside, but Arthur said he would only accept a job at the research centre which was also at Dollis Hill. Apparently, they worked on hypothetical engineering which was exactly what Arthur wanted to do. With hindsight I'm sure he later regretted turning down Mr Gee.

I went for my interview first. There was a big conference room with three desks facing a single chair. It should have been intimidating, but I had been a witness at the Crown Court. The men sitting at the desks were all managers, and had name plates in front of them. The one in the middle was Mr Gosling, he was the general manager. Mr Baily who was an exchange manager was on the right, and Mr Guy who was in charge of the external works was on the left.

They checked my name and address, and asked to see my School Certificate. Then they asked me why I wanted to work for the GPO. I said because I thought the telephone business could only get bigger. More and more people wanted a phone, and you couldn't be in business without one. I also said because it was a government owned enterprise it wouldn't go broke, which is what Dad had told me to say. They exchanged glances, and asked if I had any ideas about which branch I would like to work in. I said external works. Mr Guy nodded and smiled. "Good choice Mr Jones," he said, and made a note on his papers. Mr Gosling asked me why, and I told him I liked being outside. He asked if I had ever worked outside before? I thought for a moment, then told him that I had been employed part-time in roofing maintenance for Zimmerman's carpets.

"So you don't mind heights?" Mr Baily asked.

"Not at all, sir," I replied.

Granddad told me to say sir occasionally. "Makes the buggers feel important," he told me.

They gave me a piece of wire about eighteen inches long and a pair of long nosed pliers. "Could you copy this, please," Mr Gosling said. He handed me a similar piece of wire that had been bent into an unusual shape. It had what looked like a small coat hanger on each end, and then twisted to a diamond shape in the middle. I looked at it for a minute.

"Always take your time to think about it," had been Mum's advice before I left the house. I suddenly realised that to get it to look exactly the same it would be easier to copy a plan. I asked if I could have a pencil and paper. Again, looks were exchanged, and I was handed the stationery I had requested. I put their copy on the paper and drew round it.

Next, I had to know where the middle of my wire was to give me a starting point. I balanced the wire on the pencil until it hung without tipping. From there it was relatively easy. My efforts didn't look as neat as theirs, but they seemed very happy with what I handed back.

They asked if I could drive. I explained I was only sixteen, and because of the new driving test that had been introduced last year, I had not had the opportunity to take it. "Shouldn't be a problem," said Mr Guy. "We can test our employees, and issue driving licences. Fancy driving round in your own van, do you?" I grinned and said I did.

Mr Bailey asked me if I knew how many people in London had a phone. I took a moment to think about that, and carefully said I estimated it at around twelve per cent. They all nodded, which probably meant they didn't know either. There were a few more questions, until Mr Gosling looked at his watch, he asked me if there was anything I wanted to ask them? Granddad had told me to ask about promotion prospects. "A field marshal's baton in every knapsack," he had said winking at me. I told them this, and they all smiled.

"Well," said Mr Gosling. "You would start as a trainee technician, and you have a few years before my general manager's job comes vacant, so work hard, study and the sky's the limit." He thanked me for coming in and said they would write to me very soon and let me know how I had done. Mr Guy stood up and shook my hand; I felt confident.

Arthur was waiting on the edge of his chair. "You can go in," I told him.

"What are they like?" he asked.

"Concentrate on Mr Gosling," I suggested. "He's the one in the middle. He's the kingpin, and you'll need him to recommend you for research. Chap on the right is exchanges and the other one is external works."

Arthur looked at me and grinned. "See you later kid."

"I'll wait here mate," I replied.

Arthur told me later that his biggest problem was trying not to seem too clever. When he suggested that neighbours could share a pair of wires back to the exchange, it was as though he had mentioned flying elephants.

What saved the day was when he talked about co-axial cables, and how the electron flow at high frequency is only in the outer layer of the conductor which makes co-axial transmission possible. Mr Guy had heard of this. "It's called skin effect, isn't it," he said. Arthur then had them eating out of the palm of his hand. He was referred to Mr Tommy Flowers the head of research at Dollis Hill for a one-to-one interview the following day. He passed.

My invitation to join the GPO came three days later. It said I was to report to Wood Green yard at seven thirty the following Monday. My manager would be Mr Roberts, and my starting wages would be one pound two shillings and three pence a week. I was going to be a jointer. Mum and Dad both looked very proud.

I liked Mr Roberts as soon as I saw him, he was one of those larger-than-life characters that could deal with anything; master of all he surveyed. He was called an inspector, and was in charge of all the men who worked out of Wood Green Telephone Engineering Centre. He got me to sign lots of papers and talked about what I would be doing on the job. He got down some big pieces of cable, and explained how to navigate around them. "So," Mr Roberts said. "There is no reason to ever get your bloody wires crossed." He thought this a great joke, but I suspected it wasn't the first time he had used it.

We went to the stores and I was introduced to Mr Yarrow the store manager. He measured me, and his deputy, Ian Brown, wrote down my sizes. They got me two sets of bib and brace overalls, a pair of wellington boots some gloves and a waterproof coat.

"Sign here," said Mr Yarrow. "We'll let you know when all your tools start to arrive."

Mr Roberts and Mr Yarrow went into the office for tea and a smoke, Ian found me a bag to put all my new stuff in. "So, you fancy yourself as a jointer," he said.

"Yes, seems like a good job," I replied. "I like being outside."

"Let's see if you're still as cocky in midwinter," he said. "Last year we had a jointer frozen to a pole, took three days to find him and get the poor bugger down."

I got the feeling he didn't like me, and asked if I had done anything? "No, mate," he said. "Always pleased to see a proper English lad get work." Before I could ask what that meant Mr Roberts came back and told me to go with him.

"Who you going to put him with?" Mr Yarrow asked.

"Ron Gillroy" said Mr Roberts.

Mr Yarrow gave me his opinion. "You'll be all right then Mr Jones, Ron Gillroy is one of the best. He was a sergeant in the war. Keep your nose clean, do what he tells you and you'll do well."

"Come on then," Mr Roberts called. "I'll take you out to meet Ron." We drove in Mr Roberts' Woolsey Wasp car, it had leather seats and the speedo went up to eighty miles per hour.

I felt very grand, and Mr Roberts told me stories about jointers and what they did. The new thing was going to be putting all the main cables underground. He asked me if I knew why they would do that, considering the huge expense? It seemed silly, but I couldn't come up with a sensible answer. "Snow," he said. "When a mile of cable gets covered in snow and ice, the weight doubles. And when that happens, all the bloody poles break, and the cable tears into lots of bits. The powers that be, had finally listened to those who know, that's us, and once the cables were underground in ducts and manholes, they would be bloody bulletproof." It was an education just driving round with Dick!

We arrived at a road in Bexleyheath where a big GPO van was parked. There was a large man in the back making a sort of lead chimney, and another man on top of a pole, leaning back on a big leather belt. "Right, Jimmy, this is Ron Gillroy, he's a T1 jointer, which means he knows nearly as much as what I do," said Mr Roberts.

Ron looked round a smiled. "Best to humour him Jimmy," he said. "Are you my new trainee?" I said I was. "Right let's start the training as we mean to go on," he said. "This is our kettle, this piece of iron work is the stove, and the tea kit is in that tin with the scantily clad young lady on it. Make four mugs, and then give George a yell to come down. You do know how to make tea, don't you?" I said I did, and boiled the kettle.

The bottle of milk was in a big lead tube full of cold water, and Ron told me to use six spoonfuls of tea in the battered old kettle. "Mr Roberts will have four spoons of sugar and George and I will have three." I made the mistake of remarking that would be too sweet for me. Mr Roberts smiled, exchanged looks with Ron, shook his head and told me about 'Gang Tea'.

Apparently, the men who got the cable up on the poles, or pulled it in underground were called 'The Cable Gangs'. They had a full galvanised metal bucket boiling away all day, it contained a packet of Lipton's tea, two tins of condensed milk and two pounds of sugar.

"All stirred with a dog's tail," said the new man stealing Dick's thunder, while taking off his leg irons. "Hello mate, I'm George, pleased to meet you." I thought I was going to enjoy working with jointers.

Chapter 7
Girls

There were girls. Well of course there were girls. Even Arthur's thoughts were turning to members of the opposite sex. We were seventeen, we were full of testosterone, and we had Brylcreem. We joined the Eltham youth club and would go down on the bus to listen to jazz. I didn't enjoy the music as much as Arthur, I preferred swing, but anything that put me in close proximity with young ladies, was fine with me. At our age it was like being let loose in a sweet shop, treacle toffee could seem like the best thing in the world, but there was always the hope of coffee creams. I fell in love an awful lot and, as each girl broke my heart, I had to move on and find someone new. Arthur appeared to be more interested in the music, but I suspect that was just to cover his nerves. For me Charley Parker and Bessie Smith couldn't hold a candle to the likes of Muriel Spencer or Bridget Tulley.

There was one girl that I really liked, she was called Judy Richards. She wasn't very tall, but all the boys called her 'Little Miss Dynamite'. She wore clothes that were different from all the others, and always exuded style. It might have only been the addition of a ribbon, or some coloured buttons, but all the other girls made sure they knew what she was wearing. The next week they would be wearing ribbons and buttons, but by then she would have lace. She turned heads.

Once I decided I was in love with her, all the others paled into insignificance, and my mind was made up. Unfortunately, there were two problems. I found it difficult to be at ease in her presence, I always seemed to be trying too hard. She had that effect on lots of people. The problem was compounded by her friend, Janet. Janet wasn't interested in fashion and always wore a trench coat and a beret. They went everywhere together, and to say that she cramped my style was a gross understatement. Janet neither liked nor approved of me, and consequently all my attempts to get Judy alone met with abject failure. I needed a plan.

There was a pub outside the Welling railway station that would serve Arthur and I. The landlord probably knew we were underage, but was prepared to turn a blind eye if we didn't cause any problems. Arthur had developed a taste for mild and pickled eggs, which is not to be recommended. I borrowed five shillings off Granddad and took him to the Railway for a boy's night out.

I insisted on getting them in, and even suggested he got a couple of eggs, I declined the suggestion that I join him. Burton's best bitter and pickled eggs have an explosive effect on my digestive system.

Over his second pint I explained my problem with Judy. "I thought you were in love with Bridget Tulley," he said.

"No that was two weeks ago mate, and it wasn't love. I was blinded by lust," I explained.

"Turned you down, did she?" he grinned putting a third pickled egg in his mouth.

"Well yes, but it's Judy I need help with."

His jaw stopped masticating. "If you're going to suggest, what I think you're going to suggest, the answer is no!"

"Oh, come on, Arthur, I'd do it for you, look if we go out as a foursome."

His eyes came up from his pint and they didn't look friendly. "Are you seriously suggesting I go out with Janet?"

"She's not unattractive, mate," I pleaded.

He looked me in the eye. "She wears a beret and she's a communist," he said.

"Yes, yes that's very true, but you deserve a woman with intelligence and opinions, it's never just been about sex for you. You need intellectual stimulation, Arthur, she could have been made for you mate." While he hesitated, I went to the bar, returning with two fresh pints and a winning smile. I waited for him to speak.

"Where would we take them?" he said.

"Well, I thought we might go to the pictures. There's a new film on at the Granada next week."

He looked unimpressed. "What Film?"

"Oh, it's called *Mr Deeds goes to Town*, it's got Garry Cooper in it."

Arthur tried a different gambit. "I think they've got *Flash Gordon* on at the Gaumont, we'd both like that."

I was patient. "Yes, we both would prefer *Flash Gordon*, but I'm trying to organise a double date; that means all four of us want to go. I can't see Janet sitting through an outer space film, can you?"

He contemplated his pint. "Probably not."

"Right, that's agreed then, I'll ask Judy to get Janet to come. We'll meet them outside the flicks at seven o'clock."

Arthur nodded. "Will we have to pay?"

I grinned. "You are a mean sod, of course we pay, but think of my love life."

He finished his beer. "Come on then, I've got notes to write up."

"So we're on for this Saturday are we?" I asked.

"I'll tell you what kid, if you can get Janet Thompson to agree to come out with us, I'll pay for everybody, and get choc ices," he answered. Sometimes Arthur had no faith in my masculine charms.

Sometimes the fates just smile down on you. Two days later I was working with Ron and George in Sidcup high street. We had to cut a new cable from the bus depot into the main. For afternoon tea Ron was feeling magnanimous and sent me down to Lyons' corner house to buy iced buns for all of us. "Make sure you get big ones," he instructed. "You're a good-looking lad, Jimmy, smile at the nippy, and tell her you're in big trouble if you can't produce anything that isn't huge!" George laughed. I took a shilling out of the tea club box, and walked to the cafe. As I walked in, I saw Judy and Janet sitting at a window table. It was too good an opportunity to miss.

"Good afternoon, ladies," I said sliding into the seat next to Judy.

Janet gave me a black look and both barrels. "Oh, Christ on a bike, what do you want?" Judy at least looked a little shamefaced at this attack.

"We were just going Jimmy," she said.

"That's right, Al, we are off," Janet agreed.

"Al?" I was genuinely puzzled.

46

"Al Capone, you know Scarface." Janet grinned. My scar was part of me, and I just didn't think about it, but now I touched it self-consciously.

Judy seemed a little shocked. "Janet," she said, with an edge in her voice.

"Yeah, all right, sorry," Janet said, though I think she was more concerned about annoying Judy than me. "So how did you get it?" she continued. I didn't say anything for a moment, and then explained it was the fascists. I had been in a fight with them when I was thirteen. It was a fight that cost my friend his life.

It's one of those moments I will always treasure, Janet was so filled with remorse, she leant across the table and squeezed my arm. "Jimmy, I'm so sorry, please accept my apologies, I just didn't know." More importantly Judy also leaned across the table, gently touched my cheek, looked me in the eyes and told me how brave I was. I didn't disagree.

They ordered more tea, and I had to tell them the whole story of Mr Zimmerman. Judy had tears in her eyes, and Janet looked fiercely revengeful. "Bastards," she said. "Utter bastards."

It turned out Janet was a member of the Anti-Fascist League, which was affiliated to the young communists. Judy wasn't, but she was truly moved by the death of Mr Zimmerman. "So, they never caught the third man?" she said.

"No, the other two are still doing time, but we never found out who the ringleader was," I told them. I suddenly realised that I had been rather too long getting Ron his afternoon buns.

"Look, I've got to go," I said. "My friend Arthur and I are going to see the new Gary Cooper on Saturday, how about we all go together? Then we can come back here and have tea afterwards." I crossed my fingers.

"I'd love to," said Janet. "What do you think Judy?" I don't know who was the more surprised, but Judy said she would, so we arranged to meet at seven outside the pictures on Saturday. Arthur was going to be buying choc ices.

Ron was not happy when I returned, and had made himself tea with no buns. I explained that Lyons had advised me to wait for the new batch that were not only fresher, but bigger than the previous delivery. George examined his suspiciously, but I maintained my innocence and eventually they were both chatting to me through mouthfuls of iced buns.

Later I told Arthur, and suddenly realised what the expression, 'Knock me down with a feather', meant. At first, he thought I was, "Lying through my teeth." This changed to, "Having a laugh at his expense." Which eventually became, "She's all right that Janet, what shall I wear?" I told him his suit would be fine, but told him to be careful. "What of?" he demanded.

"Getting choc ice down the front," I told him, and dodged.

We met the girls as planned. Judy was wearing a tea dress with big wooden buttons and green shoes. Janet was in her trench coat, but had put a broach on the lapel. Arthur told her she looked smashing, and true to his word bought all four tickets. We sat, not in the back row, but close to it.

The film was actually very good. Gary Cooper inherits millions of dollars and, after nearly being tricked out of it, is saved by Jean Arthur who persuades him to use the money to set up farms for the recession hit farmers. When we came out, we made our way to the Lyons Cafe I had seen them in on Wednesday. Janet was very taken with the film, as she said it showed how communist principles are brilliant, and Gary Cooper had saved all those farmers by sharing his wealth.

"To each only his needs," she said to Arthur. To my horror Arthur disagreed.

"I know communism is theoretically the best of all worlds, but you're not equating in human nature." There was a long pause while Judy and I waited for her to explode, but she didn't. She stood up, took off her coat, pulled up the sleeves of her jumper and sat opposite Arthur to begin the first of many political arguments they were to have over the next few months.

Judy and I exchanged glances, and mutually exhaled a sigh of relief. If they were getting on, then we could leave them to it. "So, Judy, where do you get all your wonderful clothes from?" I said, looking into her eyes. The night was a success, everybody had a good time and the tea and cakes were brilliant. We walked arm in arm back to the bus stop.

"Shall we do this again?" I ventured.

"Well, I'd like to," said Judy. "Can we choose the film next time?"

"OK," said Arthur. "Anything in particular you want to see?"

"Well," said Janet. "There's *Flash Gordon* on at the Gaumont."

When the bus arrived, Janet gave Arthur a firm handshake. I got a kiss. We both went home grinning.

Chapter 8
Cable Street

By 1936 Arthur and I had reached seventeen, and life was good. We were both doing well at work. I was still with Ron Gillroy, but George had been promoted to a T1 jointer, and now had his own van. On Ron's recommendation, Mr Roberts had promoted me to be a technician 2A and made me Ron's mate, which increased my pay to two pounds twelve shillings and six pence. I gave mum one pound a week, but that still left me enough to take Judy out, and get some decent clothes.

Arthur didn't talk about his research a lot. He was working directly to Mr Flowers, and from what I could make out it was pretty high tech. A lot of it was theoretical. After a particularly good night at The Railway, Arthur tried to convince me that they could make a machine that would chop up hundreds of telephone conversations and mix them all together, send them down one pair of wires, then un-mix them at the next exchange. Flash Gordon seemed more believable! He was, however, earning very good money and there was talk of sending him to university. He had taken to wearing a long scarf, and carrying a leather briefcase.

Our love lives were also doing all right, sort of. After the initial six weeks of double dating, we started to see the girls on their own. On Tuesday nights, Judy's mum went to the church hall whist drive with her neighbour. Her dad and brother Nigel played for the Red Lion darts team, so we would sit on her sofa kissing until my lips were numb. I desperately wanted to carry her upstairs, but she was having none of it. "Too many girls ended up in the family way," she told me. So I had to make do with a lot of fondling. It was so frustrating. I think she felt the same, but she had more willpower than me.

Arthur and Janet's romance was an ongoing argument. They saw each other a lot, but couldn't agree. On the other hand, they saw each other pretty regularly, and they seemed very happy together.

Occasionally we would still meet up as a foursome. Judy's birthday was on Saturday the third of October, and we had arranged to go out for a fish supper together.

There was a new fish and chip shop in Welling high street, where you could eat in. They had proper tablecloths and metal cutlery, it also did some continental fish sauce made of salad cream and gherkins to go with the salt and vinegar. It cost more than the one next to the betting shop, but it was her birthday. I had bought her a single pearl on a chain from Johnsons in the high street.

Arthur and I met at the Railway, for a quick one first. The girls were supposed to meet us in the restaurant at seven thirty so we had plenty of time. I asked Arthur if he had got Judy anything, he looked annoyed. "Of course I have," he said. "Look." And he showed me a fancy package with three pairs of silk stockings in it. I felt annoyed, that he had bought her something that intimate, but then I remembered this was Arthur.

When we got to the restaurant, we were both surprised that Judy was there but without Janet. I kissed her and wished her happy birthday. Arthur did the same and asked where Janet was. Judy said, "Oh probably kept late at work." It didn't seem like Janet, but as she hadn't contacted any of us, we just had to speculate. The restaurant was licenced so we ordered two beers and a glass of sweet white wine. Judy said to give her another half hour. When she did eventually arrive, she was angry, very angry. She thrust a pamphlet at us, and demanded that we read it. It was only when Arthur took it, that she apologised to Judy.

"Sorry Judy, I know I'm late, but this is the absolute end!" Another communist, called Phil Piratin, had been printing the pamphlets, and Janet had been helping.

I glanced down at the pamphlet Arthur was holding. It was printed by the London Communist Party, and called for an, "All out protest against Fascism". Apparently, Oswald Mosley, the leader of the fascists, was going to lead a march of his supporters in their black shirts through the East End tomorrow.

"Why the hell would he do that?" I asked the other three. Arthur told me it was a show of strength.

"There must be thousands of Jews living in that area, Mosley is showing the world that he can scare them." Janet's anger was contagious.

The pamphlet called for a counter demonstration to intimidate the fascists.

Judy turned to Janet. "I can't see the police allowing this," she said. "There is bound to be violence."

"Oh, it gets better," Janet replied. "A petition of ten thousand signatures was organised by the British Jews, they sent it to John Snow the home secretary."

"Well, there you are then," said Judy. "It will be called off."

No!" Janet's eyes blazed. "His response was to send seven thousand extra police to escort them, and that includes mounted police to guard the scum."

Arthur looked up. "What time are we meeting?" he said coldly.

"Are we going?" I asked.

"They killed Harry Zimmerman, they marked you for life, I am not letting these bastards walk unopposed where I live." This was the Arthur that had stood up to Derek Murphy, I wasn't going to disagree. Despite Janet's protests, we told them that Arthur and I would represent all of us. It probably would turn violent and neither of us wanted the girls there. Arthur and I were adamant, we told them that was the end of the discussion, they would not be going.

The four of us met at eight o'clock at the famous Sid's Cafe in Christian Road. I'm not sure Judy would have gone on her own, but having made the mistake of trying to ban her, there was no way she was going to sit at home. Janet found four pence and phoned her communist friend, Phil, who told her they had planned to build a barricade at the junction of Christian Road and Cable Street. By the time we got there, there were hundreds of angry people outraged at Mosley's affrontery. Even the cafe owner said he was closing up, and going to take eggs down to throw at the blackshirts. As we finished our tea there was an almighty crash from the end of the road. Janet got up and stuck her head outside.

"Bloody hell," she gasped. "They've only gone and pushed a bus over." We all made our way to the junction where a double-decker bus was laying on its side. Oil and petrol leaked out of it like the dying blood of a huge animal. Dad wasn't on duty that day, but I was still pleased to see the driver and conductor unhurt.

"Well, there'll be hell to pay for this," the driver proclaimed to the world in general. "Who's going to tell my inspector that I didn't crash it?"

I stepped up to him. "Do you know Stanley Jones?" I asked.

"Oh, aye number three-four-seven out of Dartford," he said.

"Well, I'm his son, Jimmy. If you need anybody to say what happened, I saw it all," I lied.

"That's decent of you Jimmy, why the hell are they doing all this?" I explained about the blackshirts. "Yes, I've heard about that Mosley, sounds just the sort of bully we fought over in France. Can't believe they got it in for the people round here, they're descent sorts mostly."

"I'd get back to the depot, if I were you," I said. "They reckon there's going to be thousands of police with them. Could be a bit awkward with your bus as part of the barricade."

"Aye happen you're right," he replied. He stuck two fingers in his mouth and gave a piercing whistle, the conductor turned round. "Come on Ken, were going back to the depot," he shouted. The conductor turned and gave him the thumbs up.

By now there were hundreds of local people who had come out to see what the anarchists and communists were doing. Janet's mate Phil was trying to organise them. "Come on everybody, we're not letting Mosley and his bully boys march through our streets are we! Bring down anything you can to block the road." To be fair, he did motivate them, people dragged down furniture, dustbins and building material to block the blackshirts, I even saw a piano being added. By the time they had finished, the barricade looked quite impressive. Arthur and I had been helping to drag stuff down, Janet had been supervising and Judy had been hovering with intent. Suddenly it seemed to go very quiet, we had done all the hard work and nothing was happening, I felt a bit foolish, what if the march took another route?

I realised that Janet's friend Phil had got his information right when, as if on cue, we heard a rumble of noise like fast water boiling towards us. It was the march coming our way. At the head of it was Mosley standing behind his driver, in the back of his open-topped car. Behind him were at least a couple of thousand marching men dressed in brown trousers and black shirts. They were chanting, "Jews out, no Jews in London town."

Marching at the sides of the column were the police. Many were on foot, but there were mounted officers as well. If its purpose was to terrorise, it was working. Mosley was giving a strange, straight arm salute, as he shouted at the crowd. You couldn't make out what he was saying over the noise coming from ten thousand voices, but when he reached the road block, it all went quiet. Everyone was waiting to see what happened next. In a voice that was surprisingly powerful, he turned to a mounted policeman and demanded he be allowed to continue. "Tear that damned pile of rubbish down officer, so we may lawfully proceed," he commanded.

There was a moment's silence, then a single voice came from the back, "You're not proceeding through here you fascist fucker."

It was the signal the crowd had been waiting for. A half brick arced out of the crowd, it bounced off the bonnet and broke the windscreen. Mosley fell back into the rear seat as a shower of bricks, stones and bottles were hurled at him. Police whistles were blown, and the blackshirts charged.

It is difficult to imagine what close quarter violence is like unless you have experienced it first-hand. I know why many men would not talk of it when they came home from war. It is frightening. You imagine you will be brave and in control, you will be neither. Survival is the only thing that matters, and you will do anything to stay alive.

The noise was overwhelming, and it all happened so fast. One moment I was screaming abuse at the fascists, the next I was thrown to the ground. A boot caught me in the ribs, making me draw my knees up in agony. As I tried to get to my feet, a body crashed down on top of me. It was a policeman that had been clubbed from behind. He was extremely heavy, and completely unconscious. I managed to roll him off of me, but took another kick from one of Mosley's men. In desperation I scrabbled round for some sort of weapon that would allow me to get back up. Rule one in a fight is always get back up. The boot came again and caught me near my eyebrow, tearing skin so I could feel the warm blood running down my face. Then my right hand found salvation. It closed round fourteen inches of steel hard ebony, the policeman's truncheon. It was difficult to see, but when the boot came in for another kick, I swung with all my strength and caught the shin above it. Even above the noise of battle I heard the scream.

The blackshirt fell, but in rage still tried to grasp me. I managed to turn my head and was shocked to discover I was looking at Ian Brown, the storeman from work. He didn't seem to recognise me, but by then most of my face was covered in blood. As his hand reached out to grab me his arm extended out of his cuff and I saw the same tattoo I had last seen on Boxing Day 1932, the blue broken square. I felt like I had been kicked in the chest, but this time it was only shock. I was prevented from doing anything else when another blackshirt tried to pull Ian to his feet. He couldn't walk, but managed to hop away from the crowd that was baying for their blood.

I managed to crawl to a doorstep, and sat there trying to make sense of what I had seen. I looked up to see the police heading my way. I had blood all over my face, and I was holding one of their truncheons. I didn't look like an innocent bystander.

It was Sid the cafe owner from Christian Street that saved me. He hauled me to my feet, and half carried, half dragged me back to his place. It wasn't an act of personal friendship, it was just that he had seen what the police were doing to the walking wounded. Apparently, they had had chamber pots emptied on them, and were exacting vengeance on any one they could.

I stayed there for the best part of the day. It wasn't safe outside, as everybody was still angry. My new friend Sid washed the blood off my face and put a bandage round my wound. He had a big first aid kit as he was in catering, he told me. He looked at my ribs and told me he didn't think they were broken, but I ought to go up the hospital and get them checked. Sid also gave me hot sweet tea and brandy, as he reckoned, I had earned it. I asked if had seen anything of the others I had come in with that morning? He asked me if I was joking, and told me, "It was a bloody war zone out there, worse than the trenches." He advised me to go home and meet up there. Apparently, Mosley had called off the march, and had changed it to a rally in Hyde Park. "So go in the opposite direction, stick to the main roads and put the truncheon in your pocket," he advised. I did as Sid said, and made it home without any more trouble.

Mum and Dad were a bit shocked when they saw me. I explained to them that the same people that had killed Harry had tried to march through the East End, and the four of us just couldn't sit back and let that happen. Mum said it had been on the wireless. They said that three thousand fascists had caused six thousand policemen to act as protection against twenty thousand protesters. "They threw chamber pots over them," Mum said.

"There's no call for that," Dad said. "Let Jimmy tell us what really happened." I tried, but other than the bus going over and building the barricade, I didn't really know a lot. I deliberately didn't mention Ian, I don't know why other than I wanted to talk to Arthur first. Dad said I did the right thing over telling the driver I could be a witness, but didn't think the company would disbelieve him. I asked Mum if they said how many had been hurt, and how many arrests had been made. She said she thought it was one hundred and fifty arrests and one hundred and seventy-five injured, but throwing chamber pots over people, what was the world coming to? Dad asked if I knew what had happened to the others. I told him that I had been knocked silly, and had just wanted to get home. Mum said, "Quite right," when she took my bandage off. "Doctors for you my boy," she said. "This is going to need a stitch."

"So two one to the fascists," Dad said. I knew better, Ian wouldn't be swaggering into work tomorrow.

Chapter 9
It Looks Like War

Monday morning, I went to work and saw Ron, he took one look at my black eye and hunched walk and said he was driving me round the hospital. "Got involved in Cable Street, did you?" he asked. I nodded. "Well after what you told me about your Mr Zimmerman, I can't say I blame you. Best not mention it to Dick Roberts, he's already got Ian Brown from stores off for weeks with a broken leg." He turned and gave me a careful look. "You wouldn't know anything about that I suppose?" I denied all knowledge.

"Was it the blackshirts that got him?" I asked.

"No, you idiot, he is a bloody fascist, didn't you know?"

I told him I didn't. "He's just a bloody awful storeman and a worse human being as far as I'm concerned," I said.

"Well take it from me Jimmy, you're right on that score he's a bloody nasty piece of work. You stay well clear of that bastard," he replied. "Now get in: hospital!"

I had my ribs checked, they weren't broken but, because of the interesting colours, the nurse covered me in embrocation and strapped me up with a half dozen yards of bandage. I also had two stitches in my eyebrow. "You're beginning to resemble a quilt, Mr Jones," the doctor said. Easy to be funny when you're the one holding the needle! I was handed a bill of three shillings for the repair work and had to borrow sixpence from Ron.

I made my way back to the van, and Ron drove us to Blackheath to start a repair on a damaged cable. Over afternoon tea he asked me about the riot. I explained that apart from building the barricade, and shouting at Mosley, I had spent most of the day laying under an unconscious policeman and having the crap kicked out of me by an unknown assailant. He nodded. "Sounds like it wasn't a barrel of laughs, but I have to say Jimmy, I'm quite proud of you for standing up to those bastards.

How are your mates?" I confessed I hadn't made contact with them yet, but intended to straight after work. Ron thought they would be fine, but I was secretly a bit worried, nobody had been safe out there.

Before I started clearing up, I got a pencil and paper and on sudden impulse drew the strange broken square I had seen on Ian's wrist. "Ron, do you know what this is?" I asked. He glanced over, and gave me a hard look.

"Yes, I do," he picked up the paper and studied it. "It's called a swastika, and it's the symbol of the German Socialist Party. They're also called the Nazis. Jimmy don't even think of getting mixed up with this lot, they're worse than the bloody blackshirts." He looked at my picture again. "Where did you see this Jim," he asked.

I explained I had seen a man wearing it at the fight. "Seriously Jimmy, you stay away from anything to do with the Nazis. You mark my words, there'll be some in Germany who want to go to war again, and those evil shits would love to lead them." He took a long pause, then slowly looking up gave me the killer question. "Did you know Ian from the stores has one of these on his wrist?" That was the trouble with Ron, nobody thought of him as being particularly clever, but that was just because that's what he wanted you to think. He might not have had a lot of qualifications, but George had told me he had been a sergeant in military intelligence during the war. The one time I asked him about it he just laughed and told me that was an 'Oxymoron'. I didn't know what that meant so I changed the subject to the new price of a Charlton ticket.

Ron didn't ask me a lot of questions, but I found myself telling him more than I had intended to. He would pause, and just look at me, and I found myself telling him about the 1932 Boxing Day, the third BUF man and suddenly seeing the same tattoo at Cable Street.

Ron lit his pipe. "What are you going to do about it?" he asked. I said I didn't know, and I was still trying to think it through. He nodded. "Tell you what," he said. "Get your mate, Arthur, and come round the working mens' club in Hook Lane, I'm a member there and I'll sign you in. About eight?" I said we would try, but I needed to find out if Arthur was all right. "Right," he replied. "Eight, if you can. Now get those ladders put away, we'll call it a day."

I went round to Arthur's house as soon as I got off work. He wasn't in but his mum let me in. She gave me an old-fashioned look, taking in my new stitches and black eye. "How is he, Mrs Wells?" I asked.

"Well considering he got in at two o'clock in the morning when the police eventually let him go, and considering he has a black eye bigger than yours, and considering his spectacles were broken and his good jacket torn, and considering this might stop him going to university, he's fine, thank you very much," she replied.

"I'm sorry," I said. "It was a bit crazy out there, if I could have stuck with him and protected him, I would."

She stopped, "I know you would Jimmy, thick as thieves, you two. It's just he's never had any dealings with the police before."

"Is he being charged?" I asked.

"Thirty shilling fine and bound over, that's where he is now, paying it off."

"Do you know what happened to the girls?"

She folded her arms. "As a matter of fact, I know they both got home all right, but what were you thinking taking two young ladies to a street riot?" It was a fair question. While I was trying to compose a believable answer, Arthur saved the day and came in. We surveyed each other.

"Mine's bigger than yours," he grinned.

"Blackshirts?" I asked.

"No police," he said. "The one that grabbed me was covered in something horrible from a po, I suppose he thought I was taking the piss!" We both laughed.

"Arthur," said his mum. "You can't talk like that at university."

"Yes mum," he agreed.

"What happened," I asked.

"Well after I was clobbered, I was carted off to the police station in a Black Maria with loads of others. It was the sheer numbers that stopped it getting nasty, they couldn't duff us all up. I was 'processed', which means they took my particulars, then I was photographed and fingerprinted. At half twelve the station was filled to overflowing, so they threw me out and I had to walk home." Arthur grinned. "We look like a couple of desperadoes, don't we?"

I laughed. "Can we meet up tonight? My boss wants to talk to us both."

"Trouble?" said Arthur?

"Good God no, Ron has only ever helped me. I'd really like to go. The Hook Lane working mens' club at eight."

Arthur nodded. "Yes of course I'll go, but you might have to get my round in, I just gave the justice of the peace thirty bob."

"He'll probably be in there spending it," I said. We laughed, and he showed me to the door. "Have you seen Janet?" I asked.

"Yes, both of them are fine, but you might like to go and check on Judy."

"I'm on my way," I told him.

Judy flew into my arms when I rang her bell. She covered me in wet kisses and tears in equal measure. In my worry about her, it never occurred to me that she would have been anxious about me. I was Jimmy Jones Esq., indestructible seventeen-year-old, well nearly indestructible. Judy studied my stitches.

"Did it hurt awfully?" she asked. I told her that in the heat of battle it didn't, but sitting in Sid's Cafe it was like having a hot soldering iron pushed into it. She pushed herself against me, and promised my bravery would be rewarded. I kissed her back, and hoped the bingo and darts were on for tomorrow night.

Arthur and I met at Ron's working mens' club. I briefed him about Ron before we went in. "So ex-military intelligence," he remarked. "Sergeants were generally interrogators, that's a job for a man with a very high IQ, do you trust him, Jim?" I told him one hundred per cent. "Fair enough," said Arthur. "Do they do pickled eggs here?" The man at the bar had been told we would be coming, and after signing us in took us through to a little snug where Ron sat alone.

Arthur stepped forward. "Good evening Mr Gillroy, I'm Arthur Wells, Jimmy's friend. Nice to meet you."

Ron rose to his six-feet-two height and turned to Arthur. "And good evening to you, Mr Wells. Jimmy tells me you're one of the very bright sparks working up at Dollis Hill, so we're all GPO engineers working together." He extended his hand. Arthur nodded, and voluntarily placed his hand into Ron's. Not a thing I had seen him do too often. They shook hands.

We settled down with three pints and Ron lit his pipe. "Have you told Arthur about Ian?" Arthur turned to look at me.

"Ian who?" he said. There was nothing for it but to go through the whole Cable Street battle. I told it exactly like it happened, no heroics, no bravado, just the truth. Neither of them spoke, until I had finished. Arthur had gone pale, "Are you sure Jimmy?" he asked. I said I was.

Ron said, "Well now we know that much, it's up to you gentlemen to decide the next course of action. That's why I wanted you to come and have a bit of a powwow." There was a moment's silence.

"We could go to the police," I said. "They put the other two away."

"Well yes that's option one and would be the sensible thing to do," Ron agreed. "But think about your evidence, a tattoo seen briefly four years ago under hugely stressful circumstances.

"A tattoo that isn't even unique, and it's a pound to a penny, that he will come up with a string of witnesses saying he was at a bible reading meeting with them on that Boxing Day."

I got angry. "But it was him Ron, I know it was him."

"And I believe you," he replied. "But will the police?" Arthur put his arm round me.

"Mr Gillroy's right Jimmy, they'd throw it out of court. We got the other two because we were fast, this Ian has had too long to cover his trail."

"Well, what can we do?" I demanded.

"We could wait for him with a snooker ball in a sock," Arthur suggested.

Ron nodded. "That of course is option number two," he said. "You're bright boys, can you see any problems with doing that?"

"I suppose it puts us in the wrong," I said.

"Well leaving right and wrong aside, do either of you have any experience of clubbing a man to death? I take it you are going to kill him, because if you don't, you will be forever looking over your shoulder. Make no mistake lads, the Ian Brown I know wouldn't rest until he'd stepped out of a dark alley and slipped a knife between your ribs."

Now Arthur looked perplexed. "I didn't mean kill him," he said. There was another long silence.

"Is there an option three Ron?" I asked.

"I thought you'd never ask," he said. "Look, gentlemen, the reason I asked you both to come and have a chat, was to stop you acting on impulse. If you go to the police and it doesn't work you can't do it twice. If you kill him, you'll find the police take a dim view of that, and they're pretty good at catching the culprits, which would mean the rope. I should also add that he is a big bloke, and I'm not sure you'd win in a fight. You don't have that sort of education: he does."

"So option three?" I asked.

"Option three," said Ron. "Is to do nothing." There was a pause, while Ron drew on his pipe.

"Nothing!" exploded Arthur. "You can't expect us to do nothing, that scumbag murdered Harry Zimmerman, you know it, I know it, why would we do nothing?"

The barman came round into the snug. "Same again gents?" he asked. I paid out of the five shillings I managed to get Granddad to lend me, and we waited to hear Ron's thoughts.

"Let me rephrase that," Ron said, sipping his pint. "Option three, Do nothing, yet." We both sat expectantly, waiting for Ron's guidance. He took a long drink from his new pint, then spoke. "As we have agreed, if you go to the police with your mixture of hearsay and speculation, they won't manage to get a prosecution, let alone a conviction. If, however, you could gather some evidence to present them with, well then, the force of his Majesty's constabulary would be behind you, and our Ian would be looking at a very long sentence."

I knew that Ron was right, but asked, "How would we get evidence?"

Ron smiled. "You use your heads," he said. "You keep this completely to yourselves, you watch, you wait, and sooner or later you will find he's made a mistake, they always do."

He finished his pint. "During the war I learned that once they think they have got away with it, they let their guard slip. I caught a lot of them like that. Watch him and be patient. Right?" he looked at both of us in turn.

"Looks like war then," said Arthur.

Ron nodded. "I'm afraid you might be right on more than one level Mr Wells, the lights are going out all over Europe, again!"

Arthur looked very thoughtful. "Let's hope not Mr Gillroy," he replied.

We thanked Ron, and made our way home. On the way out I turned to Arthur, "Bloody hell Arthur, he can't mean going to war again. It's only eighteen years since they came home from France, nobody would want to repeat that surely?"

Arthur nodded his head. "That would have been my opinion, but if that's what Ron thinks, I wouldn't bet against it, would you?"

We walked to the bus stop in silence.

Chapter 10
The New Haircut

On Tuesday, I was due to go round to Judy's house. I considered my options and decided that all the planets had aligned and, provided her family was out, this could be 'the night'. I knew Judy wanted to as much as I did, but the horror and shame of having a baby at seventeen was making her very cautious. Obviously as the man it was down to me to stop that happening, so I decided that I should buy some French letters. Granddad had told me about these, they are rubber sheaths that fit over your knob and prevent you catching anything, and stopping the woman getting in the family way. He was issued with several packets while serving in France, and reckoned they were made of melted down tractor tyres. He told me it was like paddling with your socks on, but unfortunately the mademoiselles that worked in the French bordellos would not entertain you without one.

I had two options, the chemist near the library or a choice of three gentlemen's hairdressers. Considering one of the ladies who worked in the chemists was Mrs Gordon who knew my mum, it made my decision easy. I had never bought them before, but how hard could it be? As I walked to Albert Coopers Gentleman's stylist, I became a little concerned about various previously unconsidered questions. The size, did they come in numbers like shoes or small to extra-large like underwear? How much were they? Would they demand proof that I was over twenty-one, would they want the lady's name? It suddenly became a lot more daunting than I had first imagined. I decided to answer medium or average to everything, and make names and addresses up if necessary.

I took a deep breath and walked into Albert Coopers. There was one man in the chair when I walked in. "Take a seat sir, be with you in two shakes of a lamb's tail," said Albert. There was a copy of *Practical Motorist*, *Punch* and *Screen Pictorial* on a low table, I picked up the

Screen Pictorial and sat down. A young lad came in from the back room, gave Albert a cup of tea and then proceeded to sweep the floor.

"That's got the story behind Anna Neagle and Anton Wallbrook," he told me conspiratorially. "They reckon they done it while she was playing Queen Victoria, and he was Prince Albert."

"Yes, thank you Raymond," said Albert. "We'll keep our opinions to ourselves, shall we?"

"Yes, Mr Cooper," Raymond agreed, but he gave me a knowing wink.

The man in the chair examined the back of his head in Albert's handheld mirror. "Very nice Albert," he said. "How much do I owe you?"

"Oh, just one and nine for a regular cut," said Albert applying cologne. "Anything for the weekend, sir?" he enquired.

"Yes, please, Albert," the man replied. Raymond scuttled out the back and reappeared with a paper bag. A ten-shilling note was handed over and change received.

How easy was that I thought, my nerves vanished, now I knew the secret code, 'something for the weekend'. It made me feel like I could be very debonair about it. Why had I ever worried! The man retrieved his hat and coat from the pegs near the door and left.

Albert shook out the slightly off-white cloth and motioned me to the chair. As I sat, he whirled the cloth around me like a magician covering his assistant. "And what can we do you for, sir?" he smiled. The daft thing was that I had been so busy thinking about French letters, that I had completely forgotten about actually having a haircut.

Normally I would have said, "Just a short back and sides please," but now Albert was ahead of me. He lifted some of my hair as though examining it for nits.

"I could do a really good Clarke Gable, for you?" I said no.

Raymond came round to look at me. "How about a forward combed boggle," he suggested. He and Albert looked at each other before both shaking their heads.

"No, he's not got the jaw line for it," he concluded.

"A crew cut," said Raymond.

"Yes, yes we could get away with that," agreed Albert.

"What's a crew cut," I asked.

"Military" said Raymond. "Like Ray Milland had *in Wings over Honolulu*, you know when he was with Wendy Barrie. She was hot for it."

Mr Cooper sighed. "Look Raymond, just because actors make a film together doesn't mean to say they are leaping into each other's beds, now does it?"

"Oh, you should read some of the inside information in *Screen Pictorial*," Raymond replied. "You would not believe what they get up to, I never miss a week." Albert shook his head.

"I know," he said. "An undercut."

"Oh yeah," agreed Raymond. "He'd look dead good with one of them." They both turned to me.

"OK," I nodded. "Just remind me again what an undercut is?"

"Well," said Raymond. "Short on the sides, but quite long on top, like Ronald Coleman in *Lost Horizon*."

That didn't seem too bad. Albert then informed me that not many young men had discovered the new fashion, so I would be able to surprise my young lady as a trendsetter "Sir does have a young lady?" Sir agreed he did. "Splendid," said Albert. "I can guarantee she will be delighted." I didn't have a way out so agreed to an undercut, and hoped for the best.

Sitting in the chair was very relaxing, Raymond put the wireless on and it was playing slow dance music. My eyes felt heavy, and I felt myself nodding off, the relief of finding a male establishment where French letters could be purchased discretely was huge. Albert worked round me with the most delicate of touch, all I heard was the buzz of his electric clippers. Occasionally he would tilt my head, but other than that I was blissfully unaware. The sound of the shop doorbell roused me out of my torpor as a new customer walked in.

"Be with you in two shakes of a lamb's tail," said Albert. I looked in the mirror and to my horror saw the new customer was a young mother with her eight-year-old son.

"Be all right if I wait with Sydney?" she asked.

No, no, no. I couldn't possibly discuss French letters with a woman present. It was then that I saw my hair, or rather my lack of hair. Albert had shaved both sides to a minute stubble whereas the top had been plumped up to resemble a Red Indian Mohican. He brushed the hair from my neck, squirted cologne all over me and removed the sheet with a flourish.

Holding up his mirror for my inspection, his teeth gleamed in the knowledge of a job well done. I noticed the young mum's eyes widening as she took in my new haircut.

"Just a trim for Sydney," she said.

As Mr Cooper brushed me down, he said that immortal phrase that I had been both wanting and dreading. "Anything else, sir? Something for the weekend perhaps?" I mumbled the affirmative. "Raymond, sort the gentleman out for me please. Now, Sydney I'm going to let you sit on my special seat," he said placing a padded plank across the chair's arms.

He lifted Sydney aboard and started to discuss his sartorial repertoire with the young mum. She kept glancing at me while repeating, "Just a trim, please." Raymond fetched a paper bag from the back and with a palaeolithic leer demanded a total of four and six. It seemed a huge amount, but I was in no mood to argue. I might look like an escaped convict, but I had my French letters without having to reveal any personal information. I bid them good day and escaped back to the high street.

I looked at my reflection in a shop window, only to discover the shop girl was staring open mouthed back at me from the other side, perhaps Albert was right, I had become a fashion icon.

I put on extra aftershave, my best suit and brushed my teeth before I headed over to Judy's. Dad remarked that I seemed in a good mood considering my bloody silly haircut. "Laugh, and the world laughs with you, cry and you cry alone," I told him; it was one of Ron's sayings. He looked puzzled. There was a flower seller near the bus stop, so I bought Judy a bunch of freesias, they were her favourite. Even the conductor remarking that I looked like a new recruit who had gone AWOL halfway through his first haircut failed to dampen my mood. On arrival I shot my cuffs and knocked on Judy's door, my heart was beating faster than normal with the anticipation of a night of passion. The door was opened by a lady I didn't know.

"Now then, ee but that's a haircut and a half," she said. "Hast thou been to sheep shearers?" I must have looked surprised, because she shouted behind her, "Blanche I've got a young man at t'door with a mouth that could catch flies and a haircut that's bin done for a bet, shall I fetch him in?"

Judy's mum appeared. "Bloody Hell, Jimmy what on earth have you done to your hair." I told her it was the latest fashion and it was called an undercut. She smiled, and told me she was sure that it was very nice. "This is my sister, Ethel," she said. "She's down from Yorkshire."

I began to feel anxious. "Going to the whist drive with you then Mrs Richards?" Ethel put her arm through mine.

"Nay lad, haven't come a hundred miles t' sit in some draughty hall and play cards. My sister and I are having a proper catch up. Haven't seen each other for six years. Do you like faggots? I've done enough to spare. I expect you're our Judy's young man. Now't as queer as folk I say. Well don't just stand there, put wood in t'ole and come in."

I was left reeling under this verbal onslaught. I didn't understand everything she had said, but I knew my night of passion had been replaced with a night of faggots. I followed her in with a heavy heart.

Judy was sitting with her dad and brother in the kitchen, I gave her the flowers, but she kept her eyes on my haircut and didn't even look at them. "Evening Jimmy," her dad said. "Come to join us for a spot of Ethel's cooking?" Judy gave me a lopsided grin and rolled her eyes.

"It's a surprise visit from my Aunty Ethel," she told me. "I was eleven the last time she came down."

"That's right," Ethel agreed. "Now don't be mythered, I expect thou was going dancing or the like, don't get monk on, my faggots will leave thee feeling the bedside table, drawers and wardrobe, see if they don't." You couldn't argue with that.

It wasn't an unpleasant evening, I sat next to Judy at the kitchen table. She held my hand undercover of the crisp white cloth Mrs Richards had laid in honour of Aunt Ethel's faggots. Her dad told me to call him Ron and proceeded to tell me why I was an idiot to support Charlton instead of Fulham. Judy's brother, Nigel, had once had a trial for Gravesend and joined in berating the pair of us for failing to support the best team in the country, Tottenham. Football can be a great leveller, if you realise everybody else is wrong!

Judy's mum and Ethel reminisced about the good old days. As far as I could make out these were the days when we had the Great War, Spanish flu, rickets and poorhouses. Ethel spoke in a strange dialect full of e's and thous, strangely I seemed to be the only one not able to translate. Judy would nod, turn to me and give the London version. Apparently, the remark about bedroom furniture meant to be full to bursting. Once she had explained, they would all look to see if the idiot boyfriend had understood before moving off at speed again.

The food was actually extremely nice and Ron went to the coal shed for three bottles of porter to wash it down with. The girls drank gin and orange. There was rice pudding for dessert which, as predicted, left me full to bursting. At ten o'clock I thanked them all for their hospitality but explained I had work in the morning. Judy saw me to the door and gave me a very long and lingering kiss goodnight.

"Sorry Jimmy," she said. "I thought we would be on our own tonight."

I kissed her back, told her I loved her, and said there would be other nights. "Yes," she said. "But do something about that haircut, Mr Jones." I swear I floated six inches above the pavement on my way back to the bus.

Chapter 11
And Then There was Three

On Friday Arthur came round to see me. I thought he wanted to know how it had gone with Judy, but he had far more important news. He had been summoned to see Tommy Flowers, his boss at the research station. The GPO board had decided on Tommy's recommendation, that it would be mutually beneficial for Arthur to be sent to university, on full pay. He would still be required to put in appearances at work, but the bulk of his time would be on study leave. It meant he would be travelling to Bloomsbury every day, so he was hoping to get digs and stay closer to his, 'college', as he put it. Arthur was definitely going up in the world. His mother, as expected, had taken on the persona of junior royalty and was still floating on cloud nine. Her son was going to have letters after his name, and that automatically elevated her to at least the minor nobility.

I asked how Janet had taken the news, he went quiet and explained that she had not been happy. To her it was selling out, and he was definitely not flavour of the month. I was very taken aback when he added that as they had spent several nights together, he thought she would have been happy for him. She wasn't, and had been talking of going to Spain. I thought he meant a holiday, and asked how on earth they could afford the boat passage. He rolled his eyes. "I'm not talking about a beach holiday, bullfights and foreign food, you idiot. She meant enlisting in the International brigade, and going to fight Franco." I was incredulous, she was a girl for heaven's sake. I had seen news reels about the civil war and it looked bloody awful.

"Arthur mate, you can't let her go, she'll get herself shot," I told him.

He looked at me desperately and said, "How the bloody hell do I stop her Jimmy, when her mind is made up? You know what she's like."

"We need to talk some sense into her," I told him. "If all three of us tell her that she would be crazy to go, well that will do the trick, she just doesn't know what war is like."

Arthur did not look convinced. "Could you get Judy to meet us at the Railway tonight? It's got to be worth a try Jimmy, hasn't it?" he wasn't far off of tears. I gave him a punch on the shoulder.

"I'll go round to Judy's now, we'll meet up about seven OK?"

He forced a grin, and I got a, "Thanks mate."

As I made my way round to Judy's, I ran through all the new news. It was a lot to take in, Janet fighting for the international brigade, Arthur going to university, but most of all they had been doing it without mentioning it to me, bloody hell! Judy's mum let me in.

"Oh, hello Jimmy love, she's just taking Ethel to the station with her dad. Don't suppose they will be too long. Would you like a cup of tea and one of Ethel's Eccles cakes, they aren't too bad?" I said I would, and was moved into the sitting room to wait. "Well, what did you make of my sister then," she shouted through from the kitchen.

I said, "I think she comes from a family of strong women, and I liked her for that, I suppose that's why I like your Judy, and you Mrs Richards." Granddad had once told me to never miss an opportunity to compliment a lady. Granddad knew his stuff because when Mrs Richards appeared with my tea, she had a big smile, and she ruffled my undercut.

"You're a kind lad Jimmy, you look after our Judy, and she'll be a good friend." I nodded. I was rescued from further advice by the arrival of Judy and her father. Her dad threw his hat onto the hall stand and glared at the world in general.

"Well bloody hell fire, that sister of yours can talk the hind leg of a bloody donkey, we didn't get to speak except to say goodbye, and that was only after the bloody train door shut."

Judy rolled her eyes at me. "She sends her love, Jimmy, taken a shine to you apparently."

"Well," said Judy's mum. "I expect it will be a few years until she comes down again, unless we go up to see her?" The implied threat had the desired effect, and Mr Roberts' anger receded. He retrieved his *Evening Standard* took a pencil from his pocket and headed for the toilet.

He liked to do the Quick Crossword at his own sedentary pace in the solitude of the outside lavvy.

Judy sat next to me and stole a bit of my Eccles cake. She addressed me in a good parody of Ethel's northern twang. "E, well she might have opinions on every subject known to man, young James, but by hell that woman can cook, I say our aunty Ethel can cook; faggots, Eccles cakes and fricassee of pansy southerner, delicious!"

I didn't laugh and she gave me a look. "What's the matter Jimmy?" she said cuddling up to me. I told her about Arthur, and Janet.

Surprisingly she didn't seem very shocked. "Oh, that's just Janet," she told me. "Always going for the dramatic gesture."

I told her Arthur was extremely worried. "Right," she said. "I'll get Janet, you collect Arthur and we'll meet at the Railway at seven. Then Arthur will be able to move to darkest Bloomsbury with a clear conscience after he sees El Janeto is safe at home." It all seemed very reasonable.

Arthur and I got there ten minutes early, I got us two pints but refused to indulge him with a pickled egg. "Shall I get Janet a glass of vino tinto?" I asked. He told me to piss off. I was dying to ask about his love life, but it didn't seem appropriate. I tried to think of other topics but couldn't think of anything else. After a moment's pause, I went for the jugular. "You and Janet have been sleeping together then?"

He looked up smiled, and said, "Yeah, I love her, Jimmy, I really bloody love her."

Our conversation was interrupted when Judy burst into the bar. She ran into my arms and let out a long shuddering sob. "She's gone Jimmy," she sobbed. "She's gone." Arthur stood up, he looked very pale.

"Where has she gone Judy?" he said with a hollow voice, although we all knew the answer.

"Spain," Judy sobbed. "She's gone Jimmy, she's gone." She thrust an envelope at Arthur and retreated into tears. I held her while Arthur opened the letter, he slowly sat and read it out loud to both of us.

My darling Judy, you know I could never face long goodbyes so better that I tell you this way. I have been thinking of going to fight with the international brigade for some time. Phil my friend from the communist party has organised a truck to take a group of fourteen of us down. We are catching the ferry across to Calais, then driving down to Spain. The boat leaves at three o'clock tomorrow, so I suspect by the time you read this I will be near to Paris, "Oh la la!" I have taken out all my savings to help with the cost, and packed what few clothes I will need, if there is anything in my wardrobe you would like, please take it with my love. I am doing this because I believe that fascists like Franco can't be allowed to bully a whole country into submission. As a member of the communist party, I have a duty to fight for what I believe is right. I know it will upset Mum and Dad and you and the boys, but it is something I have to do, I hope you understand and will forgive me.

Please tell Arthur that he is one of the most caring, intelligent and loving men that I have ever met, and I hope to see him again when I come home.

I hope you and Jimmy will be happy together you both deserve it. You are still my best friend and I love you very much, I will try and write when I can. All my love and friendship Janet.

We sat in stunned silence. "When did she leave do you think?" asked Arthur.

"Her mum said she hadn't slept in her bed, so I suppose she set off yesterday." Judy reached over and took Arthur's hand. "She'll be back, Arthur, you know she will." Arthur made a noise halfway between a snort and a cry of pain.

It took weeks for Arthur to get over it, if he ever did. He went into GPO approved digs in Bloomsbury and started work on his degree. He still came home at weekends but somehow it was all different now there were only three of us. Judy and I became closer and, on one glorious passionate night, spent the whole night together making love. Her parents and brother went away for a long weekend to Ramsgate, and we had her house to ourselves. She let me in then fell into my arms covering my face with kisses. We took each other's clothes off without hesitation or embarrassment and somehow made it to her single bed. The amazing feeling of sharing every sense with another person and being so totally immersed in love was something neither of us had ever done. Later laying there in the pitch black holding her sleeping body, I realised that this was all I ever wanted, to love and be loved, perfect.

Surprisingly life still went on as usual after Janet and Arthur had left, and Judy and I became lovers. The mundane still had to be done and I still had to go to work. By 1938 I had taken my driving test and was well on my way to becoming a jointer. I had done several courses, and received a really good appraisement from Mr Roberts. I had even received a visit from Mr Guy, the head of external works. He rolled up unannounced in a brand-new AC Greyhound saloon. Ron made him tea, and admired the car. Mr Guy examined the joint I was making, he nodded to himself and asked me how many twists to the inch I was joining the wires with. I told him ten. He nodded again.

"How about the brown paper you wrap the joint in, any precautions with that?" I told him I would bake it out over the paraffin stove to ensure all the moisture had evaporated, he nodded again. "One last question Mr Jones, what would you do if you put a split in your joint?" he asked.

A split is an illegal method of crossing the wires, it causes huge amounts of crosstalk. I thought for a minute. "Well, Mr Guy, I'd run like fuck in case Mr Gillroy caught me," I told him.

He roared with laughter. "Knew I'd made a good choice with you young Jimmy, you keep this up and you'll go far. Good work here," he said. We talked motorcars over tea. Mr Guy confided in Ron that as his duties required him to travel quite extensively, he felt he should do it in style.

When he had gone, Ron told me he had left his wife for a younger woman, and the car would have been her choice. "He had a standard eight for years," he said. "Never gave a toss for style then!" I didn't care, I had got a 'Good Work' from the head man and that meant a lot.

Chapter 12
The Diary

In all the time I had spent with Ron, I had never seen him loose his temper. He was a big man, so he didn't attract physical trouble. He was a master jointer so nobody queried his decisions at work. Mr Guy and Mr Roberts knew his worth so heaven help the planner or exchange man that held his job up. Ron knew his place, which was naturally in the right. He seemed indestructible to me, and I just expected him to always be there. I got to the yard at seven o'clock and was met by Dick Roberts, he told me Ron was sick, and that he wanted me to stand in as the senior technician for a changeover job the following night. I'd done them before with Ron directing, but never as the lead man.

Dick asked me if I needed him on site to help me, I asked who would be working the job with me and decided that the names he had given me were all good men who wouldn't cause trouble. I told Dick I would be pleased to do it on my own. We started at eleven o'clock at night and had two tents set up at the changeover points. I decided to forget I was the youngest one there, and give commands like a veteran; it worked. I chatted over a communal phone system and soon got everyone into a rhythm. When I called a break at three o'clock, we had broken the back of the job. I made tea and called the pair of jointers at the far manhole down to join us. I then offered slices of my mum's Dundee cake, as a thank you for their help. That was Granddad's idea, well he actually suggested a bottle of rum, but Mum thought a cake would be safer.

We finished at half past four. I notified the exchange and we cleared up. The best bit of the whole night came when I was locking up the yard. As Charley McCree, the senior man from the far end manhole was getting on his bike to go home, he gave me a clap on the shoulder. "You done well young Jimmy, Ron Gillroy couldn't have done a better job," he said. I mumbled my thanks, but I knew compliments like that were earned. I couldn't wait for Ron to recover, so that I could tell him.

He turned up two days later limping heavily. "What on earth have you done Ron?" I asked. He sat heavily on a chair in the jointers' meeting room.

"Gout," he told me. "Bloody painful, the doc doesn't seem to think there is a lot to be done, he's given me some tablets, but they don't seem to help."

"I thought you only got that if you ate pheasant and drank too much port."

He glared at me. "No Jimmy, it's equally as common with us corn beef and best bitter types." I made him wait and told him I would get the stores, and then drive us both to the job, it seemed appropriate to mollycoddle him a bit.

I went to the stores with my list, after having filled our paraffin can on the way. I put the can on the counter and joined the queue to get my stores. Eventually Mr Yarrow served me, and started to build up a pile of our items. It was quite a big job, so it took some time. Ron limped in, to see why I was taking so long, he certainly wasn't in a good mood. I explained there had been a few in front of me, but we were nearly done. He looked at his watch, but didn't comment. Then it happened. Ian Brown limped through on his side of the counter. Without pausing he gave my full can of paraffin a hefty push.

"Get that fucking thing of my counter," he told me. It was unexpected, so none of us, including Ron, had time to react. The can landed directly on to his inflamed toe.

With a roar like an enraged bear Ron, with a speed that defied his size, threw himself after the departing storeman. He closed his left fist on Ian's collar and lifting him bodily off his feet slammed him face up on to his own counter. His right fist was drawn back into what was going to be a bone breaking punch. Thinking back, I still don't know how or why I did it, but as Ron's fist came back, I grabbed his elbow with both hands. It was like trying to stop a train. He pulled me off my feet, and on reflection I suppose I was lucky he didn't deal with me first. I think it was my scream, "No Ron, it's your fucking job," that penetrated his pain-induced rage.

The GPO are very specific about violence at work, they do not tolerate it under any circumstances. Had Ron's punch landed, he would have undoubtedly been sacked. He shook me off, released his death grip on Ian's overalls and stormed out. The silence was deafening. "Did you see that," demanded Ian trying to get his store coat back to something like its original shape. "He bloody attacked me, unprovoked assault. I'm reporting that."

Mr Yarrow walked over to him. "Good thinking," he said. "You will of course need a witness."

"Well, you saw everything Mr Yarrow," Ian demanded.

"Not me," said Mr Yarrow. "I was collecting Mr Jones' stores. Anybody else see anything?" he enquired. Nobody spoke.

"Charley," Ian appealed. "You saw it?"

"Saw what?" Charley replied.

"Oh, I see, just because its Ron bloody Gillroy, he gets away with attempted murder. If I hadn't got this bad leg, I would have shown him."

"That's right," Mr Yarrow told him. "I hear he's a real pussy cat, now if you just wait until your leg is completely healed, you probably wouldn't," and he indicated Ian's trousers, "piss yourself; again," Ian disappeared into the back of the storeroom to the sound of stifled laughter.

Ron was waiting for me by the van. He looked horribly uncomfortable. "Jimmy mate, I'm so sorry. If you hadn't stopped me I could have been down the road." He looked shocked. I took him into the back of the van and made hot sweet tea. I assured him, that I wasn't hurt and that every man present, including George Yarrow, had not seen anything.

"You've got a lot of friends," I told him. "But just to put this to bed, I'll collect our stores for a bit, and I'm going to go back for them now and offer your apology." He started to protest, but I pointed out that we all had to work here together.

He eventually nodded. "Thanks Jimmy," he said.

I went back, and found Ian on his own. His trousers were stained, and he smelled unpleasant. He met me with, "Come back to smirk, have you."

I told him, "No." I also added that, "Ron realised he shouldn't have done that, but the pain of his injured foot had caused a completely out of character reaction."

"Does that mean he won't come looking for me," Ian asked anxiously.

"No of course not," I told him, he just wants to put it behind him.

"Well, all right then," Ian agreed. "Tell him I won't do nothing for now."

With my arms full of our stores, I turned to look at him, "For now?" I asked.

He looked furtively from side to side. "Yeah, well I've been told I'm going up in the world, Jimmy Jones, and when us fascists are the ones in power, I've got a lot of old scores to settle. You should join the party, mate, you could do well."

I was grasping for a suitable reply, when he went on. "I got this diary see, and everything what I done for the party, and everyone who has opposed us, it's all down in black and white. Dates, times, all the details. I got chapter and verse on everything, back to 1931 when I joined."

I couldn't believe what he was saying. "So something like the Cable street riots?" I asked.

"Oh yes," he told me. "I know who was there fighting for, and against us. It's all written down. I just wish I knew which fucker broke my leg, but I expect I'll get a medal for that."

"Bloody hell, Ian, you take this really seriously, don't you?" I said. "How about all the scraps you got into for the party?"

He nodded. "All documented," he told me. "Every punch up and injury I got, every kike, queer and gyppo that got taught a lesson, it's all there, signed and dated for when I can report to the new powers."

I nodded. "That sounds like military history in the making, I don't suppose I could see it?" He stopped, realising that perhaps he had gone too far.

He shook his head. "No, I don't show it to no one," he told me.

"Oh, go on," I said. "It could be really interesting, a real war document; is it here?"

"Don't be a prat," he said. "I don't take it out, too much information. Anyway, I got to get on, tell Gillroy I won't press charges." I thanked him, and went to find Ron. I wanted to get his opinions on this new development.

Ron listened as I drove us to the job. He nodded. "It's a fairly common condition, the need to keep mementos from your own private fantasy. We caught a lot of 'good men' because they kept a little souvenir. Had this Welsh guardsman as a suspect for a series of rapes in Amiens. His officer swore he was the most devout man in the regiment, Chapel, a father figure to the new recruits, a good man. He nearly had me convinced until we found a box with the girl's underwear hidden in his kit bag."

I thought for a moment. "So do you think he would have documented the attack on Harry Zimmerman?" I asked.

"Hard to say," Ron told me. "He's stupid enough to have done it, but how much of what he told you do you think was bravado?"

I considered. "I reckon he was telling the truth, he looks on this as his chance of promotion when the fascists come to power. If Mosley gets to be prime minister, he thinks he'll be doing Bill Guy's job."

Ron thought for a moment. "Do you know where he lives?" he asked. I told him I didn't. "He's got a grace and favour flat in the Bexleyheath exchange," he said.

"How the hell did he get that?" I asked incredulously, they were normally reserved for employees of outstanding character.

"His dad Henry ran the exchange for years, moved in there in 1912, now he was a nice guy, old school, would help anybody. Trouble is he never came home from the war. When his wife died, Ian stayed on, took it over and, as he was a GPO employee, they just let him carry on with the tenancy."

I thought for a moment. "Ron, can you forget what I just told you?"

He gave me a sideways glance. "You wouldn't be thinking of a bit of breaking and entry, would you?"

I shook my head. "The thought never entered head," I lied. "I'll have a chat with Arthur this weekend."

He gave me one of his 'interrogating sergeant', looks. "You just be careful, this could be big trouble." He never spoke a truer word. "Now then, Mr Jones, tell me how you managed to not make a balls-up with Tuesday night's no break changeover."

I grinned, somebody had told him.

Chapter 13
Arthur's Infernal Cardboard Machine

Arthur came home on Friday night, after he had dropped his laundry off, he came round to see if I wanted a pint. He still wasn't his old self, and since we had heard no more from Janet, he had taken on a lugubrious mantle of one who had caused it all. I assured him Janet would write, if only to keep Judy informed, but Spain was a long way to get letters home. I told him Granddad had once received a postcard from a mate in Ireland that had taken two years to cross the Irish Sea. That got 'half' a grin out of him: progress!

Over our drinks I told him about Ian, Ron's injured toe, my bravery at wrestling Ron off, and the diary. Arthur listened in silence.

"I believe everything apart from you grappling with Ron," he said. "Now if you had an ear missing or some part of your anatomy in a sling, it would be a bit more credible." I admitted it had been my girly scream rather than my manly strength that had dislodged Ron's hands. Arthur nodded and went to get a fresh round. He recapped. "So you think he has a diary in this flat with a signed confession about killing Harry?" I said I did. "And you want us to break in and steal it?" Again, I said I did. "Are there any nights he goes out, party meetings? Pub nights? Storeman's tea dances? It would be easier if he wasn't there." I admitted I didn't know.

"Well," said Arthur. "We know where he is during working hours, could we get in then?" I told him the flat was actually inside the exchange, and there would be GPO staff coming and going until late in the evening. He started to draw a pattern on the table with spilled beer suds. "Could we overpower him, if the two of us went at him together." I wasn't sure, but my main concern was that he would know it was us and set the police on us. We had this conversation a long time ago with Ron, I reminded him.

"Right, best thing is to try and find a night when he's out. Could you watch the flat for a week?" I didn't fancy it but agreed I could. "I'll come back early Friday and give you a couple of nights off." We agreed, and I took Arthur home via Bexleyheath exchange. The flat was on the second floor, and from the bus stop you could see the lights on.

Arthur took a long time looking over the building. "Tell me," he said. "If it's a GPO flat, would it have a phone?" It seemed a strange question, but Arthur rarely asked anything that wasn't relative.

"Yes," I told him. Ian was the second call storeman after George Yarrow to open up the cable depot for emergency repairs. The phone was a service line, that wasn't charged for. Arthur thought for a moment.

"Do you know the number?" I said I had it in my notebook. "You're going to need another notebook to record when he goes out," he said. "We'll do a second week just to be sure, then we'll break in. Can you get us into the exchange Jimmy?" I told him I had keys that would get us up to the flat's front door.

"Do you have a sledgehammer in your kit?" Arthur asked. I told him I could get one. "Well, we won't have time to be subtle, so I reckon a good hard bang on the lock should see us in." You would think Arthur was a seasoned criminal the way he planned everything.

It sounded quite adventurous, spying on Ian from across the road, like something from a Sam Spade story. The reality was several cold and uncomfortable evenings loitering by the bus stop. I found that Bexleyheath at night was a different world. I was approached by a man in a lavender coloured shirt who asked if I'd like to go to a club with him, I nearly accepted just to get the feeling back in my toes. The second night a lady walked past, looked back at me and enquired if I fancied, "a good time," underneath the make-up she looked older than my mum, so I thanked her but declined. The pattern of Ian's night life was dull and invariable by comparison.

He got in about six o'clock and went to bed at ten thirty. After that I went home, nobody went out that late. Discreet enquiries about the Union of Fascists revealed there was no regular meeting times, and nobody seemed to know how he spent his nights. This was not a man with a great many friends. The two he seemed closest to were now being detained at his Majesty's pleasure, largely because of me. The rest of the week was the same, he stayed in. By Thursday I had a head cold and was feeling thoroughly miserable.

I reported all this to Arthur when he came back from Bloomsbury on Friday afternoon. He told me to go home and take a Beechams powder for my cold, I did. On Sunday evening he came round with equally bad news. Other than short shopping trips, Ian didn't seem to leave the flat.

Arthur told me he had an idea. He wanted to keep up the surveillance, but if it appeared there was no clear window of opportunity, well, he had a plan.

I continued for the next week, but it was hopeless. He went to the pictures one night, but that was obviously just a random visit. I tailed him to the Majestic, and more to get into the warm and dry sat in the one and threes, six rows behind him to watch Errol Flynn in *The Adventures of Robin Hood*.

The film was so good, I nearly forgot I was supposed to be a spy. When the national anthem was played at the end, he left early attracting malevolent looks. I had to drop my raincoat, to bend down out of his sight. Predictably once outside he went straight home.

We carried it on for the whole of the second miserable week before concluding it just wasn't possible to predict when he would go out. On Sunday afternoon Arthur and I sat in his lounge, and he told me it was time for Plan B.

"Look," he said. "This is going to sound strange at first but stay with me on the technical side OK." I wasn't in the mood for a lecture but decided to humour him.

"Go on then," I told him.

"Right, are we agreed that we're not going to get in with a guarantee he won't be there?" I said we were. "How about if we could knock him out before we break in?"

"Yes, that's great mate," I told him. "Is it going to be a big hammer on a long stick, or some Woolworths knock out gas that we squirt through his letter box?" I was always good with sarcasm.

He shook his head. "Look I shouldn't even be talking about this, but I have been working on the possibility of focusing and amplifying third harmonic sound waves." I must have looked even more stupid than I normally did when he got technical. "Better if I show you," he said. He disappeared into his mum's kitchen only to reappear with a cardboard box, a role of masking tape, a toilet roll inner, some scissors, an elastic band and a piece of greaseproof paper. I sat and watched slightly mystified as he covered the end of the toilet role in the greaseproof paper, securing it with the elastic band. He then carefully cut a hole in the box just big enough to fit the toilet roll in so that the covered end protruded. Finally, he closed all the flaps on the box and taped over every opening.

"And this is going to knock the bastard out, is it," I said. "It strikes me we would be better off filling the box with bricks, then dropping it on him when he leaves the flat."

Arthur sighed. "This is just a very crude way of demonstrating what I can do electronically. Now, the box is full of air, yes?" I shrugged an agreement.

"And because the atmospheric pressure is the same inside and outside the box, there are no forces in play, agreed?" I gave a second shrug. "But, if I increase the air pressure inside the box, a wave of air will expand outwards exerting a force in all directions." I went to speak, but he held up a hand like a traffic policeman to silence me. "And," he continued, "as we have left one area of weakness the wave will be concentrated, and that allows this to happen." With that he brought his raised hand down sharply on the top of the box. The toilet roll left the box with a pop and shot across the room.

I didn't know whether to laugh or not. "So, we're going to shoot him with a toilet roll tube, are we?" He picked up his bullet, and grinned.

"No Jimmy, the toilet roll was just there to demonstrate the force of the invisible pressure wave. It's that wave we are going to shoot him with, only mine will be a sound wave and it will be a lot more powerful than the one I just generated, but the principle is the same." I knew this was what Arthur did best, but I still couldn't fathom what he was trying to show me.

"So how do we shoot the wave at him?" I asked. Arthur's grin widened.

"Well," he said conspiratorially. "He has this special device in his flat that he will hold to his head for us when we want him to."

It took a second for the penny to drop. The telephone, of course, the telephone. Arthur nodded. "Well, what would you do if your phone rang? You'd pick it up and hold it to your ear, which is an unobstructed passage to the brain, and that," he concluded, "would be a big mistake."

"And that will knock him out, will it?" I asked.

"Almost certainly," Arthur said. "Depending on how far away we are with my wave generator, it will do the job if I adjust the power levels correctly."

"Where were you thinking of setting it up?" I said.

"I thought the exchange," he said. "You've got keys, haven't you?" I said I had.

"Just one more thing Jimmy."

I looked up. "What?" I said.

"I need you to help me transport my wave generator from my lab in Bloomsbury when it is finished, can you borrow a van?" I thought of the implications, taking a GPO van without permission could mean the sack, but then I remembered the picture I had in my head of Harry Zimmerman laying in the urinal at Charlton, with his blood slowly staining his coat black.

"When do you want me there?" I said.

Chapter 14
Flash Gordon

On Friday Judy received a letter from Spain. It had been posted over a month ago but, considering how long the previous one had taken, this seemed express delivery. It wasn't from Janet, it was from a man called Jose Fernandez. He had been fighting with Janet, and she had asked him to tell Judy her news. It wasn't good. Janet had been wounded, and they had left her to be captured by Franco's troops. She had ordered Jose to leave her but had given him an address to write to her friends in England. Jose told us how fearless she was, and an inspiration to all freedom fighters. He said her wound was unlikely to be fatal and told us because she was a foreign woman, she would receive treatment from Franco's medics. He begged our forgiveness for leaving Janet and swore he would try and find what had happened to her. Judy was shaken to the core, Janet shot, captured and in a Spanish hospital.

I told Dad, and he said we should invite Judy round. It would show her we cared and thought of her as one of the family. So, on the third of October Judy came round to Sunday lunch. Mum had managed to buy a joint of beef, Granddad had bought a crate of beer and Nan made one of her trifles. Despite the news about Janet, it promised to be a good day. All of us apart from Mum and Nan who were cooking, sat round the kitchen table and the mood lightened considerably. Granddad showed Judy a game where you peeled the paper from the silver foil in a packet of Woodbines. You then stretched it over a pint glass and held it in place with an elastic band. Finally, Granddad put a sixpence in the middle. One at a time we had to touch the paper with our lit cigarettes. This caused a hole to form and expand, the loser was the one who made the sixpence fall into the glass. After three Dubonnet and bitter lemons, Judy was taking no prisoners. She accused us all of cheating and wouldn't give Granddad his sixpence back. I just remember laughing a lot and thinking how good life could be with her and my family. I poured Mum a Guinness and tried to explain Granddad's silly game.

Nan looked up from her Yorkshire puddings. "He used to play that in the trenches to see who would go on reconnaissance," she said.

It was only an idle remark, but I felt like somebody had walked over my grave. The horror of another war had vanished for that hour of beer and laughter, but like a silent and unwelcome guest at our meal, it was still there.

Granddad put the wireless on as Chamberlain was going to make another broadcast about Poland. The set warmed up, and we heard what must be the most infamous wireless broadcast of all time. I can still remember most of it to this day. We waited in silence for the prime minister to speak and, on the dot of eleven o'clock he did.

He said, "I am speaking to you from the cabinet room at ten Downing Street. This morning the British ambassador in Berlin handed the German government a final note, stating that unless we heard from them by eleven o'clock that they were prepared to withdraw their troops from Poland, a state of war would exist between us. I have to tell you now that no such undertaking has been received, and consequently this country is at war with Germany."

There was more about how he had tried desperately to avoid this, but few people in the country took that in after the enormity of what we had just heard. War, only twenty-one years since the death of sixteen million people, we were at war again. Granddad wept.

At work I was told that for the moment we would be considered reserved occupation, but if we wished to sign up, our jobs would be safe. I asked Ron if he would go back. He said he would, but not until he had talked to his old regiment. I suspected he would go straight in as a sergeant, they always needed sergeants like Ron. I thought about the RAF and wondered if I could get to fly. Granddad had told me about the Royal Flying Corps. He reckoned if they got shot down, they went to big parties in the German officers' mess, and then got exchanged with massive hangovers the next day. In between flying over the trenches, they lived the life of Riley, well better than the infantry he reckoned. I suspected this was based on opinion rather than fact, but it had to be better than sitting in a trench like him and dad. Pilot officer Jones, Judy would like that, and I could grow a moustache.

We had just gone back to work after the Christmas holiday when, on the Thursday evening, there was loud knocking on our front door. I went to see who it was, to my surprise it was Arthur grasping his briefcase. He usually stayed in his digs until the weekend unless something important sent him home. As I opened the door, he unleashed a tirade of excited information that was obviously whirling round his head.

"Jimmy, I've cracked it, I've only bloody done it. The problem was the source signal, too many harmonics causing signal decay and deterioration, had to be something simple and pure. You'll never guess what I used, well of course you won't, but it works Jim, it only bloody works."

We looked at each other for a moment. "Well, hello yourself Arthur, and what brings you out on this fine night?" I asked. He shook his head and pushed past me.

He managed a, "Hello, Mr Jones," to Dad, as he headed for my bedroom. As soon as he got there, he opened his briefcase and spread a series of circuit diagrams out. He always got a bit frustrated when I couldn't keep up with the maths and science but he kept it simple to try and get me to understand. Apparently, the theory was good, but he had suffered many failures in trying to build a sound wave generator that didn't destroy itself. He explained that he had been lying in the bath on Tuesday night desperately trying to think what the problem could be. He had been very still, lost in thought, with the surface of his bath water completely flat. A single drop of condensation had fallen from the ceiling into the bath which caused ripples. Then another drop, then a third, the combined ripples merging together to absorb one another. And that was when he realised. You must only have the single pure wave as the signal source. A Eureka moment that had caused him to leap from his bath, run past his startled landlady and her sister who were having afternoon tea, and head for his bedroom to scribble notes. I asked if the landlady or her sister had since mentioned the incident. He paused, thought, then shook his head.

"No, why?" I told him it wasn't important.

From what I understood he needed a single tone with absolutely no harmonics as the source for his generator. That way it didn't shake itself to pieces electrically. He beamed at me. "And do you know what I used?" I admitted I didn't. "Well," he said, "do you remember Christmas 1932?" I had no idea where this was going but said I did. Arthur beamed. "We got crystal sets, didn't we?" Again, I agreed.

"Well don't you see, those same simple crystals are perfect for the tone, look!" He opened a notebook covered in sketches, maths and diagrams. "Look Jimmy, the Piezo electric effect is exactly right for regulating a tone so that no matter how many times you amplify it, or apply phase distortion, you get no second or third ripples in the bath!" This was obviously of great importance, and he looked up at me from his notes desperately wanting congratulations for solving an impossible problem.

"Arthur, that's just unbelievable," I told him. "So cut to the chase then Flash Gordon, what can this do?" I asked.

He closed his notebook and looked me in the eye. "It can knock seven bells out of our Mr Ian Brown, and when he's out cold we can get the evidence that he killed Harry."

I nodded. "Then you have done an extraordinary job and I don't have the words to thank you."

He smiled. "You don't need them Jimmy, can you come to the college Sunday afternoon with a van?" We agreed four o'clock.

Luckily, I had a job not far from Bloomsbury, so by slipping in to get the van I could always claim I was returning to it. On Sunday at three I collected my van and drove round to meet Arthur. He directed me round to his workshop, and I managed to park close to the rear doors. He was the only one there, nobody worked at the college on a Sunday. He took me into a large room with several benches adorned with test equipment. The walls had big shelves bolted to them with wracks of tools and electrical apparatus on them.

At one end there was a canteen with two tables, a few chairs and a marble cold shelf. There was a gas cooker with a grill and a kettle. On the back wall was a fish tank full of small tropical fish. One bench had an aluminium box about four feet square and three high. It had about twenty valves sticking out the top, and an array of switches and dials on the front. This was Arthur's death ray. He touched it with a lover's caress.

"It works Jim, there were times when I thought I'd never crack it, but it works. Let me show you." He plugged it into the mains and then wheeled a large speaker in a box over to the bench. This he connected to two terminals on the front of his invention. Next, he went outside and reappeared dragging a large sack of sand. "Here Jimmy, give us a lift," he wheezed. "It's bloody heavy." I got the other side and we lifted the sack onto a stool so it reached about five feet off of the floor. The speaker faced the sack which stood in front of the canteen area and was about eight feet away from us. Opening a small plate on the top Arthur rummaged in his pocket for an old tobacco tin. He grinned. "My first crystal from Father Christmas, 1932."

He gently inserted the crystal into a fuse holder and allowed the jaws to close on it. "I can't use a telephone at point blank range, so I have calculated the same impact if we use a speaker, obviously as it's further away I'll have to allow for signal attenuation through the air, but I'll set the power output higher than normal to compensate."

He measured the distance between the sack and the speaker and was going to move the sack until I pointed out the speaker was on wheels. He might have been a genius, but the common sense still needed a bit of work. He grinned, moved the speaker, and played with a slide rule for a bit making notes as he went.

Finally, he set three of the dials on the front and adjusted the pressure on the crystal using a micrometer. The final adjustment was to a lever that I recognised, it had cost me one pound fourteen and six from a store on the Tottenham Court Road. The shop assistant had explained it was so expensive because it was 'the bee's knees' of variable resistors, and very accurate. He had offered me a standard rheostat for a quarter of the price, but Arthur's directives had been very specific. I had parted with my twenty-four and six and, unsurprisingly, Arthur hadn't even had the decency to be overwhelmed by my generosity.

He looked up again. "Ready?" he asked. I nodded, my resolve was beginning to waver.

"Arthur, this is safe, isn't it?" I said, my voice sounding a bit strange.

"Of course, it's safe, you dick," he grinned. "Look put these ear protectors on if you want." He handed me a pair of metal headphones with no wires. As soon as I put them on, he threw the big switch on the top.

I admit that when he did that, I bent both my knees, and brought my right arm up to protect my face. He looked at me and shook his head, motioning me to lift the ear protectors. "It's not a bloody howitzer Jimmy, we have to give it a few minutes to charge, then when this meter shows a reading over this point here." He indicated a voltmeter, I nodded and pushed my headset back to look a bit more casual. "Then," he continued, "we unleash the wave, and that's when you throw yourself to the floor," he grinned. He was enjoying himself.

The machine started to make a low hum. The frequency increasing as the needles on all his meters began to climb. He now had to raise his voice to make himself heard. "The power levels should all be within my safety parameters," he shouted giving me the thumbs up.

"What happened last time you did this," I shouted back.

He looked at me in surprise. "Last time?"

"You said you got it to work," I yelled.

"Well yes, the theory all works perfectly now I'm using the crystal." I knew the answer before I asked the next question.

"You've never done this for real, have you?" He shook his head. "Oh, bloody hell Arthur, we're going to die, aren't we?"

He shook his head again and shouted, "Not this side of the speaker we're not." As he said that the machine stopped. One moment it was winding itself up to a crescendo, scaring the shit out of me, the next it just stopped. The silence was deafening. Arthur looked worried and grabbed a multi meter, he bent over the machine and went to say, "Oh for fuck's sake," only he didn't get that far. On 'fuck' the machine gave an audible noise like somebody spitting. Both my ears popped very painfully and a wave of shimmering air left the speaker; it burst every light bulb in the room

It was then like watching through an iridescent wall of water as the sandbag changed shape, it was as though a cannon ball had hit it. GPO sacks are made of hessian, and that's pretty tough, but the sack burst open firing the sand into the canteen.

Worse, the fish tank changed shape, it bent inwards at an impossible angle until it imploded into a thousand shards of glass. Water, dead fish and glass cascaded onto the floor. I looked in horror at the destruction we had caused but, even then, I couldn't help but grin at my friend who had used his genius to make Flash Gordon come true. We had a death ray.

Chapter 15
The Break In

It was seven o'clock by the time we had cleared up the workshop. The sand and glass ended up in a second hessian sack, but the dead fish were a problem. Arthur tried to pick them up and put them in a kitchen washing-up bowl, but when you have literally been blown out of the water, the chances of survival are low. Eventually he agreed with me that we had no survivors, so the bodies were swept up and unceremoniously dumped with the sand and glass. Arthur decided to claim he had caught the fish tank with the edge of a toolbox, and however unlikely that sounded, offer to replace the whole aquarium. I found a cupboard of light bulbs and replaced all the broken ones, while I was doing this, I heard Arthur give a low whistle.

"Come and have look at this," he said. He showed me the large speaker that he had attached to the machine. The wood of the box was fine, but there was no speaker, only the screws that had held it in position remained.

"It must have been blown out," I said.

Arthur shook his head. "It's been vaporised, kid," he told me. "Hell, that thing is a bit more powerful than I realised, it's literally shaken itself to pieces, down to a molecular level."

I felt a twinge of alarm. "Look Arthur this is a bit much isn't it? I mean popping the cones out of the speaker is one thing, but shaking them into vapour, that's a bit 'Ming the Merciless'. Don't you have a volume knob on it somewhere?" Arthur put down his slide rule and explained that he had used a speaker because there was a big air gap between the source and the target. I didn't like the use of 'target', but he carried on.

"I admit I underestimated the full power at focal length, but I can compensate for it. Of course, when we send the wave through telephone wires it will be close to the minimum settings, say one hundredth of today's demo. It won't be as spectacular, but it will do the job, trust me."

By now the college was completely deserted. We loaded the machine on to a trolley and wheeled it out to my van. Arthur recovered the crystal and replaced it in his tobacco tin. "I'm rather fond of that little fellow," he confided. "I first got the World Service with him." We tied the box down to the floor of my van, returned the trolley, and set out for Bexleyheath exchange.

The traffic was light and we did the sixteen miles in half an hour. I unlocked the gates and drove up to the exchange door. We found an unused trolley by the canteen and, despite Arthur's protests, manually heaved the machine on to it, we then pushed it through a maze of corridors to the cable chamber door. This is a basement room where the new underground cables entered the exchange. It is very rarely used by the exchange staff. Despite the size and weight, we eventually got Arthur's machine down the steps.

We were both breathing heavily by the time I got it positioned where the local cables came down through the ceiling. The records revealed which cable the flat's phone was in, so I cut out the pair and connected our leads to it.

I then collected a field phone from my van and connected it to a spare live pair. When I lifted the receiver, I got dial tone. "Right, you can still call the flat on this, that's Bexleyheath five-four-two-six, and connect your Ming the Merciless machine on these two wires here, OK?" Arthur gave me a thumbs up. "I suggest we do this later tonight, if we have to break the door down, we don't want any witnesses."

Arthur agreed. "We'll want a sledgehammer, and we both want to wear gloves." I knew this made sense but couldn't seem to lose the apprehension.

There was one last thing I had to do. "Arthur, mate," I said. "You don't have to do this. It's breaking the law, and it could go wrong. If you show me how to start up your death ray, I'll do it." A look of shock crossed Arthur's face.

"Bugger off," he replied. "I designed and built this, and Harry was my friend as well as yours. We are doing this together or not at all, are we clear on that?" I knew he would react like that, but I had to try.

"Sorry Arthur, I just had to… "

"I know exactly what you 'just had to'," he grinned. "But this is a two-man job. Now don't get all slushy on me kid all right?" I nodded. "Right let's go and have a pie and a pint, we'll come back when the pubs shut, OK?"

I parked the van out of sight round the back and noted that the flat's lights were on. We walked to the Goat and Compasses, a pub recommended by Fat Terry from planning. Fat Terry was a name to be respected in the world of culinary recommendations, he did not disappoint.

They did hot pies and mash with mushy peas and liquor; there is probably better food, but just then I couldn't think of any. They also did Burton's ale and London Pride, so Arthur and I settled ourselves by the fire in the snug and sank into a companionable silence while we ate our supper.

Before he sat down Arthur took a large brown paper bag from his jacket pocket and put it on the seat next to him. "What's that?" I asked.

"Pudding," he replied. "My mum gave me some more oranges because I was going to be out in the cold, vitamin C, you know, fight off colds and flu. She gets them off her mate down the market, they're Egyptian." He had the decency to look a little abashed, his mum still saw him as the eight-year-old cub scout. "Do you want one," he offered. I didn't.

He was just explaining over our third pint that the Goat and Compasses was a bastardisation of the religious phrase, 'God Encompasses us', and I was telling him he was full of shit, when the landlord called last orders. I couldn't believe it, how had two hours flown by like that? Arthur scuttled to the bar and got our last pints in; I think it was really a bit of Dutch courage for both of us. "We'll drink these, then go back to the exchange," Arthur told me.

I agreed, but said, "You sure about this mate?"

Arthur nodded. "I saw Harry after those bastards had kicked him half to death, but I told you then that the three that did it would be sorry. Two of them are doing hard labour, the last one is carrying on as though nothing happened. Well tonight, Mr Ian Brown, justice is coming. So yes Jim, I'm bloody sure." There wasn't anything else to say.

We walked out into the cold night air and made our way back to the exchange. I unlocked and went to use the toilet, checking there was nobody else about. The lights were out in the flat but at ten past eleven we agreed he wouldn't be in too deep a sleep to miss a potential call out. Arthur powered up the machine and attached the connection leads to the pair I had provided. He looked up from the orange he was peeling.

"If you call him," Arthur said, "I'll work this, I will need a couple of minutes to reach the right power level, how long do you think he will take to answer the phone?" I considered, he was probably asleep, but even so I reckoned he would answer it within twenty seconds.

"So I have about forty seconds to build the charge up before your first ring," he said. "This is going to be tighter than I imagined." He proffered his bag of oranges again. "Want one?" he asked.

"No, Arthur, put the bloody oranges down and concentrate on the job in hand, we have to get this right." He sighed and put them down. I did some mental arithmetic and reckoned that by the time I had dialled the number, and the receiver being picked up, it would be close to thirty seconds.

"Start the machine, Arthur, I'm going to dial when you tell me we are thirty seconds off firing." He nodded, removed the tobacco tin from his inside pocket and inserted the crystal. He then adjusted the dials and after much calculation with his slide rule set the vertical resistor to near the maximum resistance; the arm was almost vertical.

"Ready?" he said.

"Ready" I replied.

Arthur threw the big switch on the top, and for the second time we watched the needles starting to rise. There was no speaker involved this time, but the machine still made an unnatural hum. The confines of the underground chamber seemed to make it worse, and as before the noise level increased. Arthur shouted, "Dial Jimmy, and for God's sake remember not to hold the field phone anywhere near your ears when it goes off." I hadn't thought of that and wished he had told me earlier. I dialled Bexleyheath five-four-two-six, silently counting in my head and, after six seconds I heard the ringing tone.

Arthur was alternating his head between looking at me, and the voltmeter that was crawling up to maximum. The machine was rocking and the sound it produced was hurting my ears. "Come on, come on, answer," he pleaded, but the ringing tone carried on. Suddenly, as before, the machine stopped.

Everything was eerily quiet, then in that split second Ian Brown lifted the receiver and said, "What?"

I spun round desperate to get away from the phone, I probably did it too fast, because the next thing I knew I had trodden on something that threw me completely off balance. I dropped the receiver and crashed into the machine, hitting the vertical resistor before I fell to the floor. There was a huge bang and the entire top half of the field phone handset exploded. There was a sharp pain as the phone's metal diaphragm sliced into the top of my calf. I hit the floor. I couldn't hear anything but a monstrous ringing in both ears. Arthur was calling, but he seemed a long way away.

After a few minutes, my head cleared. Arthur was sitting staring at his machine, removing the crystal, he looked awful. It seemed a strange thing to be doing, but Arthur had a pattern that had to be completed for every task, he had always been like that. I felt the sticky blood from my leg and got up to try and find a bandage. I saw then why I had tripped, Arthur's oranges, they were squashed where I had trodden on them, and the survivors had been kicked across the floor.

"You all right Jim?" Arthur asked, he looked grey.

"Yeah, I'll live," I told him. "What the hell happened?"

"It was my fault, Jimmy, you trod on my stupid oranges, and as you fell you altered the output resistor setting." I found a piece of rag in my bass and tied it round my wound.

"So this hasn't worked then?" I asked.

Arthur looked up. "I'm afraid it's worked too well," he told me. "Can you walk so that we can find out?" I said I could.

We made our way up the stairs and along the corridor, I carried the sledgehammer. Neither of us could hear properly, and consequently we spoke louder than normal. "Knock on the door," Arthur shouted. "Let's see if he's still conscious." I put the sledgehammer down and banged hard on the door, there was no reply. We waited, then Arthur said, "Right, knock the door in and we'll get the diary."

I put my gloves on and swung the hammer at the door lock, it only took one good hit, and the lock burst inward. There was a cold draft in the entrance hall, but other than that everything looked normal.

The first room on the left was the lounge, Arthur pushed the door open and looked around, it was empty. There was a mess that only a man living alone can achieve. Fish and chip papers and empty beer bottles, copies of girlie magazines and thick dust were on every surface. The ashtrays were overflowing and a general air of neglect hung over the whole place.

We then found the bathroom, kitchen and dining room, all could have done with a damn good clean but showed no sign of life. That only left the bedroom. "Where would he have the phone?" Arthur asked. I pointed to the main socket in the hall with an extension cable running through the door frame of the last room.

"In there," I said. "He would have it next to the bed so he didn't miss any work calls." We exchanged looks and I gathered my nerve to throw the door open. There was some resistance to the door opening, and it took both of us to push it in. It was Ian laying on his side with his feet against the door. He did not look good. He had obviously climbed out of bed in his pyjamas, the trousers of which had fallen to his knees. We were literally horrified, not because he was exposed, but because half of his head was missing. The wrist of the right hand grasping the receiver showed his swastika tattoo dark blue against the translucent skin: he had bled out.

It looked like the left side of his head had exploded outwards; there was blood and brains everywhere.

"Oh my God, Jimmy, what have we done?" Arthur fell to his knees and tried to feel for a pulse. "Do you think he's dead, do you?" I'm no expert on mortality, but when most of your brain is on the carpet, I'd rate survival chances as slim. I held Arthur's shoulders.

"He's dead as mutton, Arthur. Harry can rest in peace now." He looked up at me with horror in his eyes.

"Jimmy, oh God, Jimmy, what have I done?" I squeezed his shoulders and got him to his feet.

"Come on Arthur right now we need to get the hell out of here." He didn't move.

The reason for the draught was also fairly obvious, the bedroom sash widow had been blown out, and an icy wind was flapping the curtains as it blew into the bedroom. An alarm across the street was ringing loudly.

"Right, get up Arthur we are getting out of here now. The police will be here soon, and we need to be somewhere else. Have you had gloves on all the time you have been in the flat?" He said he had, but shock had taken over, and he wasn't thinking clearly. "Let's have a quick look for the diary, then we skidaddle, we'll clear up everything later when we can get back in. There's no reason for them to look in the cable chamber." He just nodded, again this was a difference between us, he couldn't believe what had happened, I could.

We couldn't find the diary, there were so many places he could have hidden it, and we had so little time. After a cursory look I decided we had to get out. I wiped down everything I could think we might have touched with a greasy tea towel from the kitchen. I then collected the sledgehammer and got back to the cable chamber. I pushed the machine into a corner, threw a tarpaulin over it, put my tools in my bass and, dragging Arthur, headed for the back door.

As I tossed the tools into the back of my van, we heard the police car bells. We were fugitives. I had to make a split-second decision, did I abandon the van and try walking away dragging Arthur with me, or did I brazen it out and drive a GPO van out of a GPO exchange. The decision wasn't difficult. I bundled Arthur into the passenger seat and started the engine. The bells were coming a lot closer as I pulled out into the main road and headed towards Wood Green. As I turned left two police cars shot past me all bells and flashing blue lights. I thought we might have made it.

I dropped Arthur off at his house, he had gone very quiet. "Just go to bed, try and get some sleep and we will sort this out tomorrow," I told him. He nodded and went inside. It was a long drive to the yard and my head was pounding. After I had parked and locked up, I headed for the station, too late now for a bus. I can't say I felt remorse for Ian Brown's death, but I didn't want to be caught. I didn't think the police had a lot to go on.

Chapter 16
Arrested

It was a long ride home. I managed to catch the last train, but I had to sit on the platform for forty minutes. I went over and over the night's events, had we left any clue as to what had happened? Try as I might, I couldn't think of any reason the police could pin it down to us. I wish I felt as confident as my conclusion directed me, but I just didn't know enough about police methods to be sure. Mum and Dad had both gone to bed by the time I got home. They had left the outside light on for me so I could get up the steps safely. I made myself a cup of tea, and then went to bed. Sleep was a long time coming, I couldn't shift the picture of Ian Brown laying with his pyjamas down and his brains spilling out. I still didn't feel remorse, but I was scared of retribution.

Mum woke me with a cup of tea. "Come on Jimmy, you have overslept," she told me. "It's seven o'clock." I stumbled out of bed, washed and dressed as quickly as possible, Dad had made me a bacon sandwich and a flask to have on the bus.

"Not like you, old man," he said. "Must have been a hell of a night last night." I grunted an agreement, gratefully took my breakfast and ran to the bus stop. The normality of doing something ordinary like going to work seemed to lose the horrors of the night. I resolved to go round and see Arthur as soon as I had finished work. I just wanted to talk through our options. It would be all right.

"Worse things happen at sea," Granddad used to say.

When I got there a lot of the other vans had gone. Some of the men were loading stores or filling the vans from the pump. I was halfway through the job near Bloomsbury, and I had everything I needed, so I elected to sneak out and hope nobody had noticed my late start. I slipped out of the yard making my way through the traffic to Gower Street. I parked by the manhole and put some guarding round the van. There had not been a lot of rain so the manhole didn't need pumping out. I unwrapped the joint and decided to have a cup of tea before I started work.

I had just poured myself one and lit a cigarette when the van doors opened. I looked up in surprise to see Mr Guy, Charlie McCree and another man I didn't know standing by the back door.

Mr Guy came up the steps with the stranger, while Charlie waited outside. My mouth went dry. "Morning Mr Guy, you must have smelt the kettle going on," I said, fixing my face into a smile. "Can I offer you one?"

"No Jimmy not right now," he replied. "I have to ask you some questions, Jim, and I can only advise that you need to be completely honest with me." I knew then that this was serious.

"This is Detective Sergeant Tennison, he tells me your van was seen out last night on the Bexleyheath Road. I've looked through the work sheets, and there is no reason you should have been there Jim, what were you doing?" The silence stretched out while I desperately tried to think of a good reason why I had been at work on a Sunday night. The policeman broke the silence.

"Look, Mr Jones, we think we understand most of it, but it will go a lot easier on you and Mr Wells, if you help us with our enquiries."

Bill Guy nodded. "He's telling the truth Jimmy, far better to make a clean breast of it now, rather than come up with some cock and bull story."

"Did you find the diary?" I asked. Both men exchanged looks,

"What diary would that be?" DS Tennison asked. I stubbed my cigarette out.

"Ian Brown kept a diary of all his fascist activities, including the murder of my friend Harry Zimmerman. We tried to break into his flat to get the diary for the police." even I didn't think it sounded convincing.

Sergeant Tennison looked straight at me. "Did you break into the GPO flat in Bexleyheath telephone exchange last night Jimmy?" he asked me.

"Well yes, but it isn't like it seems," I tried to say.

He stopped me with an upheld hand and told me, "James Jones I am arresting you for house breaking with criminal intent, and as a suspect in the murder of Ian William Brown. Do you wish to say anything?" I looked at Bill Guy who shook his head. Sergeant Tennison continued, "You are not obliged to say anything unless you wish to do so, but whatever you do say will be taken down in writing and may be given in evidence against you." He produced a small black notebook, and looked at me expectantly. I just shook my head. "Right Jimmy, we are going to Crayford police station where I'd like you to tell me exactly what happened," he said. I know it sounds stupid, but all I could think about was the joint that needed finishing. As if reading my mind, Bill Guy put his hand on my shoulder.

"Jim, I don't know what this is all about, but you need to go with Detective Sergeant Tennison. Charlie McCree will finish up here and take your van back to the yard. I'll let Ron know, he's still got some legal friends from the war, and it sounds like you can do with all the help you can get."

The shock was beginning to set in, I just nodded. Sergeant Tennison lead me by the shoulder to a police car. A constable got out of the driver's seat, and showed me a pair of handcuffs, he looked at me, not unkindly, and said, "You're not going to give me any trouble Mr Jones, are you?" I shook my head and he put the handcuffs away and helped me get in the back seat. DS Tennison sat beside me. I wondered if Arthur was also under arrest. At the police station I was told to turn my pockets out. My belt and shoelaces were removed and the imposing desk sergeant behind the front desk recorded all my details. I was photographed and fingerprinted, then locked in a cell. Not knowing what was happening was the worst. Would they tell Mum and Dad? Would Judy be told? Where was Arthur? It was just so horrible. Without a watch it seemed like forever until I heard footsteps approaching the door. It was the desk sergeant with an enamel mug of tea.

"Here you are Jimmy," he said. "It's hot and sweet, get that down you, then you can come and have a chat with DS Tennison." He locked me in again, but the tea was a lifesaver, I thought I was going to cry, this just couldn't be happening, could it?

I heard the footsteps coming down the corridor, and then the rattle of the keys in the lock, it was the desk sergeant again. "Right, let's be having you Jimmy," he said. "Time to come and have a little chat." He collected my mug and lead me to interview room number three. This was a room with a bright electric light but no windows. There were four chairs and a wooden table with a Guinness ashtray on it. The sergeant indicated I should sit. Another policeman came in, the desk sergeant gave him a nod and left. The new man stood by the door, he didn't acknowledge me or say anything. I didn't even try talking.

After about twenty minutes the door opened and in came Detective Sergeant Tennison and another man in a suit. He put a large manila file on the table and sat opposite me. "Want another cup of tea Jimmy?" he asked. I nodded. He signalled to the policeman standing by the door. "How many sugars Jimmy?"

I told him, "Two please."

He turned to his colleague. "Three teas please Vic, two sugars for Mr Jones none for Henry and three for me." Vic left.

Tennison indicated the new man. "This is Detective Constable Talbot, Jimmy, he will be helping me with your interview. He's an Arsenal supporter, but other than that he's all right," he continued. Detective Talbot smiled and pulled the file towards himself. The sergeant then produced a packet of Player's Weights and offered me one. I gratefully accepted, he proffered a lighter and pushed the ashtray into the middle of the table. Henry apparently didn't smoke. "Listen Jimmy, while were off the record so to speak, there are a couple of things I would like to have a chat about. Firstly, your lawyer." I looked up. "Seems you've got a brief organised for you."

"What's a brief?" I asked.

Detective Talbot answered, "It's what we call the solicitor who prepares your case for a barrister. They mean well," Sergeant Tennison said conspiratorially, "but they can stop two blokes just trying to sort things out, know what I mean. Best we have a little chat before he arrives."

I didn't reply. "So, this solicitor, Jimmy, who is he?" I said I had no idea. "I mean you're not a bad lad Jimmy, and I'm sure this was all a horrible mistake, but I need to know exactly what happened to try and get you and Arthur off the hook, because I tell you, at the moment it don't look good for either of you."

Detective Talbot looked up from the file. "You blew his brains out, Jimmy, that's first-degree murder." He paused and turned to look at

Sergeant Tennison. "Is there anything we could do to help him Sarge? You did say he's not a bad lad."

"Well, it all depends on how much he's willing to help us constable, if he did, we could put a word in with the judge, see about getting the charges reduced."

"But he'd have to cooperate," Talbot affirmed. Sergeant Tennison nodded. It was well done, but I suspected they had used this routine before.

"What is it you want to know?" I asked.

"Well, what would be really helpful Jim, is if you tell me what you did with the gun."

I shook my head. "We didn't have a gun," I told him.

He stubbed his cigarette out. "Jimmy, we found the body of Ian Brown in the flat you admitted breaking into. Half his head was blown off. The doctor tells us he died because somebody shot him in his ear. So try and help me out Jimmy, what did you do with the gun?" The door opened and the second policeman returned, he put two mugs of tea on the table and resumed his position by the door. "Don't worry about Constable Higginbottom," the sergeant told me. "He's blind deaf and dumb, when required, isn't that right, constable?"

"Sir," Higginbottom replied his eyes fixed on the wall behind me.

"So come on Jimmy, where's the gun?" I looked at the cigarettes, and he offered me a second.

"Right, sergeant, listen carefully, I will tell you the truth." He pulled his chair forward and Constable Talbot got out a writing pad and pen. I started by telling them about Harry at the Boxing Day match. A half hour later I explained about how the sound wave had killed Ian, and that he was only supposed to have been knocked out, not killed.

The silence when I stopped talking stretched out beyond being comfortable. Eventually Sergeant Tennison spoke, "Well Constable Higginbottom, what do you make of that?"

He turned his head to look at me. "Biggest pile of monkey poo I've heard in my twenty-two years on the force, sir," he replied.

Sergeant Tennison nodded. "Of course the police doctor could have got it wrong, the mysterious diary might turn up, the sound wave death ray thing might advance science into the next century and pigs might fly.

I'm sorry Jimmy, if you want me to help you escape the gallows, you'll need to come up with a better story than that. Take him back to the cells, constable, and we'll see what a few hours of contemplation will do." The constable placed a hand on my shoulder and walked me back to the cell.

"You stupid idiot," he said as he pushed me inside. The door slammed leaving me alone and frightened, all I could remember was that he had said the word 'gallows'.

Chapter 17
The Truth, the Whole Truth and Nothing But

I sat on the cell bed contemplating my future. I had told the truth, the whole truth and nothing but the truth, but they all thought I was lying through my teeth. I just couldn't think of what to do. I decided I didn't like Detective Sergeant Tennison, he seemed a little over friendly to a prospective murderer. I decided to say nothing and place my hopes in Ron who had apparently organised a solicitor. I started to need the toilet, the flask of tea Dad had made me, the pot I had made myself and the two large cups I had been given were having an adverse effect on my bladder. In the corner of the cell was an enamel bucket with a lid. It had to be the toilet, so reluctantly I removed the lid. The smell was overpowering, but needs must, and I undid my fly and started to fill the bucket. I was halfway through when the cell door was opened, the desk sergeant stood watching me.

"You splash any on my nice clean floor and I'll use your guts to mop it up," he told me. At least he wasn't pretending friendship. I carefully put the lid back on, buttoned my fly and turned to face him. He nodded with approval at his pristine floor. "Your solicitors are here," he told me. "Two of the buggers, you must have more money than sense. Right smarten yourself up and come with me." We walked back to the front of the station and I was directed into another interview room. This one contained a window, a big table and Ron Gillroy with an older man.

The older man looked up from his notes, he was dressed in an old suit that could have been his demob issue from 1918. He had a yellow cardigan that was covered in pinhole burns from the constant cigarette clamped in his nicotine-stained fingers, and a shirt whose grey collar was what my nan would have called a disgrace. Surprisingly he had a military looking tie complemented with an egg stain. His hair was greasy and unfashionably long, it badly needed the attentions of Albert and the boy, Raymond. Overall, he radiated an air of cultivated neglect. He looked me up and down and then said, "Thank you, sergeant, we'll give you a call when we are finished." The sergeant inflated slightly and informed the whole room that a murder suspect had to be guarded at all times.

The man with Ron nodded his head. "Quite right, Sergeant Davis, if you would, however, care to guard him from the other side of the locked door, that would give my client his confidentiality to which the law says he is entitled." It was a battle of wills: Sergeant Davis lost.

With a parting, "Don't be too long about it then," he exited locking the door behind him.

Ron came round the table and took me by the shoulders. "You silly sod, what the hell have you been up to?" he demanded.

The man with him coughed. "Mr Gillroy, shall we use our time to try and establish just that," he said. He extended his hand. "I am David Robinson," he said. "I am a solicitor specialising in criminal law, and our mutual friend Mr Gillroy has asked me to help you." I shook his hand and thanked both of them.

It turned out that Mr David Robinson had previously been Major Robinson in the intelligence corps with Ron. He had told the police that Ron was on his staff, which had gained entry for both of them. Mr Robinson produced a large pad of paper and his fountain pen. "Will it be all right if I call you James?" he said.

"Everybody calls me Jimmy," I told him.

"I bet your mum doesn't," he smiled. "Right Jimmy, the bad news is you are being held as a suspect in a murder case. Ron tells me that is highly unlikely, so I suggest you tell me your story, and I'll interrupt you if necessary, would that be all right?" I said it would, and once again started to tell him everything, starting with the Boxing Day football match and ending with the death of Ian Brown.

Mr Robinson and Ron both listened in silence. Occasionally Mr Robinson would ask a question either about the diary or the wave generator. I explained I wasn't the technical one, and Arthur should be consulted for anything relating to the machine. Ron asked me where it was, and I told him we had left it under a tarpaulin in Bexleyheath cable chamber. As if by telepathy both men exchanged looks. "I'll check it out," said Ron. Mr Robinson nodded.

"I'm not happy about the doctor deciding death was caused by gunshot," Ron told Mr Robinson. "We've both seen enough wounds to know they're pretty unambiguous, even a thirty-eight would leave entry damage and powder burns."

Mr Robinson thought for a moment and said, "Unless they're suggesting one of the lads was capable of deliberately firing directly into the ear from a distance."

Ron grunted, "Never saw that in four years at the front. Can we ask for an independent post-mortem?"

Mr Robinson scribbled briefly on his pad. "I'll see to it," he said.

"How about the diary?" I asked. It seems my story would be a lot more believable if we could produce that. Ron told me the police had closed off the flat while the forensic police went through it.

"I reckon if it's there they'll find it," Ron told me.

"And if they find it, we would hope they will disclose the content," Mr Robinson added. "Now Mr Jones, the next thing that happens is you will be interviewed under caution. Don't worry, I will be here to advise you. My considered advice at this stage, however, is to say nothing, you are entitled to do that. After your interview it is likely you will be charged and taken to court, that is just a formality so that the police can hold you on remand. Is there anything you want to know?"

I thought. "How about Arthur?" I asked.

Mr Robinson consulted his notes. "He is being held at Eltham," he said. "We have arranged for one of my colleagues, Mr Chapman, to represent him. He's a good man we've worked together before, don't worry." He looked up at me. "One last thing, Jimmy, Arthur isn't going to tell Mr Chapman anything different to your account, is he?" I knew Arthur well enough to know he couldn't do anything else but tell the truth.

"I'd stake my life on it," I said.

Mr Robinson continued to hold my gaze. "I think you just might have Jimmy," he told me.

Ron went and banged on the door. Eventually the desk sergeant opened it and told Mr Robinson that Detective Sergeant Tennison would be interviewing me now. Ron and Mr Robinson had a brief whispered conversation, Ron nodded then came over and put his arm round me.

"Nil desperandum Jimmy," he told me. "Major Robertson is the best legal man I ever worked with. Trust him and we've got a fighting chance." I felt the tears coming but managed to stave them off. Worse things happen at sea.

Ron left and the desk sergeant took Mr Robinson and me back to interview room three. Eventually the two detectives came in, they had mugs of tea, a thick file and Sergeant Tennison had a lit cigarette. He sat opposite us. He stubbed the Player's out, then took a deep breath and said, "I wish to put some questions to you about the offence with which you have been charged. You are not obliged to answer any of these questions, but if you do the questions and answers will be taken down in writing and may be given in evidence. Do you understand?"

Mr Robinson leaned forward. "We do," he said. He then produced a packet of Senior Service cigarettes offered me one and pulled the ashtray towards us. Sergeant Tennison was not included, battle lines were being drawn. I was told that I was jointly charged with the death of Ian Brown and larceny with intent. Sergeant Tennison laid out the evidence against me, by consulting his file. We had admitted breaking into the flat, and by our own admission we were there to steal the property of Ian Brown. He had been woken by us breaking down the door, and when he confronted us, we had shot him in the head. We then ran off in panic leaving him for dead.

He looked up from his file. I didn't quite know what to do as my solicitor seemed more interested in drawing small intricate pictures of Alice in Wonderland on his pad. There was a long silence until Mr Robinson at last looked up and said, "Oh sorry, Detective Sergeant, I didn't realise you had stopped fantasising. Surely, you're not going to court with those accusations, I mean it's your career of course, but I'd have thought a man of your age would have his eyes on a detective inspector's job."

Tennison looked aggrieved. "And what exactly do you mean by that?" he replied.

Mr Robinson smiled. "Just sort of thinking out loud really. I'm no judge, or senior policeman, but…" and here he paused. "For an officer of your experience, you're putting forward a case you could drive a bloody double-decker bus through." A piece of burning tobacco had fallen on to his cardigan, and his attention was diverted into extinguishing himself.

Sergeant Tennison leaned forward. "Seems pretty straightforward to me, what makes you say otherwise?"

Mr Robinson also leaned forward, and ticked points off on his fingers. "One, I don't believe you can show me a signed copy of any alleged confession my client made. You do know you're not allowed to withhold evidence, don't you? Two, if nothing has been taken from the flat, accusing my client of theft seems optimistic, to say the least. Why not accuse him of buggery, bigamy or running a house of ill repute, you would have much the same chance of success."

At that point Constable Higginbottom at the door seemed to have breathing troubles, he snorted something unpleasant out of his nose and had to scrabble through his pockets for a handkerchief. Tennison glowered at him.

"Three," Mr Robinson continued. "You accuse my client of smashing down the front door, yet the body was found in the bedroom twelve feet away. Do you think he sat in bed waiting for them to come in? And four I would go back and double check with your police doctor. He's telling you that the cause of death was a gunshot wound. Tell him we will be requesting an independent post-mortem, gunshot wounds are irrefutable, he might want to reconsider his conclusions before he is cross examined in court."

The silence that followed was too long. Sergeant Tennison eventually sighed. "All right Mr Robinson, what exactly do you want? We both know there is no way on God's earth that these two are going to walk. We might not have a bulletproof case yet, but we will get one. What can I do to make this as professional as possible between us?"

Mr Robinson smiled. "OK, cards on the table time, Detective, I need more time for investigation. I won't make life difficult if my client here can be reasonably looked after whilst in your care. No interviews without me present, no confessions and access to all your evidence."

Sergeant Tennison sighed again. "Anything else?" he asked.

"Well yes, my client has been in custody since ten thirty this morning, you could get him some fish and chips from that excellent shop just down the road. A bottle of beer to wash it down would be appreciated as well."

DS Tennison shook his head. "No alcohol in the cells," he said.

"If you brought him out here, he wouldn't be in the cells, would he," said Mr Robinson gathering up his papers. He pushed five shillings towards Sergeant Tennison and the packet of Senior Service to me. "I'll be back very soon Jimmy," he told me. "Chin up."

I lay on my bunk and went through the events over and over until the desk sergeant opened the door. I sat up. "Right sir, if you like to follow me, dinner is served," he said, adding a, "Very irregular," as he shook his head. I was taken back to the room with a window where to my delight a fish supper and a bottle of beer had been laid out. "I take it sir does not want to see the wine list," the sergeant said with beetled brows; he really didn't approve of this.

There was not enough vinegar and the beer was a bit warm, but I decided not to complain. Good old Mr Robinson.

Chapter 18
On Remand

I didn't sleep well that night. There were a lot of nightmares, and I woke feeling exhausted. At eight o'clock Sergeant Davis brought me a mug of tea and a slice of toast with potted meat on it. He told me my dad had been in and brought me a wash kit and a change of clothes. He said I was due in court at ten o'clock, and Mr Robinson would meet me there. After breakfast I was taken back to the interview room without a window and formally charged with larceny with intent, and the murder of Ian Brown. I was taken to a washroom where my toothbrush and safety razor were laid out. There was a towel that must have been in use since the turn of the century and a sliver of soap. I shaved and brushed my teeth. When I was escorted back to my cell, I found my best suit, a clean shirt and tie, underwear and socks had been laid out for me. I changed and started to feel a bit more human. Constable Higginbottom then took me to the police van parked at the back of the station. I was locked in the back and Higginbottom got in the front with the driver.

We drove to Woolwich magistrate court, and I was taken through a back entrance to a room where Ron and Mr Robinson sat talking. Constable Higginbottom ushered me in and then stood guard outside, that seemed to be his primary duty in the war against crime. Ron and Mr Robinson stood as I walked in. "Morning Jimmy, sleep well?" enquired Mr Robinson offering me a cigarette.

"Yes, not bad," I lied. Ron looked at me, I think he knew.

"Now this morning," Mr Robinson continued, "you will only be asked to confirm your name and address. After that you will be asked if you want to plead guilty or not guilty, and you will tell them not guilty, OK?"

I nodded. "Have there been any developments overnight?" I asked Ron. He looked at Mr Robinson who nodded.

"They found your machine in the cable chamber," he told me. "The problem is they didn't know what it was so they called the bomb squad to give it the once over. The army put it in a Bedford truck and it's gone off for investigation. It's not dangerous Jimmy, is it?" I said I didn't think so, but it would be best to check with Arthur.

"Is he here?" I asked.

"He is, yes," Mr Robinson replied. "But he's being held in another room with my colleague Mr Chapman. You'll be in court together, but they don't like you conferring before your magistrate appearance. Mr Chapman tells me that Arthur is going to plead not guilty as well."

I nodded. "Will they take me back to Crayford when we're done here?" I asked.

Mr Robinson put his hand on my shoulder. "I will ask for bail Jimmy, but it's very unlikely the magistrate will grant it, this is a murder case. You will be held on remand, which means you have not yet been found guilty, and taken to a prison." The word prison was like a kick in the chest, it all seemed horribly real. "Now although you will be kept in prison, they will treat you as though you are innocent. That's the rules. So you will be OK, and Ron and I will start building your defence case. It will be all right Jimmy, trust me." Strangely I did. Ron told me that this morning was a formality, he had been to see my family, and explained as best he could, what had happened. Mrs Wells had been there as well as Judy, so everybody knew what had happened. I suspected Mrs Wells would blame me, and hoped Judy could forgive me, but there was no turning back now. I asked if the diary had been found.

Mr Robinson shook his head. "Not that we have been told," he said. "But apparently the police were still looking for evidence, so it really was only a matter of time."

We went through the build up to the break in again, Mr Robinson was very interested in how I had inadvertently turned the power up on the wave generator. "You slipped on oranges that Arthur had dropped on the floor," he repeated. I agreed, and he wrote a lot in his pad. "Involuntary," he muttered.

The door opened and Constable Higginbottom told us we were being called to court number one. We stubbed out our cigarettes and walked down the corridor together. The court room was impressively and intimidatingly large and, as I looked round, I was delighted to see Arthur standing in the dock. Constable Higginbottom escorted me to stand beside him. Mr Robinson and Ron went to the lower desks facing the bench with another man who I guessed was Arthur's solicitor, Mr Chapman. "All right Kid?" Arthur said, he looked terrible.

"Yeah, all right mate," I replied. The clerk of the court at the front then told us to stand and three magistrates came in, two men and a woman who sat in the middle. They shuffled some papers around and the usher told them it was the Regina against Jones and Wells. There was a bit of conferring, then the clerk of the court looked up and asked me if I was James Jones of seventy-six A Bellegrove Road, Welling. I said I was.

He turned to Arthur and asked if he was Arthur Edmund Allenby Wells of sixteen Selwyn Crescent, Welling. I couldn't help it, I knew we were in court, I knew it was not the time or the place but I had only ever known him as Arthur. "Who?" I spluttered.

Arthur glared at me. Under his breath he muttered, "He was the field marshal who led the Egyptian expeditionary force in Sanai against the Ottomans. Dad was a big fan."

The magistrate leaned forward and with a cold look told us, "Silence in court." I think nerves must have got the best of me because I really wanted to laugh out loud, and I had to stifle the giggles that threatened to have me disciplined. Arthur Edmund Allenby on the other hand looked very contrite. The clerk of the court then turned to me.

"James Jones you are charged with larceny with intent and murder, do you plead guilty or not guilty?"

I looked up at the lady magistrate and told her, "Not guilty."

She raised an eyebrow and turned to Arthur. The clerk repeated, "Arthur Edmund Allenby Wells, you are also charged with larceny with intent and murder, do you plead guilty, or not guilty?"

Arthur swallowed and told her, "Not guilty." She nodded, made some notes and then told us we would be sent for trial by jury at the crown court.

Mr Robinson got to his feet and asked if both Arthur and I could be released on bail. He informed her we were both of unblemished character and neither of us possessed a passport. He said he could produce several character witnesses to speak for both of us. The three magistrates went into a huddle. The shaking of heads did not look good. The centre magistrate then addressed Mr Robinson and Mr Chapman who now stood beside him.

"I am aware that this is the first time either of your clients has appeared before the bench, and if it were a less serious crime, I would consider your application. However, the seriousness of the police allegation prevents me from considering bail." She turned towards us. "You will be held until your trial at a prison. However, as you are on remand, you will not be subjected to normal prison discipline. You will be held for about six weeks to allow the police and your defence to prepare for a jury trial. Do you have any questions?"

Arthur looked at me. "Can we go to the same prison?" he asked.

The magistrate nodded. "I see no reason why you should not. Yes, you will be held on remand together. A brief word of warning gentlemen, do not show contempt in the crown court, it could prove expensive!" We mumbled our thanks and were led down to the cells together.

The two solicitors came down to see us before we were driven away. Mr Chapman told Arthur that his wave generator had been taken away by the army. He asked if there was anything dangerous that the army engineers should know about. Arthur considered and then started to explain about attenuation coefficients, and focused wavelength frequency. Mr Chapman held a hand up and passed Arthur a pen and pad.

"Could you write it down, Arthur, and I'll make sure the army engineers see it," he said. "I'm a legal man not an engineer and I'm sure I'd get it all wrong."

"It's not difficult," Arthur told him.

Mr Robinson leaned across. "If you could just humour us Arthur, we don't want anybody getting hurt." Arthur shrugged and started to write. The cell door opened and Ron came in.

"I've had a word with the duty officer, the lads are being sent to Wormwood Scrubs," he told us. "I'll let your families know."

Constable Higginbottom came in. "Right, you two, it's about that time," he said. "We're off to the Scrubs."

Chapter 19
The Scrubs

We were led to the Black Maria parked at the rear of the courts. There was one other man sitting in the back. He was over six foot, had a torn lapel on his jacket and a black eye. As we climbed in, he introduced himself. "Morning Lads, I'm Merion Williams, sorry we're meeting like this, bastards just sent me down for a twelve month for declining to fight for them. Although they thought it was all right for the coppers to rough me up a little," he grinned.

Arthur looked up. "Are you a conscientious objector?" he asked.

"Bloody right," Merion replied. "Asked me if I understood the charge, and before I could explain that I understood it, but objected to its capitalistic principals, the old bitch sent me down for a year. That can't be right, can it? What you two up for?"

Arthur indicated me. "This is Jimmy and I'm Arthur, we're on remand until our trial."

"Oh, trial is it," Merion said. "What you been up to then boys?"

Arthur looked at his boots. "Murder," he said.

Merion looked aghast. "Murder?" he said. "No, I mean look at you, you're not the type boys, I seen some rough old types in the valleys where I come from, but, well you're just not the sort to do that. How on earth do they think you done that then?"

I could tell Arthur wasn't in the mood to discuss it so I told Merion. "We blew a man's head off with a death ray that he invented."

There was a pause. "Oh, death-ray is it? Well yes, I suppose that would go for trial. Funny old world hey, me going down for not fighting, and you for inventing death rays. Blew his head off you reckon?"

I nodded. "Brains all across the carpet, they reckon some of his skull was found on the other side of the road." We descended into companionable silence.

The journey took an hour as the twenty miles seemed unusually full of cars and army trucks. Merion decided we had been silent long enough and explained that, although he was not prepared to fight for his country, he was more than prepared to take on the boys in blue who had taken the piss out of his ancestry and his pacifist beliefs.

"Called me a cowardly Welsh sheep shagger and decided to teach me how to fight. See it's not that I don't know how. It's just that if I fights, it has to be for something I believes in. Look what the bastards did to my good coat." He displayed his torn lapel. We agreed it was unfair.

"You boys not been called up then?" he asked. We said we were both reserved occupations for the moment. "So other than build death rays, what do you do?" he asked.

"We're both GPO engineers," I told him.

"Oh, wish I'd done something like that," he replied. "Could have stayed out of jail if I'd done something like that, difficult to get in the GPO is it?" We were spared further career discussion with Merion as the van pulled up outside the prison gates.

Wormwood Scrubs has to be one of the most iconic prisons in the country. Inside it is a maze of Victorian corridors and cells, but the main gates are imposing and impressive. We pulled up in front of them and a warder came out to check who we were. He read the court orders then opened up the main gates. We drove through and stopped by two men in prison uniform. Constable Higginbottom unlocked the rear doors and we climbed out.

The warder at the front took a proffered clipboard and signed it for PC Higginbottom. He was then handed his own board and called out, "Jones?" I raised my hand, he ticked the board. The same procedure was repeated for "Wells?" and "Williams?" He looked us up and down. "I am Mr Lucas, a senior warder at his Majesty's prison Wormwood Scrubs. You will address me as either Mr Lucas or sir. Follow me, we will now go and see the deputy governor." He turned left and swinging his arms led the way, the other prison officer brought up the rear. I was thinking ex- military from his bearing and gait. We later found out he had been a drill sergeant in the Black Watch. He marched us through a selection of tiled corridors and empty rooms unlocking as went with the big bunch of keys that hung from his belt. Eventually we went up a flight of steps to the governor's office.

We halted outside. He knocked on the door and was told to, "Come." Mr Lucas opened the door and shepherded us all inside.

Behind a large desk sat a man in his mid-forties. He had horn-rimmed glasses, receding hair and his shirt sleeves held up by metal garters. His jacket was hung on the back of his chair. He screwed the top back on his pen and looked up expectantly. We were told to stand on the line which was a narrow piece of well-worn wood screwed to the floor.

We shuffled into position, while Mr Lucas introduced us. "This is the deputy governor, Mr Rexford, you will address him as sir. Sir, these are Merion Gwyneth Williams, twenty-three, twelve months for conscientious objection."

Merion raised his hand. "Morning, governor," he greeted him.

Mr Lucas took exception to this. "That man, you will speak only when spoken to, you will address the deputy governor only as sir, and you will keep your fucking hands by your sides at all times. Do you understand?" Merion lowered his hand and told Mr Lucas he did. Unfortunately, he then thought it was necessary to apologise.

"Oh, sorry about that, see," he told Mr Rexford. "Only I'm new and this is all a bit, well strange isn't it, but don't worry boy, I'll get the hang of it." I thought Mr Lucas was going to have apoplexy, but fortunately the deputy governor had dealt with this sort of thing before. He raised a hand to prevent Mr Lucas extracting a horrible revenge for this insubordination. He then removed his glasses and addressed Merion.

"Did you refuse the medical for your military enlistment Mr Williams?"

"I did, yes," Merion replied.

"Well can I suggest that when released from here you accept it next time; and bear in mind Mr Williams, there will be a next time. Many of our medical officers served in the last war and are not unsympathetic to genuine conscientious objectors. You can serve your country without bearing arms you know. I suggest that you make good use of your time here to improve yourself educationally."

"That's what I thought," Merion confided. "I'm a bit of a writer you see."

"Excellent," Mr Rexford acknowledged. "Remember John Bunion wrote *The Pilgrim's Progress* whilst incarcerated in Bedford jail."

Merion considered this. "Well yes, but Dante wrote a great deal and he had all the freedom of Europe."

Mr Rexford's indulgence now ran out. He indicated the end of the interview to Mr Lucas, who gestured that the other officer should escort Merion out of the office. The verbal abuse diminished in volume as he was marched away. The governor replaced his glasses, and looked at Arthur and I. Mr Lucas read from the clipboard. James Jones and Arthur Edmund Allenby Wells. "On remand awaiting trial for murder, sir."

Mr Rexford nodded. "The Egyptian campaign I take it?"

Arthur looked up. "Yes, sir, my father was a great one for military history, he considered Allenby to be a great military strategist."

"Quite right," Mr Rexford agreed. "Now, as you are on remand, you will be treated as those who have yet to have their fate decided. Innocent until proven guilty so to speak. You will therefore be held on the remand wing with others who are awaiting trial. You will not be issued with prison uniform but you will receive a bible.

"You will be fed the same as everyone else, but you may have unlimited access to the library, and you may retain fifteen shillings for luxury items such as soap and cigarettes. Other than your legal representation you are allowed ninety minutes of visiting times and two letters a month. Do you have any questions?" We said we didn't. He looked at us for a moment. "Very well, if I may pass on my considered advice to young men newly delivered into my care. Do not try and fight authority in here, read your bible, do not get into fights and refrain from masturbating too much. You will find your legal representatives offer good advice, heed it. That is all gentlemen, thank you."

Mr Lucas ushered us out. "At least you two had more sense than that Welsh bastard. You'll find in here it pays sometimes to just shut up and listen. Now you get to see the padre. If you want a long chat, he'll be the shoulder to cry on, but not today, all right!" Neither of us being particularly religious, agreed. We were led to the chapel by the arm-swinging Mr Lucas. He opened the door and ushered us in.

The padre was a big overweight man with bad teeth. He wore a black shirt with a dog collar and a grey cardigan. He liked to touch. To Arthur's discomfort he tried to shake hands with both of us. I explained Arthur wasn't comfortable with physical contact. He gave my shoulder a lingering squeeze and told me that was all right as a he was sure a good-looking young man as myself wouldn't mind an old padre reaching out to a member of his flock. He asked us what we were to be tried for, and I told him we were accused of murdering homosexuals. He took a chair and sat a comfortable distance from us both.

"What religion are you boys?" he asked. It was like a label we had carried through school and career.

"C of E," I told him, he nodded, no problems there then.

"We have a service, Sunday mornings at ten," he told us. "You will be given a bible, and I am always here for advice and comfort." he caught my eye as he told us that.

"Thank you, Padre, that is reassuring," Arthur told him. We backed out and were collected at the chapel door by Mr Lucas.

"The padre means well," he told us. "But probably best to visit him together if you get my meaning."

"Don't think either of us is that much in need of spiritual guidance," Arthur replied.

He nodded. "Right just a quick shower and you can join Saville Row."

We exchanged looks. "Saville Row?" I enquired.

"Oh yes, you don't have to wear prison uniform on remand, so all the other occupants of the remand wing are walking about in their best suits that they wore for the courts, just like you two. Prison uniform is grey flannel; underwear, shirts, trousers and jackets. Compared to the regular inmates you lot look like you just stepped out of the Ritz."

He opened a door with his ring of keys, it was a washroom with sinks, toilets and about twenty shower heads. He handed us both a bar of soap and a towel. "Right, strip off and shower."

Hanging the towel with our clothes we stripped and took the bar of carbolic into the showers. I expected the showers to be cold, they weren't. Feeling a lot refreshed I walked back to our clothes. Mr Lucas was waiting. He held a fat tube with a sort of pepper pot on the front and a handle on the back. "Hands above your head and shut your eyes," he told me. I didn't know what was coming next but being naked dissuades you from arguing with a six-foot prison officer in heavy boots. He pumped the handle and covered me from head to toe in a fine powder, it was delousing powder and considered necessary in all his Majesty's prisons. If any got in your mouth you never forgot the taste. No matter how demeaning this induction was, it was still bloody funny to watch Arthur having to go through the same process. He arrived seconds after I had been powdered. I turned my back as Mr Lucas ordered him to raise his arms and close his eyes. A huge cloud of fine powder encompassed him, turning him light grey from head to toe. I laughed out loud. It didn't matter that I had just been through the exact same process, seeing Arthur crouching naked in monochrome was funny. He didn't see it, but it was. Mind you, when he eventually opened his eyes, he laughed at me. Welcome to Wormwood Scrubs. After we had managed to get our clothes on again, we were taken to Saville Row. We had been allocated a double cell. In a small room measuring about twelve feet by eight, they had squeezed a pair of bunk beds each with a bible on it.

A small table sat under the high window on the far wall, the enamel bucket was in the left-hand corner under a small shelf and a single chair was placed near the door. This was to be our home until the trial. I fought against the rising despair. It would not have been good for Arthur to see how I felt. As the door slammed behind us, and the keys rattled in the lock he took a deep breath.

"All right, kid?" he asked.

"Yeah, all right, mate," I replied.

We were fed in our cell that night, a thin lamb stew and a small loaf. Another inmate brought it in a tin bowl with a spoon as our only piece of cutlery, he did not speak. It lacked salt and virtually all taste, neither of us finished it. We later learned like every other inmate, to eat anything that was offered. Arthur found if you climbed on to the chair, you could look out of the window. The view was rather pleasant, meadows and open farmland. Even central London still had some open spaces. I took the top bunk and, surprisingly, we both slept well. I suspect it was mental exhaustion.

Chapter 20
Prison Life

We were released at six thirty to empty our bucket and wash, we joined the queue not really knowing where we were going. It turned out it was the same communal shower room we had been deloused in yesterday, only this time it was full of other remand prisoners. The only wash kit we had was the bar of carbolic soap and the towel we had been given.

I had a shower as it had definitely made me feel better yesterday, and I wanted to remove the grey delousing powder that seemed to have penetrated every orifice. Strangely most of the other men opted for a sluice down in the sinks. I found out why when I turned the shower on, this time it was cold. It seemed to cause general amusement that as a new boy I didn't know all the hot water had been used by six. There were a lot of other men in different wings, and only one boiler room. When I emerged shivering another man offered me his razor. "Bloody cold in there wasn't it?" he grinned. "I did exactly the same thing on my first morning. Here you won't have had time to visit the shop, do you want to use my razor?" I thanked him and tried to work up a lather with the carbolic, I wasn't very successful. "When you have had breakfast, you can go to the shop, watch out for Nigel if he's on duty. You want to buy a toothbrush, tooth powder, a razor and cigarettes. Lots of cigarettes. They're like money in here, you want something, you pay for it with cigarettes, got it?" I thanked him for the advice. Arthur had kept his clothes on and had washed only his face and hands, the grey powder still showed under his collar.

"You have a distinctly grey tinge," I told him.

"Well better than blue," he replied. "Did you realise your todger practically vanishes when you're in water that cold? God, I'd like to brush my teeth." I told him that after breakfast we could visit the shop, and the advice to stock up on cigarettes. He used the edge of the towel to rub his teeth with and told me he was starving. I was too.

"I wonder what's for breakfast," I said.

The man who had leant me his razor heard me. "Well," he mused, "it's Tuesday, so it's either kippers or poached eggs."

Arthur immediately cheered up. "I hope there are still some kippers left, I'm not over fond of poached egg." The man using the sink next to him, spat out his toothpowder and told Arthur not to be such a prat.

"Breakfast is porridge, it's always bloody porridge. It's cheap it stops you being hungry, and there's lots of it."

"No kippers then," Arthur said.

"No kippers, no devilled kidneys, no kedgeree and definitely no bleedin' bacon. Porridge. Porridge Tuesday. Porridge every fucking day. Porridge."

Well, you couldn't argue with that. The first man looked a bit abashed. "Sorry, sometimes trying to be clever doesn't work. Yeah, it's porridge, but it's not that bad. What you need to do is drop your wash kit off in your cell, bring your bowl and cutlery down to the canteen. Get your breakfast and ask before you sit down, OK?" I told him we understood, and we returned to our cell.

When we were alone Arthur told me he really fancied kippers now that the other bloke had spoken about them. I sighed. "Yeah, kippers would be nice, but it's not a hotel mate, it's going to be porridge." He too sighed. "And another thing, have you been looking at my old man?"

He grinned. "Well after all the years of you bragging about it, I found the reality reassuring. Nothing like the small elephant you've told all the girls about."

"It was freezing in that bloody shower, you wait until you have one, then see how yours perishes."

Arthur grabbed his bowl and spoon. "Come on, Jim, breakfast first, we can discuss willies later." The breakfast hall was full of men eating at trestle tables. Most of them were dressed in grey flannel, few had any item of clothing that was a good fit. We joined the queue and were issued with a tray, a mug of tea, a piece of bread and a dollop of porridge in our bowls. Arthur asked if there was any golden syrup. There wasn't, but it did raise a lot of smiles.

Bearing in mind our advice, I stood behind two empty spaces. "You gentlemen mind if we join you," I asked. A big man with a shaven head and a lot of tattoos looked over his shoulder at us.

"That's a nice suit," he told me.

I nodded. "Court appearance," I told him.

He nodded back. "All fresh meat has good suits, what you charged with, theft?"

"No, theft would be better, we're waiting trial for murder," I told him. He raised an eyebrow and exchanged looks with the other men sitting with him.

"Well sit down before your breakfast gets cold and tell me all about it. I'm Mosher, Mosher Abrahams."

"Thank you, Mr Abrahams, I'm Arthur and he's Jimmy," Arthur explained taking a seat.

Mosher reached into his pocket and extracted a tobacco tin which he offered to Arthur. "Here Mr Golden Syrup, you can have a little of my sugar, a little mind!" Arthur smiled and took a small pinch from the tin to sprinkle on his porridge. He returned it to Mosher with a nod of thanks. Mosher nodded back and the tin vanished into his pocket.

"So murder, what you pleading?" he asked.

"Not guilty," Arthur told him through a mouthful of porridge.

"Good boy," Mosher agreed. "You got a brief?"

"Yes, one of my workmates is ex-army, his old major is now a solicitor and he's helping us," I explained. Mosher grinned revealing teeth that were probably beyond dental resurrection.

"You listen to what your brief tells you, this place is full of innocent men who didn't." I nodded.

"What are you in for Mr Abrahams?" Arthur asked. As if by magic the atmosphere changed, conversations halted, and our neighbours drew back. Mosher shook his head. "Look you're new, so you need things explained to you. Rule one, never ask a con what he's locked up for. If they care to tell you, fair enough, but don't ask. Right?" Arthur nodded. He continued. "Me I'm doing an eight stretch for selling fire insurance." It was Arthur's turn to raise an eyebrow. Mosher held his gaze. "I told them if they took my insurance plan, nothing would happen to their business, if they didn't; well third-party fire and theft takes on a whole new meaning."

Arthur didn't blink. "You mean extortion?"

Mosher nodded. "That's what the judge called it. My brief told me to plead guilty, I thought I knew better and had my friends visit a witness, they got a bit over enthusiastic, and here I am. Like I say, listen to your brief boys. Come and see me in the library about four o' clock, I'll see what I can do for you." Mosher got up and the two men sitting with him accompanied him out of the dining room.

"Well, he seemed quite nice," Arthur remarked mopping up the last of his porridge with a crust of bread.

We washed up our bowls, mugs and cutlery and went to find the shop. Arthur asked one of the warders where it was. He directed us down a series of corridors, until we found a cell that had been converted into a small shop. A prisoner with a big white patch sewn to his jacket served us. He explained he was a trusty, and was given privileged jobs like this, because of his unblemished record. We bought two combs, toothbrushes, toothpowder, a razor to share and a small stick of shaving cream. They only had Woodbine cigarettes but we bought three packs each. Arthur also bought a small packet of castor sugar. "For the breakfast," he explained. The bill came to twelve and six. Arthur handed over a pound. The trusty counted change out of his till and handed Arthur five and six. Arthur kept his hand out. "What?" said the trusty.

"I gave you a pound," Arthur told him.

"No mate, you gave me eighteen bob, don't try the old Jerusalem on me, I'm a trusty and if I call for a screw your feet won't touch, understand."

I watched with interest as Arthur walked back and closed the door. He then returned and stood very close to our new friend. His voice wasn't raised but it was spoken with sincerity. "What's your name mate?"

The trusty looked uncertain his eyes darting between us, but eventually turned to Arthur and told him, "Nigel, Nigel Fosser."

Arthur continued. "Well, Nigel, unfortunately I am in here for murder. I don't want to be, and…" he glanced back at me, "if he hadn't lost his temper I might have got away with it. I mean look at him, you'll never guess how he got that scar." He sighed, then continued. "Now me,

I'm probably not big enough or angry enough to get my two shillings back, but if Mad Dog there realises you have deprived him of money, I don't think I can help you, Nigel."

Nigel looked at me. "Mad Dog?" he asked.

"Woof," I replied also moving in closer.

Arthur continued. "I know two shillings isn't a lot, but if you think it's worth pissing blood for Nigel, that of course is entirely up to you. I'm going to go outside now, because I don't want to get any bodily fluids on my shirt." Arthur turned towards the door.

"No wait," Nigel said, his eyes fixed on me. "Here I must have made a silly mistake." He tried to give Arthur a florin. I started making growling noises and tried to push Arthur out of the way. "No, keep him off," Nigel pleaded. "Here, take this, here." He offered Arthur his pound back. I stopped pushing and barked at Nigel.

"Oh, look Nigel, he likes you," he told him. "Now that is very generous, and Mad Dog and I appreciate it. But Nigel if you make silly mistakes with any other new boys, well Mad Dog might just come walkies down to see you, OK?" Nigel just nodded and retreated into a corner as we left.

We walked in silence until we had turned a corner. "Mad Dog?" I asked.

"Well, I sort of made it up as I went along," Arthur told me. "Worked, didn't it?" I glared at him. "Woof," he said, and we both dissolved into a fit of giggles. We made our way back to the cell.

Mr Lucas was waiting for us. "You have a legal visit at fourteen hundred," he told us. "Be back here by thirteen thirty, and I'll escort you down." He looked at our purchases. "So been down the shop then, was Fosser on duty when you went?" Arthur told him that he had been. "Did you have any trouble?" Mr Lucas asked.

"Not at all," Arthur told him. "He was as nice as pie."

There was a moment's silence. "You remember what Mr Roxford told you; no fighting. You could end up in a world of trouble." Mr Lucas glared at us.

"Fighting?" I said. "Last thing Arthur and I want to do is get in your bad books, Mr Lucas. Go and have a look at Fosser, you won't find a mark on him."

Mr Lucas looked at us in turn and in silence. "Be back here at half one," he said, he swivelled on his heel and marched off in the direction of the shop.

"Do you think he will say anything?" I asked Arthur.

He snorted. "What and risk a visit from Mad Dog, I don't think so," he grinned. "Come on, I'm going to clean my teeth and have a smoke."

We played cards until Mr Lucas came back at half one. He eyed us suspiciously. "I don't know what you said to Fosser, but he has had a change of heart, asked for a transfer to the farm, not like him at all."

"Still, nice that he'll be in the fresh air," Arthur commented.

"Don't give me no trouble, that's all I'm saying," Mr Lucas replied. "Now follow me." We fell in behind him as he marched to another block.

Mr Lucas unlocked a door and ushered us into a large hall filled with chairs and tables. Sitting in the middle was Mr Robinson and Mr Chapman; they stood up as we approached. "You've got forty minutes," Mr Lucas informed us, before leaving and locking the door behind him.

"Come and sit down, lads," Mr Chapman said and proffered a packet of Player's.

"How you getting on?" Mr Robinson asked. "Any problems?" I told him we were fine.

We sat and smoked while Mr Chapman outlined the progress that had been made. The police doctor had reconsidered his findings and had now concluded that death had been caused by an applied unknown force to the head. It had not, however, been caused by a firearm. The army had taken away the generator but nothing had been heard from them other than thanks for Arthur's technical notes. Best of all, though, was that the police had found Ian Brown's diary. I saw Arthur sit up.

"Was there enough in it to show he killed Harry?" he asked.

"Well," Mr Chapman said. "The entry for the 26th of December 1932 is…" and he consulted his notes. "'Give an old Jew a damn good kicking, Pat used his blade. Pete got punched, so we didn't hold back. Two — one against the Yid boys, and we got clean away, good result all round'."

"That's good isn't it," I asked. "That backs up everything that we told you?"

Mr Robinson held his hand up. "It's certainly good they found it, but I'm afraid he's no Samuel Pepys. There's a lot of fantasizing about his rise to high rank with the fascists, but this it's not specific. Old Jew could be one of thousands, Pat using a blade, could have been sharpening pencils and two — one against the Yid boys is circumstantial. However, on the bright side it does exactly match your statement, and I think it will be accepted as evidence.

"We are going down to see Peter Summersgill on the Isle of Wight, he's still locked up in Parkhurst, doesn't get out for another two years. Unfortunately, Patrick Murphy was released in 1938. We are still trying to find him."

"Where was the diary?" Arthur asked. There was a pause.

"It was hidden in a briefcase behind the bath with a pile of magazines that had photographs of women in them," Mr Cooper told him. He blushed slightly "Filthy photographs."

"Anyway," Mr Robinson interrupted. "Is there anything you need in here?" We told him a change of clothes would be good, and he told us our parents had applied for a visit and would bring them in tomorrow. Mr Chapman told us the most important thing was not to lose hope, they were building a strong defence case, and had negotiated with a really good barrister to present it. We shook hands all round and our solicitors left.

Mr Lucas escorted us back to our wing. We asked him where the library was. He told us we could visit it without having doors unlocked and gave us directions. At ten to four we went to see Mosher, we both realised you need all the friends you can get when you're banged up with bad guys.

Chapter 21
News of Janet

We eventually found the library and, to Arthur's delight, it had a few books on technical engineering, I settled for an Agatha Christie. Mosher occupied a corner table, with his two friends, they looked like Tweedle Dum and Tweedle Dee. "Boys come on and sit with us," Mosher ordered. He looked at my Agatha Christie. "The butler done it," he told me.

"Well thanks Mosher, I'll put it back," I told him.

"A joke, you can't take a joke?" he grinned exposing his brown stubs of teeth, the Tweedles laughed a little bit more then was necessary. Mosher was definitely the alpha male.

Mosher explained that he 'looked after' a lot of stuff in the prison. "You boys want anything, you come and see old Mosher," he told us. "Cost you a few fags like, but I'll always do you a reasonable rate. You got a visit coming up?" I said we both had a parent coming tomorrow with clean clothes. Mosher nodded. "Yeah, your old cacks will need a change soon. Listen boys you could do me a big favour."

"What's that, Mosher?" I asked.

"I want to put a bet on the three thirty at Newmarket on Friday" he confided in us. "Big Bad Wolf, should be able to get at least eight to one."

"How do we do that?" Arthur asked.

"No, you pudding, you don't do nothing. You ask your lovely parents to do it. It's all kosher, and if they want to put a few quid on, well good luck to them. Here," he slipped an envelope into my book, "A pony on the nose, Big Bad Wolf, three thirty Newmarket, Friday, OK?" There are times, when the most sensible course of action is to say no. This wasn't one of them.

Mosher was being nice, but we both knew it wouldn't take a lot for that to stop. "Leave it to us Mosher," I told him.

"Good boy," Mosher said. "Big Bad Wolf, right up your street hey Jimmy, woof." He must have talked to Nigel. He laughed again and he and his two companions rose and left.

The worst aspect of prison is not being deprived of your liberty, it's boredom. We walked down to the recreation area and found a chess set, it had a pawn missing, but we substituted a match box for it. I lost three straight games. "No, honestly Jim, your strategy is getting better," Arthur consoled me. "A year ago, you were falling for everything, now you have a long think before falling for it." I threw the matchbox at him.

The evening meal was cottage pie. It wasn't going to win any culinary awards, but it was edible, and we were both hungry. Afterwards we talked to Earnest Spencer, the man who had leant me his razor. He told us that he was on remand for theft from the shipping company he had worked for. It was a sorry tale. He had been caught red-handed and was now terrified that his fiancé would break off the engagement. His prospective mother-in-law had never approved of him since a Christmas when he had too much port wine and put his hand up her skirt.

"Bloody hell, Earnest, your mother-in-law!" Arthur said, half in awe, half in incredulity. "Are you joking?" Earnest told us he wasn't. We were spared the rest of the tale as the bell rang for lockdown. We told Earnest 'not to worry', but on reflection decided that was probably his best option.

On Friday we both had visitors, Mum and Dad came to see me, they brought a parcel of new clothes some more toiletries, cigarettes and a letter from Judy. Arthur's mum came with them but she sat alone with Arthur, she had been crying. Dad explained Ron Gillroy had been round to see them. He sent a message that Mr Robinson was making progress and had found Patrick Murphy who had joined the army, he hoped to visit me later in the week. Dad said that he and Ron had discussed the death of Ian Brown at length and were both of an opinion that the very worst we would be charged with was manslaughter. I know it was supposed to cheer me up, but anything that made me think I might be wearing the grey flannel uniform for years had the opposite effect. I think Mum sensed that because she put a hand on Dads' arm to shut him up.

They asked me if we had made any friends, as though this was a new school. I told them about Mosher, that he was one of the men who were looking after Arthur and me, but he had asked a favour. Mum told me to go straight to the governor if I had any problems, not to rely on 'rough types', and certainly do no favours for them, they were criminals. Dad refrained from pointing out that I was to be tried for murder and, ever practical, asked what the favour was.

I told him about placing the bet. He nodded and took the twenty-five pounds with a slight of hand that was surprisingly practiced. Mum told me that Judy was coming to visit next time, only two visitors at a time were allowed. They chatted about normal life until the bell rang and it was time for them to leave. Mum gave me a kiss on my cheek, and Dad shook my hand. "Chin up old man, worse things happen at sea," he told me. I think we all had moist eyes.

Judy's letter was wonderful. It was full of news, love, gossip and what was on the pictures. She had also sketched some new outfits that she was going to make to wear on our first date out together. Not a word of recrimination, I loved her so much. There was some bad news, and she asked me to tell Arthur that she had received another letter from Spain. It was from a doctor who worked in a hospital in Cordoba. The hospital was a state-run facility, but the doctor was not unsympathetic to those opposing Franco. He had been asked by Senor Fernandez, the man who had brought Janet in, to let her family know what had happened. The only address he had was Judy's and he had asked the doctor to write. Janet had suffered a bullet wound to the left wrist.

Under normal circumstances the injury would have responded to medical attention. Unfortunately, Janet had taken far too long to get treatment and gangrene had set in. The doctor explained that there had been no choice and he had amputated her hand above the wrist. He expected her to make a full recovery and had hinted that there were 'friends' who would get her out of Spain. It put our own miseries into perspective.

That night I broke the news to Arthur, he was obviously in shock, but took it well. "Why the hell did she go Jim?" he demanded close to tears.

"Because she had to mate, you know that," I told him. He shook his head.

"But she will have to go through the rest of her life with one hand," he whispered.

"A lot of brave men came back from the last lot with arms and legs missing, you know Janet's as brave as any of them."

He nodded. "Oh, bloody hell, Jim, what's happened to us all, this is like a bad dream." I pulled his blanket over him and hoped he would sleep.

Chapter 22
The Offer

We fell into the routine of prison life. It was ritual boredom punctuated with odd moments of relief. Visits from Mr Robinson or Mr Chapman brought either hope or despair. On the bad side they had located Murphy, he had enlisted in the army and was stationed at Catterick. Mr Robinson had visited him and, despite veiled threats from his CO, he still claimed he had no memory of anyone else being present when he had assaulted me all those years ago. He said it was just some other man who happened to be having a piss when the fight started. When they told him Ian Brown had been killed, he had turned very pale and had obviously been shaken but continued to claim no knowledge of anyone of that name. Mr Chapman was of the opinion that he would not make a good defence witness. Peter Summersgill was still in prison on the Isle of Wight and had just under two years to serve. He had been aggressive since his arrival and had been flogged again for assaulting a prison officer. Mr Robinson had shaken his head and concluded Summersgill was a habitual criminal and would not be moved from his. 'Don't know nothing', reply. When told of the death of Ian Brown he had shrugged and said, "War's coming and a lot of men are going to die, know what I mean boss." Again, they thought it would not be a good idea to call him as a witness.

The good news was that they had managed to get the diary accepted as evidence, and the more investigation the police did, the more they believed our account. That, Mr Robinson told us, meant we had a good chance of convincing the court of our innocence. The date for our trial had been set for three weeks. We were to be tried at the Old Bailey. Somehow that seemed to make it more real, we weren't just playing at being prisoners, it could mean the death penalty if it all went wrong. I tried not to think about it, but sometimes in the early hours, it was hard not to.

At the end of the week, I had a visit from Judy. She looked beautiful and smelt so clean and fresh that it made me aware of the standards of hygiene we had come to accept. Despite the disapproving coughing from the supervising prison officer, she gave me a long and tender kiss before we sat opposite each other.

She had brought me cigarettes, a clean shirt, some homemade cakes and a picture of us taken at Southend. We chatted easily as though I wasn't being held on a murder charge. We talked of Janet, and she told me she would almost certainly now be sent home, what else could she do? All too soon the bell went and Judy had to go. She kissed me again and, under cover of our embrace, slipped a fat envelope into my pocket. "Your Dad says thank you very much, he put five pounds on," she whispered. She blew me a kiss as she left.

When I got back to our cell, I shook out the contents of the envelope, there was two hundred and twenty-five pounds in five-pound notes and a betting slip. Mosher had been right, eight to one. Arthur gave a low whistle. "How long would it take you to earn that?" he asked.

"A year with a bit of overtime," I told him.

Arthur grinned. "Right let's tell Mosher we're buying a cruise on the Queen Mary," he suggested.

"Depends if you want to continue," I told him.

"Continue what?" he said.

"Breathing," I explained.

We put the money in my Agatha Christie and went in search of Mosher. As usual he was with the Tweedles in the library. An older man sat between them, his forehead glistened with perspiration, his eyes darting between them like a cornered animal. "Boys, boys, come and join me," Mosher waved us over. He was all smiles. "Big Bad Wolf hey! Did your parents have a little flutter? Seven to one, got to be better than working?" He turned his lupine smile on the man between the Tweedles. "So let's just have a little recap shall we Dave, you will pay me the outstanding balance on your account or," and he then turned to the henchman on his left, "Maurice here will break something dear to you; like a shin."

Dave nodded his head violently. "Yes Mr Abrahams, I will pay you, I swear." Maurice rose and allowed Dave to scuttle out from behind the table. Maurice placed a hand like a hock of ham on Dave's shoulder.

"Don't do nothing stupid Dave, Mr Abrahams knows where your family is." Dave nodded and made for the exit.

"Sorry about that, boys, a small matter of an overdraft facility getting a little out of hand. Occasionally it's necessary to remind my clients how the penal fiscal system operates. I'm sure Dave there is now a reformed character. Now," he spread his fingers wide and gave us an unrestricted view of his dental problems. "Do you have something for me?" I pushed the book across to the middle of the table. His smile grew. "No need to ask who done it, Big Bad Wolf bloody done it at seven to one." I put my hand on the book and stopped him picking it up.

The eyes that came up to stare at me were no longer friendly. "What?" he said.

"It's not seven to one Mosher," I told him. Maurice changed his weight to the alternative buttock; he didn't know yet if he would be required to adjust my internal organs. Arthur put his arm round Maurice's huge shoulder.

"It's all right Maurice, it's eight to one." Suddenly the atmosphere was all sweetness and light, Maurice looked to see how Mosher had taken the news, he was rewarded by a face of benevolence.

"You boys," Mosher told us. "Always the good joke." He opened the envelope and flicked through the notes at impressive speed. "Two twenty-five," he smiled. "Your parents must have got that on quickly, the odds changed the next day. When's your next visit?"

"Sorry Mosher, that was a one-off act of friendship," I told him. "My dad isn't becoming your bookies runner." Mosher shook his head.

"Now listen, Jimmy Jones, when you are in the Scrubs, you are on my territory." He wiped his hands together as though he was washing them, "One hand washes the other, you understand? You could have an easy time in here as my friend; or not."

He looked me in the eyes. "If I just want the occasional bet placing, or message delivering, well that's not too much to ask for your health and wellbeing, is it?" Somehow delivering a large amount of cash to Mosher had become confrontational. Maurice sensing it was time to apply brute force rose to his feet, his counterpart did the same. I don't think he had worked out what was happening, but if Maurice got up, then he got up. That's how it worked.

We were saved by Mr Lucas, he entered the library and glared at us all. "Right, Wells on your feet, you have a visitor, move it, move it."

Arthur and I exchanged looks. "Be all right if Mr Jones comes with me Mr Lucas?" Arthur asked. Mr Lucas had been a prison officer long enough to interpret the situation.

"Yes, the pair of you follow me," he ordered.

He swivelled on one foot and led us at a fast march out of the library and out of trouble. "See you boys later," Mosher called after us. We were still in trouble.

"Is it my mum?" Arthur asked, as we marched along. Neither of us could think who would visit Arthur on his own.

"Not your mother, Wells no," Mr Lucas told him. "Military gentleman. You two in trouble with Abrahams?"

"Not really," Arthur sighed. "Just a disagreement over favours."

Mr Lucas nodded. "Stay clear of him, he's bad news. He won't do anything where he could be caught, but we have had one or two, slip over in the showers, after disagreement with Mr Abrahams."

"What does the military want with me?" Arthur asked.

"Oh, I should think they want you to parachute into Germany and bring Herr Hitler back over here! How the hell would I know? I don't know what's going on but it's highly irregular. The governor got a call telling him it was necessary. Not seen him put out like that in a long time." We were ushered into the visitors' hall still wondering what this was about.

There was a single table with two men sitting straight backed. One was a major, the other a civilian. As we approached, they stood, the major nodding to Mr Lucas. "Thank you, officer, that will be all for now," the major told him. "We'll call when we need letting out."

"Sir," Mr Lucas replied, wheeling on his heel as though back on the parade ground. I think he was enjoying this.

The major consulted a clipboard. "Which one of you is Arthur Edmund Allenby Wells?" he asked.

Arthur raised a hand. "That would be me, sir," he told him.

The major looked thoughtful. "Did a study of a chap called Edmund Allenby at Sandhurst. Field Marshall, Egyptian campaign, fought the Ottomans in Sanai."

Arthur nodded. "My dad was a bit of a military history buff, thought he was the greatest strategist in the army."

The major contemplated this. "Well, good yes, bloody good in fact, but greatest, well I could contest that. Anyway, sit down, Wells." He looked at me. "And who is this you've brought with you?"

"This is Jimmy Jones, sir, we are on remand together, I thought this might have been about the trial, so I asked Mr Lucas if he could come with me."

The major considered that for a moment then nodded. "Very well, as you are both being charged, he might be of use. Sit down Jones." I did.

"As I understand it, you are being charged with murder caused, you claim, by a wave generator that sent a sound wave through the telephone network powerful enough to blow a chap's brains out?" He looked up.

"That's correct, sir," Arthur replied.

The major exchanged looks with Mr McRae and produced a packet of cigarettes which he offered round. "Gentlemen, I am Major Jefferis, and this is Mr Stuart McRae. We have a few questions for you about the wave generator you built."

Arthur interrupted him. "Excuse me sir, but are you the Stuart McRae who writes for *Armchair Scientist*?"

Mr McRae smiled. "I am, or should I say I was, I now work for the major here."

Arthur nodded. "I've read a lot of your articles, Mr McRae, very impressive."

The major continued. "Well having established our credentials, would it be all right for me to continue?" Arthur and I sat in silence. "Good," the major continued. "Now I wonder if you can explain this Mr Wells." He produced a leather briefcase and extracted a circuit diagram, which he passed across to Arthur.

Arthur studied it for a moment. "Oh, this is the initial separation filter to remove harmonics," he told them.

Mr McRae leant forward. "Yes, but it doesn't work." Arthur looked puzzled and returned to scan the diagram.

"You don't have a slide rule on you?" he asked. Major Jefferis delved into his bag and produced one. Arthur took it and in silence began to make calculations. The major then produced a notebook and pencil which he pushed towards Arthur. After five minutes Arthur looked up. "The reason this circuit doesn't work, gentlemen, is that somebody doesn't know the difference between capacitors in series and parallel."

Major Jefferis and Mr McRae again exchanged glances. "Show me," the major said. The three of them poured over the diagram and slipped into a sort of electrical engineering talk.

"He's right," Mr McRae informed the room. "God Almighty I should have seen that."

Arthur looked puzzled. "Why didn't you check it against my prototype?" he asked.

The major sat back. "Because the staff officers in REME decided they would have your generator stripped down, and then couldn't get it to function."

Arthur looked aghast. "Didn't they take notes?" he asked.

Mr McRae pushed the diagram towards him. "They did, and this is an example of their work." There was a long silence while we all absorbed this.

Eventually the major spoke. "Thing is, do you see, we work for a government department called MD1. That's Ministry of Defence One. One of our functions is to come up with new ideas to use in the war effort. I was hoping that this generator of yours might be a candidate, but I fear that is probably not practical, unless…" Here he paused, and looked up at Arthur. "You come and assist Mr McRae here in putting a mark two together."

I have had Arthur Edmund Allenby Wells as my good friend since 1926 when he rescued me from Derek Murphy. What he did next, however, went beyond friendship. "Would working on the development of this mean release from prison?" he asked.

The major took a moment to consider this. "Dependent upon results, it might," he told Arthur.

"And would charges be dropped?" Arthur continued.

The major smiled. "I work for a very powerful commanding officer, I suspect he might be prepared to arrange that, but again wholly dependent upon results. Is there anything else Mr Wells?"

"Just one thing," Arthur told him. "I will build a generator that will be fully functional, I will do whatever you ask, but I need Mr Jones to come with me." There was another long pause while options were considered.

"And if I say no?" the major asked.

"Then I wish Mr McRae luck, it will be like doing a jigsaw puzzle without a picture: possible but very, very time consuming."

The major glanced at Mr McRae who nodded. "He's right," he told him. "It could take forever with the shit that REME have given us."

The major rose to his feet, a clear signal that the interview was over. As he put things back into his briefcase, he addressed one last remark to me. "How do you feel about that Mr Jones, what can you bring to the table?"

I thought, this could be important, Mum had always said, "Take your time and think things through."

"Well sir, Arthur and I have been a team since 1926. He is the genius, but I am the common sense. If you want this to work, you're going to need my practical skills to compliment your mad inventor. I want to get out of here, and like Arthur I'll work round the clock to do it."

The major nodded. "What did you do before you ended up in here Mr Jones?"

"I was a GPO jointer," I told him. "A good one."

He paused for a moment but didn't look up. "I'll be back this afternoon, people to see if I want strings pulled." Mr McRae gave us a smile as he left.

Chapter 23
The Three Wise Men

As the major and Mr McRae left, Mr Lucas marched in to escort us back to our own wing. As we tried to keep up with him, Arthur asked a question. "Mr Lucas you're ex-military, what's the Ministry of Defence?" Mr Lucas stopped and, comically, Arthur and I nearly collided with him like a scene from a Laurel and Hardy film.

"Ministry of Defence, there is no ministry of defence. They're creating lots of new positions in the war cabinet, but that's not one of them," he told us with authority.

"It's just that the major told us that's who he worked for," I replied.

Mr Lucas thought. "There is a minister of defence, but he hasn't got a ministry yet, least nothing that has been in the papers."

"Who's that then?" Arthur asked.

Mr Lucas looked at us incredulously. "There's a war on you know, why don't you two keep up with current affairs? Our minister of defence is Churchill, the only one with enough balls to win this war if you ask me." He pivoted forward and shaking his head, continued to march us at speed. I think the kettle must have been on in the warders' canteen.

We said nothing until we got back to our own wing. Arthur went first. "Bloody hell Jimmy, only bloody hell. We could be out of this, we could be free. Oh, bloody hell, Jimmy, what do you think?" I found it hard to hold the jubilation back, but realised we were a long way from being clear.

"It's a hope Arthur but we're not out of this mess yet. Can you make another death ray thing?"

Arthur was still on cloud nine, but given this practical problem, the analytical part of his brain cut in. "If they let me have my old notebooks, and will supply all the bits I need, I don't see why not, what do you think Jimmy?"

I thought, but only for a moment. "This is obviously all top-secret operations. If they really want to use your death ray, then I think they might just let us out of here. What we have to be careful of is that they don't throw us back when they have got what they want." That seemed to bring Arthur down with a bump.

"They wouldn't do that would they?" he asked.

"Could you put some sort of circuit in place that will only operate if you unlock it?" I suggested.

Arthur thought for a moment. "A sort of random code lock that only opens to a pre-set key you mean?

"Yes mate, that's exactly what I mean. If we are the only ones capable of setting it off, then I reckon we are irreplaceable, what do you reckon?" I think both of us felt better that we had a plan B.

The bell went for lunch, and we took our cutlery down to the canteen block. On joining the queue, we found we were behind Merion our Welsh friend from day one. His face lit up when he saw us. "Well, lovely to see a pair of friendly faces, isn't it, how's it hanging then lads?"

Arthur clapped him on the shoulder. "Merion old mate we're fine, still got the soft life of those on remand, library, choice of fine wines with the evening meal, dancing girls in the cell every night, you know."

Merion grinned. "Oh, just so long as it's not too arduous for you. Got a date for your trial yet?" I nudged Arthur firmly in the back,

"Yes, were up at the Old Bailey in two weeks. The briefs are confident that we'll be OK." Merion held his tray out to receive a portion of fish pie, he looked at it sadly.

"Know what I miss?" he asked. "Chips, I loves chips, my mum did them by boiling them up first then frying them in beef dripping, served with loads of bread and butter, smothered in salt and vinegar. Oh, I could kill for some good chips."

We received our portion of fish pie, it was grey. "I wish you hadn't said that about chips, now you've got me wanting some," I told him.

"And me," said the man behind me. "Just shut up about chips will you."

"Oh sorry," Merion replied. "But you know what I mean?" We all nodded.

We sat with our lunch and chatted about what our prison experiences had been like. By mutual unspoken agreement neither of us mentioned the possible escape route through Major Jefferis. We couldn't, however, help but notice Merion's grey flannel uniform, the shirt and jacket were not a bad fit, but the trousers ended at his shins.

"Merion, are they long shorts, or short longs you've got there?" Arthur asked.

"Oh, I know," Merion told us. "See what happens is you're given a pile of clothes after your first shower, shirts, socks, under-cacks, jacket and trousers. Trouble is they are the first ones off the pile, nobody measures you or nothing. I explains to the idiot that I'm six foot two and these trousers were made for one of Snow White's mates. All he says to me is 'swap'. Well, I've been hunting little fellows with sixteen-inch turn-ups ever since." We promised to help him find one.

He had been set to work sewing mail bags. He told us that provided you used a good pad to guard your fingers, it wasn't too bad at all. He had been resented at first for his beliefs, but as with us, he had won over all comers with his sheer exuberance. There were regular discussions on the merits of rugby verses football, The Pembroke coast versus Southend-on-Sea and the merits of Welsh choral music. I almost wished we could go and sew bags with him, it seemed better then endless games of chess and cards. We told him about our visits and putting the bet on for Mosher. He whistled when we told him about the two-hundred-pound win.

"How did he know?" Merion asked.

"You don't want to know," Arthur told him. "He's not a man whose secrets you want to pry into." As we spoke the man himself entered the canteen, as always accompanied by his wall-to-wall muscle. He brought his food over and asked if he could join us. You didn't refuse Mr Abrahams' company, so we moved up to allow them room.

"Boys, I hope you have reconsidered my proposal," he started, digging into his fish pie. "We don't want to spoil a beautiful friendship now do we? We could be together for a long time, so better you do me the odd little favour, than we fall out." He reached out and took the salt from Maurice and shook it all over his lunch. "I just need somebody on the outside to do little jobs for me. How about that lovely young lady who came to see you, Jimmy? I'd make it worth her while, if you get my meaning?"

I looked him in the eye, and told him, "No."

Mosher shook his head. "That's a wrong decision Jimmy, a man could get badly hurt making a decision like that, what do you think David?"

Tweedle Dum gave the matter some thought. After a moment he said, "Yeah." He then pushed his plate to the side and waited for orders. "Want me to do him Mr Abrahams? Ain't nobody looking."

Mosher looked at Arthur. "Tell your mate he's being stupid, Mr Golden Syrup, no need for a world of pain." Arthur didn't get the chance because Merion got to his feet.

"Now hang on, boy," he said to Mosher. "This is all getting a bit over enthusiastic isn't it, there's no need for all this hard man bluster. If the lads don't want to do you favours, then why the hell should they?"

Mosher turned to Maurice. "I don't like being interrupted Maurice, shut him up will you."

Maurice got to his feet and moved his bulk round the table. The rest of the canteen, realising Maurice was about to hurt somebody, and not wanting to be part of it, fell into silence as they concentrated on their fish pie. Merion tried one last time to avoid confrontation.

"Oh, come on now, Maurice, is it? We don't want to fight because of him, do we? You seem like a reasonable chap, let's just sit and have a bit of a chin wag, what do you say?"

Maurice had always been employed because of his brawn, never his brain. In fairness he was an impressive size, standing about five feet ten high and three feet wide. He had a chest measurement that must have been at least forty-eight inches, arms like a gorilla and hands that could encompass a pint pot. He was unencumbered by pity or morals. Told to hurt somebody he would do so until told to stop. He was good at his job.

Merion turned to Mosher. "Oh, come on now, what on earth are you doing?" he demanded. "No need for this, do you really think that violence is the answer?"

Mosher held his hand up to stop Maurice. He considered. "In your case you Welsh conchi, I think it might be. If you can't fight don't get involved, just like your call up."

Merion spread his hands wide. "No see, it's not that I can't fight, it's just I don't want to, it never does any good as far as I'm concerned."

"Yeah right," Mosher answered, and dropped his hand. "Maurice."

I had hoped it wouldn't come to violence because even with three of us I thought Maurice or David would put us in the hospital wing. These people did broken bones for a living. Before I could get up from the table, Maurice and Merion had squared up to each other. To my surprise, Merion had assumed the classic boxing stance, both fists in front of his face, and balanced on his toes. Maurice totally ignored this and threw the first punch. If it had landed, it would have broken Merion's jaw because it had all his weight behind it. The fight should have been over, as so many of Maurice's other battles had been. One mighty punch and whatever additional punishment Mr Abrahams decreed. Not this time though. Merion swayed a little to his left and Maurice stumbled as his blow punched through the space where Merion's head had been a moment before. Merion's left fist flashed out and hit Maurice twice in the face. Blood poured from his nose. Maurice shook his head and turned towards his opponent. Merion moved back dancing lightly, unhurried.

"See, this is all wrong Maurice, I'm guessing that you have never boxed before, not proper like. There are three things my Uncle Evan taught me. Let me show you; the three wise men he called them. Timing," and here Merion hit him again, a double jab with his left hand. Maurice's head flew back, blood now coming from a split eyebrow. "Footwork," he danced in and punched Maurice in the kidneys with a blow that would have brought a smaller man to his knees. Maurice was obviously in a great deal of pain and tried to twist away. "And last of all stamina, you're breathing hard there Maurice, it's all about fitness do you see." Over the next few minutes Maurice never came close to landing a blow, he kept his head down and launched decreasingly effective haymakers that Merion sidestepped with ease. He had obviously never been in a fight that lasted this long. As it progressed, he took more and more punishment to the face and body. Eventually he just stood with his arms hanging by his side. Merion hit him in the belly and, as he fell to his knees, he hit him again with an uppercut that snapped his teeth together. Maurice was unconscious before his head hit the canteen floor.

Merion turned and faced the astonished Dave. "No need to go through all that again now is there?"

Dave looked at his unconscious partner, and shook his head. "No," he said, picking up his plate. He left the canteen.

Mosher was still trapped behind the table. "I thought you was a fucking conchi," he said, his voice sounding a little forced. Merion sat beside him.

"Being a conscientious objector, means you don't want to fight for something you don't believe in see, it's the wanting, not the doing. I was telling the boys here, my uncle Evan runs the Aberystwyth boys' boxing club. My mum used to send me every Saturday, two bob and my uncle Dai's old gloves. I was middleweight champion for a couple of years. Should we get some help for Maurice here?"

Mosher looked at his unconscious henchman. "No, he's had worse, he'll come round. What do you want?"

Merion raised himself to his full six feet two and leaned over Mosher. "I don't want nothing from you Mosher, just leave the lads alone, and stay well away from me. I used to pay two bob for the boxing, but I'm willing to wave your fee if I have to. Do you understand?" Mosher told Merion he did. Arthur fetched the aluminium jug full of drinking water and poured it over Maurice.

It washed a lot of the blood off him and made him cough and splutter, but to our relief he did come round. We helped him up, he didn't look well. Merion addressed Mosher again.

"I reckon you should give him a hand to get to his bunk Mr Abrahams." Mosher got Maurice's arm over his shoulder and half carried him out, he glanced back. Merion was finishing his dinner. "Don't worry about this," he said. "The boys and I will clear up the table." A strange thing then happened as Mosher left, a spontaneous round of applause broke out as others in the hall rose to applaud Merion's bravery, for a despised conscientious objector, he was suddenly very popular. We thanked Merion again, and left for the remand wing. We had an appointment with Major Jefferis.

We sat in our cell as the afternoon drifted slowly by. Arthur must have asked me at least six times, if I thought he was coming. I told him there were people to see, and these things never happened quickly. We returned to the dining hall for our evening meal, there were no signs of either Mosher or Merion, but the talk was of little else. Those who had seen the fight were enjoying celebrity status, and we noticed several re-enactments being demonstrated. After our 'toad-in-the-hole', we returned to the wing at eight o'clock and, I too was getting apprehensive. I would have bet money that department MD1 would have been back for Arthur. After lights out we talked for a bit and then drifted off to troubled sleep. At six o'clock the cell door crashed open and a warder I had never seen before stood there. "Right, wakey, wakey you two. Get yourselves dressed and come with me, quick as you like now." It looked like Major Jefferis had returned.

Chapter 24
The King's Shilling

After hurriedly dressing we were marched down to the governor's office and told to wait. After ten minutes the door was opened by the governor himself. He looked harassed and dishevelled as he ushered us in. Major Jefferis and a corporal sat in chairs at the governor's desk. The major turned and addressed us, "Ah, Mr Wells, Mr Jones, good morning gentlemen. I apologise for the early hour, but lots to do, lots to do. You will be pleased to know that I eventually managed to persuade my CO to agree to your recruitment."

The governor shook his head, and muttered, "Very irregular, very irregular!" The relief was like being lowered into a hot bath. I heard Arthur exhale the breath he had been holding.

The major continued. "However, he stipulates certain conditions if you are to be released under my supervision." This didn't sound so good. "If you accept these conditions, then you may leave today under the custody of Corporal Taylor here."

"Brilliant," Arthur told him. "Thank you Major."

"I wouldn't thank me just yet," he replied. "Let's go through these conditions first, shall we?"

The governor steepled his fingers and lent forward to address Arthur and I. "I'm not sure you realise exactly the enormity of what you pair are responsible for. I have here a piece of paper signed by the secretary of state for war, Mr Hore-Belisha. He authorises your release from prison so that you may assist with," and here he glanced down at the paper he was holding, "the war effort. In my twenty-seven years' service, I have never seen this done before, it is most irregular. Apparently the major here has the authority to ride roughshod over the country's judicial procedures and if he so wishes, throw open the gates of Wormwood Scrubs." He paused.

"I do," Major Jefferis confirmed and opened his briefcase to produce a pile of official looking forms. "Firstly, it would be impossible for you to work on top secret military projects as civilians, so I need to recruit you into the army. If you agree, you will become members of the Royal Corps of Engineers, my regiment. You would be inducted as privates and given basic training. As privates you will be subject to army discipline and required to follow the chain of command. Is that all clear?"

"What chain of command?" I asked.

The corporal leaned forward. "The army chain of command you knob head," he told me. "The brass tells the officers what to do, the officers tell the NCOs and the NCOs make you do it. If I shouts jump, all you want to know is how high, clear?"

I told him it was. "So," Major Jefferis asked. "Are you prepared to sign up?"

"Before we do, can I have your word that we will be released from prison, and charges will be dropped," I asked.

The major spent a moment looking at us both. "Released from prison, yes. Dropping the charge of murder will be conditional on results, and that of course could mean re-arrest, are we clear on that, gentlemen? On the other hand, if we can get this sound generator of yours to do what you tell me it can, then yes, all charges against you will be dropped." I exchanged looks with Arthur, he leaned forward and asked for a pen.

The major gave him several forms and a fountain pen. "Sign here," he said.

"What am I signing?" Arthur asked.

"This is your 'King's Shilling', it's an application to join the armed forces." We shared the pen and both signed. "And this," the major continued. I raised my eyes. "Your medical fitness examination," he told us. "You will both be pleased to know you are A one."

The governor snorted. "A retrospective medical?" he queried.

"In times of war certain procedures fall out of sequence," the major replied. "And finally, this." he pushed the last forms towards us. "That gentlemen, is the Official Secrets Act. It means if I even suspect you of talking about our work to anybody at all, I now have the authority to shoot you!" We signed.

He put the forms in his briefcase and extracted another small pile, which he signed and handed to the governor. "This absolves you, Governor, these men are now under the authority of his Majesty's army and me in particular. Do I have your permission to take these men with me?"

The governor shrugged. "I suspect there is little I can do to oppose the secretary of state for war, so please take them away. The meeting was over."

Corporal Taylor stood up. "On your feet you horrible men, left wheel and follow me." We tried to copy him but ended up doing a parody of his precise movements. Major Jefferis held a hand up, and the corporal slammed his boot down bringing us to a halt.

"Take them for breakfast, Corporal." He handed over a ten-shilling note. "As way of apology for the unearthly hour."

"Sir," the corporal replied.

Once outside, Corporal Taylor lost the army automaton mindset and became more of a human being. "Right lads, you better call me 'Tinker' everybody else does. Did you want to get any personal stuff out of your cells before we go?" At the last visit we had both been brought a change of clothing. Mum had taken both our suits and replaced them with comfortable clothes. I had on a pair of corduroy trousers, a woollen shirt and an old sports jacket. Arthur was similarly attired in tweed trousers, an Aran pullover and a casual jacket. Other than these few things we had very little to take with us. We had pocketed our cigarettes and matches, leaving everything else. I thought about our soap, tooth powder and the last of the sugar left in the cell. The desire to get out of the prison overcame our greed for possessions.

"No, you're all right, mate," I told him. "Where are we going?"

"Well first to a little transport caff I know on the North Circular I'm bloody starving, then I'm to take you to get kitted out and after that to see Sergeant Major Hunt. He's been told you're coming, it's a big old house out Bedford way, and we're building huts in the grounds."

"Do they want us to help with the building?" Arthur asked.

"Don't think so," Tinker told us. "They don't tell me a lot, it's the army way, you'll get used to it. Requisition transport, meet Major Jefferis here and drive you back to the stores and the park. Come on, the staff car is round the back." Tinker's staff car was a six-wheel Scammell Pioneer. It was a cross between a lorry and a jeep and had all the worst characteristics of both. It was slow, old and draughty. The gear box required the driver to execute a tap dance on the pedals as he double declutched. On the other hand, we loved it because there was room for three in the cab, and we were heading away from Wormwood Scrubs. We grinned like schoolboys as Tinker drove us through the gates.

The cafe was wonderful, they didn't do kippers, or porridge, but they did a big fry up, with toast and huge enamel mugs of sweet tea. It took us forty minutes of companionable chewing before we sat back with cigarettes. Tinker mopped up the last of his egg and turned to Arthur. "Rum old do this, you two get sprung from the Scrubs by the bleedin' secretary of state for war, so what do they want you to do?"

Arthur leaned forward and conspiratorially told Tinker, "The only thing we heard one of the screws saying, was something about parachuting into Germany to kidnap Hitler."

Tinker's last bit of egg fell off his crust of toast and onto his battledress. "Never!" he said.

"Well, they didn't discuss it with us," I told him.

Tinker lowered his voice. "Listen lads, I really wouldn't tell anybody else, old Jefferis really can shoot you if he wants." We agreed it would be foolish to give the Third Reich any warning.

Tinker paid the bill, pocketed the change and drove us north sixty miles through pleasant countryside to a suburb of Bedford called Kempston. We pulled up outside one of the most impressive army barracks I had ever seen. It looked like a medieval castle. Tinker grinned. "She's a sight for sore eyes, ain't she? I done all my basic training here. It's over one hundred and fifty years old, imagine! Anyway, time to get you kitted out," he said. We followed him through the security checkpoint after he had produced identification for all of us.

He seemed to know where we were going, so Arthur and I just followed. The barracks was a hive of activity with building work going on everywhere. Tinker pointed out the new sergeants' mess and the site where a lot of new married quarters were to be built. He told us that he had heard rumours that all the existing staff were going to be sent to Bury

St Edmunds. He indicated his opinion by sticking an index finger against his head and corkscrewing it round.

"That can't be right though, can it? They wouldn't do all this construction then move away, surely?" Arthur commented.

Tinker laughed. "You really are new boys, aren't you? The army don't do nothing because it makes sense. The day they put the last lick of paint on them new married quarters is the day we'll all march off somewhere that ain't been decorated since the first lot." He spat. "Bloody army."

We were taken to an enormous building that was the stores. Tinker approached the sergeant in charge, saluted and handed him yet more paperwork. The sergeant read this through then summonsed another corporal over to help. Tinker saluted again, then led us away with the new corporal. Our new guide shouted for 'Geordie' to give him a hand; when Geordie appeared, they began to measure us. It was quite an efficient process, and they had obviously done it many times.

"Shoe size?" Geordie asked. We told him I was an eleven, and Arthur an eight. Geordie grinned. "Why aye, you know what they say man don't you?" We admitted we didn't. "Away," Geordie laughed. "Big shoes; big fucking feet!" This caused a certain amount of merriment between the three of them.

"Yes, the old ones are still the best," Tinker laughed. Uniform was now piling up on the counter. I was wondering how we were supposed to carry it all when Geordie threw a pair of kit bags on the pile.

Eventually we were equipped with everything a modern soldier needed to survive, from shaving gear to khaki socks. Tinker signed for it all and we stuffed it all into the kit bags.

"Where are you taking them next?" Geordie asked.

"Over to the park to meet Hunt," Tinker told him.

Geordie sucked his teeth. "Listen lads he's an RSM and he hates everybody. Stay away from him as much as you can, we do!"

Tinker handed us our kit bags and told us to fall in. "Come on it's not all bad news, should be there in time for grub." We hefted the bags and followed Tinker back to the truck.

We threw the kit bags in the back, climbed into the cab and, after a few backfires she started up. Tinker then drove us thirty miles further north to a small town called Bletchley. From the town centre we drove up a hill and turned right into Wilton Avenue, the approach road for a military camp.

"Welcome to Bletchley Park," Tinker said.

We stopped at the barrier and Tinker handed over his own identification and a slip of paper presumably authorising our entry. The sentry came round to inspect us, noted something on his clipboard and waved us through. On our left was a country mansion with corner towers and a grand front door. To its left was a newly constructed wooden hut about eighty feet long, it looked strangely out of place, presumably this is what the Royal Engineers had been building. On our right was a duck pond surrounded by neatly cut grass and a lot of flower beds. We drove through more manicured lawns until we came upon another group of huts under construction. Tinker parked the Scammell and ushered us out. "Word of advice lads, you are going to have the pleasure of meeting Regimental Sergeant Major Hunt. He is not a nice man and does not like any disruption to his military life. You are being thrust on him, and he will not want you. Stare at a spot eight inches above his head, keep your thumbs in line with your trouser seams and answer with either 'yes sir' or a 'no sir', nothing else, understand?"

We thanked Tinker, he gave us a wink and returned to army mode. "You horrible men, fall in and follow me, lefright, lefright." We marched behind him into the huge hut, down a long corridor and eventually to a door with Regimental Sergeant Hunt's name on the door. Tinker stamped to a halt and knocked.

"Come," a voice called out. It did not sound inviting. Tinker opened the door, went through and stood to attention on the left.

"Lefright, lefright," he shouted, and we shuffled in. "New recruits, sir," Tinker informed the RSM.

We stood in silence before the biggest desk I had ever seen. It was mahogany, and immaculate with all the stationery neatly aligned. There were family photographs, and pictures of the royal family in silver frames. Behind it was Regimental Sergeant Major Hunt. He was not a particularly large man, but he had the most impressive collection of medal ribbons I had ever seen adorning a uniform. He continued to read the document in front of him. When he considered we had been intimidated enough, he looked up. "And who the feck are you?" he asked, his perfectly clipped moustache bristling.

"Good afternoon, sir, I'm Arthur Wells and this is my colleague, Jamie Jones. A pleasure to meet you." Out of the corner of my eye I saw Tinker wince.

This seemingly harmless introduction had an alarming effect on Sergeant Major Hunt. He went through a strange transmogrification, the veins in his neck stood out, his colour turned from puce to beetroot, and his voice went up at least an octave. He rose to his full height of five feet four and, leaning on his desk, gave Arthur a spittle flecked tongue lashing. "You, you horrible feckin man, you stand to feckin attention when you feckin address me, I am a feckin Regimental Sergeant Major, that's feckin God to you, you feckin piece of shit."

He drew breath and directed his rage towards Corporal Taylor. "Are you having a feckin laugh at my feckin expense Corporal, because if you feckin are, I shall personally rip your feckin balls off and stuff them down your feckin throat. Tell me Corporal that you have not feckin brought me this pair of feckin Nancy boys with no feckin uniform, and no feckin idea."

Tinker brought his right boot down so forcibly, that I wouldn't have been surprised to see blood gushing out of the lace holes. "Sir, no, sir," he barked.

There was a moment of calm. "Tell me, corporal, are these men standing in front of me dressed in the uniform of his Majesty's feckin fighting forces? He enquired.

"Sir, no, sir," Tinker replied.

"Well why feckin not," the RSM balled as his blood pressure turned his colouring up a notch.

"Orders, sir," Tinker bawled back.

"Orders, whose feckin orders?" the RSM snarled retaking his seat and tidying his papers.

"Major Jefferis', sir, I was to collect them from the prison, get them kitted out at Kempston and then report straight to you, sir. Their gear is in the truck, sir, but I thought report straight to you was important, sir."

He offered the RSM a chitty. Regimental Sergeant Major Hunt snatched the paper and read it, he shook his head. "Feckin officers, I've feckin shit them! Take these two jailbirds, get them in feckin uniform and report back here zero seven hundred hours tomorrow sharp, dismissed."

Tinker threw the RSM an inch perfect salute and drove us back into the corridor. "Lefright, lefright, lefright."

Once outside, he glared at Arthur. "What did I tell you?" he exclaimed. "You only say, yes sir or no sir, nothing else. Thank God, we caught him on a good day! He's just got that new desk, and he's like a dog with two pricks."

"Sorry mate," Arthur told him. "At six o'clock this morning I was a civilian, we'll learn, but it will take a bit of time."

Tinker nodded. "Well thank God you're going on that mission what you said, somebody will be wanting to keep you alive until then." I just prayed he was right.

Tinker took us to another hut that was serving as a dormitory. We were taken to a small room with two bunk beds similar to our cell. It also had a kettle, a selection of tin mugs, tea and a small bag of sugar. We obviously weren't the first occupants. "This is you," Tinker told us. "Dump your kit and we'll go to the canteen." We walked to the entrance barrier where the canteen stood. The setting sun still had some warmth, and we no longer faced a possible death sentence. Despite RSM Hunt, things didn't seem that bad.

The canteen provided lamb chops, spotted dick and lots of tea. After a smoke Tinker took us back to the room. He spent an hour going through the basic requirements of putting on an army uniform. At the end of it, it was seven o'clock and he decided that we had all had enough. "I'll be round at zero six hundred hours to get you presentable," he told us. "I'd get some sleep lads, could be a long day tomorrow." We thanked Tinker and watched him stride away. At least we seemed to have one friend.

Chapter 25
The Eight Bells

As we watched Tinker go, both Arthur and I physically deflated. We had both had one hell of a day. Sergeant Major Hunt wasn't our flavour of the month, but we both appreciated he was a sort of pantomime character who couldn't ever lose the foul-mouthed persona. We had been given plenty of dressing downs, but nothing quite as vitriolic as RSM Hunt's verbal assault. Arthur turned and managed a grin. "Well, I think that confirms it," he said. "You're in the army now, still all in all he seems like a kindly old gentleman."

It was the right thing to say as we both needed something to lighten the mood. "Tell you what, let's leave the spit and polish until the morning, sod Sergeant Major Hunt and go and find a pint."

"What about the uniforms?" I asked.

Arthur was adamant. "Bloody horrible itchy things, I'm not going out in that." I shrugged, what else could possibly go wrong? We walked to the main gate trailing a middle-aged man with a waxed military moustache. He was dressed in a double-breasted pin stripe suit and a trilby. We attracted one or two looks as civilians strolling round a military establishment, but nobody challenged us.

A tall thin lance corporal with bad acne came out of the hut by the barrier, his beret was tucked into an epaulet. "Evening gents, papers please." I looked at Arthur, who produced his GPO identification pass. He handed it to the lance corporal while I hastily found mine. "What the fuck's this?" he demanded.

Arthur lent forward looking at his pass. "Ah, now do you see the big words across the top, they mean I work for the General Post Office, which is of course a government run organization. The bit across here says 'Arthur Wells', that's me do you see? I, Lance Corporal, am a consultant to a project so secret you would have to be court marshalled, dishonourably discharged, and shot if anybody suspected you of interference. Now put your beret on properly, salute the major here and open the bloody barrier."

I desperately kept a straight face, you just can't pull a stunt like that with the army, can you? After a moment's hesitation while Arthur held the lance corporal's gaze, he saluted and scrabbled to get his beret on. He then told Arthur, "Sorry sir, didn't realise, sir."

"Perfectly all right Lance Corporal, no doubt you'll be briefed tomorrow. Bloody army comms hey."

The lance corporal looked relieved. "Yes sir, thank you sir." As we strolled under the raised barrier, I noticed the man in the trilby hat was leaving a phone box just outside the gate, and briefly wondered how he had got through.

"Come along Major, do keep up," Arthur called.

"Hang on a minute Arthur, how many pennies have you got?"

He went through his pockets. "Eight," he said holding the coins in his palm. I took the money and went into the phone box, leaving the door ajar for Arthur. I put four pence in, dialled, then as the phone was answered pushed button B.

"Can I speak to Mr Jones from the Greenwich route?" I said. There were a few moments until I heard a familiar voice.

"Who is this please," he said.

"It's me, Dad, we're free."

I had not heard Dad swear often, but I distinctly heard a, "Jesus fucking Christ. Jimmy, is that really you, did you say you are free?"

I told him as much as I could, both of us taken out of prison to do 'war work', charges to be dropped, joined up, all top secret. He must have had a thousand questions, but when I put the second four pence in, he realised we had limited time. I asked him to tell Judy, Ron Gillroy and Mrs Wells.

"Where are you, Jimmy?" he asked.

"Don't think I can tell you Dad, but we're OK, everything is going to be OK. Tell Mum I love her, and I love you, Dad." Then the pips went.

We went down to the junction, past the church and left to the nearest pub, it was called The Eight Bells. It didn't seem a particularly pleasant place to spend the evening but being within walking distance of an army training establishment didn't give it a need for charm. Both of us felt a lot happier now we had told the families we were no longer in prison.

The landlord kept the conversation to, "What will it be then?" We ordered two pints of best (which was an exaggeration) and some crisps. We then found a table near the back of the pub and settled in to lick our wounds and drown our sorrows. After a refill, Arthur went to the toilets, on his return he mentioned that the man in the trilby was sitting in the front room nursing a whisky.

"Well, there you go, perhaps he crossed swords with Sergeant Major Hunt as well," I said.

Arthur grinned. "Do you think they will all be like him?" he asked. I told him that my granddad had explained to me that to become a sergeant major you had to have a deep and pathological hatred of mankind, a vitriolic liver and piles.

Any deviation from those conditions would turn you into a 'bleedin' Nancy boy'. Regimental sergeant majors have, in addition, a pineapple inserted in their fundamental orifices to make them permanently unhappy. It's King's regulations. By the third pint the world didn't seem too bad a place. We were just considering returning to our hut when four soldiers came over, they were all privates and dressed in khaki kit and big boots; they didn't seem friendly.

"This is our boozer," the leading one told us. "Army boozer, you ain't fucking army, what you doing here?"

Arthur gave me a look. "What we are doing here, gents, is the same as you, we are having a pint at the end of a long and nasty day." The second one took a pace forward, he was smaller and rather rat-like with darting eyes and protruding teeth. I could imagine him bayonetting the wounded.

"Fuckin civvies," he spat. "Why ain't you doing your bit?"

It was not going to end well. Like those playground fights we had long ago there seemed no reason, but we both recognised the inevitable. The landlord also sensed trouble. "Take it outside, lads," he told us.

His word seemed to have more sway with our quartet, they exchanged looks, and told him, "All right Bill, just don't want these nonces spoiling your pub." They left.

Arthur shrugged "They won't be waiting for us outside or anything, will they?"

"Two on to one," I said. "Better reduce the odds quickly." He nodded. "You all right?" I asked.

"I'm fine Jimmy. Now if you were going to lay in wait for somebody going back to the camp, where would you go?"

I thought. "Well certainly away from the camp, somewhere quiet and somewhere four of them could hide."

Arthur nodded. "The bus shelter by the church?"

"Well, that's where I'd go," I said.

"So if we hop over the church wall a bit further back, we could come out behind them." Arthur suggested, and gave me a strained grin. "We can't afford prisoners Jimmy, not with four of them. I know they're army, but I'm betting without orders they'll panic."

"Come on then, mate," I told him.

"Coming, kid," he said as we left the Eight Bells. The gent with the trilby had long gone.

We climbed the church wall three hundred yards from the bus stop, it was undergoing repair and several large cobbles were amongst the building materials. I saw Arthur scoop one up. Then as quietly as we could we approached, crouching to try and blend with the darkness. We heard them before we saw them.

"So we get four quid just to give them a good kicking."

"Well, that's what Hunt says, I'm not going to argue with him, are you?" There were sniggers.

"They're only two civvies, probably queers, you know Hunt can't stand queers."

"Tommy would know, wouldn't you, Tommy. You like a good bumming."

This got a bit more laughter until Tommy told them to, "Fuck off."

"Right shut up, they should be here any minute." With that they all went quiet. As agreed, Arthur went to the left and I went right until we were up against the back of the bus stop. It was one of the older ones built like a large shed with only the front open. I saw Arthur weigh the cobble in his hand, one of the soldiers had stuck his hand out of the shelter and was holding the entrance, his fingers curling round the edge.

Arthur caught my eye and put three fingers up, then two, then one. As the last digit fell, he brought the cobble down hard on the protruding hand. I had taken a deep breath and as the scream came from inside the shelter, I matched with one of my own swinging myself inside. I was met by the startled face of their leader and smashed my forehead into his nose. His hands flew up to his broken nose and I kicked him hard in the balls. Two on two.

Unfortunately, we had now lost the element of surprise, and learnt that the two squaddies who had stood at the back were ready for us; they were also armed. One had an axe handle, I remember thinking, "Where the hell had that come from?" The other had a big sheath knife. They came out facing us, circling with the knife and the handle poised to strike. The other two had fallen to the floor nursing their injuries, I briefly wondered about recovery times, we really had to finish this fight fast. I decided to rush the one with the handle and try and use it against the one with a knife. Arthur must have been thinking the same because I saw him come up on the balls of his feet. We were just about to commit when the voice came from behind us.

"Good evening gentlemen, could I ask you to put down your weapons and stand apart." It was the man with the trilby hat. It wasn't spoken very loudly but it was said with authority. Arthur dropped his cobble, and I took a step back. The two remaining soldiers didn't.

"Fuck off, Granddad," the one with the knife told him. "We're teaching these two bastards a lesson."

The man with the trilby shook his head. "Not tonight you're not, son," he told him, and walked towards them.

"Look, sir, please don't get involved in this," Arthur told him, "Don't want to see you hurt."

"Well, that's very considerate of you," Mr Trilby replied. "Now ground your weapons, Private, before somebody goes to hospital." The one with the axe handle took exception to that and, losing patience, took a swing at him. He was young fit and very fast; unfortunately, he didn't stand a chance. Mr Trilby stepped inside his guard and, with his left hand, hit the inside of the descending wrist, the handle flew out of the man's grasp. At the same time Mr Trilby's right fist flashed out and caught the soldier just below his left ear. He went down like a sack of potatoes. The knifeman now lost all reason and charged holding the knife out in front of him intent on impaling Mr Trilby.

When you watch martial arts performed by an expert it almost seems as if the victim is cooperating. Mr Trilby moved very slightly to the side, his left hand overlaying the back of his opponent's knife hand, he then pulled the accelerating man further forward throwing him completely off balance, until he suddenly whipped his body round causing the man to somersault backwards accompanied by the wet crack of his wrist breaking and the ensuing scream of pain. It had taken him under thirty seconds to overcome two men and probably save our lives.

He adjusted his hat, stroked his moustache and said, "Right gentlemen, if you would like to accompany me, my name is Warrant Officer Pomeroy, and I will be your personal instructor."

"What about them?" Arthur asked.

Mr Pomeroy gave the injured soldiers a brief inspection. "Broken fingers, broken nose, broken wrist and concussion. Walking wounded gentlemen, they can make their own way back to the care of Sergeant Major Hunt."

"What's he got to do with all this?" I demanded.

"Well, when I was told I had to train you two up, I wanted to know what you could do. No good wasting time if the raw material is no good."

Arthur turned to face him. "So you set this all up?"

"Not at all," Mr Pomeroy replied indignantly. "RSM Hunt was told to send a couple of his men to give you a hard time, four was a little too enthusiastic for my liking, so I intervened."

"Couldn't we have done this in the gym?" Arthur said. "We could have been stabbed for Christ's sake!"

Mr Pomeroy smiled. "There are parts of the world, Mr Wells, where someone trying to stab you would be the least of your worries. There will be numerous people who will wish to do far worse to you than that. Besides you can't reproduce street violence in a gym. Now fall in and follow me." Open mouthed we accompanied Mr Pomeroy back to the camp.

Chapter 26
Things that go Bump in the Night

Mr Pomeroy escorted us back to the main gate. He held up a single card in a leather wallet and the same lance corporal we had seen earlier snapped to attention. As I walked under the barrier, he gave me a brief nod and an, "Evening Major sir."

Mr Pomeroy turned his head and waited for me to catch up. "Mr Jones, I am certain that you will eventually rise to the rank of Major, however it is probably best if you wait for your commission to come through official channels. Impersonating an officer in times of war could mean facing a firing squad. Pity to have escaped the hangman for that!" I mumbled my apologies and glared at Arthur. Mr Pomeroy led us up to the mansion and through the front door. The guard came to attention and opened the inner door for Mr Pomeroy. He then led us up the stairs and down a first-floor corridor to the right. He extracted keys from his pocket and unlocked a door with MD1 on it.

"We tend to be a bit informal in MD1," he informed us, taking a seat behind his desk. He reached into one of the drawers and extracted a bottle of whisky and three glasses, pouring three generous measures. He removed his trilby and ushered us into seats. "Off the record gentlemen, how likely is it you can get this sound wave generator to function?"

Arthur took a tentative sip of his scotch and looked up at Mr Pomeroy. "I would need to recover all my notes from home, I would need access to a wide range of electronic components and I would need Mr Jones here to help me. If MD1 can help with that, I guarantee success."

Mr Pomeroy nodded. "And how long would it take you, Mr Jones and Mr McRae to complete it?"

Arthur shook his head. "Not sure, my original took six months, but then it was all experimental, and I was building it on my own."

"That's a bit longer than we were hoping," Mr Pomeroy told him.

"Can I ask a question?" I said.

"You can, Mr Jones," he told me. "As I said, we can be informal when it suits us."

"All right then, what are we now? Are we squaddies who will have to drill and march around the parade ground, or are we members of MD1 who will build death rays?"

Mr Pomeroy topped up his glass. "Technically both. You signed up as soldiers, but we want you to work on a specific project, which neither of you will speak of outside this room!

To overcome this anomaly, Major Jefferis has decided that I will train you in specific skills that will be of practical use until we can move to a new workshop which is being set up near Aylesbury. Your training will be in field skills, not drill. From what I witnessed tonight, you have a lot to learn, but you might just survive. That was good problem solving tonight, and that's what we specialise in at MD1. Tomorrow you will present yourselves in shorts, singlet and running shoes at seven o'clock at the gate house. I will be waiting."

Arthur coughed. "Excuse me, Mr Pomeroy, but we're also supposed to present ourselves to RSM Hunt at seven o'clock. Which one shall we do?"

"A good question," Mr Pomeroy agreed. "And a problem that needs resolving. As members of MD1 I will leave you to sleep on it, but beware of things that go bump in the night. Now gentlemen we have an early start, I bid you goodnight."

As we walked back to or hut, Arthur asked which I thought was the worse fate, ignore RSM Hunt and fail to turn up for his kit inspection, or disregard Mr Pomeroy's invitation and risk mutilation.

"We could do one each," I ventured.

"That's the worst of both worlds," Arthur countered. "If we do that, we're going to have both of them after us." He was right of course.

"Oh, sod it, let's sleep on it," I suggested.

"Right," Arthur said. "What could possibly go wrong?" I should have stayed awake worrying, I didn't. I was asleep as my head hit the pillow.

At ten to six there was a loud banging on our door. I struggled out of bed, and found Tinker standing outside, he looked ready for a royal parade. Every last piece of his uniform gleamed or had razor sharp creases. His boots looked like they were made of patent leather, but he seemed strangely agitated. "Right let's get you two stood down, no appointment with the RSM this morning."

Arthur emerged from under his blankets. "Then why are you waking us up Tinker?"

"Because I didn't want you spending hours getting ready for inspection, and turning up only to have your heads bitten off," he told us. I put the kettle on to make black tea.

"What's upset him this morning?" I asked. Tinker sat down looking shell shocked.

"The reason RSM Hunt is in a rabid dog black mood this morning, is that last night somebody blew up his new desk and wrecked his office." There was a lengthy silence while we absorbed this.

"What!" we both said together.

"Well apparently somebody got past all the sentries, broke into block D, picked the lock on his door and used explosives to blow his office to hell," Tinker told us. "Apparently the whole camp is walking on eggshells. He's looking for somebody to kill."

"Blimey! Who's in charge of security?" Arthur asked.

Tinker grinned. "He is."

I know it was childish, but I had to suppress giggles all the way to the toilets to relieve my bursting bladder. Who on earth could and would do something like that? Then I remembered the conversation from last night. MD1, problem solving, informality, bump in the night! It couldn't be, could it?

We arrived in our new singlet and shorts three minutes early, to find Mr Pomeroy and another man in PE kit waiting at the main gate. Mr Pomeroy was in his usual double-breasted suit and trilby hat. He looked at his watch. "Good morning gentlemen, nice to see you here on time. This is Corporal Russell, he will be assisting you with your morning's exercise. We will start with a short run to a lovely little village called Drayton Parslow. It is now 07.02, shall we meet here at ten o'clock? Corporal Russell, you have my permission to kill them, if you consider them slacking. Clear?" Corporal Russell assured Mr Pomeroy it was.

"Did you hear about RSM Hunt's office?" I asked before we set off.

"Never listen to tittle-tattle," Mr Pomeroy advised me. "Plastic explosives! Probably a gas heater malfunction." It later occurred to me that the only heating in the huts were small portable electric fires, and nobody had previously mentioned plastic explosive. I concluded I was better off not asking.

Unlike Tinker, Corporal Russell did not have a nicer side, he was a PT instructor and merciless in his training. We did a slow run to loosen up, then after about a mile he began introducing short sprints for twenty or thirty yards. At three miles I was afraid Arthur was going to die, at four miles I no longer cared and was selfishly hoping I went first. Corporal Russell not only ran without breaking into a sweat, he managed to chat at the same time. "We're going through a little village called Newton Longville next. Lovely place to live, my missus has got her eye on a cottage down there, that's why I suggested this route to WO Pomeroy. I'll take you on a little detour to show you." Neither of us had the wind to kill Corporal Russell, otherwise we would have.

At five miles Arthur was sick. Corporal Russell produced a canteen and let him swill his mouth out. He told me to keep running on the spot so I didn't seize up. We reached Drayton Parslow and collapsed on the village green. Sucking in huge breathes to try and calm our racing hearts. The corporal looked at his watch. "Well not bad lads, it's 08.20 that's just over four miles an hour.

Let's see that gives us a hundred minutes to get back. Come on, don't want to keep the WO waiting." I was in despair, it never occurred to me that we would have to run back. I thought some form of transport would be waiting for us. Arthur was beyond despair or caring.

How we somehow managed to get back without dying remains a mystery to this day. Corporal Russell now had to resort to shouting a lot to stop us lying down and giving up the ghost. He would run back to whoever was trailing, scream at them to, "Pick your bloody feet up," and then run with them back to the front. Unbelievably he interspersed bringing our parentage into disrepute with normal conversation. "I blame the cigarettes myself, well that and the beer of course. Treat your body with respect and it will repay you a thousand times. I mean look at the WO, he must be forty if he's a day, but with all that meditation and martial arts exercises, well there isn't a man on the camp he couldn't take on with one hand tied behind his back. You all right there, Private Wells?" Arthur resorted to dry retching as he had long ago emptied his stomach. "Come on Wells not far to go now, look there's Wilton Avenue, right heads up, chest out, show a bit of pride for the WO" He looked at his watch. "Now sprint, let's get there by ten, run." We collapsed at Mr Pomeroy's feet; they could have stuck a bayonet in me and I wouldn't have got up.

Mr Pomeroy looked at his watch. "O nine fifty-eight, well done Corporal, didn't think you'd get them back on time, outstanding. Tell them they have until noon to recover, then they are to meet me on the lawn by the duck pond for a little hand to hand combat."

"Yes, sir, thank you, sir," Corporal Russell replied. I knew if I could raise my head, he would be grinning.

Chapter 27
Who done it?

It took us a quarter of an hour to recover the power of speech. Corporal Russell encouraged us to take small sips from his water bottle and to do some winding down stretches. He was actually quite good at his job, and we began to feel we might survive. He explained there was a minimum standard of fitness we would need to achieve but doing a ten-mile run in under three hours was not bad for a first attempt. He told us we had to build up stamina, muscle tone and lung capacity. He advised giving up smoking and reducing alcohol intake. Neither of us liked his advice or the prospect of achieving army fitness. We got to the canteen and managed to scrounge some tea and toast from one of the ladies behind the counter. Arthur told me he wasn't sure getting out of the Scrubs was as clever as we thought. As we had an hour before we were to report to Mr Pomeroy we walked back to the dormitory block. I wanted a shower and Arthur wanted to start making a list of the more obscure components he thought would be needed. We walked past block D, and noticed a military police truck parked by the blackened hole where the explosion had come through from the RSM's office. We stopped to gawp with another soldier. "Does anybody know what happened?" I asked.

"I heard it was an assassination attempt on the RSM," our new friend told us. "German spies broke in and lobbed a grenade through his window, only he was too wily an old bird, and he'd gone home. Least that's what my mate Nobby reckons."

"How does Nobby reckon they got past the sentry?" Arthur queried.

"Probably dressed as nuns," he told us. Put like that it became so obvious.

We went back to our own hut, showered away the sweat and Arthur started to compile his list. "How specific do you think I need to be?" he asked.

"Well personally I'd give your list to Mr McRae, at least he knows what you're talking about, and if there is a query, he can at least speak 'techno talk' to you to sort it out." Arthur nodded, stuck his tongue out and scribbled a shopping list.

We presented ourselves at noon on the lawn with the duck pond, in front of the mansion. Mr Pomeroy was not yet there, but Corporal Russell was. He had laid out six large, padded mats to form an oblong about twelve feet by eighteen. "Hello lads, how are the muscles?" he enquired.

The truth was that my calves felt like they had been kicked by a horse, but I wasn't going to admit to it. "Oh, not too bad I suppose," I lied.

"Well just in case you were feeling a bit sore, I brought you some of my magic embrocation." He pulled a bottle of green liquid out of his kit bag.

"I'll try some, please," Arthur told him. "My calves feel like I had an elephant jumping on them."

"Good man," the corporal told him. "Now lay on your back and put your heel on my chest." Arthur did and got his leg smothered in the green liquid. It smelt medical. Corporal Russell then began to kneed the muscles, and rub the medication in. "How does it feel?" he asked.

"Wonderful," whispered Arthur. "Oh, that is so good."

"Steady now," laughed the corporal. "I'm a married man!"

When he had done Arthur's other leg, he looked at me. "You sure you're OK?" he asked.

"Oh, go on then," I told him, and took over from Arthur. It was magical, the dull ache vanished, and a warm tingle took over. I was just having my second leg finished when a voice cut through the calm.

"That man, feckin stop rubbing my privates, it's against King's feckin regulations. I will not have sodomy in my feckin camp." We all stood to attention as Regimental Sergeant Major Hunt marched towards us. "I know you Corporal Russell, never took you for a feckin shirt lifter," he barked as he stood in front of us.

"No sir, just trying to get the men ready for WO Pomeroy's unarmed combat demonstration. Embrocation for muscle strain, sir."

"Feckin embrocation, what sort of a feckin idiot do you think I am?" the RSM demanded.

"Well," a voice from behind us answered. "Personally, I would say you are, as 'feckin idiots' go, outstanding. Corporal Russell was acting under my orders to get this pair ready for training. If that includes massage so that I can turn them into lethal killing machines, then he is doing his job. You on the other hand, are a foul-mouthed caricature of a soldier, and you will leave my dojo and keep your half-witted opinions to yourself." WO Pomeroy seemed very clear on that point. You could cut the atmosphere with a knife, RSM and WO are very close in authority and power in the army. I suspect the RSM was no coward but brawling in front of junior ranks was not an option.

"Going to teach them how to waggle a feckin wooden sword are you? Fat lot of good that will do them on a real feckin battlefield." He turned on his heel and marched away.

Mr Pomeroy watched him go. "Right gentlemen, now we have increased the average IQ of our group, let us begin. What do you think the first thing that I teach you should be?"

"How to shoot?" Arthur ventured.

"No Mr Wells, this is unarmed combat, that's how to fight without a gun or a knife."

"How to stand?" I guessed.

"Not a bad idea Mr Jones, wrong, but not a bad idea. Show me your fighting stance, take your plimsolls off and get on the mat." Self-consciously I got on the mat with bare feet. I adopted the same stance I had seen Merion use when he dealt with Maurice. Mr Pomeroy joined me and, walking round me, gave a running commentary. "Very good," he said. "Knees bent, feet nicely spaced and at about sixty-five degrees, you've done this before Mr Jones." I grinned. "Unfortunately," and with this he gave a sharp tug to the back of my singlet causing me to fall heavily on to my arse, "we are not tripods, and therefore always have a weakness, but more of stance later. No gentlemen, the first thing I am going to teach you is how to fall over."

It was a long and painful afternoon. We were supposed to land on the tip of our little finger, then doing a forward roll transfer the point of contact along the arm, across the shoulders and then the hips until the momentum of our legs brought us upright to face the next threat. That sounds quite simple, it isn't. Unfortunately, when we had mastered the basics by throwing ourselves over, Mr Pomeroy and Corporal Russell assisted with a little more power. We were subjected to hip throws, shoulder throws and, in one extreme case, Corporal Russell placed his foot on my chest and fell over backwards launching me into the air. By four o'clock I could barely stand.

"I think we'll call that a day," Mr Pomeroy told us. "Thank you, Corporal, much appreciated. If you would like to take these two for a little run tomorrow morning, I'll see you here, same time afterwards."

"Sir," the corporal acknowledged, throwing a salute. Mr Pomeroy vanished in the direction of the mansion still with a bounce in his step.

"I hate that bastard," Arthur told the world, from his sitting position.

"Well," Corporal Russell told him. "That bastard might just save your life one day. He's the best I've ever seen, studied in the Orient I believe. Now give me a hand to store these mats."

We made it back to our hut, Corporal Russell gave us the remainder of his magic embrocation and left to go home. "Let's make it seven thirty shall we lads, have a bit of a lie in." We grunted our thanks and headed for the shower.

After getting myself cleaned up, I lay on my bunk with a copy of a book I had found. It was called *The Hound of the Baskervilles*, and was an exciting adventure but I didn't make it beyond chapter two.

Arthur shook me awake, it was seven o'clock and he was starving. We just made it to the canteen in time. In the evening we passed the time by strolling through the grounds of the park. Inevitably we walked past Block D with the blackened hole looking like a missing tooth against the rest of the huts' pristine paintwork. A military policeman stood guard. We wished him a good evening, and he nodded back. Arthur lit a cigarette, and on impulse offered the MP one. He glanced around and, as we were the only ones around, took the proffered Player's. "Made a hell of a mess," Arthur commented. The red cap took a light and looked around.

"Plastic explosive tends to do that," he said.

"Look I'm sorry, but we've only been in the army for a day. What on earth is plastic explosive?" Arthur asked. The military policeman grinned with the smile of a man who knows a little more than others.

"New development for secret agents," he told us. "Apparently it's very stable and very powerful. I heard the boffins say it would only take a piece the size of a Brussels sprout to do this."

"Yes, but how do you know it was this plastic stuff, it might have been a stick of gelignite," I said. The policeman came up on his toes and delivered the punch line.

"We know it was plastic explosive, Private, because the silly sod left another small bit stuck in the back of his top drawer. Now that's top secret, so don't you go telling no one." We thanked the MP and strolled towards the far end of the park.

"Who do you think did it?" Arthur asked. For somebody with an IQ the size of an elephant Arthur could sometimes be slow on the uptake. We sat on an upturned cable drum and lit cigarettes.

"Look mate, it's new and experimental stuff this plastic explosives, you can't just stroll into the stores and sign for a couple of pounds of it!" Arthur shrugged. "So," I took a deep breath. "Now let's consider who hates the RSM enough, and who is brave enough to do it to him."

Arthur thought for a moment. "Well, the whole world hates him, but I can't think of anybody stupid enough to try and blow him up."

I began to feel like the detective in the last chapter when he has them all gathered in the drawing room. "The explosion took place late on Wednesday night, so late everybody had gone home, and Block D was unguarded. They weren't trying to kill Hunt, just to teach him a lesson."

"Go on," Arthur said.

"You heard what Tinker said, new desk, like a dog with two pricks, imagine what he felt like when he discovers the pile of matchwood where his pride and joy used to be!

"Now remember the problem that we had, report to the RSM at the same time we were to report to the WO. How do you solve that? Simple you destroy the place we were meant to report to, problem solved!"

Arthur had his mouth open. "You don't mean?"

"I do," I said. "I think Mr Pomeroy 'done it'. Not only did it resolve our problem, MD1 specialises in problem solving remember. It also settled a lot of old scores between them. The clever bit though was to leave a little bit of this explosive to be found. Looks like the RSM had it in his desk all the time. I'd say game, set and match to the warrant officer."

"So what do we do?" Arthur asked.

I looked at him. "We do nothing, Private Wells, we do what my granddad told me. 'Never volunteer', and that includes information!"

He started to say "But—" but I led him back to the hut, I wanted some embrocation and an early night.

Chapter 28
The Forty-eight-hour Pass

Training followed this routine for two weeks. We both gave up smoking, and neither of us had taken a drink since our night at the Eight Bells. Our running was definitely improving as it was now no longer just pure pain. Remarkably we could both actually get our heads up to look around whilst gasping the odd word with Corporal Russell. The unarmed combat, on the other hand, had mixed results. In a way it was like learning to dance, but with knives. If you put your foot there, I will move mine here. I struggled, whereas Arthur seemed to find the rhythm. He grabbed Corporal Russell's wrist as he made a grab for Arthur's throat. Spinning through one hundred and eighty degrees so they were front to back, he kept the corporal's arm extended. He then took a sharp step forward, while thrusting back with his buttocks. The corporal took off over Arthur's shoulder, and was slammed to the floor. I don't know which of the two was more surprised.

Mr Pomeroy released the neck hold he had on me and walked over to Arthur. "Been reading up on it Private Wells?" he ventured.

"No, sir," Arthur told him. "

So who showed you how to do that?" he asked.

"Nobody, Mr Pomeroy, it just seemed to happen, I'm sorry, sir."

Mr Pomeroy glanced over to Corporal Russell. "You didn't see that coming Corporal?"

"No sir," the corporal replied. "It was very fast and quite unexpected. I would have been dead."

Mr Pomeroy nodded. "I think we might have a natural." Arthur looked as though he wasn't sure if they were taking the mickey. Mr Pomeroy shook his head. "I'm not taking the piss, son. Occasionally I've seen fighters who don't think, they just do what their mind and body wants. Those people are hard to kill."

Arthur shook his head in disbelief. "I'm not a fighter, Mr Pomeroy, what my body tells me in most of the violent confrontations, is run."

"You didn't run that night at the Eight Bells Private Wells, did you?" Arthur looked over to me for help, but I couldn't think of any worthwhile contribution.

"Well, that was different, sir, no way of avoiding it, so best meet it head on. I suppose it's a sort of mental acceptance."

Mr Pomeroy nodded. "The mind doesn't always accept what the body can't do. If you can use that in unarmed combat, you will be hard to beat. Now gentlemen, help Corporal Russell clear away, then come and see me in my office."

We made our way up to the MD1 office in the mansion. Mr Pomeroy told us to come in and shut the door. He indicated a pair of chairs and waited for us to sit. He then closed a file and told us, "I have been speaking to Major Jefferis, he is very pleased with my report on your physical training. As recognition of your hard work, he has authorised a forty-eight-hour pass. You are to go home, see your families and you, Private Wells, are to collect any notes and diagrams that you think will be useful to the generator construction."

He paused. "You will under no circumstances tell anybody about MD1, or anything you have seen here at Bletchley Park. Are we very clear on that, gentlemen?" We said we were.

"Please be under no illusion, the odd lack of discretion will see you back in Wormwood Scrubs first thing Monday morning." We both knew he meant it. "As far as your friends and family are concerned you have enlisted in the army, following the court's decision not to charge you with murder." He looked up.

"Yes, Mr Pomeroy, sir," we both acknowledged. He pushed an envelope across the desk. "Here are your travel warrants and an advance on your pay. Be back here Sunday night." We stood, saluted and marched out.

"Bloody hell, Jimmy, we're going home," Arthur told me, putting his arm round my shoulder. "I really didn't think that would ever happen. Come on I'm going to put my civvies on."

"No, you can't do that mate, we are supposed to be new recruits. Squaddies travel in army issue."

Arthur frowned. "Oh well, I'll change when we get home." We packed a small bag each and made our way down the footpath that linked the park to the station. We caught the half past three train to Euston and then used the bus to get us back to Welling. Arthur left me outside Harry's old shop. As discussed on the train we agreed to meet at eight in the Railway. Celebrations outflank abstinence.

What we had, of course, forgotten to do, was to warn our family we were coming home. Mum and Dad were sitting having a cup of tea, and as I came through the door, Mum knocked the lot over as she charged to hug me. "Oh Jimmy, Jimmy, you're home," she told me. She was crying so much that was all she could say. Dad joined us as soon as he had sponged down the hot tea Mum had emptied in his lap. Mum reinstated the tea, and although she kept touching me and saying, "Oh Jimmy," we ended up sitting round the dining room table just like we used to do.

I explained that I was under strict orders not to reveal where or what Arthur and I were doing. They, however, weren't stupid and had guessed it was to do with the machine that had killed Ian Brown, but agreed not to ask further. I explained that a major had arranged for us to be released on condition we signed up. Dad wanted to know which regiment I was with as our uniforms had no identification badges. I told him I was a Royal Engineer, which seemed to keep him happy.

When I mentioned my forty-eight-hour pass, Mum flew into a frenzy of planning meals. I told them I had agreed to go to the pub at eight and asked if they could come. They both seemed very pleased and asked if Mrs Wells would be there. I said she would, and then asked if they minded if I went and saw Judy. They told me to go now, but to be back by six, Mum had a steak and kidney pie that would be ready. I made my way to Judy's and hoped like hell that she would be in.

She was. She had been washing up when she opened the door, and simultaneously threw her wet arms round me, leapt up to encase me in her legs and scream. I stopped the scream by kissing her with all the passion and fury of many weeks' enforced separation. She eventually broke from the kiss to draw breath and sob, "Oh Jimmy, oh God Jimmy, Oh Jimmy." Not very literal, but I knew exactly what she meant. Her parents had gone to see her brother Nigel play football, and without thinking she dragged me upstairs where we made love on her bed. It was the best. All the fear, all the anxiety we had both suffered since my arrest dissolved in a frenzy of passion. We had each other, and nothing in the world was more important than that. Afterwards she lit a cigarette and was a little surprised when I told her I had given up. We lay together, letting the sweat from our love making cool.

I went through all the things that had happened, the prison fight, the army wanting to build Arthur's machine, our release and our brief experiences as soldiers. Judy listened in silence. "Why have they made you enlist?" she asked.

"Well, they can't have civilians working on top secret projects," I explained.

"How about this Mr McRae?" she asked. "Is he in the army?" I had to admit he wasn't. Judy was right, the army don't do unnecessary stuff like that, I couldn't think why, but there would be a reason for it. "And you're doing all this fitness training with your own instructor?" she queried. I had to admit that put like that it did seem a bit strange.

The clock downstairs chimed, I glanced at my watch, it was half five. "Bloody hell Judy, Mum is cooking for six, I've got to go. Do you fancy a steak and kidney pie?"

Judy kissed me again. "Would there be enough to go round?" she said.

"Of course, you know Mum, she can't cook for anything less than a football team," I told her.

"Right, I'm just going to leave a note, get changed and do my hair: ten minutes!"

We were late, but Mum and Dad were too tactful to ask. They were genuinely pleased to see Judy and made her feel welcome. Talk over dinner was of the war, petrol rationing and Charlton.

Dad also told me Ron had been round to see him. Our solicitors had been told of our release, and enlistment. They too had worked out that our skills were required for the war effort but had been gently advised not to pursue the matter. Ron had asked if Dad could let him know if he heard anything. He was genuinely concerned that we were safe. I asked Dad to let him know we were both fine. Judy asked about Arthur and I told her we were all meeting up at the pub at eight. The evening was wonderful, I was surrounded by the people I loved, we were no longer under a possible death sentence, and we had decided that abstinence in a pub was just not an option. Mrs Wells was so happy she had three gin and limes and wanted to sing. There were tears, laughter and hugs to spare, but in the back of my mind was the grain of sand in the oyster of reason. What were we being specially trained for?

Our forty-eight hours of freedom went too quickly. Arthur, Dad and I went to the football on Saturday. I went round to see Judy's parents in the evening. They also seemed to realise that Arthur and I were doing something secret for the war and didn't push me on my new army career. Surprisingly they never condemned me for the murder I had committed. It was only briefly mentioned when Nigel, Judy's brother, told me he was pleased that all the stupid charges against Arthur and I had been dropped. Judy's mum put her hand on my arm and told me, "That's what we all think Jimmy, we never stopped believing in you."

I could feel tears coming until Judy intervened. "Oh no, our soldier has an empty glass, come on Dad, drinks all round please." Mr Richards went out to raid the coal shed and returned with fresh bottles for everybody. He filled all our glasses, then proposed a toast.

"To our Jimmy, back with his friends." I took a long drink.

Mum and Mrs Wells somehow managed to put together a Sunday lunch. Arthur had walked over with her in the morning and we had another good day catching up. Judy was also invited as it was now clear that we were 'Walking Out'. The piece of pork Mum had managed to get was just about big enough for six, but Dad had done potatoes for ten.

I didn't want to leave, but Dad glanced at his watch, and told me, "The three-four-seven was due in ten minutes and that would take us to Euston." I kissed the girls and gave Dad a firm handshake.

"I'm not sure when we will get leave next Dad, but I'll try and give you some warning next time." He seized me in a bear hug and told me just to keep safe.

Judy didn't say anything other than, "I love you." It was enough. We kissed, then Arthur and I walked down from the flats and over to the bus stop.

Chapter 29
The Firs

It was wonderful to have seen our loved ones, just to have had the reassurance that the world was still normal and we no longer had a death sentence hanging over us. Within hours of returning to Bletchley Park, however, we were back in our army routine. The big news was, in our absence, RSM Hunt had been moved out. Nobody knew why, but it was definitely a better atmosphere without him. Mr Pomeroy later told us that personal possession of secret explosives was actually a court martial offence. However due to his exceptional service record and written depositions by fellow Bletchley Park staff, Mr Pomeroy included, it had been seen as more diplomatic to post him elsewhere. He even had the decency to keep a straight face when he told us.

We persuaded Corporal Russell to have a night out with us to celebrate, not to the Eight Bells, but to a nice little pub in Newton Longville where his wife had aspirations to live. He told us he wasn't a drinker, but as a gesture of solidarity he would allow himself a shandy. We went in civilian clothes and were collected by Corporal Russell in his Austin 8. It wasn't the fastest of cars, but it was better than running any day of the week. We sat in the garden and sipped our drinks. He told us as we were off duty to call him John. Arthur and I got a second pint, but John nursed his, and declined a refill.

"How did you end up as a PT instructor, John?" I asked.

"Oh, usual way," he told us. "I always liked sport, had a trial for Gravesend as a kid. I joined up in '35, seemed like a good career move, the army were still short of men after the first lot, and I was thinking about getting married. Got picked out on my basic training at Catterick and offered a position as an instructor."

"How about the unarmed combat?" Arthur put in. "That's a bit advanced for a PT instructor?"

John smiled. "Well, I did a bit of boxing, nothing too flashy, but I won a couple of inter regimental bouts, and Mr Pomeroy happened to see me fight. He pulled a few strings, got me transferred, and started to teach me. He studied in Shanghai, he was a member of the municipal police force out there, Christ they were a bunch of hard bastards. If you can get him to talk about it, he has some pretty bloodthirsty tales.

"I had always been interested in self-defence, and the WO took it to the next level. You should see him when he fights for real."

"We have," Arthur told him. "He took down two men without taking his hat off."

I thought back to the conversation I had had with Judy. "I can see why you and Mr Pomeroy would want to be able to fight like that, but why are you training Arthur and me? I mean we're just here as technicians really, aren't we?"

John shrugged. "I don't know why Mr Pomeroy wants you trained, I just get orders lads, get you to the peak of fitness and very competent at unarmed combat. It's the 'very' that makes you different."

Arthur shot me a sideways look. "So this isn't normal procedure for new recruits?" he asked.

John grinned. "There's nothing 'normal' about you two is there? Recruited from prison, not in any regiment, basic training at Bletchley Park. That's special treatment all the way down the line. Look, I don't know what they have in mind for you, but it isn't a career in the infantry. Now let's have one more beer, then I should be going. Don't forget lads, we have a long run tomorrow, how about halves?"

At the end of the week, we were again summonsed to Mr Pomeroy's office. When we marched in Major Jefferis was already ensconced behind the desk, Mr Pomeroy stood to the side. "Good morning gentlemen," the major greeted us. "Mr Pomeroy here tells me you are a damn sight fitter than when I first saw you. He also tells me you are resourceful cheats and liars."

I started to protest, until the major raised a hand to stop me. "That's not an insult, Major Jones, that's a compliment. You two strolled out of a top-secret establishment by showing the guard a GPO identification pass! You survived an attack by four soldiers who had been trained in combat, and you worked out exactly what happened to RSM Hunt and kept quiet about it. I am pleased with your progress." Mr Pomeroy touched the side of his nose with an index finger, we knew it meant shut up and agree. We did.

The major continued. "Your training will carry on under Warrant Officer Pomeroy and Corporal Russell, but not here. We are re-locating to a new headquarters at an establishment near Aylesbury.

"The generator and all the associated paperwork will be there tomorrow, so will you. Mr Wells, did you collect everything you will need on your forty-eight-hour pass?"

Arthur nodded. "I will require access to other components though."

The major smiled. "You have no idea how much you sound like Mr McRae. He is constantly demanding, and I'm sure he believes thermionic valves grow on trees. Very well, you and McRae make a shopping list, and I'll see what I can do. Now get your kit packed, have some dinner then you can travel down with the Warrant Officer to your new billet. Any questions?"

"Sir," Arthur said.

"Yes, Wells," the major replied.

"Sir, I know our main job is to build you the sound wave generator, so why are we being taught advanced self-defence?" A silence followed.

"You are members of MD1," the major told him. "All our team are trained to deal with any eventuality, that's standard practice for us." He looked expectantly at Arthur.

"Sorry, sir, I think that's bollocks, sir." I noticed Mr Pomeroy's cheeks blowing out, but he remained silent. Major Jefferis exhaled through his nose.

"Listen Private, if a major tells you something, you accept it, do you see?"

Arthur turned towards him. "That's not what you want from us Major, is it? You got us out of prison to do a specific job for you, that job shouldn't include breaking a man's arm to take a knife off of him. We are useful because we are intelligent, please do us the courtesy of telling the truth. Sir."

The major leaned back and glanced at Mr Pomeroy. "Very well," he said. "Again, this is top-secret. If you and Mr McRae can get this sound thing of yours functioning, there is a good chance it will be used on a

178

mission behind enemy lines. Mr McRae pointed out that it would be relatively easy for you to build a lock into the mechanism so your usefulness would not end after completion. We really don't want extra complications, so in order that you feel you are still part of MD1, and not scheduled for a return to prison, Mr Pomeroy came up with the solution. You will be part of the team that goes on the mission."

It seemed so bloody obvious, once McRae knew how to build Arthur's death ray, we were expendable. We were both young and fit, so they could afford to use us up the sharp end. It had all the hallmarks of a secret service plan, and there was nothing we could do about it if we wanted to stay out of jail.

"Good, so now you know," the major told us. "Don't worry, we'll look after you, you just get your bit done. And Mr Wells?"

"Sir," Arthur responded.

"I hope you now understand why it is imperative that you know how to break a man's arm?"

"Yes, I think I do, sir," Arthur told him. "Thank you for your candour, Major."

Major Jefferis saluted as we left the office. "Well at least we know," I told him.

"Bloody hell though, Jimmy, I'm a GPO engineer, not a secret agent," Arthur complained.

"Well actually if you think back, what was it Mr Pomeroy called you? Oh yes, A born street-fighter. Add to that the fact they took us off remand for murder, and I can sort of see their point."

Arthur nodded. "Oh, shit Jimmy, another fine mess!"

We collected all our belongings and put them in our kit bags. Walking to the canteen we dined off toad-in-the-hole, and large mugs of army tea. We speculated how we would travel to our new headquarters, I thought it would be another Scammell, Arthur thought we would be in the back of a Bedford truck. We stood waiting at the front of the mansion when a large black car pulled up, Corporal Russell gave us a grin from the driving seat of the Wolseley 18/85. It was the same model the police used. Astounded, we asked where he had got it from, he winked and told us not to ask. Mr Pomeroy joined us, and placed a large suitcase in the boot, he then selected the front passenger seat. We squeezed one kit bag in but had to sit with the second on our knees. John drove us across the rolling Bedfordshire countryside and into Buckinghamshire.

We drove for half an hour to a village called Whitchurch, and arriving at the White Swan pub, we swung into the drive of another country house on the opposite side. This one wasn't as large as the Bletchley Park mansion, and it had gardens rather than grounds, but first impressions were of a beautiful, old, half-timbered house surrounded by high walls. The sentry came forward, inspected our papers and waved us through. Corporal Russell parked and Mr Pomeroy swung out of his front seat. "Pick up all the bags and follow me," he ordered. Between the three of us we managed to keep up as Mr Pomeroy marched us into The Firs. We went down a series of corridors decorated with old family oil paintings. Mr Pomeroy told us the house had been built in 1897 and had come into possession of a Major Abrahams in 1930. He had generously allowed it to be seconded for the war effort, and Major Jefferis had managed to persuade his CO to let him use it.

We were allocated a room each, Corporal Russell was going to commute in as he lived near enough to do so. Mr Pomeroy had already chosen a large bedroom with views over the garden. We were allocated smaller rooms, but still very comfortable.

Arthur's already had an occupant, a large ginger tom, it was asleep on the bed. Arthur had never cared for cats and had always been a bit wary of them. I clapped my hands and shooed him out. He took his time and gave me a disdainful look. We later found out he was called Chester, and he didn't suffer anybody but Mrs Sansom the housekeeper gladly. Arthur said, "Well apart from him it's like a four-star hotel."

Having dropped our bags, Mr Pomeroy led us down more corridors to a large room, that had been stripped out to make a workshop and there, on a raised bench, was the cause of all our trouble: Arthur's 'Flash Gordon' machine. Mr Pomeroy dismissed Corporal Russell, with a, "You know what to do with the car Corporal?" Apparently, he did. He turned to us. "You start work on this tomorrow when Mr McRea arrives," Mr Pomeroy told us. "We will eat across at the pub, the kitchen here closes at five, and arrangements have been made. They do not

180

include unlimited beer, and don't forget your training will continue. We will meet in the pub at nineteen hundred, and you may buy me a scotch." Life seemed to have improved.

Chapter 30
Live Ammunition

The White Swan provided an excellent supper of game pie. Mr Pomeroy wouldn't let us have deserts, instead he suggested an interesting cheese board. We were allowed one drink per head that MD1 would pay for, but the ever-resourceful warrant officer had done a deal with the landlord where our puddings were magically transformed into brandy. Mr Pomeroy seemed in a much better mood now that everything he had organised was functional. He even removed his trilby. After his third 'pudding', Arthur probed him about Shanghai.

His eyes narrowed as he thought back to his past as a policeman. "I wasn't far off your age when I ended up in Shanghai," he told us. "Started when I got attacked one night by a street gang in the red-light district. I really thought I'd had it; there must have been at least a dozen of them. I hadn't really done anything other than refuse to pay an extra twenty dollars for services rendered. But being European was enough to get your throat cut in those days. I managed to put two down, but I got backed into a corner. That's when I met Mr William Fairbairn, or Dangerous Dan as everybody called him. He was a lieutenant in the Shanghai municipal police. There was just the two of them, him and a constable prowling round the trouble spots. They took on the ten remaining, cool as you like, I joined in and we soon had them on the run. I stood there gasping my thanks when one of the first ones that I'd knocked down suddenly sprang up behind me. He had a knife and would have stuck me like a Sunday joint, but Dangerous Dan saw him first. He took the knife off him, and casually sliced off one of his ears. Nobody wants to carry on with only one ear, so he did a runner. I had blood all over me, some of it was mine, and I needed a couple of stitches. Dangerous took me back to the police station, got me fixed up, and offered me a job." I have heard people brag about things before, and you can normally tell when they're shooting a line. Mr Pomeroy wasn't.

182

"What they made you a copper, just like that?" Arthur asked. Mr Pomeroy drained his brandy and put his empty glass down. I went to the bar and had it filled.

"Pretty much," he said. "There were two blokes who ran the whole show, Fairbairn and his number two, Eric Sykes. Provided they kept the crime rates manageable they were allowed to do just about what they wanted. Hard men, both of them.

"Fairbairn reckoned I had potential and I was signed on. Every afternoon one or the other would have me fighting for my life. 'Defendu', they called it, a martial art they had developed from gutter fighting. I can hear him now, as I lay face down in the dirt, 'What do I do to you now Pomeroy?' The answer was always a kick in the balls, because no matter how badly you think your opponent is hurt; a kick in the balls ends it. Remember that when you're playing for real lads, it's good advice."

"How long were you out there Mr Pomeroy" I asked.

"Too long, son," he told me. "I spent my formative years getting an education in violence. Mind you I've lived off it ever since. Now we have a long day tomorrow, meet me in the back garden after your run, then you can start assisting Mr McRae in the afternoon. I bid you goodnight gentlemen, do not be too late." We stayed to finish our drinks, then followed Mr Pomeroy back.

Corporal Russell was there at the crack of dawn and took us on a gentle six-mile run through the pleasant Buckinghamshire countryside. For April the weather was kind, you don't want it too hot when you're running, but you don't want it wet either. Our PE instructor paid no regard to the weather, to him a run was a run. Today, however, we had our first bit of sunshine, even if it was early. On our return breakfast had been laid out in the dining room, it was boiled eggs and toast with the usual big pot of strong tea and, as a luxury, a small pot of local honey.

Mr Pomeroy was just finishing his. "Get some breakfast, then meet me in the garden, I have a little present for you," he told us. It sounded intriguing. We finished up and made our way outside. Mr Pomeroy and John were waiting for us by a cloth-covered table in the garden. Mr Pomeroy addressed us. "Gentlemen, up until now your training has been self-defence, today we start on the attack. No doubt if you are sent on a mission, you will be armed. You will be given a handgun, probably a Webley revolver and possibly a machine gun." With this he pulled the cloth off the table to reveal a pistol and a strange looking machine gun with a wooden stock.

"This," he explained, "is a Webley Bulldog pistol. It holds five rounds, of point forty-four ammunition, it has a two-and-a-half-inch barrel so you can carry it in a coat pocket. They have been made in Belgium since 1872 so there a great many of them in circulation, and they have stood the test of time. They have an effective range of fifteen yards."

He replaced the pistol and picked up the machine gun. "This is a prototype Sten gun. It was designed by a Major Shepherd and a Mr Turpin at the Enfield munitions works. It's named after a combination of Shepherd, Turpin and Enfield. As you can see it collapses into quite a small weapon." He folded down the stock and rotated the magazine port to demonstrate. "It holds thirty-two rounds of nine millimetres and can fire on semi and fully automatic. These will be army issue in a few weeks, you get to play with it now. Any questions?"

Neither of us had, but both of us desperately wanted to bring the hundreds of games of cowboys and Indians to life. As children we had shot each other with sticks and fingers countless times, and now we were going to get to fire a real gun. I know I should have been more mature, but I wasn't. I guessed Arthur felt the same because as Mr Pomeroy asked, "Right who would like…" Arthur stepped forward and told him.

"I would Mr Pomeroy, please."

At the bottom of the garden was an old apple tree, growing against a high brick wall. Chester the cat lay on top of the wall, warming himself in the morning sun. Mr Pomeroy pointed at the tree. "There we are gentlemen, a German sentry. You need to kill him to get past." He picked up the Sten, clicked the stock into position and inserted the magazine indicating the firing mechanism he handed it to Arthur. "The gun wont fire until you pull back the firing pin, so in your own time, Private, deal with the sentry."

With a huge grin, Arthur pulled the firing pin back and, on fully automatic, fired all thirty-two rounds into the brick wall. I swear the cat rose vertically and, spitting brimstone, hovered as the line of bullets swung towards him. The noise was deafening. Most of The Firs' domestic staff, the landlord of the White Swan and a man who had been walking his dog all ran to see what had happened.

The sentry on the gate had a hard time trying to prevent them getting into the rear garden. He glared at Mr Pomeroy. "Bloody hell sir, let us know when you're going to start shooting will you, I nearly crapped myself." Corporal Russell, walked over to placate him.

Mr Pomeroy took the gun back, removed the magazine and checked all thirty-two bullets had been fired. He beckoned Arthur to follow him and went to examine the tree. Not one bullet had found its mark. The cat had only just escaped with eight lives and wasn't seen for two days.

"How successful would you rate your dealing with the German sentry Private Wells?" Mr Pomeroy enquired.

Arthur had the good grace to look suitably abashed. "Well, it was my first go with a machine gun," he said.

"Indeed," Mr Pomeroy agreed. "But that was a sentry I told you to deal with, sentries are there to guard things, and if in any doubt raise the alarm. He didn't bloody have to, did he? You just loosed off thirty-two rounds which has brought every bugger round here running to see what has happened. You would now be dead, which from the look of things," and here he ran his hand over the undamaged apple tree, "the sentry would not. The nearest you got to a kill, was that sodding ginger cat. Now stand here, you will now be the sentry, yell if you suspect intruders."

Arthur shuffled over to the tree and, giving me a hangdog look, stood facing Mr Pomeroy. When it happened, it was so fast that it took us both by surprise. Corporal Russell dived from behind the tree, clamped a hand over Arthur's mouth and drew a knife across his throat. They both collapsed into a heap on the ground. Mr Pomeroy smiled with satisfaction. "Now," he said. "Do you see anybody running to assist Private Wells here? Poor bugger has just had his throat cut. No, you bloody don't, and the reason you don't is because Corporal Russell killed him without making a sound. Get up you two." The corporal helped Arthur up, he still looked a bit shocked. "You're all right private," Mr Pomeroy told him. "I told the corporal to keep the sheath on, this time. Now come over here and learn something."

We went back to the table, and Mr Pomeroy produced two knives from his kit bag. They looked like brass handled Italian stilettos. "You will no doubt recall me telling you about my two compatriots in the Shanghai police, Mr Fairbairn and Mr Sykes. They have returned to this country and are now teaching killing skills up in the north of Scotland. They were asked to design a knife that would be issued to people like you. This is it." He handed one to both of us. "Now I know you both think a gun is far more glamorous, but as Private Wells just demonstrated, it isn't always the best tool for the job. Guns are noisy, heavy, and are prone to mechanical failure, they also require ammunition and maintenance. This, however, is as near perfect a killing weapon as you can get." He took mine and held it up. "It is a stabbing and a cutting knife, eleven and a half inches long with a seven-inch blade. That's long enough to penetrate winter uniforms, and sharp enough to shave with. If you tear an artery with a blunt knife, it can sometimes clot and allow your opponent to survive, this won't.

"We will be concentrating on killing with this knife, silent killing and quick killing. This design is approved by the war office and is waiting production at the Wilkinson Sword factory. Because of my past association with its designers, I managed to get you these a bit early. You look after them, they will save your bacon. Let us start with cutting a throat."

It was a long morning's exercise, and we were both glad when Mr Pomeroy decided we had all died enough for today. He allowed us to keep our knives but took back the guns. "We'll have a proper day on the range," he told us.

After dinner we went down to the workshop and Arthur unpacked all his notes and diagrams. Mr McRae arrived at two o'clock in his Austin 10, and gathered us round for a powwow. He was a civilian and consequently treated Arthur and I as fellow workers rather than squaddies. We agreed the best plan was to remake the entire machine. I would strip out the existing components, Arthur and Mr McRae would build each schematic according to Arthur's original design. We had a plan.

Once again, we fell into the army routine, we ran, we practiced knife fighting and we worked long hours on the death ray, although I wasn't allowed to call it that. The primary oscillator and filters were completed and working, but there were many innovations that Mr McRae suggested.

That meant many technical arguments as Arthur defended his original design. 'The generator', as it was now known, started to take shape. All seemed to be going well until the thirteenth of May when we received a visit from Major Jefferis. For the first time since we had met him, he looked flustered. "Afternoon, chaps," he greeted us. "May I have a progress report?"

Mr McRae took him through our procedure and technical alterations until he was up to date with our work. He didn't interrupt, just listened intently. "So," he asked when Mr McRae had finished. "Best estimate for completion?"

We exchanged looks and after some hesitancy Mr McRae suggested, "If we get the latest list of stores delivered, about ten days, I would say."

The major shook his head. "That's too long. The CO wants a demonstration of where all his faith and money has gone. He's coming Saturday morning and wants to see it work. That gives you five days including today." We all started to protest, but it was to no avail, "Gentlemen, I cannot tell the prime minister you are not ready for him."

I think my mouth did actually fall open, I know Arthur's did, because I saw it. Mr McRae grinned. "Did you not know who the CO was?" he asked. "When he was only the first lord of the Admiralty, he had the foresight to set up little organisations like ours to build innovative weapons of war. That's why Major Jefferis could get you out of prison, that's why you have become unregistered guests at Bletchley Park and here at The Firs. That's why we are going to get this damn thing working."

The major smiled. "Well said Mr McRae, Winston Churchill is travelling out to Chequers on Saturday, and will be stopping here for a spot of lunch and a demonstration. Let me ask you again, what is your best estimate for completion?"

Arthur held both his hands up. "Saturday, but no more PE with Mr Pomeroy."

The major nodded. "Agreed," he told him. "I'll chase up your stores, do you have anything else to add to the list?"

Chapter 31
Light Blue Touch Paper and Stand Well Back

We worked every day, and late into the night. Mr McRae parked his Austin round the back and took a room at The Firs. We rarely saw the light of day. Meals were hurried, and Mr Pomeroy and John both came down to help with anything they could. There were fewer arguments about technical issues, there just wasn't time, surprisingly the death ray mark II started to look achievable. By Friday lunchtime it was finished. Arthur soldered the last connections and all of us stopped what we were doing. "So," Corporal Russell asked. "This is the machine that kills with sound waves."

Arthur put his hand on the chassis. "Doesn't look particularly deadly, does it," he said half to himself.

"Well Arthur, Jimmy, I think we need to try it," Mr McRae told us.

"Mr Pomeroy could you set up a target in the garden please." Mr Pomeroy looked at me. "We used a sack full of sand last time, if you could stand it in front of a couple of mattresses that would absorb a lot of the energy."

"Give us half an hour," he replied, and he and John left to set it up.

We had pre-ordered six heavy duty speakers. The army had external, bull-horn ones that looked indestructible, I suspected, however, that they would not survive to make it back to the stores. While Mr McRae and Arthur mounted the machine on a trolley, I collected one speaker and carried it out to the garden. The sack of sand hung from a branch of the apple tree, three mattresses scavenged from the house, and two of our martial arts mats were propped up against the wall behind it.

"How's that?" the Corporal asked.

"It looks good, should do the job," I told them. "I need to mount this speaker on something, any ideas?" John thought for a moment, then vanished to the other end of the garden. He reappeared struggling to carry half a railway sleeper.

"Think they were going to use these for a raised flower bed," he said. "Any good?"

We put it on Mr Pomeroy's table, and bolted the speaker on. We then adjusted the height of the sack until it appeared to be in line. I went to tell Arthur we were ready for him. Very carefully he and Mr McRae pushed the trolley into the garden, I unreeled a power lead and Arthur plugged the device in and connected the speaker. We all shook hands, it seemed the right thing to do, you don't get too many special moments like that. "Are we safe over here?" Mr Pomeroy asked.

"Yes, if we stay behind the speaker, the concentrated wave should all be going away from us," Arthur reassured all of us.

I noted that nobody looked entirely sure Arthur had got that right. He did more calculations with his slide rule, measured the distance between the machine and the sack and showed his calculations to Mr McRae who adjusted his spectacles and nodded.

The sack was swinging slightly in the breeze so Mr McRae stepped up to it to hold it steady. "If you're going to stay there, can I have your fountain pen?" I asked. Mr McRae grinned, and stepped back behind the speaker. Arthur carefully put a crystal in the small compartment on the side, he adjusted the three dials on the front and looked up.

"Ready?" he said, his voice sounded excited.

"Go on, son," Mr Pomeroy told him. Arthur threw the large switch on the top. It was quite gratifying to see everybody except Arthur and I flinch when he did this. We were old hands! As before the voltmeters started to rise, and a low hum came from the machine, the sound again grew louder and more penetrating until it was almost painful. All the meters reached their red lines and the table that the speaker stood on started to shake. The noise from the machine seemed worse than the other two times that I had done this when suddenly, as before, everything stopped. There was a second of complete silence, and then the machine made the strange spitting noise. Absolutely nothing else happened.

It was rather like November the fifth when a firework fails to go off. Nobody really wanted to risk their eyebrows and get too close in case it wasn't a dud. Eventually Arthur picked up an Avo meter and took a panel off of one side. He was joined by Mr McRae who took notes of various readings. They conferred over the main circuit diagram, and then decided to try it again. Apparently, every stage of the machine was doing exactly what it was supposed to do, but it hadn't worked.

Arthur decided to try again so we repeated the whole of the setting up procedure until he again threw the main switch. As before, the machine made loud noises, the dials climbed up to their red lines, the vibration made the table shake until everything suddenly stopped. The strange spitting noise followed and, as before, nothing else happened.

Arthur and Mr McRae took the trolley back to the workshop, a subdued air had now descended on all of us. We knew it should have worked, we didn't know why it hadn't. We made consolatory remarks to each other but in the back of everybody's mind was the consequence of failure to show Winston Churchill what he had invested in.

We broke for a light lunch, and over soup and rolls I tried to logically go through all possibilities. Was the voltage different here? Was the fact we were outdoors a contributory factor? Was the new speaker unsuitable? It was the wrong thing to try. Arthur was under so much pressure and had of course mentally ticked off all my suggestions. "Yes, just fuck off, Jim, and let me think will you," he shouted. He got up from the table and stormed out. I got up and was going to follow him out when Mr Pomeroy put a hand on my arm.

"I'd just leave him for a bit," he said. "He's got twenty-four hours, he just needs to think it through."

"Best if we all give him a bit of room," Mr McRae agreed. "I'm going to try and see if we have made a mistake in the construction. Come with me Jimmy, you can take notes."

I followed him to the workshop. "What do you think Mr McRae," I asked. He looked up from his multi meter.

"I think we are making a single stupid mistake," he replied. "It took some effort to get my head round what Arthur had designed, but I now understand his theory; this should work." He emphasized the point by stabbing the chassis with a finger. "You've seen it work twice, so I need to find the flaw. What the hell have we done wrong? Right Jim jot these numbers down for me, primary transformer input two hundred and forty volts."

By eight o'clock we were no wiser. Arthur had still not returned, and I was a bit concerned. Mr Pomeroy told me he would be OK. "He's just going through it, over and over in his head," he said. "Man needs to be alone at a time like that. Go and get Mr McRae we're going over the White Swan. We all need to down tools for an hour."

The four of us walked across the road, it wasn't a happy evening and consisted mainly of 'What if' scenarios. Mr McRae returned from the bar with two pints, a whisky and a lemonade. "You ever read Dickens?" he asked. We all admitted we hadn't. "Well, there is this chap in David Copperfield called Mr Micawber, his maxim was 'Something will turn up', that's not a bad thought for tonight. Now I suggest we finish these then try and get a few hours' sleep before we start again tomorrow." It was good advice.

At five o'clock there was a loud banging on my door. Bleary eyed I opened it to find Arthur grinning like a Cheshire cat. "I think I've sorted it, Jim," he said as he barged past me. "We're going to be all right kid. What time is the first train to London?"

I didn't have a clue but went stumbling downstairs to make tea and find a timetable. Arthur was reborn, and full of energy despite, I suspected, having had no sleep.

He made toast to go with the tea as I checked the London trains. "First one from Aylesbury is six forty," I told him. "But how do we get to the station?"

Arthur grinned. "We borrow Mr McRae's car," he said. "He leaves the keys in the kitchen in case anybody needs to move it."

"Shouldn't we wake him up to ask?" I suggested.

"Absolutely not," Arthur had suddenly got serious. "If I'm right, there could be consequences! Look Jim, run me to Aylesbury, come back here. Then pick me up at," and he consulted the timetable "eleven forty, bugger that's cutting it fine. Tell Mr McRae to give Churchill dinner and a long technical explanation, tell him a final component is on its way. OK?" I nodded, Arthur was way ahead of me, but I knew he was the only one capable of pulling our chestnuts out of the fire. He took his tea and toast with him as I swung the starter handle with the choke half out. The car fired up straight away and we climbed in. There was no other traffic on the roads and I pulled in to Aylesbury station with ten minutes to spare.

"You got any money on you Jim?" he asked, fortunately I had two ten-shilling notes and three half crowns in my pocket; I gave him the lot.

I drove back to The Firs with mixed emotions, I trusted Arthur with my life, and if he was confident, he could get the bloody death ray working, then so was I. It was the timescale that worried me, Churchill was due for 'A spot of lunch, and a demonstration'. If he intended to eat first then we had a fighting chance, conversely if he was interested enough to demand the demonstration on arrival, we were in trouble. As I pulled into the drive, I caught sight of an anxious looking Mr McRae in his dressing gown.

I climbed out of the car and waved at him. "I'm so sorry about taking your car, Mr McRae, but when you hear why, I hope you won't mind." After listening to my explanation, he forgot all about the car.

"What did he say the problem was?" he demanded. I had to admit he hadn't told me, but that was so much like Arthur. "We don't have a plan 'B' so what I'm going to do is see if we can feed the PM first."

"I'll get everything set up for the demo, and let you do the technical explanation, which will give me time to retrieve Arthur. I will need to get to Aylesbury station to collect him from the eleven forty, so I will need to take your car again, if that's OK. If we don't hit too much traffic, I would hope to have him back by twelve twenty. Can you cover for us until then?"

Mr McRae nodded. "Let's go and talk to the kitchen staff and see what we can do."

Major Jefferis arrived at ten thirty. We made him a coffee and showed him the target and padding Mr Pomeroy had reinstated in the garden. Mr Pomeroy, Corporal Russell, Mr McRae and I had discussed what we should do, and had mutually agreed there was no point in telling anybody, especially Major Jefferis, about yesterday's failure. "So, everything set up for the CO, well done chaps, where is Private Wells I really should thank him as well?"

We all answered simultaneously.

"Shopping."

"Gone home."

"Just popped into Aylesbury."

"Out for a run, sir."

There was a moment's silence until Mr Pomeroy explained that Arthur had, "Run down into Aylesbury to get some last-minute components as back up, and probably would take the opportunity of being alone to call his mum at home." That man was not only fast on his feet!

The major looked a little perplexed, but only asked reassurance that Arthur would be back before noon. I told him Mr McRae was sending me in his car to ensure that he was. "So what's the itinerary with Mr Churchill, sir?" I asked, crossing my fingers.

"Well, I've managed to get a nice salmon, so if the cook can get it ready for twelve thirty, I think we will have drinks on the lawn, watercress soup, salmon and new potatoes, a pudding and a decent bit of cheese. I'm told he likes to dine well." We all made the appropriate noises, but the relief that we had a little extra time was tangible. The major must have sensed the tension, but probably put it down to the occasion. He went to deliver his salmon to the cook. I had planned to set off at eleven to make sure I could collect Arthur on time.

Mr McRae told me he would get the generator set up in the garden for our return. "Might as well have a rehearsal before the main show," he grinned. "Let's just hope Arthur has seen something we are all missing."

I pulled into Aylesbury station car park with minutes to spare, the train was on time, and amongst the crowd disembarking was my bespectacled friend. I gave him a wave and he ran over.

"Everything all right?" I asked.

He nodded. "I bloody well hope so," he told me. "Now put your foot down, let's get back." I drove as fast as I dared, often pushing the little Austin up to sixty. We arrived at Whitchurch at five past twelve and, as we swung into The Firs' car park, I had to break hard to avoid a large black Wolseley 18/85 that occupied the centre of the drive. It seemed familiar, but I realised that it must mean Mr Churchill had arrived before us: damn.

We ran round the back to find the rest of the team in very smart uniforms and suits standing round a bald, portly man smoking a large cigar and holding a glass of champagne; it was Mr Winston Leonard Spencer-Churchill, our new prime minister. Major Jefferis glared at us. "Ah, Prime Minister, allow me to introduce the two young men who have been instrumental in the completion of your project." The great man turned and surveyed us. He transferred his cigar to his left hand and extended his right.

"Having read your files with interest gentlemen, it is a pleasure to meet you in the flesh. Which of you is Arthur Wells?"

Arthur stood forward and said, "Good afternoon Prime Minister." He overcame his usual dislike of contact, and shook the prime minister's hand.

"So this was all your brainwave?" the PM demanded. "Had a few failures I'll be bound?"

Arthur nodded. "Yes, sir, it sometimes wasn't easy."

Churchill pondered for a moment. "There is sometimes a thin line between success and failure, I call it Hadrian's Wall." It was a joke, the prime minister was telling Arthur a joke! It took a moment for the penny to drop, but then we all laughed, genuine laughter for a good joke. The mood changed. "Think we should have this demonstration before lunch, what do you say Jefferis?"

"Of course, sir." Major Jefferis shot a glance at Arthur, who took the hint.

"I'll just set everything up Major, if you could position the prime minister behind the speaker, please."

Churchill's chauffeur carried an armed dining chair across to where the sack hung in front of the garden wall. Mr McRae also glanced pleadingly at Arthur but started to give the prime minister a broad-brush picture of how we had concentrated sound waves into a weapon.

The death ray sat in the same position we had left it yesterday. Arthur produced a slide rule and tape measure and re-inserted a crystal. He adjusted the dials and micrometres, finally giving Mr McRae the nod. "I should warn you, Prime Minister, that the machine will make an unpleasant noise, which will intensify until it fires. After the master power switch is thrown, it will take a moment to build the power up. Do not be alarmed."

Churchill took his seat and nodded. "Used to procure tanks in 1915 when I was the minister of munitions, can't be louder than that, can it?"

"A different frequency, Prime Minister," the major told him. "All right Wells, fire it up."

Looks were exchanged between Mr Pomeroy, John and Mr McRae: this was it. Arthur looked up at all of us, winked, and threw the switch. The meters started to rise, the low hum increased in volume and the whole contraption started to shake. The chauffeur stepped protectively towards Mr Churchill, as he covered his ears. The noise became very uncomfortable, almost painful, when again it suddenly stopped. I saw Churchill lean forward, probably disappointed, then came the spitting noise and the sharp pain in the ears. Followed by utter destruction.

The shimmering corridor of air appeared between the speaker and the sack, which bulged and swung away. The sack swung back as though pulled by a string until it reached the limit of its elasticity and burst, sand blasting the mattresses behind it. The gym mats burst, their padding filling the air with flock but, most impressively, the entire section of garden wall behind all of this exploded. It was as though a giant naval shell had hit it. Dust and debris floated in the air.

The chauffeur had a gun in his hand and was shouting something at us, my hearing like everybody else was not working, but I was thankful to see Mr Churchill rise to his feet, and indicate the chauffeur should put down the gun. We walked him away from the destruction and found him a brandy.

"My God," Churchill shouted. "My God, like Joshua at the battle of Jericho, my God." The chauffeur was still upset, he called us stupid idiots, and I suspect wanted to shoot the lot of us.

"Did you know it was going to do that?" he demanded. I suppose it doesn't look good being a bodyguard to the prime minister, and having him disintegrated on day three of the job.

As our hearing recovered, the mood lightened, Churchill was delighted with his new toy, and all through lunch bombarded us with questions. Major Jefferis stood behind Arthur and I and gave our shoulders a squeeze of gratitude, we had delivered the impossible, MD1 was safe.

Mr Pomeroy and Mr McRae cornered Arthur. "Well?" Mr Pomeroy asked.

"What?" Arthur replied.

"We want to know how you got it working," Mr McRae demanded. "You didn't change the circuitry, everything was the same as yesterday, but you got it to work. How?"

Arthur paused. "You're not going to like it," he said.

"Go on," ordered Mister Pomeroy.

"I changed the crystal," Arthur told them, "Eliminate the impossible, and whatever is left, no matter how improbable, is the truth. I read that somewhere.

"Anyway, I went through it a hundred times in my head, until I realised that the only thing I had changed electrically, was the crystal. I went home, collected the original one we used last time, and, well you saw the result."

"Well, that's all right then," said Mr Pomeroy. Mr McRae remained quiet. "What's the matter McRae, it worked, you're the hero of the hour."

Mr McRae looked at Mr Pomeroy. "Tell him, Arthur," he said.

Arthur nodded. "It means, Mr Pomeroy, that we can do this, but only with the original crystal. We can't build another machine."

Realisation appeared on Mr Pomeroy's face. "Let's keep that little bit of news to ourselves gentlemen, shall we."

Chapter 32
Practice Twenty-two — Rapid Fire

Mr Churchill left after lunch. The excellent soup, salmon, treacle tart and stilton had, if anything, improved his mood. Each course had been accompanied by wine or brandy which he had consumed in great quantity and without any apparent effect. He beckoned Major Jefferis over towards the end of the meal, and they talked quietly between themselves. The prime minister eventually consulted his pocket watch and rose to his feet. He addressed all of us. "Gentlemen, I am mightily impressed by your efforts. I do not yet know how I shall use this new weapon in our battle against the Nazis, but use it I shall. They will tremble before it like the Canaanites at Jericho. It will be our Joshua's Trumpet, and the walls will come tumbling down. You have your country's gratitude gentlemen, thank you." His chauffeur offered him his hat and opened the dining room door into the garden.

They walked towards his car and, as he got in the back, I realised why it had looked familiar. It was the same car Corporal Russell had driven us over from Bletchley in. I caught Mr Pomeroy's eye, he looked as though butter would not have melted beneath his waxed moustaches: guilty! Corporal Russell at least had the decency to look as though he had been caught red-handed. I mean appropriating the prime minister's car even if he was awaiting election, that couldn't be approved by MD1, could it?

The generator was carefully packed away. After it had been made secure, Mr McRae and Mr Pomeroy joined us in the workshop. Mr Pomeroy removed his hat, not a good sign! "I think we should sort something out gentlemen." He indicated a table with four chairs, we sat. "Now, if I have got this right, your sound machine will only work with one particular crystal, is that right?" Arthur told him it was. "And where is that crystal now?" he enquired.

Arthur delved into his pockets and removed the small tin. "Here Mr Pomeroy." Mr McRae leaned forward, examined the crystal and then replaced it in its cotton wool bed.

"Can we reproduce it?" Mr Pomeroy asked.

"Don't know," Mr McRae answered. "On the face of it, it's just a cat's whiskers crystal, thousands of them were sold in the twenties and thirties. We can duplicate the size, of course, certainly worth trying, but I suspect there is something unique to this particular one. We need time."

"I will give you a week, but if by then you can't produce another, I must inform Major Jefferis. If he is thinking we can knock these out like mills bombs, we need to set him right, we all owe him that."

By the following Saturday, Arthur and Mr McRae had to admit failure, they had tried electrically and mechanically to reproduce a second crystal, but none of them would work. Major Jefferis was sent for.

He arrived Monday morning for breakfast. Mr McRae broke the bad news to him over coffee. Surprisingly, he took it better than we had all thought. He asked if it would be possible to work two machines from the one primary source. I didn't really understand why not, but Arthur was adamant that it wasn't. He asked if there was a way to record the signal from the crystal and reproduce that. Mr McRae explained that they had tried that last week and again the recording had lacked the magic required to fire up the death ray. Finally, he told us, "Well gentlemen, we have a working generator, we have impressed the prime minister and we have been given a second commission. All in all, I would say you have all earned your corn with MD1." That sounded like we wouldn't be going back to the Scrubs.

"What's the new commission?" Mr McRae asked.

"Yes, we are getting a specific job together, top secret gentlemen, top secret. What I need you to make, is a device that will block radio signals to and from a military town. Something we can turn on and off, rather than just blow the masts up. I have a dossier with mast locations, frequency bands and any other information the planners thought you might need." He handed Mr McRae a leather briefcase. "I think we have a friend in Mr Churchill, he was genuinely impressed and has increased our funding as well as reducing red tape for MD1. If we want sugar buns for tea, we damn well get sugar buns, the PM says so. Let's make him happy again with this job."

The major stubbed out his cigarette, saluted and made for the door. As he got there he stopped and turned to Mr Pomeroy. "Tell me, warrant officer, are these two ready for active service?"

Mr Pomeroy considered. "I'd say they were sir, yes."

"Excellent," the major replied. He turned to us. "Gentlemen you will cease shaving as of now; don't ask! Get them on the range this week, would you."

"Sir," Mr Pomeroy confirmed. I'm sure we all then thought back to Arthur's near cat murder. Was giving him another loaded weapon really a good idea?

On Wednesday, Corporal Russell arrived in a Bedford truck. It was to take everybody apart from Mr McRae to the firing range at Kempston. Corporal Russell drove, Mr Pomeroy sat in the front passenger seat, leaving Arthur and I to squeeze in the back seats. It seemed an uneconomic way to travel until we arrived at the range and discovered the three heavy looking crates, we had bought with us. We took them to our section of the range, where a large table had been erected.

In the first crate was a selection of handguns and ammunition. We went through safety, firing stance and types of bullets. Mr Pomeroy then selected a Webley Mark Six revolver, he broke the gun and loaded it with six bullets. He then pointed to a target twenty yards away. "There you are Mr Jones, a Nazi storm-trooper, kill him." I weighed the gun in my hand, two and a half pounds and eleven inches long. I took the stance Mr Pomeroy had demonstrated and fired. "Squeeze it like a lemon," had been his advice.

What I hadn't been expecting was the recoil, the gun shot up as the bullet fired: a miss. I settled for a second shot and, bracing myself for the kick, managed to get an outer. Mr Pomeroy told me with the heavy lead bullet that the Webley fired, that would be a man down.

"Now you shoot him in the head as you advance," he advised. My third, fourth and fifth shots were on target but the sixth was a bullseye. "Not bad, not bad at all," was my reward. Arthur tried but only managed two outers. We then changed to an Enfield Number Two pistol; its range was much less at only fifteen yards, but it was lighter and the recoil was much diminished. Both of us were better shots with this gun, although I still liked the reassuring weight of the Webley.

We then moved on to the Browning automatic, this was a bit more like it. I had seen this type of gun on numerous trips to the pictures. The recoil from the first bullet causes the second to be dragged from the magazine and placed in the breach. Effectively you can just keep pulling the trigger until you run out of ammunition. Mr Pomeroy did not approve. Too many things to go wrong, he was mistrustful of the claimed fifty-five-yard range and contemptuous of the foreign calibre. Arthur and I loved it, and even Corporal Russell fired off a full ten-round magazine. I know which one I would have chosen every time.

We opened the second crate to discover the two machine guns Mr Pomeroy had shown us before. We lifted out the two Sten guns and several magazines. This time Mr Pomeroy gave us a briefing.

They were to become the new army issue to replace the more expensive Bren, Vickers and Tommy guns. In his opinion they would be even more utilitarian by the time they hit mass production. At his request the wooden stocks on ours had been replaced with skeleton metal. "They're Woolworth specials," he said. "But they do the job. Only nine pounds fully loaded and capable of up to five hundred rounds per minute." As Mr Pomeroy explained MD1 operatives rarely wore uniform, and the ability to conceal a weapon was more important than accuracy.

We spent a long time, stripping and reassembling them, they were very basic, but as Corporal Russell commented, "Less to go wrong." Targets were set up at forty yards, and at Mr Pomeroy's insistence we fired the first magazine on single shot. You instinctively wanted to hold it by the pistol grip handle and the magazine, but Mr Pomeroy made us use the left hand to support the barrel. As always, he was right. By the end of the first twenty-eight-round magazine all three of us were hitting the target. After a brief examination of the groupings Mr Pomeroy told us to change to automatic. "Short bursts gentlemen, short bursts, we do not want to jam our weapons. Do we?" The guns tended to pull to the left on automatic as Arthur and the cat had found out. Once you got used to this, however, accuracy improved considerably. It was huge fun to watch the targets disintegrate under a stream of bullets. By the time all our ammunition was gone, we all felt confident with the new machine gun.

The final crate contained rifles, two Lee Enfield 303s. We spent an hour stripping them down and reassembling. Mr Pomeroy then gave us a demonstration and from a reclining position hit targets two hundred yards away. He claimed it was the most accurate weapon the British army had ever used.

We were nothing like as good as Mr Pomeroy or Corporal Russell, but we did manage to hit some of the dinner plate-sized targets. After you fired, you had to grasp the rifle bolt on the right-hand side and pull it back and down to release the spent cartridge then push it back to reload. Mr Pomeroy asked how fast I could empty the ten-round magazine if accuracy wasn't important. I noticed that my friend Corporal Russell was grinning.

"How inaccurate can I be?" I queried.

"Well now, suppose I move a bigger target to thirty yards, and let's say anything that leaves a hole, counts. Last one to empty the magazine buys the drinks tonight?" I knew I wasn't as good a shot, but just firing off ten rounds, how difficult could that be? The target was close enough to give me confidence.

"You're on," I told him.

Corporal Russell placed a large square target at thirty yards. He loaded the rifle and handed it to me. "You have to make a hole anywhere on the card," he told me. "Good luck." He took off his watch and counted me down. "Three, Two, One, Fire." I squeezed off the first shot, a hit, pulled the bolt back and fired again, it wasn't easy, but I started to get a rhythm. Before I knew it, I had fired all ten bullets and the corporal looked up from his watch. "Thirty-two seconds, that's good shooting, Private." He walked to the target and counted the holes. "Some were near the edge, but ten hits," he told me. I actually felt quite pleased with myself.

Mr Pomeroy reloaded, and laid down facing the target. "Ready, sir?" the corporal asked.

"Ready," Mr Pomeroy replied.

"Then Three, Two, One, Fire," the corporal shouted. What happened next defied logic, it appeared Mr Pomeroy had somehow swapped his rifle for a machine gun. There wasn't a break between shots and when the wave of noise ceased Corporal Russell called out the time. "Eight seconds." I had just seen it, but I really didn't believe it. Mr Pomeroy grinned.

"It's technique, lad," he told me. "You move the bolt with your palm not between fore finger and thumb. An experience rifleman is expected to fire twenty accurate shots a minute. That's about what you did. Using this trick, you can lay down rapid fire at forty rounds a minute, and that includes reloading. In the last war it was called "Practice Number twenty-two — rapid fire. I think I shall have a large single malt!"

We made our way back to The Firs grinning like schoolboys and feeling like proper soldiers. A good day out.

Chapter 33
Bletchley Park after Dark

The war had been escalating without us. Although we listened to the news and read the daily papers, we felt cocooned and isolated in our country house. We ate well, we slept in comfortable beds and we continued with the academia of the task that MD1 had been given by Mr Churchill. It seemed as though we were observing our country's struggle for victory from the comfort of a cinema seat. It did not feel good.

The British Expeditionary Force of over four hundred thousand had been sent across the channel to fight with the French and the Belgians in the 'Battle of France'. Every day we read in disbelief how the German army out manoeuvred and out gunned the allies. Eventually three Panzer units pushed north-west to Ardennes, going round the impregnable French Maginot Line and driving everything in front of them

The head of the British forces, Viscount Gort, realising the battle was lost, ordered a retreat to the nearest port capable of evacuating the remains of the allied army. Had the Germans continued their advance, even with the siege of Lille, where forty thousand members of the French army, held back seven German divisions, all would have been lost. Instead, Goering persuaded Hitler to allow his Luftwaffe, to bomb the retreating armies into submission. The air attacks prevented the navy from getting in close enough to rescue the three hundred and fifty thousand troops dying on the beach. It looked hopeless until a call went out for all the British boats capable of crossing the channel to mount a rescue mission. Unbelievably it worked, hundreds of small boats defied the German bombs and, by the fourth of June, three hundred and thirty-eight thousand, two hundred and twenty-six men were returned to British soil.

For a lesser prime minister, it should have been a humiliating defeat, but Mr Churchill gave a speech where he told us we would never surrender, and we would fight on the beaches, the landing grounds, the fields, the streets and the hills. Damn right, Arthur and I could not wait to face the enemy. I like to think it was this message that gave him the incentive that cracked the radio mast problem.

A week later he walked into the White Swan where I sat with Mr McRae and Mr Pomeroy. He didn't say anything but laid a single sheet of maths and diagrams in front of Mr McRae. He looked like he hadn't slept for a week. The scrubby beard didn't improve the image.

We kept very quiet while the figures were perused, I went to the bar and got Arthur a pint, he looked like he had earned it. Mr McRae suddenly made a noise that was a cross between a snort and an exhalation. He stood up and addressed the entire pub. I had never heard Mr McRae swear until then.

"The boy's a bloody genius," he informed us. He polished his glasses and shaking his head went through the work again. He turned to Arthur who was halfway through his pint. "Fifth harmonic?"

Arthur nodded. "It works, I've tried it on all the mock-ups. Kills input and output dead. Turn it off and everything restores. What do you think?"

Mr McRae continued to shake his head. "I think I love you, Arthur Wells, this is an incredible piece of work, you're truly a grandmaster of the circuit diagram. Well done that man." I think Arthur slept well that night.

Mr Pomeroy reported our success back. He told us that Major Jefferis asked if we could make two devices each portable enough for a man to carry. This involved Arthur and Mr McRae spending days with blueprints, slide rules and gallons of tea in the workshop. Eventually we built a rubber covered aluminium chassis with the valves on the inside. It had a nine-foot telescopic aerial, ran off a fifty-volt battery, and was carried in a backpack. We would have liked to get rid of the battery but were told it was to be a field device, and the batteries had to stay. By the twenty-first of June, we had both sets operational. Mr Pomeroy came to inspect them.

"All right," he said. "In a nutshell good points and bad points?"

Mr McRae scratched the back of his head. "Well, first good point is that they work. Given the time we have had, it's an extraordinary achievement."

Mr Pomeroy nodded. "All right," he said. "I accept it's a miracle you managed to build them, but as this is mark one, what would you like to see in the mark two?"

Arthur thought for a moment. "Well, they're heavy," he said. "If we could ditch the battery, it would be better."

Mr Pomeroy nodded. "And?"

"Well," Arthur said. "The range isn't huge, to knock out a transceiver you would need this to be within twenty-five feet of it."

"Anything else?" Mr Pomeroy asked. We all racked our brains

"I can't think of anything else," Mr McRae told him. "They will do the job if we can carry the damn things within twenty-five feet, OK?"

Mr Pomeroy smiled. "Very OK everybody. Now all I need to do is to get a chance to use them."

Mr Pomeroy vanished for the rest of the afternoon. He later turned up in a small civilian car he had acquired. This, he explained, was to drive Arthur and I back to Bletchley Park. "Tonight, gentlemen we are mounting our first attack. You will enter the park and disable the diplomatic radio mast from 23.05 until 23.15. This is a double test, one to see if you can break into an army establishment. Be warned strolling out is a damn site easier than getting in. Two is to see if the machine you have spent a fortune on, does what you tell us it will." He held his hands up as Arthur started to protest. "I know it will, but the prime minister requires proof. He will be receiving an emergency broadcast at twenty-three hundred hours. He expects it to go off the air at exactly 23.05. Questions?"

"How do we get in?" I asked.

"Absolutely no bloody idea," Mr Pomeroy told me. "You will go in civilian clothes with no identification. There are two guards on the main gate and a two-man patrol that walks the grounds until zero seven hundred hours, both are armed. I shall drop you at Bletchley station at twenty-one thirty and wait for you until midnight, do not kill anybody, do not get caught and don't expect a rescue. This is for real."

We sat and talked through our options, my idea was to break into the GPO yard steal a van and bluff our way in as an emergency repair team. Arthur was against it, too easy to check, and we might be recognised. We eventually agreed to a straightforward breaking and entering. Arthur managed to get a detailed map of Bletchley and traced where he thought the perimeter fence now was. It was chain link but we didn't think it would be a problem. He then disappeared into Mr McRae's office for ten minutes, and emerged grinning. "All set Jimmy," he told me.

Mr Pomeroy dropped us of at half past nine as promised. It was dusk and I estimated we had a half hour until dark. Having checked with Arthur's diary there should be little moonlight. We didn't use the footpath from the station as it emerged right by the main gate, two bearded civilians carrying what looked like an army radio might cause a bit of suspicion. Instead, we walked up the main road and turned toward the park but passed the approach road.

Nobody seemed concerned about us and, presumably because Bletchley Park was known to house a lot of secret army types, nobody questioned why I had a two-foot cube strapped to my back.

We turned into St Mary's Church and sat on the bench in front of the front door. Arthur checked his watch. It was now getting dark and we made our way round to the graveyard at the rear of the church.

We followed the slope down to the edge of the graveyard and saw the concrete posts and chain link fence that bordered the park. Arthur opened his bag and produced an electric torch, a heavy pair of gloves and wire cutters. We crawled along the perimeter until we were close to the back of a storeroom, there were a lot of brambles, but that meant nobody was going to investigate that too thoroughly. I was just about to start cutting when Arthur gripped my shoulder. "Hang on Jimmy, look what the crafty so-and-sos have done." He shone his torch on a single wire that had no business being in a fence. "It's an alarm wire, cut that and somewhere in the park, a bell will ring, not very sophisticated. Would you like to deal with it, Mr Jones?" He handed me six feet of insulted wire and a penknife. I carefully cut the insulation away from the alarm wire and twisted the stripped end of our new length into it. I then moved to our right and repeated the procedure, allowing the bridged alarm wire to be cut.

I still flinched when I cut through it, waiting for the bells and lights, but of course nothing happened. Arthur then snipped a four feet vertical cut from the bottom and peeled back the edges to give us a hole big enough to crawl through. He handed me a small dark cylinder. "What is it?" I asked.

"Burnt cork," he whispered. "Rub it on your face, and you won't be seen." I did, then wriggled through into the park. Arthur pushed the generator through and followed, swearing as he caught his hand in the brambles. I was sympathetic, as I had used the heavy duty gloves he had packed. We emerged from behind the storeroom, me wearing the generator and Arthur in the lead watching for patrols. He took the burnt cork and drew a big X on the wall.

We moved silently from shadow to shadow getting deeper into the park where the diplomatic wireless mast stood. The odd hut still had lights on, but we saw no one. We reached the base of the radio tower without incident. Arthur checked his watch, 10.55, we had ten minutes to lie low before disabling the transmitter. Arthur extended the aerial fully and wrapped some ivy round it. Unfortunately, it was chrome, and shone in what little light there was. I found two old sheets of corrugated iron and formed them into an inverted V we crawled inside and, at twenty-three hundred hours, Arthur turned on the set.

The voltmeter showed a healthy fifty volts. And all the indicator lights were green meaning we were good to go. We lay there watching the minute hands approach 11.05, when there was a noise from the perimeter path.

It was the night patrol and they strolled casually towards us, chatting as they came. We froze, two minutes to go, and we didn't know what would happen when we threw the transmit switch. The first sentry was explaining how he had invested in a good supper at the Swan, and Beryl, the object of his desire, had only given him a kiss on the doorstep before vanishing into her digs. The other private was sympathetic but confided that he knew of two canteen ladies who 'would' for a couple of drinks in the Eight Bells. They walked past us without a backward glance. Arthur checked his watch, glanced at me, and threw the switch. One of the valves must have been touching the chassis because a light tinkling noise like a muffled alarm clock came from the set. It wasn't very loud, but in the still and quiet night it sounded to us like a fire alarm. The two men turned back and walked towards the mast.

"What the hell's that?" the first one said.

"I reckon it's the cable feed running up the mast," the second told him. "My old man was a ham operator and my mum used to give him hell about his kit keeping her awake. He used to be up all hours talking to Finland, Canada and the like. God knows why, I think it was to stop him going up to bed with Mum, they didn't get on that well." They continued to stare up into the darkness, while Arthur wrapped himself around the set. "I can hear the old bugger now, this is QCKfive-five-three, QCKfive-five-three, how do you copy? Over."

"My old man was into crown green bowls," the other replied. "He didn't stray far from home, and he got to have a couple of pints after, know which one I'd do. So you reckon this is OK then?"

The other shrugged. "Like getting an airlock in a pipe I reckon, they'll send the signals blokes over if it's a fault." They moved off. Arthur checked his watch again, and after ten seconds turned the machine off. The noise stopped. The departing sentries halted.

"There you are," said the first one. "It's fixed itself. Let's go and have a fag."

We packed the set away and backtracked to the storeroom with a dirty cross on the side. I was about to push the set through when a voice called out, "Halt, who goes there?" He didn't get to use the 'Friend or foe' bit because Arthur hit him. I scrabbled back to find an unconscious soldier slumped on the floor. Arthur looked at me wide eyed.

"Oh, shit, Jim, what do we do, he'll tell everybody when he comes round."

I felt for a pulse, it was nice and strong, and listened to him breath. Arthur had hit him hard, but all he would have in the morning was a bad headache. He was signals, and I guessed he had been sent out to check the mast. I looked around, leant up against the side of the storeroom were two ladders. They were wooden and must have weighed twenty-five pounds each. I pushed them until they started to slide. "Grab these Arthur, don't let them make a noise." He helped me lower them to the ground and then to pull the soldier into a position, where we could put a ladder on top of him. I bent over, undid his trousers and unbuttoned his fly. Arthur looked at me in horror.

"What the hell are you doing, Jim?" he demanded.

I grinned. "What does this look like?" I asked. He didn't get it. "He got caught short, stepped in here to have a piss, when crash bang wallop the ladders fall on him. Would you tell anybody about that?"

Realisation dawned on Arthur's face. "No, I bloody well wouldn't," he grinned. "Come on we only have six minutes."

I didn't know what for but followed Arthur through our escape hole. He helped me repair the fence with another length of wire from his bag, then strap the generator to my back. "Right come on we have two minutes," he panted. We made it back to the church entrance and Arthur helped me get the generator off. He checked his watch, "Made it," he told me.

I really didn't know what he was talking about until after a few minutes a taxi pulled over. "Mr Wells?" the cabby enquired.

"That's me," Arthur told him. "Station please."

"Need a hand with your case?" the man asked.

"No, you're OK, mate, I'll get it in," I told him. There were a lot of signals men out as we drove to the station, but nobody looked at a passing taxi. The best bit of all was Mr Pomeroy's face when we paid off the cab and got back in his car.

"Home James, and don't spare the horses," Arthur told him.

We arrived back at The Firs at half past twelve. Before we were allowed to go and clean up, Mr Pomeroy took us through the debriefing, it was basically telling him what had happened. He nodded approvingly at our approach route, he noted the alarm wire and Arthur's brief description of bypassing it, similarly the chrome aerial and the vibrating chassis. The only thing that seemed to give him concern was disabling the signals man.

"Did he see you?" he demanded with his pencil poised.

"No, I think he heard Jimmy, and challenged him, but he couldn't really have seen either of us," Arthur told him. "I came up behind him and hit him with an elbow to the ear like you taught me. He was unconscious before he hit the floor."

Mr Pomeroy looked up. "It's OK, I dealt with it," I told him, and explained how we had left him with an unzipped fly under the ladders. I swear I saw a brief smile under his moustaches. The taxi, he of course knew about. He closed his notebook.

"Well, gentlemen a good night's work. I am told the prime minister lost contact with Bletchley Park halfway through a personal message. It had to be sent again ten minutes later. They are blaming it on sun spots whatever they are. Go and get cleaned up, Major Jefferis wants to see us tomorrow. I am to take you and Mr McRae over to the park after breakfast. Now get a drink, and some sleep."

We went to bed feeling damn good.

Chapter 34
The Briefing

After breakfast we squeezed into Mr Pomeroy's car. Mr McRae had heard on the radio that France had surrendered, and that the Battle of France was over. It was a sombre moment knowing we were now absolutely alone. We pulled up outside the mansion and made our way to the MD1 office. Major Jefferis welcomed us in. A board covered in maps and photographs had been set up and, while we helped ourselves to tea and biscuits Mr Pomeroy locked us in.

The major started without preamble. "Good morning gentlemen, following your success last night, you are to be sent on an MD1 mission. It is called, at the PM's insistence, 'Operation Joshua'. This is what, where, why and when. Everything I am about to tell you is absolutely top secret. Are we clear?" We said we were.

He continued. "You will no doubt have heard that the Battle of France is over, and the French will today sign an armistice. That was sadly predictable, and counter measures have been taken. Mr Churchill's prime concern however is the French fleet, the fourth largest in the war. Should it fall under German or Italian control, we would lose our naval supremacy. That cannot be allowed to happen. At present it is split with forty per cent in Toulon harbour, twenty per cent in Britain, Alexandria and the French West Indies, but the remaining forty per cent is at a port in Algiers called Mers-el-Kébir. The French consider Algeria to be part of France, not a colony. Consequently, they feel the fleet is secure there." He indicated a map with a port in North Africa. "Our agents tell us that the Germans will agree to the entire French navy being stood down for the remainder of the war. That may sound very attractive to the French negotiators, but frankly, gentlemen, we don't believe a bloody word. We know they do not have enough Kreigsmarine to man the extra ships, but we also know the Germans and Italians have stepped up their recruitment and training to a level never seen before." He paused to get tea.

"Toulon is too well protected, Alexandria is under negotiations, but it is the ships at Mers-el-Kébir that interest us. The PM has released Paul Reynaud, the French prime minister, from his obligations as an ally, this will enable him to surrender and cease hostilities.

"In return the PM has asked that the French fleet joins the Royal Navy. Their alternative is that the fleet sails for British, American or French West Indian ports where they can truly be stood down. The final alternative being to scuttle the lot."

Mr Pomeroy puffed out his cheeks. "Can't see that happening," he told us.

"Indeed," Major Jefferis agreed. "That is why we have a Plan B. The admiral in charge of the entire fleet is this man," he indicated a photograph. "Admiral Francois Darlan. He is a highly experienced and respected sailor, he is also a master tactician, currently based in Toulon. We do not want him assisting this man," he again indicated a picture of a beefy faced sailor. "This is Admiral Marcel Bruno Gensoul. He is at present the commanding officer of the fleet at Mers-el-Kébir. He is a pompous idiot, but we believe he can be manipulated.

"Your first job is, therefore, to knock out the telephone and radio communications to the port, leaving Gensoul without the option to delegate. The exchange is here," he indicated on an aerial photograph, "and the two masts, are here and here. One of which is in the French coastal defence at Fort Santon. It has a single thirty-five-millimetre gun overlooking the harbour." Arthur went to speak, and the Major raised an eyebrow. "Wells?"

Arthur shook his head. "They're sitting on warships, Major, all of those ships will have a radio room that can communicate with Toulon despite what we do on shore."

Mr McRae stood, taking over from the Major. "It's all right Arthur, that has been dealt with. It's four hundred miles from Mers-l-Kébir to Toulon, and if they don't use the ship to shore radio links, they can only use Morse. We know the frequencies they broadcast on, and we will have our own transmitter off Minorca belting out an intercept signal. We also have a team in Toulouse who will be doing a similar job to you in removing the radio masts there."

The major looked to see if Arthur had any more objections: he didn't. "To continue, let me introduce you to this gentleman." He indicated a third photograph of a tall blonde man in the naval uniform of a French officer. "He is Jean Claude Montfort, Capitaine de Corvette; that's a lieutenant commander to you. He has worked his way up the slippery pole to become aide-de-camp to Gensoul. The admiral relies heavily on his opinions, which is bad news for us. Montfort has German sympathies, his father fought for them in the last war. He is also a supporter of Marshall Henri Petain, the man likely to be installed by the Nazis as a puppet head of the French Ministerial Council.

"Petain is an old man and will do exactly what the Germans want. We are, therefore, concerned that Montfort will do his upmost to prevent Gensoul from complying with Churchill's demands. Your second task is, therefore, to eliminate Montfort."

The sudden realisation that we were expected to kill somebody was chilling. Up until now it had all been academic and, if I'm honest, quite fun. Now, however, the reality of war had come home to roost. Mr Pomeroy now took the floor. He pointed to a photograph of a car riddled with bullets.

"Some of the Algerians also feel Montfort has betrayed their fight for freedom. This assassination attempt by Algerians took place five weeks ago, it was amateurish and failed. They killed his driver and a second passenger. Montfort escaped, but has not been seen outside since. We now can't get to him and want you to use the sound generator to kill him. After that, you will use plastic explosives to destroy the exchanges, and you will use your radio blocking equipment to turn off the two radio masts, restoring them at set times allowing communication with Gensoul."

Mr McRae now stood again. "In your absence, gentlemen, I have managed to double the effective range of the radio blockers, and we will obviously change the aerial and ensure all sets are silent."

He sat, the major stood. "Well, that's told you what, why and where. You now need to know when. You will fly out of RAF Brize Norton at twenty-one hundred hours on the twenty-eighth, that's six days' time. You will fly to Gibraltar where you will take a boat along the coast to a fishing port called Ain El Turk, it is close to the harbour of Mers-el-

Kébir where the French have their fleet. We are sending an agent with you, he speaks Arabic and French and knows the town. You and the equipment will be taken into Mers-el-Kébir where you will liaise with MD1's top operative, Aled Alemna. All your work must be completed by noon on the third of July, that is imperative. Transport home has also been arranged. Any questions about Operation Joshua?"

We had hundreds, but the major neatly sidestepped them delegating to Mr Pomeroy. We were to have instruction in explosives and fuses. Mr Pomeroy seemed to have thought of everything, but that after all was his job. We went through the rest of the day studying maps and technical information about Mers-el-Kébir's telephone system. It all seemed well planned.

"What happens on the third to make Gensoul release his boats?" Arthur asked.

The discussion paused. "I'm afraid that is the only part we can't tell you, it's classified above everybody's level but mine," the major told us. "Just make sure you are out of the town as soon as you are finished." That didn't sound good.

The next five days were spent blowing things up, throwing hand grenades and modifying our equipment. The plastic explosives were more effective if you contained the blast. If you wanted to blow up a railway track, you put the charge under the rail where the force would be concentrated upwards. This was my sort of engineering and I became quite good at it. Mr Pomeroy nodded encouragingly. The mills bombs were simple but effective. You pulled out the safety pin which allowed the lever to release and prime the fuse. The cast iron case was grooved to improve the grip, and not as I thought to allow for fragmentation. Mr Pomeroy made it very clear that the time from lever release to explosion was just four seconds. It had been seven, but too many had been thrown back. I had played cricket for the GPO team and could throw one a hundred and twenty feet. Arthur couldn't, so Mr Pomeroy suggested that he laid down covering fire while I threw, teamwork!

On our last night we all went across to the Swan for a farewell drink. It was a strange evening where we felt like condemned men awaiting execution. Mr Pomeroy put his calloused hand on Arthur's shoulder. "You look after him, Private Wells, I want you both back here, you understand?" Arthur agreed. Mr Pomeroy had consumed the best part of a bottle of brandy that he had somehow cajoled out of the landlord's private stock and was becoming maudlin.

John kept telling us he, "Wished he was going with us, and that a man should do his bit for his country, and that he wanted a chance to come face to face with the Hun," but then he had consumed a pint and a half.

Mr McRae told Arthur that, "When this lot is all over, we should set up an electronic design centre." I wasn't that sorry when the night came to a close.

After they had wished us good luck and shaken our hands they left, leaving us quietly talking about the future. Arthur sipped his pint reflectively. "You've got to hand it to them, this has all been set up very fast."

I looked at him. "When did they tell you to start growing a beard that will make you look like a native of Algeria?"

He stared at me. "But they can't have! How, I mean they wouldn't have known; would they?

He really didn't know.

"Arthur this is the secret service, they knew what they were doing the day they sprung us from the Scrubs. I think the details were filled in as we went along, but Major Jefferis knew from day one what he was going to use us for."

"Do you think it has a happy ending?" he asked.

"I think that's down to us," I told him.

He nodded. "Still cheer up Jimmy, big day tomorrow, we get to ride in an aeroplane. I'm really looking forward to that."

Chapter 35
Travelling

At two in the morning Arthur threw up again. We were frozen, uncomfortable and deafened by the constant roar of the Wellington's two engines. I don't think the ride was everything he had hoped.

We had been driven to RAF Brize Norton in Oxfordshire. Our bags of explosives, small arms and personal kit had been loaded on to our lorry with the crates containing the sound generator and radio signal blockers; it looked heavy. Everything was then transferred to our Wellington bomber and lashed down. An extra fuel tank had been fitted to the plane to ensure we had a safety margin, as Gibraltar was the maximum range for a Wellington.

We met the crew who would fly us the one thousand five hundred miles to Gibraltar at the flight briefing. They seemed a nice bunch, pilot, navigator, front and rear gunners, flight engineer and radio operator. They didn't comment on our beards as they had probably flown agents down to the Med before. They told us that they had done the run down to Gibraltar a couple of times and what an amazing place it was. Warm, cheap beer, WAAFs and exotic Mediterranean food. The only drawback apparently was gangs of monkeys who held the high ground and would steal anything. Arthur laughed at this but was put right by Rigsby the indignant rear gunner. He had a pal stationed out there who had been court-martialled for losing a complete Lewis gun to a gang of monkeys led by a big bugger who wore a flight lieutenant's cap.

Biffo, the pilot, told us his idea for a career after the war. He was going to buy a Wellington cheap because nobody would want war planes by then. Rip out all internal fittings and install twenty seats. He could then buzz people down to Gibraltar for a holiday on the Med. "Get a couple of poppsies to serve drinks," and he was damned if he could see how it could fail. Listening to Arthur wretch in the darkness made me think I wouldn't be investing in 'Biffo Air'.

We flew at twelve thousand feet over the Atlantic until we reached Bordeaux, then took a dog leg into unoccupied southern France and across the Pyrenees climbing to eighteen thousand to avoid any air traffic from Madrid. Mercifully only seven hours later we landed, without incident, and with Arthur still in the land of the living: just.

It was five fifteen local time when we made our weary way out of the bomber, to be greeted by Major Fox. Our crew made their way to the mess for a well-earned breakfast. We thanked them and wished them luck on the return leg. Biffo confided they were having a couple of nights R&R, and he had brought sunglasses.

Major Fox took us to another dining area where we were fed. Surprisingly, Arthur had got his appetite back. The major then told us to get some sleep, and report to him in room one-zero-nine at fourteen hundred hours. We slept like the dead. At thirteen hundred hours there was a knock on the door and Jose, a civilian batman, greeted us with a "Buenos Dias" and two mugs of sweet tea. He indicated a washroom with a shower, toothbrushes and soft towels, which was far better than Wormwood Scrubs. He then escorted us back to the dining area where we ate scrambled eggs on toast with a delicious coffee, then down a labyrinth of corridors to room one-zero-nine. We were met by Major Fox and another man who was an Arab. He was dressed in what appeared to be a tablecloth wrapped round his waste and a short-sleeved cotton shirt, he also had a skull cap on his head.

"Good afternoon gentlemen," the major greeted us. "I trust you slept well, and have eaten?" We said yes to both. "This is Taheen," he introduced us. "He is a member of MD1, and you can trust him implicitly. He speaks Arabic, French and English and knows the area where you will be going.

"Taheen this is Jimmy," he indicated me. "And Arthur. I am relying on you to get them through their mission." Taheen smiled with the whitest teeth I had ever seen.

"*As salaam ealaykum* Jimmy, *as salaam ealaykum* Arthur." He told us. "It means, peace be upon you, or as you say in English, watcher cock." His grin increased, I liked Taheen.

Major Fox beckoned over to a table where a mock-up of the harbour had been made out of papier mâché; it was rather good. "This is Mers-el-Kébir, the French harbour. At present it contains at least ten battleships and destroyers and numerous smaller gunboats of the French fleet.

"We have a boat for you to travel down to a neighbouring fishing village called Ain El Turk." He pointed to a small town on the Moroccan side of a low mountain range. "The French do not allow civilian boats into their harbour. When you arrive, a lorry will transport you to a safe house in Mers-el-Kébir.

"Taheen will take you to the telephone exchange here." He indicated on the model. "And the two radio masts, here, and in the fort here. There is a military headquarters here where we think your target is hiding. It is only five hundred yards from the exchange, which I understand puts it within your range?" He looked at Arthur who nodded. "The town has French military patrols, but we don't think that they will trouble you. Your equipment has already been stowed on board. I would suggest you check it is all in working order before you depart this evening.

"As you are to become Arab fishermen, I was asked to supply these for you." He went into a backroom and reappeared with what appeared to be two off white dressing gowns that stank of old fish, and two pairs of leather sandals.

Taheen held the clothing up. "This is a Thawb, traditional Arab dress, warm at night, cool in the day, and damn fetching for the ladies. Please take your clothes off." Arthur and I exchanged looks.

Major Fox shook his head. "No false modesty chaps, we want any patrol boat you might encounter to believe you are simple fishermen. If you're wearing a Moss Bros suit, it sort of spoils the deception." We stripped while Taheen helped us with a simple linen undergarment, a cotton shirt and the Thawb, topping the lot with a swathe of head scarfs. He grunted his approval.

"Now you look like Arab, but you are too white. Do not worry my friends, Taheen will soon fix." He produced a bottle and rag and began to apply a lotion. Arthur got the first treatment and as I watched he was transformed into a walnut coloured, bearded Arab. I would not have believed this was Arthur Edmund Allenby Wells of Welling in Kent.

It was then my turn and Taheen applied a liberal dose of stain to my face, hands and legs. "How long will it last?" Arthur asked.

Taheen showed his teeth again. "It does not come off Arthur, but in three months you will look like you have been on smashing foreign holiday, jolly good." The things we do for King and country.

We all walked with Major Fox down to the dock area, I could not believe how many navy ships there were moored there. I suppose this was our stronghold to the Mediterranean, but there must have been at least sixteen huge warships. Amongst them there was a strange fishing boat with a single mast, a raised stern deck and a lateen sail bobbed at anchor.

It was filthy and smelled of rotting fish, I noted the men working there gave her a wide berth. One of the sailors walking past barged me with his shoulder. "Fucking wogs," he told his companion.

Taheen and Major Fox grinned. "Well, there's proof of the pudding," he told us. "Good job, Taheen."

On board the boat, which Taheen told us was called a Dhow was Captain Abdul, he had a belly like a Buddha, receding hair, a large hooked nose, two weeks' stubble and an earring. He spoke only Arabic and addressed us as 'Eenglish'. Taheen spoke to him at length and he nodded and gesticulated until both parties seemed satisfied. Taheen turned and told us everything was ready, but Captain Abdul needed money to buy fuel for the return trip. Major Fox nodded and promised to return with some.

Below decks was surprisingly clean, although the smell of fish was certainly still there. We met the other two members of the crew, Jemmy the engineer and Hamid the cook and general hand. Hamid could speak reasonable English, but Jemmy couldn't. He seemed genuinely pleased when Arthur told him, "*As Salaam ealaykum*," smiling and bobbing while he patted Arthur on the shoulder adding a bit of engine grease to the Thawb. He took us to the forward hold where all our equipment was stowed. I checked the small arms and explosives while Arthur looked over the electronics. I noted an army loudspeaker amongst the technical gear, and wondered why Arthur had packed it. Everything was in good order and we returned to the main deck where Taheen and Captain Abdul were bent over charts. Taheen looked up.

"Jimmy, Arthur, is everything right as nine pence with your equipment?"

We assured him it was, and he then indicated on the charts the route the captain proposed to take. Basically, it was crossing the straights to Ceuta in Morocco, then following the coast to Melilla where we would sail into Algerian waters and dock at Ain El Turk. Major Fox returned with a small leather bag which he gave to Captain Abdul. It contained gold coin which caused the good captain to grin like a Cheshire cat and pump Major Fox's hand. I suspected he had been over paid. The Dhow was fuelled and victualled and Captain Abdul seemed keen to leave, as he would rather travel across the straights in daylight. Major Fox shook our hands, returned to the docks and watched as we slowly chugged out into the Mediterranean.

The straights were busy with many ships but Captain Abdul knew his trade. He turned off the engine, raised the sail and using the offshore winds navigated us towards Africa. He, Hamid and Jemmy worked as an efficient team. I stood on the deck with the warm wind blowing around me and watched the most beautiful sunset I had ever seen. Arthur was below banging around in the hold. I didn't know what he was up to, but it did spoil the tranquillity of the African night. Hamid also went below, and I was soon aware of the delicious smell coming from the galley. I hadn't eaten since our scrambled eggs and became aware of how hungry I was.

We ate on the deck under the stars. It was a large communal pot of lamb stew and another of couscous. Arthur didn't seem that hungry, and I wondered if he was suffering from sea sickness. Taheen gently reminded me only to eat with my right hand. They were all Muslims and the left hand is considered unclean for a shared pot.

It was truly a wonderful meal, and I told Hamid so. He looked pleased, but obviously wondered why Arthur wasn't eating. When I discretely questioned him, he told me he didn't want meat and tapioca. I called him a tit, and put a little of each on his plate. "Eat a little," I told him. "If you still don't want any, I'll have yours." He tentatively took his first mouthful with all four of us poised watching. He chewed, smiled, made a *mmmmm* noise and took another big handful. A sigh came from Hamid, the effendi had educated his palate. We slept on the deck with our three Arab hosts sharing the steering duties.

My Thawb seemed warm enough, but Jemmy threw me a blanket. "It will get colder," Hamid told me. "You need a woman or a blanket, this is the best we can do." I went to sleep feeling more content than I had for years.

Chapter 36
First Blood

The sun rises early off the African coast, and at five o'clock we were awakened by the noises of the boat making ready. Hamid brought us coffee and warm bread, which he served with a sort of strong cottage cheese. The wind dropped and reluctantly Captain Abdul started his engine. It was a beautiful day and I saw two large fish leading the boat. I cried out that sharks were in the water and attacking the boat. When Taheen came to see the problem, he laughed and explained that the creatures were harmless dolphins, and that they were considered lucky. It was an amazing sight and Arthur and I spent half an hour watching them flying as they leaped out of the water. Suddenly as soon as they had appeared, they vanished. I felt like applauding.

We moved at a sedate pace carving a white wake through the blue waters, above us the hot sun beat down from a cloudless sky. Arthur and I sat drinking mint tea on the raised platform, the only shaded area on the deck. At half past ten. Taheen came hurriedly up the steps. "Jimmy, Arthur my friends, there is problem." He pointed towards the horizon. We both looked, but neither of us saw anything. "Look, fast boat come this way. Abdul thinks is navy, a routine check, you will mend nets and say nothing. Maybe French, maybe Italian."

"Maybe they will go past us?" Arthur suggested.

"No, they change course; mend nets and I will tell them we are poor fishermen."

We collected the machine guns and a grenade and hid them beneath the pile of nets. To my surprise Arthur then got me to help carry the sound generator and a radio blocker up to the top deck. We covered them in piles of nets after he had connected wires between them and screwed the loudspeaker to the decking. Captain Abdul did not look pleased, but he said nothing. By now we could see the boat, it was fast and grey and flying the Italian tricolour. It had two torpedo tubes and a heavy machine gun mounted on the front deck.

There were eight men on deck some of them watching us through binoculars. They hailed us with their own loudspeaker, unsurprisingly it was in Italian. Taheen shouted back in Arabic, then French, neither seemed to get a response.

They manoeuvred very close to us and threw ropes which Jemmy reluctantly tied to our rail. Holding his hands up at them Captain Abdul went and fetched Hamid, amongst his other many skills he apparently spoke a little Italian. He came up from his galley, blinking in the sunshine, after a brief conversation with Captain Abdul, he wished the Italians good day and listened while their captain spoke slowly to him.

Taheen came and sat with me and whispered a translation of the Arabic between Hamid and Abdul. They wanted to know what we had been doing. Hamid gave a pantomime shrug, indicated the boat, and told them, "Fishing." The Italian wanted to know where our catch was. Hamid told them that, "It had not been a good night as our idiot of a captain had missed the shoal of sardines we were hoping to sell in the Algerian markets."

The captain of the torpedo boat seemed unimpressed and told Hamid he was sending a boarding party to check our boat. It didn't look good so I pushed a Sten gun across under the nets, to touch Taheen's foot. Arthur then stood up, and gesticulating uncovered the sound generator, he quietly told Hamid to tell the captain about the crate we had dredged up in our nets off Gibraltar. Hamid translated telling of, "A secret radio with many code books. Did the captain wish to buy it? It would compensate us for our poor catch, and it was very cheap." The Italians response was to point a machine gun at Hamid.

Arthur waved his hands. "*Non ce problema, capitano.*" He turned his back and told Hamid to tell them he would demonstrate this wonderful radio, then they would be willing to pay many lira for it. Hamid passed on the message whereupon the captain cocked the gun and pointed it at Arthur. "*Momento capitani,*" Arthur shouted and threw the big switch. The crew on both boats looked as our sound generator started to hum, the noise increased and became uncomfortable. Both crews covered their ears.

As it reached a crescendo the Italian captain made a cutting gesture and shouted to stop, "*Spegnerlo, spegnerlo.*" He was too late.

As always, the machine just stopped, which caught everybody by surprise, the strange spitting noise was accompanied by a wall of water that rushed from our boat to theirs. The port side of their hull buckled and tore, and all the crew were thrown to the deck.

Taheen was instantly on his feet and firing the Sten at the Italian crew, many were hit and fell back to the deck. I grabbed the other gun and caught them in a crossfire, hosing bullets into jerking bodies.

From our raised deck I threw my grenade into their ventilation shaft that went below decks, four seconds Mr Pomeroy said, and he wasn't far off. A huge gout of black smoke came from the engine room as the grenade exploded. By now the ship was sinking fast, the damage caused to the front gave it no hope. Within two minutes all that was left was a stain of oil, a lifebelt and two bodies that were wearing lifejackets, the rest had gone down with the ship. Captain Abdul came to the rail to look, he spat at the remains and said something in Arabic; it wasn't complimentary.

I felt my legs go and had to sit down. We had killed before, but that was accidental, this time I had dispatched at least five men, men that would have had families and lives that I had ended. Arthur sat next to me; he was as white as a sheet. "How did you do that?" I asked him.

He stared down at his feet. "Mr McRae and I made the battery packs interchangeable," he told me. "I didn't know the distance so I just set it all to maximum, Christ Jim, it tore the front of that boat off."

Taheen joined us. "Jolly good, Arthur," he told him. "They would have turned the machine guns on us, they sink many Arab boats, it is done for sport. Shokran Lak my friend, we owe you, our lives. I told you the dolphins were lucky."

Captain Abdul passed, patting Arthur on the shoulder. "Shokran Lak effendi, Thank you." We moved off.

Hamid and Jemmy came to look in awe at our generator. They understood guns, but something that could sink a metal boat with sound was an anathema to them. We had released a Jinni on board their boat and that was not a matter to be taken lightly. We packed the equipment away, ditching the destroyed speaker over the side. Although the atmosphere was now subdued, we kept a lookout with sharp eyes. Thankfully, the horizon remained empty. By six o'clock the captain steered us into harbour at Ain El Turk. Taheen went ashore and, within half an hour, an old lorry with much of its original paint work gone arrived at the dock.

A customs official also approached and Captain Abdul invited him aboard. He was given tea, the blessings of Allah and a small bag of gold while Taheen's two men loaded our equipment into the lorry. Apparently, the customs man was a great friend of Captain Abdul, and the pair had grown wealthy smuggling goods into Ain El Turk.

We made our farewells and joined Taheen and his men. The lorry, which I noted had the steering wheel on the wrong side, took us first to the fish market where Taheen purchased a lot of fish that was just on the turn. Crates of the stinking stuff were loaded on top of our equipment: it really didn't encourage investigation. We then took the coastal road across a range of steep hills. Driving with only one low powered headlight, we arrived two hours later at the town of Mers-El Kébir.

There was a check point on the approach road, and a French sailor waved us down. He asked to see Taheen's papers, and despite the smell asked what we had on board. Taheen threw open the tarpaulin and with his best dazzling smile showed the unfortunate sailor our cargo. "Fish," Taheen told him in French. He then took one of the largest and ugliest of the catch and presented it to the matelot. "For you my friend, so that you might have a full belly," he told him. The sailor declined, took a step back, and waved us through. We had arrived.

The streets of Mers-el-Kébir were narrow. There was no pavement and houses opened directly on to them. Cooking smells came from numerous open fires, and many dark faces glanced at us as we manoeuvred slowly through the labyrinth. There was a rapid exchange between Taheen and his friends as the lorry ground to a halt. The fish was unloaded and vanished as crowds came to claim a free meal. We then drove on, turning into a cul-de-sac where, as soon as we stopped, a door opened and our crates and equipment vanished inside. Taheen led us in and closed the door behind him when we heard the lorry depart. It was dark and cool inside and smelt of jasmine. A single hooded figure sat on a low couch. This, said Taheen, with a certain reverence is Aled

Alemna. The figure rose and turned to face Arthur, there was a brief pause. "Well, fuck me, you took your own sweet time Arthur Wells," Aled Alemna said, and kissed him hard on his astonished lips.

Chapter 37
Betrayal

Taheen and I exchanged astonished glances. It's just not a thing you expect when on a top-secret mission and a long way from home. Arthur back-peddled and fell over the couch, he was never good with physical contact and this was both unexpected and extreme. He stared up at the figure as she slowly reached up, and with the metal hook attached to her left wrist pulled the hood from her face. It was Janet Thompson. Older, more careworn, in desperate need of a good wash; but Janet Thompson from Welling in Kent. "Hello, Arthur," she said. Arthur was beyond compiling a reply.

Taheen spoke. "You know Aled Alemna!?" he asked incredulously.

"Oh yes, Arthur and I go back a long way," she replied. "Hello, Jimmy, how are you?"

I think I said, "Fine, good, yes," which is not bad considering my jaw was hanging open.

"May I prevail upon your hospitality for tea," Janet asked Taheen. "I owe these two an explanation."

Taheen fetched refreshments and we settled down for a night of long and complex explanations. Janet went first and told us her story. She had been rescued from Spain after her amputation. There were several sympathetic organisations to aid the various foreigners who had come to fight. Her friend, Jose Fernandez, had managed to get a group to extract her from the Cordoba hospital, after the doctor was satisfied she was fit to be moved. An elderly couple had taken her and travelled the one hundred and eighty miles south to Gibraltar with her in a donkey cart. Although there were still patrols on the road, they managed to avoid arrest by simply dying her skin with a blue tinge, and giving her a small jar of pigs' blood. They explained that their daughter was sick with fever, she had nosebleeds and coughing. What should they do? There were enough of Franco's men who remembered the symptoms of the 1920 Spanish flu pandemic, and consequently left them well alone.

On reaching Gibraltar she had at first been refused entry. As she said she, "didn't look like an English girl from Kent and seemed to have mislaid her passport." A Major Fox had become involved after she broke a sentry's nose. She had given the major the benefit of her Anglo-Saxon vocabulary, which convinced him she was genuine. Spanish ladies do not know words like that.

Taheen giggled. "She was very bad lady, telling Major Fox he should perform many unnatural acts." Major Fox was no fool and, realising the potential of having a female operative in North Africa, recruited her into MD1.

She was treated in the hospital and fitted with a prosthetic hook. There then followed many weeks of field training before she was sent on operations in Morocco, Algeria and Tunisia. She had become competent in Arabic, and often travelled with Taheen building a formidable reputation as Aled Alemna, the Right Hand. A week ago, she had been instructed to meet two new agents that Taheen would bring and assist them with Operation Joshua. It wasn't until she received the details including their names that she too had gasped in incredulity. She laughed and said, "If only Judy was with us, we could all go down the Kasbah for dinner."

Taheen nodded and told us, "Allah Hakim," which means God is wise. We then sat until the early hours telling Janet and Taheen our story. The killing of Ian Brown with our sound generator, the arrest, Wormwood Scrubs, our recruitment and training by Major Jefferis and our dispatch to Mers-el-Kébir. Taheen greatly appreciated the story, rocking and clicking his fingers in merriment, telling us this was truly kismet and our destinies were obviously entwined. Allah Hakim.

Eventually we all became too tired to continue and Taheen showed us our individual bedrooms. I don't know where Arthur spent the night, and it seemed wrong to enquire. The fact that at breakfast he and Janet had huge grins on their faces might just have been coincidental.

Today was the thirtieth of June which gave us two and a half days to execute our mission, and half a day to escape. Arthur laid out his big map of Mers-el-Kébir, and Taheen indicated where we were and the locations of the exchange, radio mast, Fort Santon and the naval headquarters. Janet was to take up a position near the naval building, where she could observe. Taheen indicated it. It was a strange map symbol that I didn't recognise and asked what it was.

He told me it was a minaret, a tall tower for calling the faithful to prayer built next to the mosque. It overlooked the naval building and was visible from the exchange. If we managed to kill Montfort, she would drape a red scarf from the balcony, which we would be able to see.

We needed to carry out the assassination first, as we needed the communications network intact to do so. The exchange seemed ideally placed to install the sound generator. Taheen told us he had a friend who worked there who would get us in and locate the right cable pair, as all records would be in Arabic. We both looked a little sheepish, neither of us had thought of that. At nine o'clock the lorry returned, and we loaded up. Taheen gave the driver a hug, they obviously knew each other well, there was no one else with him so the five of us drove slowly to the telephone exchange. We dropped Janet off at the minaret and continued to the exchange.

We decided it would be best to reconnoitre the exchange before setting up our heavy equipment. Our plan relied on assumptions that we both wanted to verify. Taheen went to the main door and knocked, it was opened by his colleague who kissed him on both cheeks and beckoned Arthur and I inside. We carried in our weapons and explosives. The driver stayed with our lorry. It was cool inside and after much shaking of hands we were introduced to Mohamed, "*As salaam ealaykum.*"

We told Taheen we wanted to see the underground cable chamber where the cables came into the building. To our huge relief Mohamed nodded vigorously and beckoned. Strangely there didn't seem to be any other members of staff around. He unlocked a metal door and turned the lights on, again beckoning us to follow down the stairs. As we reached the floor, a group of four men stepped out from behind a pillar, two, had guns pointing at us. They were French sailors, an officer, a sergeant and two seamen. Mohamed did a sort of bow to Taheen, I didn't know what he said, but I think it was an explanation for his betrayal. He then scuttled over to stand behind the French. We dropped our bags.

The officer spoke English. "You are spies and I am placing you under arrest, raise your hands. If you resist, I have orders to kill you." Mr Pomeroy's training cut in and I realised I had already assessed the situation.

The sergeant had not yet cocked the machine pistol, the officer's gun was pointing at my knees and the two seamen were old hands at street fighting. They had scar tissue on their faces and callused knuckles.

Suddenly Arthur screamed at the top of his voice while pointing back at the stairs "No, for Christ's sake don't." You would have had to been inhuman not to turn and look what he was shouting about. They weren't, and it was their undoing.

Taheen drew a small pistol and shot Mohamed in the forehead. Blood and brains sprayed out behind him as he collapsed on the floor. I grabbed the officer by his gun hand, pulling hard forward, he stumbled and could not raise the pistol. I grabbed my knife from the sheath on my left forearm and in one fluid movement slashed it across his throat. It severed both his internal and external jugular veins. He instinctively dropped the gun and held both hands to his wound. It did not help, and he sprayed blood four feet while making a horrible wheezing scream. Arthur moved towards the sergeant who was desperately trying to draw the slide back on his machine gun. He hit his opponent's gun with his left hand driving it to the sergeant's left. Despite this he managed to fire a short burst before Arthur was behind him and snapped his neck with a vicious head lock twist.

It was now two against two. I hoped Taheen might have used his pistol, but a brief glance revealed him slumped and bloody. The sailors had now both drawn knives and adopted the stance of experienced fighters. These men were veterans of a hundred street fights. We paired off and I realised my opponent was very good. A brief skirmish left me with a stinging wound across the bicep on my left arm. We closed again and although I managed to draw blood on his inner thigh I again was left with a shallow cut to my side. He swore at me in French, made a feint for my face and swung his boot. I instinctively threw my head back but he managed to catch me with a lucky kick to the knee and I fell heavily. I knew with a sickening certainty that I was going to die; I could not get up to defend myself. From where I lay, I saw Arthur perform the same move I had last seen at Bletchley Park. He grasped his opponent's knife hand, whirled round so they were front to back and then keeping their arms rigid he took a crouching step forward throwing the Frenchman high enough to scrape his heels on the ceiling before bringing him down head first on to the concrete floor. He used the momentum to somersault across the floor and slash his knife across my man's Achilles tendons. With a scream of agony, the sailor fell beside me, he managed to turn his head and look at me before Arthur plunged the knife into his right eye. I saw the light go out in the other. As Mr Pomeroy said, "A natural fighter."

I laid there feeling numb, Arthur scrabbled across to Taheen and propped him up, he looked over at me and shook his head. Taheen had been shot twice in the chest. He was dead.

We managed to climb back upstairs and found a first aid kit. Arthur bandaged my wounds and we assessed our situation. The driver spoke no English, all the records were in Arabic, we were dead in the water as far as our original plan was concerned. We were covered in blood and the French must know that we were here. On the plus side we were alone and probably had at least an hour before the authorities came looking for us. I cautiously opened the front door and breathed a huge sigh of relief; the lorry and driver were parked thirty yards away. As my Thawb had less blood on it than Arthur's I waited until the street was empty, ran to the van and banged on the driver's door. It made him jump, but my wild gesticulations got the message across, 'come with me, come with me'. We dashed back inside together.

His face spoke volumes, it was fairly obvious what had happened and he spoke one word, "Taheen?" Arthur shook his head and took him to the cable chamber door, as he gazed down at the carnage his eyes filled with tears. He sought for the word, then told us, "Brother." I touched both hands to my heart and lowered my eyes to try and convey we too had lost a friend. After a moment he looked at us, grasped the edge of Arthur's gore splattered robe and shook his head. He pointed to the door and made a stay gesture with both hands. He then went out closing the door behind him.

We decided, that although the assassination was now impossible, we still had time to destroy the exchange. We descended into the cable chamber stepping round the bodies and collected our explosives bag. Cables came in from the east and west, the sea was to the north and the south wall was empty. I showed Arthur what I wanted, a piece of plastic the size of a small apple fused and pushed into the duct mouth. The duct was made of earthenware pipe and would concentrate the blast. There were sixteen ducts on each of the two walls. After twenty minutes we had a charge in each one. I took four larger pieces and attached them to the support pillars.

We heard noises and went to investigate with our Sten guns. It was Taheen's brother and bless him he had brought two new Thawbs. We wrapped Taheen in the old clothing and carried him to the lorry now parked directly outside. I set the pencil fuses for four minutes and locked the exchange door behind us. We again tried to communicate, we used the word minaret which didn't seem to register, but then Arthur said, "Aled Alemna," and realisation dawned. The lorry moved off and as it rounded the corner there was a huge thump as the exchange cable chamber imploded. Telephones in Mers-el-Kébir had suddenly ceased to function.

Chapter 38
Death Rays and Explosives

Several police cars and a fire engine passed us going the opposite way as we headed for the minaret. They were speeding toward the column of smoke that marked where the exchange had been and were far too busy to pay any attention to an old lorry. When we reached the street with the minaret on it, Janet was waiting at the corner. She was squatting with a lady selling vegetables, helping to fan the flies away. As soon as she saw the lorry, she bade the lady goodbye and climbed in. Our faces must have given away our story, she spoke only one word, "Taheen?" His brother threw his arms round her and wept. She comforted him making almost maternal noises as she stroked his back. Her face was also wet with tears, and she had gone pale with shock. We asked that she would tell Taheen's brother that we would greatly miss him, and that he was truly a brave and honourable friend. She spoke softly still holding him, she told us his name was Malik and he thanked us for our kind words.

She started to explain that she had become worried and left the tower as it was nearly noon. Just as I stupidly said, "Why noon?" an awful noise started. It was a cacophony of out of tune nasal singing and it was very loud. It came from the tower above our heads.

"Because," Janet shouted, "that's when they call the faithful to prayer." Sure enough, the street began to fill with Muslims making their way to the mosque. She explained that the 'Muezzin' called five times a day for the faithful to attend the mosque: dawn, noon, afternoon, sunset and nightfall, and he would not wish to share his beacon with a one-handed Christian woman. Arthur got out and stared up at the minaret.

"Where are Montfort's offices?" he asked. Janet pointed to a group of flat roofed building fifty yards away on the other side of the road. A high barbed wire fence surrounded them.

"That's the French navy HQ. Gensoul and Montfort have the highest block near the road. It has large windows, and if the blinds are up you

234

can just see into it from the tower. You won't get inside, it's too well guarded, and he has stayed in there since the Algerians tried to kill him."

Arthur nodded. "Could I get a look up the tower when the man has finished singing?"

She told him we would have to wait until prayers were finished, but she had a key and could get him up when it was empty. We climbed back in the truck and waited. An hour later Janet decided it would be safe and she took Arthur round to a back door where they were able to gain access to the top balcony. He took a notebook and pencil with him. Twenty minutes later they were back with Malik and I. Arthur asked if we could go back to the house as he needed to do some work. Janet asked Malik and he nodded, taking us back but avoiding the police and fire brigade at the exchange. We offloaded all the equipment, and let Malik take his brother for burial after asking him to return at nine o'clock tomorrow. Janet held him and kissed him between the eyes.

Janet took me into the kitchen and inspected my wounds, neither were too serious, but she decided my arm needed stitching. She found a needle and thread which I had to thread for her. Despite my protests she put four stitches in my arm. It really hurt and Arthur didn't help by grinning like a Cheshire cat while I suffered. We prepared a light meal from food Janet and I found in the kitchen. Arthur locked himself away with a slide rule, the big map and the notes he had taken earlier. After we had eaten, he asked Janet if she could get a small block and tackle, the sort of thing used to lift engines out of cars. She said that she thought she could. He then asked if she knew a time when Montfort would be in the office block but Gensoul would be out.

She told him, "Gensoul preferred to spend his days aboard his flagship in the harbour, and Montfort had consequently taken over the whole top floor at the HQ." This appeared to be good news and Arthur returned to his calculations leaving us to do the washing up.

Janet and I reminisced about Welling, Judy, The Railway Arms and life in a more gentle time. I asked if she would return and, after a bit of reflection, she admitted that life would be very dull after becoming 'the Right Hand', but loosing Taheen had hit her hard, they had been friends for a long time. Arthur joined us again in the evening, and Janet produced a bottle of brandy and a packet of cigarettes, a rare treat in Algeria.

Although we had abstained from cigarettes since our training days the temptation proved irresistible, and we both lit up feeling both a little guilty and a little nauseous.

Realising we were becoming too maudlin Janet drew our attention to the rest of the mission. Surprisingly Arthur had hopes that we could still complete everything MD1 had wanted. In a moment of silence Janet asked why we had to close down both radio masts. Arthur, back in his element, explained that if we just closed down one, all traffic would automatically divert from military to civilian and vice versa. It was an automatic process.

Janet considered. "What would happen if one of the masts was, oh I don't know, struck by lightning?"

Arthur looked puzzled. "I just told you everything would be automatically transferred to the other mast."

"Then why are we blocking out both?" she said. "We are splitting our resources and doubling the risk of capture by having to stay close to two failing radio masts, they're bound to send people to check. Why don't we blow up one and turn the remaining one on and off as requested?" Sometimes when confronted with the obvious you can feel really stupid. These orders had come from MD1 planning and they were flawed, Janet was perfectly right.

"How much explosive have we got left Jim?" Arthur asked. I went and collected our bag,

"About two pounds, that's just about enough to knock down a mast," I told him. "And we have eight assorted fuses." Arthur studied our map.

"This one," he said. "It's next to a sports' field so less civilian casualties, and the other one is in the fort at the top of the hill. That has roads round it where we could hide the truck."

It made sense. "We'll do it first thing tomorrow." Janet said.

"No, I want to go straight back to the tower," Arthur told us. "We'll do the radio mast after, when the authorities are diverted." I was starting to ache all over, so I diplomatically told them I was off to bed.

We had coffee and the last of the bread for breakfast, just before Malik came to collect us. We loaded everything up and Janet told him Arthur wanted a chain hoist, neither knew the equivalent word and we were stuck until Arthur drew a sketch and mimed lifting an engine out. Malik clapped his hands. "*Selsla Rafaa,*" he told us. We diverted to a garage, Malik went in and came out ten minutes later with an old hoist, it had a ratchet handle with a large hook and a length of chain with a smaller one on the end. He told Janet the owner was a cousin and would ask no questions.

At nine thirty the minaret was quiet and deserted. We offloaded the hoist, sound generator and a battery pack, but stubbornly Arthur wouldn't tell us what his plan was yet. Malik parked the lorry at the end of the road, then came back to join us. He helped Arthur carry everything up to the minaret balcony as my arm wasn't up to heavy lifting. Once on the balcony we were virtually invisible to the street below which helped significantly. While Malik and Arthur caught their breath, Janet turned to face them. "All right Arthur, what are we doing?" Janet demanded. We all looked at him.

He composed himself and polishing his glasses explained. "The machine has two ways to project a concentrated sound wave. Through a cable and through the air. We had planned to send it down a telephone line, but because we couldn't identify the right cable that was abandoned, and anyway we have destroyed the exchange so nobody has a working phone any more. I used our only speaker on the Italian gun boat, but yesterday I heard those." He pointed to the four heavy duty speakers mounted on the minaret. Obvious when it's pointed out to you! I studied them; they were bolted to the walls with hefty looking pieces of iron work. They faced all four points of the compass and were of sturdy construction. Unfortunately, they were all out of reach.

Arthur pointed. "There's a junction box there. It will take the microphone lead and split it into four. Disconnect that speaker and run a lead over to me." He indicated the one facing the French military buildings. "Now, Janet, can you ask Malik to put the small hook of the hoist on the bracket where it joins the building." He had three attempts, but nearly fell each time. Janet came up with the solution. She got Malik and I to form the base of a human triangle which she clambered up to attach the hook. I took the small tool kit we had brought and separated the cable of the north facing speaker.

Meanwhile, Arthur checking his calculations positioned the hoist on the railing about twenty inches to the left of the bracket. He marked the rail and told Malik and I to hold the hoist at that exact spot. We took up the slack chain, and Arthur very slowly began to pump the ratchet. Nothing seemed to happen at first, but slowly the speaker began to move. It swung down and across. Arthur took several sightings until he was satisfied.

He then transferred the hoist four feet further along the rail. We started again, and as if by magic the speaker swung to face the navy building, we thought Montfort was in. He checked twice, then looked up wiping the sweat away. "That's about as good as I can get it," he told us. The brackets looked the worse for wear and we had lost a bolt but were still attached. Arthur turned to Janet and I. "Right tell Malik to get the hoist back in the truck and I'll finish up here." He used the tool kit to connect the battery and the speaker to the sound generator and inserted his precious crystal.

Janet and I made it back to the truck, we could just see the roof of the building from where we sat. "Do you think Montfort will be in there?" I asked.

Janet shrugged. "I just don't know Jimmy." As she spoke, we felt a change in the air pressure. My ears began to hurt and I noticed both Janet and Malik trying to cover out the intrusive noise.

It suddenly stopped and we witnessed the effect of the generator from a different angle. A shimmering wave of dust and light came from the minaret. It struck the building too high up and tore the roof off, but as we watched it lurched and dropped lower causing the walls to collapse. The noise was horrific as the entire building collapsed in a giant cloud of dirt and debris.

Malik and Janet sat open mouthed; I had forgotten they had never witnessed the effect of Arthur's death ray. It still scared me, but this was the fifth time I had seen its destructive power. I knew they probably didn't believe what they had just witnessed. I jumped from the cab and ran to the back of the minaret. Arthur appeared out of the dust and he looked like he had just been deloused at the Scrubs apart from a trickle of bright blood down his face. He was carrying the battery pack in both arms. I grabbed him and pushed him up behind Malik. "Go!" I shouted doing an appropriate gesture. A large piece of masonry had fallen across the road so he had to do a three-point turn.

Sirens were sounding, people milling around confused and curious, French navy personnel were staggering out of the gate trying to escape. Everybody was grey from the dust. We headed away from the scene just as another smaller explosion came from above us. Arthur had blown up his generator; nobody else would ever use it.

I told Malik to head for the second radio mast as every emergency service in town was heading for us. We drove slowly and considerately away, giving way to the rescue vehicles. I would have believed it was a bomb if I had not known differently, and I'm sure everyone else did. Janet used a bit of rag to clean Arthur's face; she mopped the blood up from where a piece of masonry had split his eyebrow. I wondered if he would need stitching?

He explained that his original aim for the speaker had been too high, but as the generator shook the minaret, the bracket had given way causing the sound wave to hose down the building, causing massive structural damage. Even if Montfort had survived, he was not going to be available to advise the Admiral for quite a while.

Forty minutes later we parked outside the radio station. There was a building at the base of the radio mast with several thick cables coming from it. Everything was surrounded by a high barbed wire fence with warnings in Arabic and French forbidding entry. I saw no reason why it would be manned so indicated to Malik to back the lorry up to the gate. I then attached the chain hoist to the lorry's tow bar and the gate door. Malik ripped it away. We carried the wrecked gate round the back of the mast to find ourselves looking at a deserted football pitch. Perfect!

We all agreed that removing the back left leg would cause the mast to fall on the pitch. It looked a bit like a picture I had seen of the Eifel tower, and I decided the best place for the charge would be just above the base, about twenty-five feet up. There were ladders all the way to the top, but the bottom trap door was locked. I had seen it done countless times at the pictures; the hero shoots his gun at the padlock which then springs open. I sat on the lorry roof and Malik manoeuvred me under the trap door. I then cocked the Sten and fired a single shot at the padlock, I missed. I tried again firing a short burst, one or two hit the lock but ricocheted uncomfortably close to Arthur and Janet. They ran out of range and in pure frustration I gave it a longer burst. In fairness it worked, but caused Malik to berate me in Arabic, gesticulating at two holes in the roof and floor of the truck. Sorry Malik!

He climbed with me to the second stage, and we strapped the last of the explosive inside the angle iron. I chose an eight-minute fuse, snapped the casing and went down in a hurry. We all managed to get in the cab, and back on the road, Malik reversed the lorry anxious to go, but we had to make sure before driving off. Eight minutes can seem a very long time, but as we sat in nervous silence there was suddenly a dull thump from the mast and it slowly and quite elegantly crumpled on to the football pitch. I hoped they didn't have a home game on Saturday.

We were just about to drive away when a portly middle-aged man appeared from nowhere and shouted indignantly at Malik. He stood blocking our way. Janet started to reply, but it had been a long day and I wanted to get home, so I climbed out of the cab and emptied my Sten gun over his head. He moved surprisingly fast for a man of his age and weight.

Chapter 39
Merde!

We were lucky and didn't run into any patrols on our way back. The plan had been to let Malik and Janet talk us out of it, but if necessary, Arthur and I would use the Sten guns: nobody wanted that. Once in the house, Janet closed all the shutters and gave Malik an encoded message, he was heading off to Ain el Turk on business and had access to a secret radio transmitter they used to communicate with Gibraltar.

Janet made mint tea and asked Malik to stay for a while and advise us on the final attack, as there was one more element of our plan to carry out. We had to disconnect the radio transmissions from Fort Santon at specified times. The fort was a medieval stone building, built to command the harbour as a look out and later a gun platform. It was now the main French radio station, situated at the top of the range of hills that separated Ain el Turk from Mers-el-Kébir. There wasn't a big military force there, but due to our recent activities they were on high alert. The signals men lived in quarters, inside the walls.

Using Janet to translate, we discussed our two options. Often when you speak them out loud, you realise there is actually only the one. The signal blocker had to be within sixty yards of the mast. That meant either plan A, where we could either drive round the perimeter of the fort or park next to it. Malik did the sums, the outer perimeter track was about two miles long, and we estimated being there for eight hours. Travelling at twenty miles per hour, that would mean eighty laps of the fort; he thought they might notice! Plan B then. This was to get inside the fort and hide with the signal blocker, turning it on and off as required. We would, therefore, need a reason to be there. Janet asked Malik what he thought. He told us there was nothing that we could say to persuade the sentry to let us in. Everything would be checked, and double checked. There were terrorists about. Through Janet I asked if there was any way he could get us inside. He thought, and then told Janet it would be better if we were called to deal with some emergency. His friend was a plumber and twice had been called to unblock drains on the main French camp.

If we could get in and block the drains, it was almost certain they would be desperate for plumbers the next day. They would probably welcome us with a kiss on both cheeks. If we intercepted the real men, we could take their place and spend the day digging up drains.

It sounded feasible. Janet asked if we had any ideas how to cause a big enough problem with the sanitation? Arthur asked Malik if he knew anything about drains. His look didn't need translation. He spoke to Janet. He knew there was a toilet block and living quarters near the mast, and that there were manhole covers near them. She translated verbatim, "Shit goes down small pipes into manhole, manhole feeds shit to bigger manhole and bigger manhole has pipe to sea." It didn't seem that complicated. Arthur suggested one of our remaining grenades with a fuse pencil. We had two left, with a twenty minute setting. If he removed the original fuse, it would still detonate the grenade but twenty minutes after we had gone. If we could wedge it in the pipe to the big manhole it should cause a pretty nasty blockage. The fact it was three feet underground should muffle the explosion enough for it to go unnoticed. Malik told us we would need to do this tonight as it would take time for the sewage to build up. We needed the sort of problem that you couldn't mask with potpourri.

He told us we would need to climb the outer wall. This, he assured us, was an easy job as it was only forty feet high and Allah would protect us, which was a lie. A forty-foot ascent in the dark is not easy! He also told us we would need better shoes and asked what size we were. Making a list he decided we would also need a good length of rope, manhole keys, a ladder to assist the climb, and a map that he would draw for us. Janet gave him money and he went out. His parting smile was reminiscent of Taheen.

We had very little food left so Janet decided she would go to the market. "A single woman would not cause suspicion," she told us, and could pick up the gossip about the attacks from the other shoppers. We waited until sundown then, dressed in the black robes of an abaya, she took a basket and headed out for the kasbah.

While Janet was out, we did an inventory of our munitions. All the explosive had been used but we had five fuses left. The Sten guns had three magazines containing ninety-six rounds and there were three grenades. Not enough to go to war, but we could deter most attempts at arrest. In addition, we had the two radio blockers each with a battery pack.

Janet returned an hour later laden down with food. We had bread and cake, assorted vegetables, dates, meat that didn't look familiar and two bottles of wine that she had traded a silk head scarf for. It was a local product that we realised was an acquired taste.

We helped her unpack as she told us the news from the market. Opinion was that the Germans had blown up the exchange, an Italian plane had bombed the French naval building and the mosque, but no Algerians had been injured. *Allah Azim*. Algerian agitators had retaliated by blowing up the radio mast and attempting to murder Mr Azziz the football club caretaker. I was relieved it meant the authorities wouldn't be doing a house-to-house search.

We moved into the kitchen, and Janet started to prepare a meal. Despite her having only one hand, she was extremely dexterous and soon the smell of a spicy meat stew began to fill the room. As if drawn by the aroma, Malik returned. We laid an extra place, and offered him a glass of the local wine, he declined the alcohol but tore off a large piece of bread, displaying his gleaming teeth.

When Janet came in carrying the pot, he produced two sheets of paper, a message sent by Major Fox. "Eat first, I'll deal with that after," she said. A good decision, the food was delicious. Malik drank water which given the alternative was probably a wise decision.

We finished with a plate of dates and strong coffee. Then while we cleared up, Janet took a bible and vanished into a bedroom. I must have looked a bit puzzled; Janet had never been religious. Arthur shook his head. "She's not going to pray you idiot, that will be the code book." A Christian woman travelling with a bible might not be approved off, but it was understandable. You wouldn't question a Muslim with a Koran after all.

Arthur explained they would have a pre-set text every day. The sender would write out his message, then one letter at a time, change it to a letter from the code book. Those letters were then returned to plain text using the exact same decode page.

We cleared away and Malik produced a packet of French cigarettes, although we had both agreed that last night's lapse was a one off, we once again weakened and accepted one. They were eye watering filthy things that smelt unlike anything we had tried before, but there was no alternative. When Arthur coughed, Malik grinned and said, "Excuses *ils sont affreux.*"

Arthur turned and catching Malik's shoulders asked, "*Vous parlez Francais?*"

Malik shrugged and told him, "*Bien sur, mon pays est occupe, si je ne peux leur parler, je n'ai rien.*"

"What did he say?" I asked.

"I think he said that the cigarettes are shit, and when I asked if he spoke French, he said he had to because his country is occupied. I've probably got words wrong, but I think that's the gist of it."

Janet reappeared with the message. "Malik speaks French," I told her. She didn't seem surprised.

"Most Algerians can, it makes years of being under enforced French rule more tolerable and few French can speak Arabic." She then sat us down and began to explain what the third would bring.

There was a list of times when they wanted the radio masts on or off, allowing them to be able to communicate with Admiral Gensoul when they chose, but ensuring he could not seek advice. It started at noon. Force H, a large part of the British fleet, would sit offshore as a threat, and a representative would be sent ashore to present Churchill's ultimatum. Hopefully the French ships would then sail under escort to British ports, and we could return to Ain El Turk where Captain Abdul would take us back to Gibraltar. "What happens if they don't?" I asked. "Will the navy fire on them, could be a hell of a battle."

Janet shook her head. "That would have to be a last resort, surely Gensoul couldn't be that stupid, could he!"

At one o'clock we dressed in black clothing that Janet had supplied, put on the new rubber soled shoes Malik had bought and strapped the knives to our belts. We then headed out leaving Janet behind. Once out of Mers-el-Kébir we took the mountain road to Ain El Turk but took a right turn near the summit. Malik turned the single headlight off, and we drove slowly in the darkness.

The road we were on went directly to the main gate, so Malik turned off left and followed the castle wall. We came to section where the masonry turned nearly ninety degrees and the wall was lower than that of the main structure.

Malik parked close to the angle in the wall, and produced a ladder, tools, and a length of rope. He put the ladder on the roof, which left us about fifteen feet to climb. Despite his earlier reassurances and the protection of Allah, it wasn't easy. Arthur went first carrying the rope. The stone was weather beaten and the desert winds had eroded several handholds, but in the pitch black we struggled. Arthur hit on the idea of bracing his feet on either sides of the angle and pulling himself up with his arms. It seemed to work, until his left foot slipped, sending masonry cascading down on me. He hung precariously for several seconds until I hissed instructions of where the footholds were. It dawned on me that if he did fall, I was directly underneath him, and cursed Malik for his stupid idea. Eventually Arthur reached the top, made the rope secure and helped me climb it. We both lay panting on the top.

Arthur tugged the rope, and Malik tied a canvas sack to it, which we heaved up. We then lowered the rope inside the fort with the bag still attached and climbed down keeping our feet on the wall. It was dark and deserted, so Arthur produced Malik's map and a small electric torch. I recognised the mast silhouetted against the light of the town and, taking bearings from it, directed Arthur toward the living quarters. Although it was now two o'clock there were more lights here and we had to keep to the shadows.

Once we found the toilet block it was clear where the drains ran. I pointed at a manhole twenty-five feet away that was going in the direction of the sea. Arthur nodded and whispered he had thought of a good place to hide our radio blocker. He then produced a manhole key to lift the lid. Bracing ourselves we took one side of the key each and lifted. The smell was appalling, even with the drains unblocked. Twenty-four smaller ducts fed in from the left, and one larger one exited to the right. The bottom of the manhole was full of shit up to the lower edge of this pipe. Breathing through my mouth, I produced the grenade. I was just unscrewing the fuse when we heard the noise of talking and footsteps, it was the French night patrol.

We both lay flat in the shadows, and I noticed Arthur had drawn his knife. I desperately tried to signal not to attack, if we left bodies behind there was no way we could get in tomorrow. As they approached there was a sudden change in the conversation. The expression for 'What the hell is that awful smell?' is pretty universal, and understandably they were both reluctant to approach.

"*Oh Jesus, ce sont les toilets,*" the man nearest me said.

"*Il pue de la merde,*" his partner agreed. They both turned and walked away. They wanted no part in dealing with the awful smell, and apparently were going to use the, 'It was fine when I left it,' excuse. After five minutes listening until we could no longer hear them, we got up. I resumed priming the grenade, and when I was satisfied handed it to Arthur.

"What?" he said.

"You've got to push it up the duct and break the fuse pencil," I told him.

"Why me?" he said. "I don't want to climb down there."

I'm sure when I am an old man, I shall be able to amuse my grandchildren with the story of how I lost a game of Stone, Paper, Scissors while hiding in an enemy fort. I will also tell them how I lowered myself knee deep into sewerage because my best friend Arthur decided to choose rock to my scissors. Bastard! I broke the fuse, pushed the grenade as far as I could and clambered out. I did not smell nice.

We swung the manhole lid back on, and quickly made it back to our rope. Reversing the procedure we climbed to the top, hauled the bag up then lowered it to Malik. We doubled the rope round a protruding rock and using both sides got back to the ladder before pulling one side to recover it. Malik kept sniffing with an expression of complete disgust. Arthur just pointed at me.

Malik would not let me in the cab, and insisted I ride in the back. I heard the French word '*Merde*', repeated, with an accompanying gesture of him holding his nose. We made a hasty retreat to the main road and swung left towards Mers-el-Kébir. I checked my watch and realised the grenade must have gone off by now, so either it had failed, or it had not caused the guard to turn out. I didn't much care which.

Malik drove to the sea and made me wash the worst of it off. I still stank, but now I was also wet. I swore vengeance on Arthur. We got back without running into any patrols, and at three fifteen Malik parked. Janet had waited up, and was extremely relieved that we were all unharmed, and the mission was hopefully a success.

While we were trying to tell her about the adventure, she went and ran a bath for me. She also told me to put all my clothes in a sack, which she intended to wash. Arthur gave me the last of the Algerian wine which was still awful, but I didn't care. Malik decided to stay the night, as he was tired and we needed to be waiting on the approach road early.

Chapter 40
Open Fire

Janet woke me with coffee at six. Malik and Arthur were already up and loading the truck, everything had to go as this was our last day and we weren't coming back. Malik came in, he had been topping the radiator up as the lorry had a tendency to overheat. He sniffed me and indicated I was much improved from last night by pretending to hold a flower under his nose. Arthur entered in time to witness this, but wisely said nothing other than, "Morning kid." I grunted and finished the coffee.

Janet fed us bread, dates, more coffee and a sticky honey cake for breakfast. She suggested we drive to the fork where the approach track to the fort split from the main Ain El Turk Road. Anyone going down there was heading for the fort, there was nowhere else to go. She suggested that we jack the truck up and remove a wheel which would give us a legitimate reason to be parked. At half past seven we were in position and waiting for an Algerian plumber to arrive. The heat was particularly fierce today, and we sat in the shade of the truck discussing what the day would bring and sipping water. It was a long wait, and I think both Arthur and I had given up hope. Malik told us all would be well, plumbers do not rush in Algeria, they were far too important. "Be at peace. It is the will of Allah," he told me. There was nothing I could do, so I made myself comfortable and dozed off, I had not had a lot of sleep.

A half hour later I was awakened by another truck grinding towards us. This time Allah had smiled on us because the plumber was Malik's friend, he flagged them down and they greeted each other with affection. The French had sent a motorcycle to summons him as no phones were yet working. The despatch rider had told him, "Most urgent, the drains were intolerable, and the rewards would be substantial." He had therefore finished his breakfast, collected his two men and eventually headed for the fort.

There was much shaking of hands as Malik introduced us. They seemed particularly impressed with Aled Alemna and had heard many tales of her bravery in the fight to free Algeria. Her reputation was our passport to success. Malik persuaded our new friends to lend us plumbing equipment and turn back to Mers-el-Kébir.

Janet proffered money to compensate for the loss of work. This was received with gratitude that would have won applause in any amateur dramatics production. We replaced the wheel and headed toward the fort.

At eight forty-five we pulled up by the guard house. The sentry came out and eyed us with suspicion. Malik got down from the cab and, in French, explained we were plumbers, who had been summoned to deal with the drains. The sentry inspected the back of the lorry that had drain rods, shovels, pickaxes and manhole keys. Fortunately, he didn't inspect the canvas sacks at the back that held our weapons and radio blockers. He returned to the cab and took a good look at the three of us. Janet seemed to trouble him. He indicated her and asked Malik questions. Malik became animated and gesticulating wildly he spat on the floor and raised his voice; this didn't seem prudent when facing a man with a rifle. To our surprise the sentry raised his hands in supplication, and grinning ushered us into the fort. When Malik got back in Janet questioned him about what had happened. The sentry had asked why a team of plumbers had a woman with them. He explained that Janet was his sister, and that their mother had insisted that she accompany him. She liked a boy in the next street, and to the shame of her parents had been seen making 'eyes' at him. Their mother could not cope with the humiliation, the father had washed his hands of the whole shameful episode so poor Malik had to take her everywhere with him to preserve the family honour. Arthur and I agreed, we also would have let him through.

There didn't seem that many sailors in the fort, and those that were there paid us little heed, once you were past the sentry, you became just Arab labour and practically invisible. Malik drove us to the manhole we had opened last night and parked, the smell was overpowering, but we were forty yards from the mast. It was now 08.55 and Arthur clambered into the back of the truck, attached the battery to our first blocker and carried it into the first toilet stall. He extended the aerial and turned it on.

I nailed two planks of wood across the door and Malik hung a notice on it saying '*Ferme*', we didn't think anybody would argue.

Janet had wandered to the balustrade and was looking out to sea, she beckoned us over. They were a long way off, but there on the horizon were about twenty war ships. I recognised the largest as the Hood, she must have been one of the biggest battleships afloat and the last time I had seen her was in Gibraltar. We were joined by a French signals man, he too stared at the ships. He gestured at them and said, "*Anglais, amies*," and grinned.

Malik asked him what they were doing. He told him, "Inspecting our fleet, we must now stay in harbour." He then asked if we were there to fix the drains and told us the smell had been getting worse since breakfast time.

Malik told him that yes, we were plumbers, but it looked like being a long job as the ducts would have to be dug out. He told Malik his name was Pascal and that he was just about to make coffee, would we like some?

Janet seized the initiative with a, "*Merci* Pascal," and followed him back to the building at the base of the tower. We fell in behind and to our amazement were permitted to enter. Pascal put a percolator on the gas ring and checked his radio equipment. He seemed concerned and checked all the connections, tapping dials and shaking his head. Malik asked if something was wrong, and he explained he had lost contact with the French fleet. He tried using Morse code, but that too had little success. Puzzled he poured the coffee, which I have to say was excellent. We thanked Pascal but noticed Janet looking at her watch, nine forty-five was getting close. Pascal obviously wanted to find the fault so we drank up and went back to work. A quick removal of the planks and Arthur turned the signal generator off. Minutes later Pascal came to his door and gave us the thumbs up, everything was working again.

We started to dig a trench so as to be seen doing something. It was hard work but we didn't want to finish too early. We stopped for a drink and despite the smell Pascal strolled over. He fanned the air under his nose and stood back. Malik asked if everything was now working, and he beamed and reported it was. Conspiratorially he told Malik that the radio messages between the two fleets didn't seem that friendly. Admiral

Gensoul had told the English to go or force would be met with force. Apparently, the English wanted to send a boat to bring an officer ashore, but Gensoul had ordered he was to be stopped at the harbour entrance. "Who would be an admiral with ruffled feathers?" Pascal observed.

We walked back to the balustrade and saw one of the English destroyers making for the harbour. Pascal vanished and reappeared with some field glasses. He generously shared them with Malik. The destroyer, Foxhound, dropped anchor off the harbour entrance and lowered a whaling boat. This sailed for the harbour boom where it was met by a launch from the French flagship, Dunkerque.

Pascal snorted, "*Voila, La entente cordiale.* Now they will sit in the shade and drink pastis while the English counts our boats, it is tough at the top *n-est pas!*" Arthur slipped back and turned the blocker on again. He re-joined us without Pascal noticing. Eventually we returned to the digging, and Pascal to his radio shack. He reappeared a few moments later and observed the mast with his field glasses. Nothing seemed to be wrong up there! Other technicians appeared and a major cable from the shack to the mast was changed. It took until noon. When we saw Pascal go inside, Arthur turned us off, and changed the battery pack. Pascal reappeared with a big grin, and raised both his arms in triumph, a job well done. His colleagues shook hands and left him to it. He walked to the observation point and beckoned us over. When we got there, we saw the Foxhound leaving the harbour. Pascal waved. "*Au revoir mes amis.*" He turned to Malik and explained that they had agreed on the stock take and run out of liquor." We thought it more likely that no agreement had been reached.

We stopped to eat, and I remarked how friendly Pascal was, unusual for an occupying militia. Malik snorted when Janet translated and asked if we did not have men like this in England? It took a moment for the penny to drop. He liked Malik, not Janet. Suddenly it all made sense. Apparently, it was not uncommon in Algeria, and as Janet said, Malik was a fine figure of a man. He threw his tangerine at her.

We were just about to resume when we noticed aeroplanes taking off from the British aircraft carrier. They were old biplanes and we watched them circle until an escort flight of more modern single wing planes joined them, then both flights headed for the harbour. We weren't the only ones to have seen this and six sleek French fighters were launched from the French aircraft carrier to intercept them.

At first, we thought the biplanes were bombing the harbour, but then realised they were laying mines to prevent anything leaving. Anti-aircraft fire from the French ships was ineffectual as the biplanes flew too low, but two of the French fighters attacked a British escort plane which exploded and crashed into the sea. Nobody cheered.

Feeling a little sorry for Pascal, Arthur cut the radio communication again. We guessed this was because the French admiral would be desperate for advice now shots had been fired. We resumed digging and I noticed Pascal actually kicking the new cable they had just installed. At fourteen hundred hours Arthur turned him back on, he must have been wondering what the hell was happening.

He reappeared and told Malik, "They have seen sense, and the English are sending a negotiator." He indicated the Hood. "*Mon dieu* that ship could blow up the whole fort with one shell." We watched the Foxhound return, and again drop the whaling boat off. It went into the harbour but seemed to be unable to berth. Sailors on both sides bellowed at each other through loudspeakers, but it was too distant to hear what was said. Evidently the French fleet had been ordered to make ready and the harbour was slowly filling with smoke. Eventually the whaleboat started forward at speed and made straight for the Dunkerque. Arthur and I thought they would sink it, but it was allowed to tie up, and we saw a solitary figure climb on board.

We turned the blocker on and off as instructed until half past five. The whaleboat then took the RN man back on board and sailed out of the harbour. Pascal, watching through the smoke with his field glasses, reported that he was saluted by the French as he left. "A close thing, Malik," he sighed. "I am too young and handsome to die, what do you think?" Malik told us he had assured him Allah had blessed him. He seemed pleased.

Our timing instructions had now run out, and Arthur asked Janet what she thought we should do. She told us to pack everything away, but leave the blocker running. Whatever was supposed to happen had obviously failed, and it was time for a retreat. We packed everything including the blockers and said goodnight to Pascal with the lie we would see him tomorrow. Then at seventeen fifty-five there was a very bright flash from one of the British ships.

The first salvo hit the French fleet with devastating effect, their aircraft carrier, the Bretagne and the Strasbourg all received direct hits. The noise was deafening even from our perch on the mountainside. I noticed the biplanes were back in the air, and wondered if they would drop bombs, but their purpose seemed to be directing fire. The second salvo was worse, I saw flashes coming from the Hood, and seconds later the battleship Bretagne exploded. The flagship Dunkerque was badly damaged and as it ran aground, another battleship did the same. The destroyer Mogador had its stern blown off and sank.

There was very little returning fire as most of the French warships had been tied up to the dock with their guns pointing inland. Those that did try and manoeuvre into a position to bring their guns to bear, were hampered by the sinking ships around them. The fort had a single gun mount, but it refused to turn on its mountings. Janet confided that she had managed to feed a length of rope into the gears when she had been innocently looking out to sea. It probably saved our lives.

Pascal joined us open mouthed at the destruction. It lasted nine minutes, in which we saw hell, ship after ship was hit by the huge British guns, sailors were jumping into the burning sea to escape. The French did not have a chance and it was pure carnage; we learned later, that one thousand and three hundred, unsuspecting French sailors died, and many more were injured. Then at 18.04 the guns fell silent, and the only sound was the screams of the dying coming from below.

I didn't mean to say it, but I did. I had never seen anything like the destructive power of those shells, and I think we were all in shock. I shook my head and turned to Arthur, "Bloody hell, Arthur, bloody hell; what have they done?"

Unfortunately, Pascal heard me. The shock in his face was overcome by outrage and he shrieked at me, "*Vous et Anglais, vous etes des traitres et des assassins. Alarme, Alarme.*" This wasn't something we could talk our way out off, so Janet hit him hard from behind with her hook. He went down, but his shout had been heard. We had to run.

Chapter 41
Taxi to Ain El Turk

If anything saved us in those first few seconds it was confusion. Malik grabbed the unconscious Pascal and, supporting him on one knee, pointed back to the radio mast and screamed, "Assassins, assassins." Most of the sailors ran towards the radio hut, some had side-arms drawn. It gave us a few seconds to scramble into the truck, Janet and Arthur in the back, Malik and I in the front. The ancient engine fired up and we trundled towards the guard house.

A group of five men holding rifles stood in front of the lowered barrier. The middle man raised his hand in the universal signal to stop. Malik shouted at me, but I didn't understand, thankfully Janet did, and from the back shouted to open the handle on my door, but hold it closed by the strap. It seemed to make no sense as Malik was now travelling at only ten miles per hour. As he approached the sentries, he accelerated then did an emergency stop. The door was torn from my hand and hit the two men on my side with a bone breaking impact. When I managed to get myself upright, I saw the two on the right had suffered similar injuries. There was no sign of the middle man, and I thought he must have been run over, but he scrambled out of a ditch and fired at us with a rifle. He should have hit us, but I suspect shock had affected his aim. Arthur stitched a line of bullets from one of the Stens towards him, and he leapt back in the ditch. Malik banged the truck into first and we crashed through the barrier and turned right on two wheels. Unfortunately, the French had better vehicles than us, and we knew it would only be minutes before they were in hot pursuit. I knew there was no way we could reach the maze of streets in Ain El Turk before they caught us, but there was no alternative other than to run. We pushed the lorry up to forty miles per hour and bounced along the track to the main road then turned right to Ain El Turk. We had cliffs on our left-hand side and a steep slope on our right. As we rounded a right-hand corner, I saw the French in the wing mirror. At first, I thought there was only a single jeep with about six men clinging on for dear life, but another slower vehicle came into view, it was a half tracked armoured car with a gun mounting. If that got in range it would blow us off the mountain. We slowed as the old lorry had to tackle a steep incline up a sharp left-hand bend; the temperature gauge was rising fast.

Malik had also seen them and, as we rounded the bend, he braked to a halt, leaving the lorry two hundred feet from the corner. Janet and Arthur jumped out of the back with our bag of weapons, it was going to be 'Custer's last stand'. Malik and Arthur took a Sten gun each, Janet and I got the last two grenades. We stood to either side and waited until, with impeccable timing, Malik released the hand brake.

The cliff hid us from the pursuing French so that they came round the corner at speed. Their emergency stop was pretty fast, but not good enough. The lorry had gathered momentum as it went with the wheels at just the right angle to reverse round the corner. It hit them with a great thump and transferred all the energy into the jeep. The sailors riding in the back were thrown into the air, some clattered into the road, others not so lucky went over the cliff; nobody got up. The driver and the front passenger had been decapitated by the tailgate.

The lorry had stopped with one of its rear wheels sunk in a storm drain. It leaned at an alarming angle. Malik beckoned us to push the jeep back, he pulled out the two bloody corpse and heaved the jeep towards the cliff and then pulled the handbrake on. On the front of the jeep was a winch, a common accessory in the desert. He unravelled it and attached the cable to the lorry. The engine was beyond repair, but the winch ran off of the battery. Malik turned it on and we saw the lorry leaning further and further until it fell across the road with an ear-splitting crash.

As this happened an old Mercedes taxi came round the bend in the opposite direction. The driver slowed to a halt obviously believing he was witnessing a very bad accident. Arthur stuck his Sten gun through the window. The wide-eyed driver got out of his car with his hands raised.

Malik and I retrieved a ten-gallon petrol can, and liberally splashed it over both the jeep and lorry. We could now hear the armoured car approaching. It might be able to blow the lorry out of the way, but a burning barricade would be a better obstacle. I lit the petrol.

We ran to the taxi, and Malik told the driver to get back in, the French would not deal kindly with him. He was confused and told us, "Viva la France?" Malik spoke rapid Arabic to him, he then saluted us and told us, "God save your gracious King." Friend or foe he was happy to drive us to Ain El Turk harbour, no charge.

He did a rapid three-point turn and headed back to the town. The barricade had stopped the armoured car, but I suspected not for long. We saw the plume of black smoke, and Arthur remarked that at least our radio blockers would not fall into the wrong hands. Malik urged the driver to go faster. The taxi had seen a lot of service, but amazingly it was still capable of sixty miles per hour. When we reached the top of the hill, the driver put his car in third gear and his foot to the floor. I honestly think the French armoured car was less dangerous.

The plume of smoke changed; Janet told us they had probably managed to push the burning lorry off the road. We, however, were free and clear, well we would have been, but the ancient taxi began to make strange noises. I doubt if it had been above forty miles per hour for the last ten years. It started to misfire and slow down. Malik shouted at the unfortunate driver, but there was little he could do. Knocking the car out of gear we freewheeled towards the town. As we started to slow, the driver put the car in top gear, turned the ignition on and let out the clutch. There was a backfire loud enough to get a small group of pedestrians face down in the dust. They must have thought the British war ships had come back. Mercifully, the engine caught and fired. We might only be able to move at twenty miles per hour, but it was faster than running. We limped to the waterfront and turned off along the promenade, there were many fishing boats but we couldn't see Captain Abdul and his Dhow. The noble taxi ground to a halt and with a final gush of steam expired. It had done well, but now we were on our own. We all climbed out and looked left and right for our rescue boat; it wasn't there. Our driver vanished towards the market.

I heard a powerful engine, and, as I looked at the road, my heart sank. The half-track sat there with the crew looking at us. The gun turret turned until it was pointing directly at us, nowhere to run. The hatch opened and a French sergeant appeared. It became apparent he wasn't taking prisoners. I saw his hand raised to give the order to fire, knowing there was no escape this time I dropped to my knees.

In later years I have thought about the moment, and all I can remember is a huge shrieking whistle and an explosion that blew us all backwards. The armoured car wasn't there any more, just a smouldering lump of metal. From the harbour came the whoop of a navy siren.

A British gunboat was making toward the wharf and waving from the bridge was Major Fox. "Quick as you like," he shouted indicating the jetty. We ran, we scrambled, but we all got on board. The boat turned and made speed for the open sea.

I think we all burst into laughter as a psychological release. Nothing was funny, and a great many people were dead, but we weren't. I know I was very close to tears. Major Fox made his way down to the deck and saluted us. "That's a job very well done," he told us, then as a second thought he asked, "Taheen?"

Janet shook her head, and told him, "Taheen is dead, sir, but this is his brother Malik who saved our lives many times."

Major Fox strode over and shook Malik's hand. He spoke in Arabic, but we knew it was a mix of condolence and thanks. "Get yourselves cleaned up," he told us. "There are ablutions and clothing below. We'll get you fed and then I want to know everything."

"What happened to Captain Abdul?" I asked.

Major Fox nodded. "Stood down for your ride home, no place a Dhow when the French are looking for a fight. Besides, I rather wanted to come and get you myself. By the way, you owe able seaman Giles a tot of rum, that was his rather exceptional marksmanship the disposed of the half-track." He saluted again and headed back to the bridge.

The four of us stood watching Ain El Turk disappear behind us. "Well," Janet said, putting her arms round Arthur and Malik. "That was a hell of an adventure, thank God you'll never be asked to do that again."

"I don't think we are particularly useful now that Arthur's death ray has gone," I told her. "It was a one off."

Arthur shuffled his feet, looked a bit embarrassed, and produced an old tobacco tin from under his robe.

THE END.